**Praise for *New York Times* bestselling author
B.J. Daniels**

"Daniels is truly an expert at Western romantic
suspense."

—*RT Book Reviews* on *Atonement*

"B.J. Daniels is a sharpshooter; her books hit the
target every time."

—#1 *New York Times* bestselling author
Linda Lael Miller

"Daniels is a perennial favorite on the romantic
suspense front, and I might go as far as to label her
the cowboy whisperer."

—*BookPage*

**Praise for *USA TODAY* bestselling author
Barb Han**

"Han crafts a wonderful mystery with suspense and
action. *Texas Prey* is an entertaining read that will
hook readers at the outset."

—*RT Book Reviews*

"Another thrilling yet emotional story... A page turner
with plenty of action."

—*RT Book Reviews* on *What She Saw*

WRANGLED

NEW YORK TIMES BESTSELLING AUTHOR

B.J. DANIELS

Recycling programs
for this product may
not exist in your area.

ISBN-13: 978-1-335-40665-1

Wrangled
First published in 2012. This edition published in 2022.
Copyright © 2012 by Barbara Heinlein

Delivering Justice
First published in 2016. This edition published in 2022.
Copyright © 2016 by Barb Han

For questions and comments about the quality of this book,
please contact us at CustomerService@Harlequin.com.

Harlequin Enterprises ULC
22 Adelaide St. West, 41st Floor
Toronto, Ontario M5H 4E3, Canada
www.Harlequin.com

Printed in U.S.A.

CONTENTS

B.J. Daniels is a *New York Times* and *USA TODAY* bestselling author. She wrote her first book after a career as an award-winning newspaper journalist and author of thirty-seven published short stories. She lives in Montana with her husband, Parker, and three springer spaniels. When not writing, she quilts, boats and plays tennis. Contact her at bjdaniels.com, on Facebook or on Twitter, @bjdanielsauthor.

Books by B.J. Daniels

Harlequin Intrigue

Whitehorse, Montana: The Clementine Sisters

Hard Rustler
Rogue Gunslinger
Rugged Defender

The Montana Cahills

Cowboy's Redemption

HQN

Sterling's Montanas

Stroke of Luck
Luck of the Draw

The Montana Cahills

Renegade's Pride
Outlaw's Honor
Hero's Return
Rancher's Dream

Visit the Author Profile page at
Harlequin.com for more titles.

WRANGLED

B.J. Daniels

This book is dedicated to Julie Miller and Delores Fossen, two fellow Harlequin Intrigue writers I greatly admire. I was with them in Los Angeles relaxing at the *RT Book Reviews* convention when I came up with the ending of this book. Thank you both for your friendship. I'm looking forward to our January Ice Lake anthology together.

Chapter 1

The knock at the door surprised Zane Chisholm. He'd just spent the warm summer day in the saddle rounding up cattle. All he wanted to do was kick off his boots and hit the hay early. The last thing he wanted was company.

But whoever was knocking didn't sound as if they were planning to go away anytime soon. Living at the end of a dirt road, he didn't get uninvited company—other than one of his five brothers. *So that narrows it down,* he thought as he went to the window and peered out through the curtains.

The car parked outside was a compact, lime-green with Montana State University plates. Definitely not one of his brothers, he thought with a grin. Chisholm men wouldn't be caught dead driving such a "girlie" car. Especially a lime-green one.

Even more odd was the young, willowy blonde

pounding on his door. She must be lost and needing directions. Or she was selling something.

His curiosity piqued, he went to answer her persistent knock. As the door swung open, he saw that her eyes were blue and set wide in a classically gorgeous face. She wore a slinky red dress that fell over her body like water. The woman was a stunner.

She smiled warmly. "Hi."

"Hi." He waited, wondering what she wanted, and enjoying the view in the meantime.

Her smile slipped a little as she took in his worn jeans, his even more worn cowboy boots and the dirty Western shirt with a torn sleeve and a missing button.

"I wasn't expecting company," he said when he saw her apparent disappointment in his attire.

"Oh?" She looked confused now. "Did I get the night wrong? You're Zane Chisholm and this is Friday, right?"

"Right." He frowned. "Did we have a date or something?" He knew he'd never seen this woman before. No red-blooded American male would forget a woman like this.

She reached into her sparkly shoulder bag and pulled out a folded sheet of paper. "Your last email," she said, handing it to him.

He took the paper, unfolded it and saw his email address. It appeared he had been corresponding with this woman for the past two days.

"If you forgot—"

"No," he said quickly. "Please, come in and let's see if we can sort this out."

She stepped in but looked tentative, as if not so sure about him.

"Why don't you start with how we met," he said as he offered her a seat.

She sat on the edge of the couch. "The Evans rural internet dating service."

"Arlene's matchmaking business?" he asked in surprise. Arlene Evans, who was now Arlene Monroe, had started the business a few years ago to bring rural couples together.

"We've been visiting by email until you…"

"Asked you out," he finished for her.

"Are you saying someone else has been using your email?"

"It sure looks that way, since I never signed up with Arlene's matchmaking service. But," he added quickly when he saw how upset she was, "I wouldn't be surprised if Arlene is behind this. It wouldn't be the first time she took it upon herself to play matchmaker." Either that or his brothers were behind it as a joke, though that seemed unlikely. This beautiful woman was no joke.

She looked down at her hands in her lap. "I'm so embarrassed." She quickly rose to her feet. "I should go."

"No, wait," he said, unable to shake the feeling that maybe this had been fate and that he would be making the biggest mistake of his life if he let this woman walk out now.

"You know, it wouldn't take me long to jump in the shower and change if you're still up for a date," he said with a grin.

She hesitated. "Really? I mean, you don't have to—"

"I *want* to. But you have the advantage over me. I don't know your name."

She smiled shyly. "Courtney Baxter." She held out her hand. As he shook it, Zane thought, *This night could change my life.*

He had no idea how true that was going to be.

Chapter 2

Dakota Lansing got the call at 3:20 a.m. She jerked awake, surprised by the sound of the ringing phone. She hadn't had a landline in years. Glancing around in confusion, for a moment she forgot where she was.

Home at the ranch. It all came back in a rush, including her father's death. She turned on the light as the phone rang yet again and grabbed the receiver.

As she did, she glanced at the clock, her mind spinning with fear. Calls in the wee hours of the morning were always bad news.

"Hello?" Her voice broke as she remembered the last call that had come too early in the morning.

This is Dr. Sheridan at Memorial Hospital in Great Falls. I'm sorry to inform you that your father has had a heart attack. I'm afraid there was nothing we could do. Your sister is here if you would like to speak with her.

My sister? You must have the wrong number, I don't have a sister.

"Hello?" she said again now.

At first all she heard was crying. *"Hello?"*

"Dakota, I need your help."

Her sister, half sister, the one she hadn't known existed until two weeks ago, let out a choked sob.

"Courtney? What's wrong?"

More sobbing. "I'm in trouble."

This, at least, didn't come as a surprise. Dakota had expected her half sister was in trouble when she'd asked after their father's funeral if she could stay at the ranch for a while.

"I want to get to know you," Courtney had said. But it had become obvious fairly quickly that her half sister wanted a lot more than that.

"Speak up. I can barely hear you," Dakota said now.

"I can't. He's in the next room."

Dakota rolled her eyes. A man. Not surprising, since Courtney had been out every night in the two weeks since their father's funeral.

"I think he might be dead."

Dakota came wide awake. *Dead?* "Where are you?" There was a loud crash in the background as something fell and broke. "Tell me where you are," Dakota cried as she stumbled out of bed. *"Courtney?"*

Her father's secret love child, a woman only two years younger than herself, whispered two words before the line went dead.

"Zane Chisholm's."

* * *

Zane woke to pounding. He tried to sit up. His head swam. He hadn't really drunk champagne last night, had he?

Numbly he realized the pounding wasn't just in his head. Someone was at the door and it was still dark outside. He turned on a light, blinded for a moment. As he glanced over at the other side of his queen-size bed, he was a little surprised to find it empty. Courtney had come home with him last night, hadn't she?

As he got up he saw that he was stark naked. Whoever was at the door was pounding harder now. He quickly pulled on a pair of obviously hastily discarded jeans and padded barefoot into the living room to answer the door.

"What the hell happened to *you?*" his brother Marshall asked in surprise when Zane opened the door.

"I'm a little hungover." A major understatement. He couldn't remember feeling this badly—even during his college days when he'd done his share of partying.

"Your face," Marshall said. "It's all scratched up."

Zane frowned and went into the bathroom. He turned on the light and stared in shock into the mirror. His pulse jumped. He had what looked like claw marks down the side of his left cheek. As he looked down at his arm, he saw another scratch on his forearm.

What the hell had happened last night?

"Are you okay?" Marshall asked from the bathroom doorway. He sounded worried, but nothing like Zane felt.

"I don't know. I'm having trouble remembering last night."

"Well, it must have been a wild one," Marshall said. "I hope it was consensual with whatever mountain lion you hooked up with."

"Not funny." His head throbbed and his memory was a black hole that he was a little afraid to look into too deeply.

"You do remember that you and I are picking up horses in Wolf Point today, right?" Marshall said. "I'll give you a few minutes to get cleaned up, but don't even think about trying to get out of this. I need your help and we're already running late. I told you to be ready at four forty-five."

Zane nodded, although it hurt his head. What time was it, anyway? The clock on the wall read 5:10 a.m. "Could you make me some coffee while I get ready?"

His brother sighed. "Aren't you getting a little too old for partying like this?" he grumbled on his way to the kitchen.

Zane stepped into the bathroom, closed the door and stared into the mirror again. He looked like hell. Worse, he couldn't remember drinking more than a glass or two of champagne, certainly not enough to cause this kind of damage.

He thought about Courtney. She had to have done this to him. He touched his cheek. What scared him was, what had *he* done to get that kind of reaction from her?

Emma Chisholm had been an early riser all her life. She liked getting up before the rest of the world when everything was still and dark. Since marrying Hoyt Chisholm a year ago, she especially liked seeing the sun come up here on the ranch.

As she stepped into the big ranch kitchen, she heard a sound and froze.

"I hope I didn't scare you."

Emma shuddered as a chill raced down the length of her spine. She tried to hide it but knew she'd failed when she turned to see amusement in their new live-in housekeeper's one good eye. Up before sunrise and often the last one to bed, the woman moved around the house with ghostlike stealth.

"There really is no need for you to work such long hours," she said as Mrs. Crowley stepped out of the dark shadows of the kitchen. The fifty-eight-year-old woman moved with a strange gait—no doubt caused by her disfiguring injury. It was hard to look into Mrs. Crowley's face. The right side appeared to have been horribly burned, that eye white and sightless. Behind her thick glasses, her other eye shone darkly.

"I'm not interested in sleeping anymore," Mrs. Crowley said. Her first name was Cynthia, but she'd asked them to refer to her by her married name.

The moment she'd come to the house, she had taken over. But Emma couldn't complain. Mrs. Crowley, a woman about her own age, was a hard worker and asked for little in return. She lived in a separate wing of the house and was Emma's new babysitter.

Not that Emma's husband, Hoyt, would ever admit that was the case. But last year his past had come back to haunt them. It had to do with the deaths of Hoyt's last three wives. An insurance investigator by the name of Aggie Wells had been convinced that he'd killed them.

When Aggie had heard about Hoyt's fourth marriage—this one a Vegas elopement to Emma—she'd come to Montana to warn Emma that she was next.

Aggie was dead now. While the police hadn't found her killer, Emma was fairly certain that the perpetrator was the same one who'd murdered at least one of Hoyt's wives.

Aggie Wells had originally been convinced that the killer was Hoyt, but as time went on she'd thought Hoyt's first wife might still be alive. Laura had allegedly drowned in Fort Peck Reservoir more than thirty years before. Aggie had even found a woman named Sharon Jones, whom she believed was Laura. Unfortunately, Sharon Jones had disappeared before the police could question her.

For months now Hoyt had been afraid to leave Emma alone. Either he or one of his six sons hung around the house to make sure no harm came to her.

She'd been going crazy, feeling as if she was under house arrest. Hoyt and his sons had to be going crazy as well. They were ranchers and much more at home on the back of a horse than hanging around the kitchen with her.

Finally Hoyt had come up with the idea of a live-in housekeeper. Emma was sure that Mrs. Crowley wasn't what he'd had in mind. But after all the rumors and suspicions that were flying around, it was next to impossible to get anyone to work at the ranch.

Fortunately, Mrs. Crowley had been glad to come. She said she liked that Chisholm Cattle Company was so isolated.

"People stare," she'd said simply when Emma had

asked her if she thought she could be happy living this far away from civilization.

She was an abrupt woman who had little to say. Emma knew she should be thankful, but sometimes it would be nice to have someone who would just sit and visit with her. That definitely wasn't Mrs. Crowley, but Emma kept trying.

"I see you've made coffee," Emma said now. "May I pour you a cup? We could sit at the table for a few minutes before Hoyt comes down."

"No, thank you. I'm cleaning the guest rooms today."

Emma could have argued that the guest rooms could wait. Actually, they probably didn't need cleaning. It had been a while since they'd had a guest. But Mrs. Crowley didn't give her a chance. The woman was already off down the hallway to that wing of the house.

As Emma watched her go, she noticed how the woman dragged her right leg. That's what gave her that peculiar gait, she thought distractedly. Then she heard Hoyt coming downstairs and poured them both a cup of coffee.

It wasn't until she took the mugs over to the table that she realized Mrs. Crowley always made herself scarce when Hoyt was around. Maybe she just wanted to give them privacy, Emma told herself. "Strange woman," she said under her breath.

A moment later Hoyt came into the kitchen, checked to make sure they were alone and put his arms around her. "Good morning. Want to sneak out to the barn with me, Mrs. Chisholm? Zane and Marshall have gone to Wolf Point. Dawson, Tanner and Logan are all mending fences and Colton has gone into town for feed."

She laughed, leaning into his hug. It had been a while since they'd made love in the hayloft.

Cynthia Crowley watched Emma and Hoyt from one of the guest room windows. They had their arms around each other's waists. Emma had her face turned up to Hoyt, idolization in her eyes. She was laughing at something he'd said.

Cynthia could only imagine.

She let the curtain fall back into place as Hoyt pushed open the barn door and they disappeared inside. As she turned to look around the guest room, she mumbled a curse under her breath. The decor was Western, from the oak bed frame to the cowboy-print comforter. *Emma's doing,* the housekeeper thought as she moved to look at an old photograph on the wall.

It was of the original house before Hoyt had added onto it. The first Chisholm main house was a two-story shotgun. It was barely recognizable as the house in which Cynthia now stood. Hoyt had done well for himself, buying up more land as his cattle business had improved.

On another wall was a photograph of his six adopted sons, three towheaded with bright blue eyes, three dark-eyed with straight black hair and Native American features. In the photo, all six sat along the top rail of the corral. The triplets must have been about eight when the picture was taken, which made the other three from seven to ten or so.

They looked all boy. There was a shadow on the ground in the bottom part of the photograph. Hoyt must have been the photographer, since she was sure the shadow was his.

Now the boys were all raised—not that Emma didn't get them back here every evening she could. All but Zane were engaged or getting married so the house was also full of their fiancées. Emma apparently loved it and always insisted on helping with the cooking.

Not that Cynthia Crowley minded the help—or the time spent with the new Mrs. Hoyt Chisholm. Emma fascinated her in the most macabre of ways.

The new Mrs. Chisholm had definitely been a surprise. A man as powerful and wealthy as Hoyt Chisholm could have had a trophy wife. Instead he'd chosen a plump fifty-something redhead.

"There is no accounting for tastes," the housekeeper said to the empty room as she went to work dusting. Before she'd been hired on, she'd been told about Hoyt's other three wives—and their fates.

"Do you think he killed them?" she'd asked the director of the employment agency where she'd gone to get the job.

"Oh, good heavens, no," the woman had cried, then dropped her voice. "I certainly wouldn't send a housekeeper up there if I thought for a moment…"

Cynthia had smiled. "I'm not afraid of Hoyt Chisholm. Or his wife. I'm sorry, what did you say her name was?"

"Emma. And I've heard she is delightful."

"Yes, delightful," Cynthia grumbled to herself now. At the sound of laughter, she went to the window. Through the sheer curtains she saw Emma and Hoyt coming out of the barn. They were both smiling—and holding hands.

Cynthia Crowley made a rude noise under her breath. "The two of them act like teenagers."

A loud snap filled the air, startling her. It wasn't until she felt the pain that she looked down. She hadn't been aware that she'd been holding anything in her hands until she saw the broken bud vase, and the blood oozing from her hand from where she'd broken the vase's fragile, slim neck.

Once they had the horses loaded at a ranch north of Wolf Point, Marshall suggested they grab lunch. Zane wasn't hungry, wasn't sure he ever would be again. He was anxious to call Courtney and find out what had happened last night.

Stepping outside the café to call her, he realized that he didn't have her number. Nor was she listed under Courtney Baxter. He tried the couple of Baxters in the Whitehorse area, but neither knew a Courtney.

With no choice left, he called Arlene Evans Monroe at the woman's rural internet dating service that had allegedly put them together in the first place.

"Did you set me up with a woman named Courtney Baxter?" he asked Arlene, trying not to sound accusing. Arlene used to be known as the county gossip. In the old days he wouldn't have put anything past her. But he'd heard she'd changed since meeting her husband Hank Monroe.

"Yes," she said, sounding wary. "Is there a problem?"

"Only that Courtney showed up at my door last night

saying I had a date with her through your agency and I didn't have a clue who she was."

"Are you telling me you didn't make a date with this woman?"

"I never even signed up for your dating service. I thought maybe someone had done it as a joke."

"Zane, I have your check right here."

How was that possible? He knew he was still feeling the effects of the hangover; his aching head was finding it hard to understand any of this. But all morning he'd been worried about what had happened last night. He had a very bad feeling and needed to talk to Courtney.

"When does it show that I signed up?" he asked Arlene.

"Two weeks ago."

Two weeks ago? A thought struck him. About two weeks ago he'd come home to find someone had been in his house. Like most people who lived in and around Whitehorse he never locked his doors, so the intruder hadn't had to break in. Nor had the person taken anything that he could see—not even his laptop computer. But enough things had been moved that he'd known someone had been there.

He swore now, realizing that must have been when the person had gone online and signed him up for the dating service—and taken at least one of his checks. He hadn't even noticed any were missing.

"What is the number on that check?" he asked Arlene. She read it off and he wrote it down, seeing that it was a much higher number than the checks now in his checkbook. He wouldn't have missed it for months.

Who went around signing someone up for a dating

service? This made no sense. It had to have been one of his brothers. Or his stepmother, Emma? She had made it clear she thought it was time her six rowdy stepsons settled down. Maybe she was behind this.

But neither Emma nor his brothers would have come to his house when he wasn't home, gotten on his computer and then taken one of his checks to pay for the rural dating service. Who then? And why? This was getting stranger by the moment.

"I need Courtney Baxter's telephone number," he told Arlene.

"According to the service policy you agreed to—"

"I didn't agree because I never signed up," he said, trying not to lose his temper. He caught his reflection in the café window and saw the four scratches down his cheek where someone had definitely clawed him.

"Zane, what if I call her and make sure it's all right first? Do you want to hold?"

He groaned, but agreed to wait.

She came back on the line moments later. "She's not answering her cell phone. I left her a message to call me immediately. I'm sorry, Zane, but that's the best I can do. It's policy."

He swore under his breath. The old Arlene would have handed it over. She would also have asked why he was so anxious to talk to his "date" and the news would have gone on the Whitehorse grapevine two seconds later.

"The moment you hear from her…"

"I'll let you know," she said.

Zane didn't hear anything from Arlene on the long

drive back to Whitehorse. He hoped that once he got home there might be a note or something from Courtney.

Not wanting to drag the loaded horse trailer down the narrow lane to the house, Marshall dropped him off by the mailbox on the county road.

"You sure you're going to be all right?" Marshall asked.

He'd been sick all day and still had a killer headache.

"You really did tie one on last night," his brother said, looking concerned. "What were you drinking anyway?"

"I remember having some champagne."

Marshall shook his head. "That all?"

Zane couldn't recall if it had been his idea, but he doubted it. Courtney must have suggested it. "And I only had a couple of glasses, I'm sure."

His brother lifted a brow. "You sure about that?"

He wasn't sure of anything. "Don't worry about me. I'm fine," he lied as he climbed out of the Chisholm Cattle Company truck and headed down the narrow dirt road to his house.

The early summer sun was still up on the western horizon. It warmed his back as he walked. Grass grew bright green around him, the air rich with the sweet scents of new growth. Grasshoppers buzzed and butterflies flitted past. In the distance he could see that there was still snow on the tops of the Little Rocky Mountains.

As he came over a rise, he slowed. A pickup he didn't recognize was parked in front of his house. Courtney? Or maybe one of her older brothers here to kick his butt.

He quickened his step, anxious to find out exactly what had happened last night—one way or the other.

Zane was still a good distance from the truck when he saw the woman and realized that it wasn't Courtney. This woman was dressed in jeans, boots and a yellow-checked Western shirt. Her chestnut hair was pulled back into a ponytail. She stood leaning against the truck as if she'd been waiting awhile and wasn't happy about it.

When she spotted him, she pushed off the side of the pickup and headed toward him. As she came closer, his gaze settled on her face. He felt the air rush out of him. She was beautiful, but that was only part of what had taken his breath away.

He'd seen Dakota Lansing only once since she was a kid hanging around the rodeo grounds. She'd been cute as a bug's ear back then and it had been no secret that she'd had a crush on him. But, five years his junior, she'd been too young and innocent so he'd kept her at arm's length, treating her like the kid she was.

The last time he'd seen her he'd happened to run into her at the spring rodeo in Whitehorse. He'd been so surprised to see her—let alone that she'd turned into this beautiful woman—he'd been tongue-tied. She must have thought him a complete fool.

The whole meeting had been embarrassing, but since she'd moved to New Mexico, he'd thought he would never see her again. And yet here she was standing in his yard.

"Dakota?" he said, surprised at how pleased he was to see her.

Smiling, he started toward her, but slowed as he

caught her body language. Hands on hips, big brown eyes narrowed, an angry tilt to her head. His brain had been working at a snail's pace all day. It finally kicked into gear to question what Dakota Lansing was doing here—let alone why she appeared to be upset.

She closed the distance between them. "Where is my sister?" Those big brown eyes widened, and he knew she'd seen the scratches on his face just seconds before she balled up her fist and slugged him.

The punch had some power behind it, but it still had less effect on him than her words.

"Your sister?" he asked, taking a step back as he rubbed his jaw and frowned at her. He'd known Dakota Lansing all his life. She didn't have a sister.

Chapter 3

"Courtney Baxter," Dakota said. "The woman I know you were out with last night." She looked as if she wanted to hit him again. Her eyes narrowed. "What did you do to her?"

He rubbed his jaw, feeling as if he was mentally two steps behind and had been since Courtney Baxter had knocked on his door not twenty-four hours before. "Courtney Baxter is your sister?"

"My *half* sister. Where is she?"

His head ached and now so did his jaw. Dakota had a pretty good right hook. "How do you know I was with her?"

"She called me sounding terrified. What did you do to her?"

Taking a step back, he raised both hands. "Hold on a minute. We can figure this out."

"What is there to figure out?" she demanded.

He noticed something he hadn't earlier. Dakota's left hand. No wedding ring. No ring at all. The last time he'd seen her, she'd had a nice-size rock on her ring finger. He'd heard she was engaged to some investment manager down in New Mexico.

She saw him staring at her left hand and stuck her hands into the back pockets of her jeans, her look daring him to say anything about it.

No chance of that.

"We should put something on those knuckles," he said, having noticed before that her right hand was swelling. Hitting him had hurt her more than it had him. Well, physically at least.

Dakota Lansing. He still couldn't believe that the freckle-faced tomboy who used to stick her tongue out at him had grown into this amazing-looking woman.

"Why don't you come into the house for a minute," he said, and started for the front porch.

"Zane, I'm only interested in finding my sister."

"So am I." He left the door open, went into the kitchen and opened the freezer door. By the time he heard her come in he had a tray of ice cubes dumped into a clean dishcloth.

"What did you do to her?" Dakota demanded again from the kitchen doorway.

He motioned to a chair at the kitchen table. "Dakota, you know me. You know I wouldn't hurt anyone."

She didn't look convinced, but she did sit down. He reached for her injured hand, but she quickly took the ice from him, pushing his hand away.

"Courtney said on the phone last night that she was

in trouble. I heard something crash in the background. Just before the connection went dead she said your name."

The whole time she'd been talking she was glaring at him, challenging him to come up with an explanation. He wished he could.

"Dakota, I have to be honest with you. I can't remember anything about last night. I woke up this morning alone with these scratches on my face and—" he pushed up his sleeve "—my arm."

Her eyes widened a little when she saw the scratches on his arm. He saw fear flicker in her expression, fear and anger. "How long have you been dating my sister?"

She sounded almost jealous. Which he thought just showed how hungover he was. "I had never laid eyes on her until she showed up at my door last night claiming we had a date," he said. He saw she was having trouble believing it. "I swear it. And I certainly didn't know she was your sister. So how is it I never knew you had a sister?"

"She's my father's love child." Dakota sighed and shifted the ice pack on her swollen knuckles. "I only found out two weeks ago after my father died."

He remembered seeing in the newspaper that her father had passed away. He'd thought about sending a card, but it had been so many years, he doubted Dakota would remember him.

"Are you sure she's even—"

"I saw her birth certificate. It had my father's signature and his name on it. Apparently Courtney's mother and my father got together either when my mother was dying or right after."

He could see how painful this was for her. Dakota had idolized her father, and to find out on his death that he'd been keeping a lover and a sister from her for years…

"So you're claiming that Courtney just showed up at your door?" Dakota asked, clearly not wanting to talk about her father.

Zane told her about his call to Arlene at the dating service, the check someone had used to enroll him and that he was waiting to hear from Courtney, since he, too, was worried about what might have happened last night.

She studied him for a long moment. "So a woman you have never seen before shows up at your door claiming you have a date, and you just go out with her anyway?"

He guessed Dakota had probably heard about his reputation with women. "I didn't want to hurt her feelings."

Her chuckle had a distinct edge to it, and he remembered why he'd always liked her. Dakota had always been smart and sassy. She'd been a daredevil as a kid, always up for just about anything, from climbing the three-story structure that held the rodeo announcer's booth at the fairgrounds, to trying to ride any animal that would hold still long enough for her to hop on. Since her father had raised rodeo stock, she'd had a lot of animals to choose from. He'd liked her a lot. Still did, he thought.

"How well do you know her?" Zane asked.

"Not as well as you know her, apparently," Dakota said, and shoved the ice pack away as she reached for her phone.

"Who are you calling?" He hated to think.

"I'm trying Courtney's cell." She punched in the number and hit Send. "I've been trying to call her all day and—"

At the distant sound of a phone ringing they both froze for an instant. Then, getting to their feet, they followed the muffled ringing.

Zane hadn't gone far when he realized the sound was coming from his bedroom. He pushed open the door and stepped in, Dakota on his heels.

The ringing seemed to be coming from the bed, but when he drew back the crumpled covers, it was empty. As the phone stopped ringing, no doubt going to voice mail, he knelt down and looked under the bed.

He could just make out the phone in the shadowy darkness under the bed—and what was left of the lamp that had been on the nightstand on the other side of the bed. The lamp lay shattered between the bed and the closet.

Refusing to think about that right now, he reached for Courtney's phone.

It wasn't until he pulled it out and heard Dakota gasp that he noticed the cell phone was smeared with something dark red. Blood.

He dropped the phone on the bed, realizing belatedly that he should never have touched it. He had a bad feeling it would be evidence—against him.

As he turned, Dakota took a step back from him. The frightened look in her eyes hit him like a blow. There were tears in her eyes; the look on her face was breaking his heart.

"I didn't harm your sister. Dakota, you *know* me."

"I *knew* you, Zane, but that was a long time ago."

"Not so long. I haven't changed. Drunk or sober, I would never hurt a woman. You have to believe me." But how could he keep telling himself that nothing bad had happened last night when the evidence just kept stacking up?

They both turned toward the front of the house as they heard a vehicle pull up. Zane moved quickly to look out, hoping it would be Courtney and he could get this cleared up and relieve his mind.

But it wasn't Courtney's lime-green compact with the MSU plates.

It was a Whitehorse County Sheriff's Department patrol SUV.

"Mrs. Crowley," Emma cried when she saw the woman's bandaged hand.

"It's nothing."

"Oh, here, let me see it." She reached for the woman's hand.

"I said it was nothing," Mrs. Crowley said, taking a step back and drawing her hand behind her. Her face had closed up, her one good eye glinting as hard as the tone of her voice.

Emma fell silent. She'd held out hope that she would like the woman Hoyt had hired as her housekeeper-babysitter. Being close in age, she'd thought they might have things in common.

But every time she had reached out to Mrs. Crowley, offering her friendship, it had been quickly rebuffed.

"Just let me do my work," the woman said now. Her wrecked face caught the light; the burn scars looked angrier today than usual.

Unlike Hoyt, Emma made a point of looking Mrs. Crowley in the eye. She refused to be put off by her injuries—or her manner.

Hoyt just steered clear of the woman and often apologized for hiring her.

"She's fine," Emma always said in Mrs. Crowley's defense. She suspected that the woman had trouble getting other positions and couldn't afford to lose this job. Hoyt paid her well and the living accommodations were probably nicer than any she'd had before. Not that Emma's kindness or the house or the pay had softened Mrs. Crowley in the least.

"Whatever happened to her has made her push people away," Emma told her husband. "We just need to keep trying to make her feel at home here."

Hoyt had been skeptical. "You probably pick up stray dogs, too, don't you? Honey, this time I don't think even you can make that woman civil—let alone happy."

Emma couldn't help but wonder what had happened to Mrs. Crowley that made her like this. She suspected it was more than whatever accident she'd had that had left her disfigured. But Emma doubted she would ever know. It wasn't like Mrs. Crowley was going to tell her anytime soon.

"Did you call the sheriff?" Zane asked without looking at her as Dakota joined him at the window.

"No." With a sinking feeling, Dakota watched Sheriff McCall Crawford climb awkwardly out of the patrol vehicle. Dakota saw that the sheriff was pregnant, a good seven or eight months along.

"Maybe Courtney called her, or—"

Or Courtney had been found. Dakota didn't let him finish that thought. "Courtney wouldn't have called the sheriff." If her sister had had any intention of calling the sheriff, wouldn't Courtney have done so last night instead of calling her?

Whatever Courtney was up to, Dakota suspected the sheriff was the last person she wanted involved.

"Well, if you didn't call her, and Courtney didn't…" Zane let the thought hang between them.

Dakota glanced over at him, saw his freshly scratched face in the glow of the afternoon sun coming through the window and could guess what was about to happen.

Once the sheriff saw the scratches, she wouldn't need to hear about the phone conversation Dakota'd had with Courtney in the wee hours this morning. Nor would the sheriff need to see the bloody phone from under Zane's bed before hauling him off to jail.

Common sense told Dakota, given the evidence, jail was probably the best place for him. But not if she had any hope of him helping her find her sister.

"Here's what I want you to do," she said as the sheriff's footfalls echoed on the old wooden porch. "Go in the bathroom and stay there. Let me handle this."

Zane shook his head as the sheriff knocked at the front door. "If you think I'm going to hide behind your skirts—"

"What you're *going* to do is help me find Courtney, and you can't very well do that behind bars," Dakota said through gritted teeth as the sheriff knocked again. "Turn on the shower. There's something I haven't told you about Courtney. Now trust me."

She shot him an impatient look and waited until he

disappeared into the bathroom and shut the door before she went to answer the sheriff's third knock.

As the door swung open, Sheriff McCall Crawford couldn't help her surprise.

"Dakota Lansing?" McCall said. "Haven't seen you in a while." She'd been several years ahead of Dakota and they'd gone to different schools—McCall in Whitehorse, while Dakota had gone to Chinook—but they'd crossed paths because of sports.

"I've been living in New Mexico. I only recently returned. For my father's funeral," she added.

"Yes, I heard. I'm sorry." The sheriff looked past her. "Is Zane around, by any chance?"

"He's in the shower, but you're welcome to come in." She stepped back and McCall entered the house. "He's getting ready so we can go out for dinner."

McCall glanced around the small house. There wasn't much to see. Zane Chisholm obviously wasn't into decorating. She doubted he spent much time here.

"I came out to talk to Zane, but since you're here…" McCall said. "Is there a problem I should know about?"

Dakota looked confused by the question. "A problem?"

"I got a call that there was a domestic disturbance out here."

"When was that?"

"Twenty minutes ago," McCall said.

Dakota let out a laugh. "You didn't really take that call seriously, did you? The closest neighbor is a half mile away. Hard to really see or hear a domestic disturbance, unless of course they said there was gunfire involved."

"True," McCall said. "Unless, of course, *you* made the call."

"I can assure you, I didn't call. But I suspect caller ID would have confirmed that," Dakota said.

The sheriff smiled. She remembered Dakota Lansing as being smart and capable. "Just had to check. Actually the call came from a woman who said she was your sister."

"Courtney?"

McCall saw that she now had Dakota's attention. "Is Courtney Baxter your sister?"

"My half sister. Long story. Why would she make a call like that? I haven't seen her for several days."

"Good question." McCall glanced toward the bathroom door. She could hear the shower still running. Zane Chisholm took an awfully long shower.

As she felt the baby kick, McCall rested her hand on her swollen belly. For a moment she was lost in that amazing feeling. The whole pregnancy had been like this, stolen moments from her job when she felt as if she wanted to pinch herself. She just couldn't believe she and Luke were having a baby.

"Is it possible your sister is jealous?" McCall asked as she turned to leave. "I heard Zane was out with a pretty blonde last night. Apparently they were celebrating rather hard."

Compliments of the Whitehorse grapevine first thing this morning. McCall even knew that Courtney Baxter had been wearing a very sexy red dress. Who needed Twitter? *No one in this county,* she thought.

That Courtney was Dakota Lansing's half sister had come as a surprise. The scuttlebutt now around town was that the girl was the product of an affair Clay Lansing had years ago.

"I actually set up the date," Dakota said. "I knew the two of them would hit it off. Zane and I are just friends. But I can understand why Courtney might be jealous after a date with Zane. He is a catch."

McCall nodded as she glanced into the kitchen and bedroom, saw the unmade bed and figured this was merely a case of sibling rivalry. "Well, you two have a nice supper. Have Zane give me a call when he gets a chance."

As she started for the front door, she heard a cell phone ring from somewhere in the bedroom. "If that's your sister calling, please tell her I'd like to talk to her, too," McCall said, and let herself out.

Dakota let out the breath she'd been holding since the moment she'd realized it was Courtney's cell phone ringing. Zane had left it lying on the crumpled covers of the bed. Fortunately it had been out of the sheriff's sight.

She hurried into the bedroom and gingerly picked up the phone. Private caller. "Hello?"

No answer, but she could hear breathing on the line. "Who is this? Courtney? If that's you—"

Whoever it was hung up.

Dakota stood holding the phone for a moment, then quickly dropped it back on the bed. She felt a rush of anger. Courtney was fine. She'd called the sheriff twenty minutes ago. She must have seen Dakota's pickup parked in front of Zane's house from the county road.

Or she'd called so the sheriff would see Zane's scratched face.

"What are you up to, Courtney?" Dakota said to the empty bedroom. No good, that much she was sure of. "And what really happened here last night?"

The room provided few answers. Unless you read something into the crumpled sheets on the bed. She felt a surge of anger mixed with something she didn't want to admit. Jealousy. Zane had gone out with her sister. *I didn't want to hurt her feelings.* She swore under her breath.

Too bad he hadn't felt that way when they were kids, Dakota thought, remembering how he'd pushed her away.

"You're just a kid," he'd said when she tried to hang around him at the rodeo grounds. "Go on. Find someone your own age to bug."

She ground her teeth at the memory. She'd had the worst crush on him. And, stupidly, she'd written it all down in her diary, every horrible tearful account, including her conviction: *Zane doesn't know it, but some day I'm going to marry him.*

Two days ago, when she'd realized that someone had been in her things, she'd discovered that her diary and some old photographs were missing. Courtney. She was the only one who could have taken the diary.

Now Dakota wondered when Courtney had taken it. Two weeks ago—about the same time that someone had mysteriously signed Zane Chisholm up for a dating service?

It was no coincidence that Courtney had tricked Zane into a date. Dakota was sure of that. Courtney had the diary. She knew how her sister had felt about Zane. So Courtney had done this out of meanness?

What had she hoped to accomplish by this? More than sibling rivalry, Dakota thought, remembering the scratches on Zane's face and the frantic phone call in the wee hours this morning.

Whatever Courtney was up to, Dakota was going to find her and put a stop to it. And Zane was going to help her.

Unlike him, Dakota had a bad feeling she knew exactly why Courtney had targeted him. She couldn't wait to get her hands on her diary—and her sister.

Mrs. Crowley stepped into her room and closed the door firmly behind her. She had always been so good at playing her roles—she now thought of herself as Mrs. Crowley. Smiling at the thought, she locked the door to listen. She had to make sure she wouldn't be disturbed.

It hadn't taken long to learn the sounds of the house. The older section had more to say than the newer one, but she knew all of its many voices—which floorboards creaked, which doors opened silently, which spot in the house carried the most sound for eavesdropping.

She'd explored every square inch of the house until she knew she could move through it blind if she had to. That was a possibility if the house were ever to catch fire.

Satisfied that everyone was down for the night, she stretched, relieving her back from the strain of walking hunched over. She had taught herself to move silently and now chuckled to herself at how many times she'd been able to come up behind Emma without her knowing it and startle her.

Moving just as silently now, she stepped into the bathroom and studied herself in the mirror over the sink a moment before she reached up and took out the white contact lens. She blinked, waiting for the eye to focus. Then she removed the dark brown contact lens.

She slowly began to remove the burn scar, peeling it off as she peeled away Mrs. Crowley. At last she stood at the mirror, her face scrubbed clean, her eyes blue again.

As she stared at herself, though, she felt she was looking at a stranger. It had been so long since she'd been herself, her image came as a shock.

But it was nothing compared to the shock it would give others in the house when the time came to end this charade, she thought with a wry smile.

Chapter 4

The moment Zane had gone into the bathroom and turned on the shower, he'd changed his mind about staying hidden while Dakota handled the sheriff.

He'd never run from trouble in his life, and he wasn't going to now. But as he'd reached for the bathroom door handle, he'd glimpsed his face again in the mirror over the sink. The scratches were an angry red and, maybe worse, he had no explanation for them.

Dakota was right. He needed to find Courtney and he couldn't do that behind bars. He feared anything he said to the sheriff would come out sounding like a lie. If Sheriff McCall Crawford saw Courtney's cell phone…

He'd stayed put even though it was hard. He couldn't hear what was being said. For all he knew, Courtney had been found and that was why the sheriff was here.

Zane jumped at the tap on the bathroom door. He quickly turned off the shower and opened the door.

"The coast is clear," Dakota said as he came out.

"What did McCall want?" He hated the fear he heard in his voice. From Dakota's reaction, she'd heard it too. She had to be wondering if she was wrong about him.

"Apparently Courtney called about a disturbance out here between you and me."

"*Courtney* called? Then she's all right?"

"Apparently."

He shook his head. "But why would she…" The thought struck him like a brick. "She wanted the sheriff to see the scratches on my face and arm. What the hell is going on with her?"

"She seems to have it in for the two of us," Dakota said. "That's why we have to find her and find out what she's up to."

"The *two* of us?"

Dakota looked away for a moment as if she hadn't meant to say that. "The last time I saw her was a few days ago. Right after that I realized she'd been in my house and taken something of mine." She waved a hand through the air. "The point is, I want it back. She had no business in my house, let alone taking anything of mine."

He nodded, seeing that whatever Courtney had taken, Dakota didn't want to talk about it. He changed the subject. "What did McCall make of all this?"

"She seemed to think it was my sister being jealous."

"We know better." The date last night, what he could remember of it, hadn't been anything special. In fact, he recalled before he'd lost his memory that he hadn't planned to see Courtney again. She was beautiful, but not that interesting.

His head still hurt, but a thought wormed its way through. "You said Courtney showed up two weeks ago. That's the same time someone broke into my house and used my computer to set up the rural dating account. Could she have been planning this that long ago, trying to set me up for more than a date?"

"Why go to the trouble?" Dakota asked, frowning as if she was trying to work it out herself.

"Why me at all?" It didn't make any sense to him either. "The requirements I put down for the perfect date apparently made Courtney the perfect match."

Dakota raised an eyebrow.

"I didn't put down *any* requirements, but whoever signed me up must have rigged it so that my requirements matched Courtney's. It had to be Courtney."

"A lot of trouble and to what end?"

"I guess that depends on what happened last night," he said as he glanced around the living room. Nothing seemed to be missing, but then he'd made that mistake before.

"You really don't remember what happened after your date?" she asked.

"I've never had a hangover like this before."

Dakota was looking at the scratches on his face again. "Maybe you should get a drug test at the hospital."

Dakota was willing to consider that he'd been drugged? Zane was surprised and relieved. But why hadn't he thought of it? Because he'd been running scared from the moment he'd opened his eyes this morning.

He had to know what he was dealing with. Courtney Baxter seemed to be setting him up. But why? He was just grateful that Dakota seemed to be on his side. If he'd just gotten drunk and didn't remember, that was one thing. But if Dakota was right and Courtney had drugged him...

"I think a drug test is a good idea," he said, but Dakota didn't seem to hear him.

She was looking at Courtney's cell phone. She had picked it up by two fingers. He could see the smeared blood from here.

"Any idea how it got blood on it?" she asked. "Or how it ended up under your bed? I noticed there was also a broken lamp on the other side of the bed. You probably don't know anything about that either."

He shook his head. "You said you heard something crash in the background when you were on the phone with her."

"Could have been the lamp." She looked down at the phone again. "Maybe we should see about getting DNA off this phone to find out if it is even Courtney's blood. We can have a doctor run a blood test on you at the same time for possible drugs. Do you have a small plastic sandwich bag we can put this in?"

"Top drawer on the right." He watched her head for the kitchen, trying to figure out what about Dakota was bothering him. She certainly was taking all this better than he would have thought.

"I doubt there will be fingerprints other than ours, but..." She stopped on her way back from the kitchen, the cell phone in a plastic bag she'd found in the drawer. "What's wrong?"

He wasn't sure. "You just kept me out of jail—at least temporarily—and now you're going to help clear me? What's going on, Dakota?"

"I told you. I need your help to find Courtney."

"Because she took something of yours that you want back. If you just wanted to find Courtney, you could have told the sheriff everything you know and thrown me to the wolves," he said. "The sheriff, with all her resources, would be looking for your sister right now. So why didn't you? It wasn't just to keep me out of jail so I could help you find her. I hate to sound suspicious, but I have to wonder why you're so anxious to find her that you would throw in with *me*."

"She's my sister."

"Uh-huh."

Dakota sighed. "Okay, maybe I've suspected she was up to something from the first time I laid eyes on her."

"You said your father's name and signature are on her birth certificate. Are you saying you're questioning that?"

She shrugged. "All I know is that something's wrong with her story. After what you've told me, I'm even more convinced."

"But not enough to go to the sheriff."

"I want to do some investigating of my own before I get the sheriff involved," Dakota said.

He suspected there was more, something she was hiding, but right now he was just glad he wasn't in jail. "Then you believe me?"

"I'm willing to consider you were set up." She

stepped to the door and opened it. "On the way into town, I think we should see who Courtney's been calling—and who's been calling her."

Dakota hadn't been completely truthful. Not that she didn't have her reasons for wanting to believe Zane and, if she was being honest with herself, some of them had to do with the crush she'd had on him when she was a girl.

He was even more handsome now. Not that she was the kind of woman who was overcome by good looks. Zane hadn't made fun of her like the other boys when she'd been the skinny, freckle-faced, buck-toothed, mouth-full-of-braces girl who'd hung around him like a lovesick puppy.

Nor was she that smitten girl anymore. But she also believed that Zane, while no longer the lanky boy she'd known as a girl, was still honorable and decent. She had to trust her instincts. Her instincts told her that Zane was telling the truth.

"I'll drive," she said, and Zane didn't argue. He looked like death warmed over, making her also believe she might be right about him having been drugged.

She could tell that his greatest fear was that something really awful had happened to Courtney last night. Dakota told herself it was more likely, after what the sheriff had said, that Courtney was up to her pretty little neck in this and not as the victim. Another reason Dakota wanted to find her as quickly as possible.

As she drove, she watched Zane out of the corner of her eye as he began to check the numbers on the cell phone through the plastic bag.

"There are no contact numbers," Zane said. "I get the feeling this is a fairly new phone, since there are so few calls and messages. The last outgoing call was…" He read off the number.

"That's the number at my ranch from when Courtney called last night. Do you recognize any of the other numbers?"

"As for incoming, there are calls and messages from you and Arlene Evans Monroe. I had asked her to call Courtney and get back to me when she heard from her." He studied the numbers for a moment. "Otherwise there are two incoming calls from numbers that I don't recognize. Courtney returned one of those calls, but not the most recent one."

Dakota realized she hadn't told Zane about the phone call earlier. "Someone was looking for her. Before the sheriff left your house, Courtney's cell phone rang. I answered it. I could hear breathing on the other end of the line, but the person didn't say anything before hanging up."

"Courtney? If she was the one who called the sheriff about a disturbance at my house," he said, his brows furrowing.

"Or someone else looking for Courtney."

"Do you recognize either of these numbers?" He read the numbers off to her.

"Sorry, they don't sound familiar. There's a notebook and pen in the glove box," she told him as they neared town.

Zane jotted down the numbers as Dakota pulled into the back of the hospital.

Whitehorse County Hospital was small. As they

walked in the back door, Zane spotted Dr. Buck Carrey. He looked more like a rancher than a doctor. A big man, he had a weathered face wrinkled from the sun and from smiling. His gray hair was uncharacteristically long for Whitehorse and pulled back in a ponytail. Today he was wearing jeans, boots and a Western shirt, with his white Stetson cocked back on his head.

He greeted Zane warmly, then shook hands with Dakota, whom he hadn't had the pleasure of meeting before, and invited them into his office. "You said this was a confidential matter?" he asked, closing the door.

Dakota listened while Zane gave an abbreviated version of what they needed. Doc raised a brow when Zane showed him the phone. "Let's start with the blood test. As for the DNA, I need something to compare it to."

"I'm her sister. Well, half sister. Will that work?"

"Close enough." Doc left and came back with the items he needed to do both tests. He took blood from Zane, then a swab of Dakota's mouth and another swab of blood from the phone.

"I'll have to get back to you on your blood test," he told Zane. "Same with the blood on the phone." Doc seemed to study Zane's scratches for a moment. "You sure you don't want the sheriff in on this?"

"If we can't find Courtney, we'll go to the sheriff," Dakota promised. Her sister was in trouble, she'd bet on that. But she feared it was Courtney's own making.

"I'm sorry about all this," Zane said as they left the hospital. "First your father's death, then a sister you never knew you had and now this."

Dakota shrugged as she opened her pickup door and

slid behind the wheel. "I think what hurt the most was that I'd always wanted a sister and apparently I've had one since I was two—I just didn't know it."

"Why do you think your father kept it from you?"

She shook her head. "Guilt maybe. Everyone says he adored my mother, but when she got sick, I don't think he could handle it."

"I can't imagine your father living a double life, not the way he felt about your mother." He also couldn't imagine Clay Lansing keeping all of this from his daughter. There had to be more to the story. "So what do you know about Courtney's mother?"

"Nothing, really," Dakota said. "Courtney said she died and that she doesn't like to talk about it."

"Did she mention where she was raised, at least?"

"Great Falls. She wasn't even that far away, just a few hours. My father must have seen her when he went there, since she was at the hospital when he died."

"He died in Great Falls?" Zane asked in surprise.

Dakota nodded and seemed to concentrate on her driving. "All of it has come as such a shock—his death, Courtney, the lie he lived all these years." He could hear the hurt in her voice. "She had more time with him at the end than I did," Dakota said, voicing her pain.

"If she's telling the truth," Zane said as he looked over at her. "You suspected something about her story was a lie, didn't you?"

She glanced at him in surprise.

He smiled. "I know you, Dakota. You wouldn't have believed me so quickly if you didn't suspect your sister was up to something." True, they hadn't seen each other in years, but in so many ways she was that kid he knew from the rodeo grounds. She'd always seemed too smart for her own good.

"If you're right and you were set up, then Courtney is in on it," Dakota said. "I can't imagine any other reason she would sign up for Arlene's rural dating service. One look at her tells me she's never had trouble finding a date."

Zane had been one of those men. He cursed himself for it. "I need to see her room where she was staying."

"She's not there," Dakota said. "I checked and her car wasn't there before I came looking for you."

"She might have dumped her car somewhere."

"Why would she do that?"

He shook his head. "Why would she pretend we had a date and possibly drug me?"

"You don't know she was the one who signed you up for Arlene's rural dating service," Dakota pointed out.

"No, but she had to be in on it. That's the only thing that makes any sense. You didn't check to make sure she wasn't at home, a friend maybe had given her a ride home?"

Dakota shook her head. "She doesn't have any friends here."

"That you know of," Zane said. "Let's try her room first. If she set me up…"

"You think she's cleared out."

"Yeah, that's exactly what I'm thinking. I'm sure there's more, but I have a feeling this next part is her being scarce until the other shoe drops," he said.

They reached Chinook, a small, old town along the railroad, down the Highline from Whitehorse. She turned north on a dirt road toward the Lansing ranch, traveling through the rolling prairie.

It had been a clear blue day, the kind that are almost blinding. Now the sun had dipped behind the Bear Paw Mountains, the sky a silken blue-gray and still cloudless. A meadowlark sang a song that traveled along with them as she drove.

"You say she doesn't have any friends," Zane said as he watched the countryside roll by and tried to get a clear picture of what Courtney Baxter was really like. He couldn't shake the feeling that he hadn't been out with the "real" Courtney last night. "No one you've seen her with, no phone calls?"

Dakota shook her head.

"When I woke up and Courtney was gone, I just assumed she'd left on her own," he said. "But what if there'd been someone else with her at my house last night after I passed out?"

He felt her studying him again, stealing glances at him as she drove. "Dakota, you know me. I wouldn't have hurt her."

She let out a breath. "I know."

"Thank you for believing in me. I suspect whatever this is, Courtney isn't in it alone and I have a bad feeling your sister doesn't realize how dangerous the person she got involved with really is."

"Oh, I don't know about that. I get the feeling Courtney can take care of herself."

Dakota drove past the large old, white, single-story ranch house to the small matching guesthouse out back. Zane remembered when they were kids and Dakota had told him that her father had built a house on the ranch for her to stay in when she reached sixteen. He recalled her excitement because she was like him. She never wanted to leave the ranch; she just didn't want to live at home.

But something had changed for her to end up in New Mexico, engaged to a guy involved in investment managing.

Zane saw as they climbed out of the pickup that Courtney's compact car was nowhere in sight.

Dakota knocked at the front door. "Courtney?"

He held his breath, praying she would open the door. Dakota knocked again, then pulled out a key and opened the door.

As the door swung in, Zane caught the scent of perfume, the familiarity of it making him a little sick to his stomach and increasing his dread. What had happened last night? The harder he tried to remember, the worse he felt.

The guesthouse was small, one bedroom, one bath with a kitchenette and living area. The bedroom door was ajar. Dakota stepped over to it, carefully pushing the door all the way open to expose an empty, unmade bed.

"It doesn't look like she's been back," Dakota said as he headed over to the closet and eased the door open.

Only a handful of clothes hung there. He frowned and moved to the chest of drawers. The top drawer held a few undergarments. The next drawer had even less, only a couple of tank tops and pajama bottoms. The third drawer had two pairs of jeans, and the bottom drawer was empty.

He closed the last drawer and turned to look at Dakota. "What woman has so few clothes?"

She shrugged. "Maybe this is all she owns."

"Or maybe she left most of her belongings somewhere else. Does she have a job?"

"She said she's been looking locally."

He smiled at that. "Not looking very hard, right?"

Dakota sighed. "I got the feeling she was waiting for me to offer her half the ranch."

If Courtney Baxter really was Clay Lansing's love child, then she could probably legally force Dakota to split the ranch and the rough stock business with her. He swore under his breath. How could Clay have done this to Dakota? Worse, he'd kept her sister from her—and let Dakota learn about her after he was gone. Didn't he realize the repercussions of his actions?

Zane moved to the bed. A clock radio sat on one of the bedside tables, nothing else. He bent down to look under the bed and was hit again with the smell of Courtney's perfume. For a moment he thought he would be sick. He stilled his stomach and squinted into the darkness under the bed.

Something glinted. Reaching in, he felt the cool, weathered vinyl surface, found the handle and pulled the old suitcase from under the bed.

He glanced at Dakota.

"Maybe you'd better make sure it isn't ticking before you open it," she said.

He popped the latches on each side. The suitcase fell open.

Emma Chisholm glanced out the window, surprised to see Mrs. Crowley silhouetted against the fading twilight.

Instinctively, Emma stepped back, afraid the woman might have seen her. She was relieved when she stole another glance and saw that Mrs. Crowley had her back to the house.

What was she doing out there? The woman never went outside. At least not that Emma had ever noticed.

Peering around the edge of the curtain, it took her a moment to realize the housekeeper was on a cell phone. Emma had never seen her make or take a call. No cell phone had ever rung while Mrs. Crowley was working. Emma was actually surprised that the housekeeper even owned one.

She couldn't help but wonder who the woman was talking to. Mrs. Crowley made it clear she had no one who would interfere with her ability to stay at the ranch and work every day except one each week.

When pinned down, the housekeeper had said she was widowed, no children. She'd quickly made it clear she thought Emma had stepped over some invisible line by even asking.

"It could be a friend," Emma muttered to herself. But even as she said it, she had her doubts. "Maybe a friend from before the accident."

That was something else that Mrs. Crowley made clear she wasn't going to talk about.

"People don't just stare at me," she said, her voice sharp with bitterness and anger. "They want to know what happened. Like vultures, they would love to hear every horrible detail." Mrs. Crowley's one good eye glinted like granite. "Well, they won't be hearing it from me and neither will you."

With that, she'd turned and limped off.

Emma watched now from the edge of the curtain as Mrs. Crowley finished her phone call and stood for a long moment as if admiring what little remained of the sunset.

As she turned to come back to the house, her gaze rose to the second floor as though she sensed Emma watching her.

Emma jerked back, heart hammering. The last thing she wanted Mrs. Crowley to think was that she was spying on her, true or not.

After a moment, Emma dared to take another peek. Mrs. Crowley was still standing in the same spot. The harsh glow of the sunset fell across the woman's disfigured face. She was smiling her crooked half smile, her gaze mocking as she looked up at the second-floor window, making sure that Emma knew she'd been caught spying on her.

Chapter 5

Empty. The suitcase was empty? Dakota laughed, letting out the breath she'd been holding. She'd been so afraid of what they were going to find. "It's just an old suitcase. Looks like it belonged to another generation."

"Like her mother?" Zane said with the lift of an eyebrow.

"More like her grandmother." Dakota leaned over it and caught a whiff of stale air that reminded her of her own grandmother. "My nana had a similar suitcase. It even smelled a little like this one."

The suitcase had been expensive because it had been made to withstand even a fall from a plane, supposedly. She realized what Zane was getting at. These particular suitcases, because of their expense, often had the name and address of the owner engraved on a plate inside.

She peered into the silky lining. Her fingers brushed

over something cold and slick at the edge. She looked up at Zane and smiled as her fingers found the engraving. Turning the suitcase to the light, she read, "Frances Dean, 212 W. River St., Great Falls, Montana."

"Don't get too excited. Your sister could have picked this suitcase up at a garage sale," Zane said.

"Or this could be a relative." As she started to pull her hand back from the metal tag, her fingers caught on the lining. It tore. When she looked down she saw why her fingers had caught. The lining appeared to have been cut.

"Well, would you look at that," Zane said as he peered into the space between the lining and the hard cover of the suitcase.

He reached in and drew out a thin stack of hundred-dollar bills.

Dakota felt her eyes widen. "Do you think Courtney knew the money was in there?"

Zane sent her an are-you-serious look. "Who do you think put this money in there? The bills are new."

"How much is it?" Dakota asked as he began to dig out the stacks.

"I'd say at least ten thousand."

Ten thousand dollars? "I don't understand this. Courtney let me think she was broke. She'd been borrowing money from me until she could find a job, she said."

Zane shook his head sympathetically. "Apparently your sister took us both in. Any idea where she might have gotten it?" He tossed the money into the suitcase, snapped it shut and grabbed the handle.

"Probably from whoever put her up to whatever no

good she's involved in," she said, still in shock. Courtney had played them both. "You're taking the suitcase?"

He smiled. "Looks like we're going to Great Falls to find out if Frances Dean knows where we can find Courtney. In the meantime, we have the money. Which means it's only a matter of time before Courtney comes looking for *us*."

Dakota glanced at her watch. It was several hours to Great Falls. There was no way they would get there in time to talk to anyone—at least not tonight.

"Don't you think we should wait and go in the morning?" she asked.

He shook his head. "I'm afraid of what Courtney will do next if we wait. This way we can try to track down whoever lives at the address on the suitcase first thing in the morning. You don't have to come if you don't want to."

No chance of that. "Just let me go over to the house and throw a few things into a bag."

"Dakota," he said as she started to turn away. "Thank you. I'm glad you're in this with me."

She felt a stab of guilt. *Tell him about the diary. He needs to know that you're the one who involved him in this.*

"Give me ten minutes," she said, and hurried across the yard, telling herself that Courtney had to have more of a motive for involving Zane than sibling rivalry. Dakota hadn't even seen Zane in years.

But she realized as she packed a few items of clothing in an overnight bag that Courtney might be using Zane because she felt cheated. Maybe she thought she should have had everything Dakota had since she didn't get to live on the ranch with their father.

Who knows what made Courtney do what she has, let alone what she is planning to do next, Dakota thought. Zane wasn't the only one worried about that.

On impulse, Dakota went into her father's den. Once she'd realized that Courtney had been in the house and taken her old diary, she'd been so upset that she'd only given a cursory look for what else her sister might have taken.

Now she had a bad feeling as she went behind her father's desk and saw that the bottom drawer was partially open. There were gouges in the wood where someone had used something sharp to break the lock.

With trembling fingers, Dakota pulled the drawer out, knowing what had been inside was gone—and who had taken it.

Zane found Dakota standing in her father's study. He tried to read her expression, but the afternoon light cast her face in shadow.

"Is everything all right?" he asked.

She looked up and seemed surprised to see him, as if she'd forgotten about him. He figured she was thinking about her father, missing him. He regretted interrupting her but they had to get going.

"I hate to rush you—"

"You're not," she said quickly. "I'm ready."

He saw her overnight bag by the door and picked it up. "Anything else?"

She shook her head. She seemed distracted, but he didn't press her as they walked out to her pickup.

"I thought we'd go to my place if you don't mind. I can pack a few things and we can take my truck. I'm feeling much better."

"Whatever you think," she said. He could tell wherever her mind had been, it was still there.

They were both quiet on the drive back to his house. It wasn't until they were on the road to Great Falls that Dakota broke the silence.

"You think Courtney was paid to set you up?" she asked.

That's exactly what he thought. But ten thousand dollars? That was a lot of money. Way more money than he was worth setting up.

"I just can't understand why anyone might have paid your sister to do this," he said. "Especially that *much* money. And other than me looking like I got into a cat-fight and feeling hungover, what was the point? Unless she was supposed to kill me…."

"Don't say that. Even if Courtney drugged you, I'm sure she didn't mean to take it that far."

Zane looked over at Dakota. "I thought her phone call to you was part of the setup, but what if she really was in trouble? What if she *was* supposed to kill me and couldn't go through with it? That could explain why she's disappeared. She's hiding from whoever paid her to do the job."

"Why would she want you dead? And why didn't she come back for the money? Unless the money wasn't her real reason for what she did."

"That's why I don't think she acted alone. But it has to be someone with a grudge against me." He glanced over at Dakota and gave her a crooked grin. "As I recall, you had quite a temper when I riled you up. You out to get me, Dakota?"

"That's not funny." She turned away.

Zane stared out at the Montana evening as they drove through the rolling green prairie. This was such a beautiful time in this part of Montana. The mountain ranges were capped with pristine white snow from the last snowfall in the high country. The snow and deep blue mountains were in stark contrast to the lush green of the prairie. Creeks ran wild with the beginning of summer runoff and there was a feeling of new beginnings in the air.

It was the kind of evening he loved and yet he was too aware of the woman sitting just inches away from him.

Dakota didn't seem to be aware of him. Something was bothering her. But apparently it wasn't anything she wanted to share with him. He'd been joking earlier about her being a part of this. What if she was?

Dakota was furious with her half sister and couldn't wait to find her. If Courtney even really was her sister.

She'd been so shocked when she'd first learned about Courtney that she now realized she should have demanded more proof. All she'd had was a glance at Courtney's birth certificate. Once she'd seen her father's name and his signature…

Why hadn't she questioned that the birth certificate might have been a fake? She'd invited Courtney to come live at the ranch—a stranger. Now she regretted that terribly. What else had Courtney taken from the house? Dakota didn't know. Just as she didn't know why Courtney was doing this or what she had to gain other than possibly ten thousand dollars.

Dakota had put off telling Zane what she'd discovered missing in her father's den. She needed time to let all of this sink in so she could sort it out. At least that's what she told herself. But she hadn't sorted it out and Zane needed to know. He already suspected that Courtney was supposed to kill him last night. What if he was right? What if Courtney tried again?

"There's something I need to tell you," she said as they left the meandering Milk River behind and headed south toward the Missouri—and the city of Great Falls. "I told you Courtney took something of mine."

"But you don't want to tell me what she took."

She knew it was silly not to confess about the diary. But she was embarrassed by all the things she'd written. With luck, she would get it back and Zane would never have to know.

Letting out a breath, she said, "Courtney took some old photos along with a pistol my father kept in the bottom drawer of his desk. It's a .45."

Zane let out a curse. "You're just now telling me about this?"

"I didn't check until I went in to pack for this trip. But after everything that has happened…"

"Wait," he said, holding up a hand. "You came looking for her because of something she took, right? Something that had you upset enough that you actually believed I had been set up."

"Courtney had also taken some personal things of mine, including some old photographs."

"Old photographs?"

"Some of my father at several rodeos and one of you and me."

He blinked at her. "She took a gun and a photo of your father and one of the two of *us?*"

"I'm sorry. I should have told you."

"You think she *targeted* me because of a photograph of the two of us? That's why you believed me! That's why you're so anxious to find her and why you didn't want the sheriff involved." He shot her a look, then laughed. "Dakota, you aren't responsible for this. Seriously. You can't believe that's all that's behind this."

She shook her head, feeling close to tears.

He grinned. "You had a photo of the two of us?"

She brushed at the tears. "It was a good one of *me.* You just happened to be in the picture," she said, and looked away, but she knew he was still grinning. Just as she knew he was wrong. She *was* responsible somehow for what was happening.

Emma Chisholm heard the steady throb of an engine and slipped out of bed. At the window, she saw one of the ranch pickups pull around to the side of the house. She glanced back at the clock beside the bed. 2:11 a.m.

As the driver cut the engine, she thought it must be one of her six stepsons. But since they each had their own homes it would be unusual for one of them to come by this late—unless there was trouble.

Emma was surprised when Mrs. Crowley stepped from the pickup.

"I will need a vehicle at my disposal," Mrs. Crowley had announced the day she'd appeared at their door.

"I'd prefer not to drive my own car given the condition of your…rural roads."

Emma had to shoot Hoyt a warning look to keep him from saying what she knew he was thinking.

"There is always a ranch pickup around. Will that do?" Emma had asked the woman. She was determined to make this work, one way or the other.

Mrs. Crowley had turned her nose up, but said that would have to do.

"Who the hell does she think she is?" Hoyt had demanded later when the two of them had gone out to the barn. That was where they escaped to, knowing that Mrs. Crowley wouldn't set foot out there. "If you knew what I was paying her…" He'd broken off, looking chagrined.

"It's all right. I know she didn't come cheap." Emma appreciated that he'd gone to so much trouble to make sure she was safe. She knew that Hoyt would pay any price for her safety.

"Yeah, well, the problem is that no one wants to work for a murderer. Even an acquitted one."

"Stop that," Emma had snapped. "The problem is that no one wants to be more than a mile from a mall." She'd laughed. "They just don't realize that there isn't a mall anywhere that can beat being out here."

Hoyt had smiled as he'd cupped his hand behind her neck and pulled her close. "How did I get so lucky with you?"

Emma could have told him, since he was the sexiest man she'd ever known and the biggest-hearted. Any woman would have been a fool not to love this man and appreciate the land that he loved. But she'd bit back her words. His first wife, Laura, hadn't appreciated either.

Now Emma wondered what Mrs. Crowley was doing out at this time of night. She didn't seem like the type of person to close down the bars in Whitehorse, but as secretive as she was, who knew her type?

The woman reached back into the pickup cab for the large purse she carried. It was more like a carpetbag, and tonight it seemed fuller than ever. What did Mrs. Crowley carry in there, anyway?

With a start, Emma realized that the woman could have a secret life at night. It wasn't the first time she'd taken off after supper without a word. She could have come in late all those nights as well and Emma just hadn't heard her before.

Still, as she watched Mrs. Crowley carefully close the pickup door so as not to disturb anyone and then disappear into the lower floor of the house, Emma was amazed at the woman's stamina. As hard as she worked, refusing even a break, how could she stay out this late and still be up before the sun in the morning?

On her day off, Mrs. Crowley stayed in her room, not even interested in food. Everything about the woman was a mystery to Emma. The weather was beautiful this time of year and yet she showed no interest in the land right outside her window. In fact, the drapes on her windows were always closed.

Maybe the sunlight bothered her burned skin and eye, Emma thought, chastising herself for finding fault with the woman. Mrs. Crowley had made it possible for Hoyt to return to work with his sons. No more babysitting Emma day after day.

Emma stepped back from the window, telling herself it was none of her business. Climbing back into bed beside Hoyt, she snuggled closer. It didn't matter what the woman did late at night or on her day off in her room.

But Emma had a terrible time getting back to sleep. What did they really know about the woman who lived in their house with them?

Zane frowned as he took in the house. The house at 212 W. River Street was a narrow, two-story wood structure that had once been white before all the paint had peeled off. Like the neighborhood, it had an abandoned look.

He glanced over at Dakota. They hadn't said much since he'd knocked on her motel door to see if she was ready for breakfast. Last night when they had stopped at a motel, it had felt awkward.

He'd stopped thinking of her as a kid and that was part of the problem. She seemed embarrassed and clearly hated admitting that she'd kept a picture of the two of them from when she'd had a crush on him. He couldn't help being flattered that she'd kept it. He'd always pretended to his friends that Dakota hanging around bugged him. But he'd been sorry when her father had moved his rough stock part of the ranch to New Mexico and Dakota had gone with it.

Right now, he was glad that they had that history together. True, she had her reasons for wanting to find her sister, but he doubted she would have believed him about Courtney otherwise. Just as he was sure she wouldn't have wanted his help if she didn't somehow feel responsible.

But Zane didn't believe that Courtney Baxter had come after him because of some photo she'd seen of the two of them from years ago. If Courtney wanted to hurt Dakota, the best way was to try to take Lansing Ranch. Not only would it kill Dakota to lose it, the ranch was worth a lot of money, not to mention the rough stock business. Worth a lot more than ten thousand dollars.

The question still remained though: Why come after *him?* What was to be gained other than the money?

The money alone meant Courtney hadn't come up with this by herself. He suspected Dakota was right about the phone call from her sister. Maybe Courtney really had been scared and crying out for help. Or maybe that had been part of the setup. Maybe Courtney wanted to throw the two of them together. He felt foolish this morning for ever suspecting Dakota.

Now, as they climbed out of his pickup, he feared the address they'd found in the suitcase was a dead end. He'd hoped the name plaque might lead them somewhere, but it appeared the house was empty and had been for some time.

Everything around the house was overgrown to the point that the vegetation was slowly taking over the structure. No one had lived here in a very long time.

"Hello?" The voice was small, just like the woman whose head barely topped the fence between the properties. "Can I help you?" the neighbor asked.

She had a shock of white hair that seemed to float like a halo around her head. Dressed in worn blue overalls, a red long-sleeved shirt and tennis shoes, the woman stepped out from behind the fence. She surveyed them with keen blue eyes. In her hands was a hedge trimmer.

"You live next door?" Zane asked, unable to hide his surprise. He'd thought for sure that the entire neighborhood was abandoned.

"Have for almost ninety years," she said proudly. "I was born here. But you're not looking for me, are you?"

"We were looking for Frances Dean," Dakota said, stepping forward.

"Dead, I'm afraid," the woman said. "Entire neighborhood's been dying off for years now. I'm about the only one left. A developer is just waiting for me to die so he can tear down what houses haven't fallen down and build a bunch of condos."

From her tone it was clear she was holding out until her last breath. "You aren't with that low-life vulture, are you?"

"No," Dakota assured her. "Did you know Frances Dean well?"

"All my life."

"Did she happen to have a daughter?" Zane asked.

"Camilla," the woman said with a nod. "Married one of the Hugheses. Widowed, I'd heard. Nice girl."

"Do you know if she has a daughter by the name of Courtney?" Dakota asked.

"Can't say. Last I heard of Frances she was worried because Camilla was having trouble getting pregnant." The old woman shrugged. She eyed Zane's scratches. "You look like you tangled with a rosebush. Did that once. Nasty thorns on those little devils."

"Well, thank you for your time, Mrs...."

"Miss. Abigail Warden." They introduced themselves. "Pleased to meet you. I suppose I should ask why you're looking for Frances's kin."

"A woman named Courtney Baxter has gone missing. We're trying to find her mother and we have reason to believe she might be related to Frances Dean," Dakota said.

"Might be. Might not. Good luck to you." Miss Warden turned back to the hedge with her clippers. As they left, they heard the *snap, snap, snap* of her blades.

"You know they're going to find that poor old woman under that hedge someday," Dakota said.

"There are worse ways to go," Zane said as they got back into the pickup. When his cell phone rang he pulled it out of his jacket pocket, hoping it was Courtney.

"It's Doc," he said to Dakota, then snapped open the phone. "Hello?"

"I got back your blood test," Doc said. "There were a variety of drugs in your system."

"One that would cause memory loss?"

"Several that would. You're lucky that mix of drugs didn't kill you."

Maybe it was supposed to. "What about the DNA on the phone?"

"I put a rush on it. We can get a basic preliminary test within twenty-four hours, so we should be hearing soon."

Zane thanked him and hung up, more upset than he wanted Dakota to know. Her sister had targeted him. To what end, he couldn't imagine. In fact, knowing what he did now, he was surprised he hadn't heard from

Courtney. He wouldn't have put some sort of black-mail past her.

Of course, there was another option. That the reason Courtney hadn't turned up was because of whoever had put her up to this. Someone she hadn't trusted entirely and that's why she'd taken the gun from Clay Lansing's desk drawer. It made sense—if Courtney had feared she was going to need it.

Chapter 6

At a convenience store, Dakota borrowed a phone book. There were a half dozen Hugheses in the book, but only one C. Hughes. She jotted down the address, opting not to call first.

Fortunately, when they arrived at the address, there was a car in the driveway.

The first thing Dakota noticed about Camilla Hughes when she answered the door was how little she looked like Courtney. Camilla was a petite woman in her late fifties with dark brown hair and eyes. There was a cultured softness to both her manner and her speech. Again nothing like Courtney.

"May I help you?" Camilla asked, looking from Dakota to Zane and back.

"Hi, we're friends of Courtney's, just passing through

town and we were hoping she might be around," Dakota said.

"Oh, I'm so sorry," Camilla said. "Courtney isn't here. Did she tell you she was going to be here?"

Dakota stole a look at Zane, pleased that she'd been right about the suitcase. Still, Courtney's lack of resemblance to this woman worried her. That and the fact that their last names were different.

"No," Dakota said. "Since we were in town we thought we'd just take the chance that she might be."

"Have you tried calling her?" Camilla asked.

"I'm not sure I have her number with me," Dakota said.

"Come in." Camilla waved them into her spotless, well-furnished home. "I'll get it for you." She went to a small desk just off the living room. As she was writing a number down for them on a notepad, Dakota moved to the fireplace.

There was a line of framed family photographs along the mantel. Dakota picked one up and turned it so Zane could see the woman in the studio shot. It was the same woman who'd showed up at Dakota's father's funeral, the same one Zane had taken to dinner last night. Courtney Baxter.

The other photographs were all of Camilla, a tall slim man with red, thinning hair and beautiful Courtney at various ages over the years. Dakota put the photo back on the mantel as Camilla Hughes came over to hand her the piece of notepaper.

The cell phone number Camilla had written down was different from the phone they'd found under Zane's bed. *Was that phone even Courtney's?* she wondered with surprise.

"Your name is Hughes but your daughter goes by Baxter?" Zane asked, expressing what Dakota had been wondering.

All the color washed from Camilla Hughes's face in an instant. She took a couple of steps to the side and lowered herself into a chair. "That's the name she's going by?"

He nodded, and Dakota could see that like her, he was surprised that the woman had become so upset. As Camilla waved Zane into a seat across from her, Dakota joined him on the couch. "I'm sorry. I didn't know she was doing that. Baxter was her biological mother's name."

"She's *adopted?*" Dakota asked, unable to contain her surprise even with the obvious difference in appearance between mother and daughter. It explained why Courtney didn't resemble either her mother or father, though. But then Courtney didn't resemble their father or Dakota either. That meant she must have taken after her mother. Her *biological* mother?

"Yes, Marcus and I adopted her when she was only a few days old," Camilla said, still looking shaken.

"Her mother couldn't keep her?" Dakota had to ask, wondering about the mystery woman who'd had an affair with her father.

Camilla looked even more upset. "A nurse told me in private that the mother didn't want her, wanted nothing to do with her." Camilla instantly bit her tongue. "I've never told Courtney that, of course. I shouldn't have told you either. I'm just upset that Courtney has chosen to go by a woman's name who didn't want her."

"It's all right," Zane said. "I'm sorry this news has upset you so."

"Courtney has always known she was adopted, but she never seemed to have any interest in finding her birth parents," Camilla said. "I didn't even know that she knew her birth mother's last name." She seemed to shake herself out of her thoughts. "I'm sorry, but how is it that you know my daughter?"

Dakota felt telling Camilla about her relationship to Courtney would upset the woman further. Not to mention finding the ten thousand dollars tucked in the suitcase and the fact that her daughter seemed to be missing.

"We only recently met her," Dakota said. "Your daughter has been staying with me up north of Chinook."

"Staying with *you?*" Camilla asked, frowning.

"In my guesthouse. When we met, she said she needed somewhere to stay until she could find a job and get a place of her own," Dakota said.

Camilla shook her head in obvious bewilderment. "A few weeks ago she told me she was going on a short trip. She came over and borrowed her grandmother's suitcase. I haven't heard from her since and she hasn't been answering her phone…." She frowned. "If she's been staying up north, then why were you looking for her here?"

"She didn't come home the last two nights," Dakota said. "We were coming to Great Falls and thought she might be here. I wanted to let her know that a man at one of the jobs she'd applied for wanted to do a second interview."

She hated lying but the explanation seemed to relieve Camilla a little—that is, until she took a good look at Zane's scratched face.

"Rosebushes," Dakota said.

"Are there any high school friends or college friends she might be staying with?" Zane asked.

"She really hasn't been in touch with any of them that I know of." Camilla looked close to tears. "They all have jobs. Courtney was still trying to figure out what she wanted to do." She pursed her lips. Dakota could tell that she hated telling complete strangers such personal information. She only did so because of her obvious concern for her adopted daughter.

"Is it possible one of her birth parents contacted *her?*" Dakota asked.

Camilla seemed surprised by the question. "I hadn't thought of that. Maybe that's where she is now." She brightened at the thought. "Now that you mention it, Courtney hasn't been herself lately. She's been distant, secretive. I thought it was just growing pains, a sign that she wanted to be more independent from me."

"You said 'lately,'" Zane asked. "The past few weeks?"

Camilla nodded. "She even purchased a second cell phone a couple weeks ago. I thought that was odd. Clearly she didn't want me to know who she was calling—or who was calling her. I thought it might be a young man she wasn't ready to tell me about."

"Do you have that number?"

She shook her head. "She said she needed space.

We've always been so close. Marcus and I spoiled her, no doubt about that. But maybe we should have pushed her out of the nest sooner. Then after Marcus died… I know I leaned on Courtney more than I should have."

"What about Courtney's birth father?" Dakota asked, trying to keep the emotion out of her voice.

Camilla shook her head. "The nurse I talked to didn't know anything about him."

"Isn't his name on the birth certificate?" Zane asked.

"No. Courtney's birth certificate shows my name and Marcus's."

"I'm confused," Dakota said. "Where was Courtney born?"

"It was a home birth somewhere in Montana. We got a call. We didn't even realize that anyone knew how much we wanted a child and hadn't been able to have one of our own." She looked worried now. "It wasn't through an adoption agency exactly."

The Whitehorse Sewing Circle, Dakota thought. That group of old women had been secretly orchestrating adoptions for years. "Did your daughter get a quilt shortly after she was born?"

"Why, yes," Camilla said.

"So you don't know the names of her birth parents?" Zane asked.

"Just the mother's name. Lorraine Baxter."

Dakota recalled now that she had only glanced at the mother's name on the birth certificate that Courtney had shown her. It could have been Lorraine Baxter.

"You never tried to find her then?" she asked.

"Good heavens, no! That's why I was shocked when you told me that Courtney was going by the woman's name. You must be right about the woman contacting her. But why now? She didn't want her when she was born, why would she contact her now?"

Dakota knew there could be all kinds of reasons. She feared, though, given what they now knew, the reason wasn't a good one.

"When she picked up the suitcase, she didn't say where she was going?" Zane asked.

"No. That was something else that worried me. She said she had something she needed to do." Camilla's voice broke and tears welled in her dark eyes. "When she left, she hugged me and told me how much she loved me. But I had the most horrible feeling that she wasn't ever coming back, that she was telling me goodbye."

Zane could see that Dakota was upset as they left. She'd promised to let Camilla know if they heard anything from Courtney.

"That poor woman," Dakota said as they climbed back into the pickup. "What if something bad has happened to my sister?"

"If she *is* your sister," Zane said.

Dakota frowned. "Courtney offered to take a DNA test anytime I wanted, but I didn't see any reason since she'd already showed me the birth certificate with my father's name and signature."

"I suspect that birth certificate could be a fake."

"I'm not sure how the Whitehorse Sewing Circle operates. But wouldn't there be an original birth certificate with the birth parents' names on it?"

He shrugged. "Maybe. If the mother thought she was going to keep the baby, then changed her mind, and the women of the Whitehorse Sewing Circle found the Hugheses, who were ready to adopt the baby, and saw that another birth certificate replaced the first. You heard what she said about the quilt. The Circle makes every baby it handles a quilt."

"If the mother didn't want the baby, then why would she keep the original birth certificate?" Dakota asked.

"Maybe she thought it would come in handy someday."

"Those women in the Circle have placed a lot of babies illegally and gotten away with it. If Courtney was my father's daughter then she was probably born somewhere near Whitehorse. Anyone with relatives or friends in Great Falls could have known about the Hugheses and their desire for a baby."

Zane nodded. "Your father would have known about the Whitehorse Sewing Circle, which means that Courtney's mother would have probably known as well."

"Or maybe he sent her to the women so she could get rid of the baby," Dakota said.

"You know your father would never have done that."

"Do I? What if it was a woman he never should have gotten involved with?"

"A married woman?"

"Possibly."

Zane shook his head. "We won't know until we find Lorraine Baxter." He started the truck engine and drove, wondering where to go next. "This birth certificate Courtney showed you, did you ask Courtney for a copy?"

"I was so shocked I didn't ask for anything. But why

put his name on the birth certificate if he isn't involved in this?"

Zane shot her a look. Was she serious? "He had money, a ranch, a good business."

"Still, Lorraine Baxter would have had to know him. She had to get a copy of his signature if she was going to forge his name. She didn't just pick his name out of thin air."

"Okay, let's say she knew him. Maybe had been intimate with him. Maybe Courtney *is* your half sister. The only way we're ever going to know everything is if we can find this woman. Don't look so skeptical," he said, glancing over at her. "If we're right, she's been in contact with Courtney and recently."

Dakota smiled at him. "You amaze me."

"Really?" he asked, grinning at her.

"You're a lot smarter than you look."

He had to laugh because he knew how he looked with his face scratched up. He really wanted to find Courtney and get some answers, Dakota's sister or not.

"We need to try the numbers we found on her phone," he said.

"It might not even be Courtney's phone."

"Or it could be the extra phone she bought."

"So Courtney could talk to her birth mother without Camilla knowing about it," Dakota said.

"You're pretty sharp yourself," he joked as he pulled over. No reason to keep driving when they didn't have a clue where to go next.

He shut off the engine and turned to look at Dakota. He still wasn't used to the woman she'd grown into—or his reaction to her. He felt so close to her and yet they hadn't been around each other in years.

"Courtney must have gotten the birth certificate from her biological mother," Dakota said, frowning. "How else could Courtney have known about her birth father? Her adoptive mother didn't know his name and, apparently, neither did the nurse who delivered Courtney."

"If the birth mother was telling the truth and your father is really Courtney's father, then I doubt he ever knew he had a second daughter," Zane said. "I spent a lot of time around your father when I was rodeoing. Your father adored you. I can't believe he didn't have plenty of room for another daughter in his heart. He wouldn't have kept her a secret, and he wouldn't have given her up for adoption."

Her eyes filled with tears. "I want to believe that. I know he had wanted more children. If my mother hadn't gotten sick…"

Zane saw the pain behind the tears. She had hated the thought that Clay had kept Courtney from her. Dakota had idolized her father. He'd been everything to her even before her mother died. To have a sister sprung on her like this must have been more painful for her than he could imagine.

But if Courtney really was the daughter of Clay Lansing, then her mother had had an affair with him either while his wife was dying of cancer or right after.

Zane just hoped the whole thing was a scam and that Courtney Baxter shared no blood ties with Dakota.

Dakota reached over and took his hand. "Thank you," she said, her voice breaking. "I've been struggling with this for weeks. I hated that I was suspicious of Courtney and I've been so angry with my father for keeping it from me."

Zane squeezed her hand. Leaning toward her, he drew her into his arms. He hadn't planned to kiss her. But at that moment, it seemed the most natural thing in the world.

Her lips parted, her breath warm and sweet. He felt a quiver run through her; his pulse kicked up as his mouth dropped to hers.

Dakota gently pushed him away. "Sorry, but your reputation precedes you."

He heard the slight tremble in her voice. She pulled free of his arms and he leaned back, telling himself he shouldn't have kissed her. Especially given why they were together. Didn't he have enough woman problems right now?

"You're going to believe rumors about me?" he joked as he tried to cover up how even that quick kiss had affected him.

She smiled, but there was hurt in her gaze. "Let's not forget that you went out with a woman who simply showed up at your door."

"Yeah," he said, sobered by the memory. And not just any woman. Possibly Dakota's half sister. "You make a good argument." His gaze caressed her face for a moment before meeting her eyes. "But that kiss? I was just fulfilling a promise I made you before you moved to New Mexico. Remember?"

Dakota felt her face heat with embarrassment. Oh, she remembered all right.

"Don't you want to be the first boy I ever kiss?"

Zane looked down at her, sympathy in his gaze. "Your first kiss should be with someone special."

"That's why I want it to be with you." Her voice cracked, her eyes filling with tears. *"I'm moving away and if you don't kiss me..."*

"Dakota." He touched her shoulder, crouching down so that they were at eye level. His voice was soft. *"That's real sweet, but there are going to be so many boys who want to kiss you. Boys you're going to want to kiss, too."*

"Then will you at least save a kiss for me?"

Zane nodded and smiled, the caring look in his eyes making her love him all the more.

"Promise me that you'll kiss me one day. Promise?"

"I promise."

"I was just a silly kid," she said now.

"Yeah, you were. But you aren't anymore, are you? And I'm not sorry about the kiss."

Courtney's cell phone rang—the one they'd found under Zane's bed and at least believed was hers.

The sound startled Dakota and yet she'd never been so glad for the interruption. She had wanted Zane Chisholm to kiss her since she was that silly kid who hung around him at the rodeo grounds.

But the phone was a good reminder that Zane had been with her sister two nights ago. She knew his reputation, and while she'd thrown herself at him when she was a girl and he was a teenager, she was no longer that starry-eyed tomboy. And Zane was definitely not that still-innocent teenager.

As for the kiss… Dakota told herself that as nice as

it had been, it was just a kiss. But the purring of her pulse beneath her skin, the erratic beat of her heart, the quick breaths, all of those spoke of the true effect that Zane Chisholm's kiss had on her.

Dakota only hoped Zane hadn't noticed. Or if he had, that he thought it was the phone ringing that made her hand tremble as she pulled the bagged phone out of her purse.

She looked down at the phone as it rang again. "It's the same number calling from before, the one that hung up when I answered. What should I do?"

The phone rang a fourth time. "Don't answer it. Maybe they'll leave a message."

The phone rang once more, then fell silent.

Sheriff McCall Crawford stood in front of the mirror, studying her changed figure.

"It's beautiful. *You're* beautiful," her husband, Luke, said as he came up behind her and placed his palms over her bare, round abdomen. He kissed her on the back of the neck, then peeked at her in the mirror.

"Why are you frowning?" he asked.

"Was I?" she asked, quickly checking her expression. "I'm just so…big. I'm going to have to get a new uniform."

"Or you could go ahead and take maternity leave," Luke suggested.

She met his gaze in the mirror. "I have another month before the baby's due." She wasn't telling him anything he didn't already know. McCall turned in his arms to face him. "You want me to quit."

"No, I…" He sighed. "I just don't want anything to

happen to you and the baby. I know that is horribly self-ish. Sorry. It's just how I feel."

She started to tell him that she was the sheriff and had a job to do and that he knew that when he married her, but she stopped herself. She had to admit that lately she'd been feeling the same way.

She would be out on a call and feel their baby move inside her and all she could think about was that little life. The thought of putting their baby in jeopardy scared her. She didn't want to be afraid to do her job. If that happened, she told herself she would quit.

"Nick will be back in a few days." Her undersheriff would be filling in while she was on maternity leave. "I'll see about taking my leave then."

What she couldn't tell Luke was about her fears. Ruby hadn't been a bad mother, just not a great one. McCall wanted to be a great one.

But that was only one of her fears. She was afraid that she wouldn't want to go back to being sheriff after their daughter was born, that she had worked this hard to be the best law enforcement officer she could only to give it up. She felt torn and hated that feeling. Why couldn't she have it all?

Her cell phone rang.

Luke groaned. "Duty calls."

She kissed him and reached for her phone, listened, then said, "I'll be right there."

As she snapped the phone shut and reached to put on her clothing she saw her husband's expression. "A lime-green compact was found south of town in a ravine," she told him. "I'm sure there is nothing for you to look so worried about."

But as she climbed into her patrol SUV and headed south toward the isolated wilderness of the Missouri Breaks, McCall had a bad feeling about the car and driver.

The deputy had told her the car was registered to a Courtney Hughes. But in the purse found inside, he'd discovered a credit card under the name Courtney Baxter—the woman who'd been seen out with Zane Chisholm two nights ago.

McCall hated to jump to conclusions. But neither Zane Chisholm nor Courtney Baxter had called her back, she reminded herself as she drove the narrow dirt road south into the rugged breaks country.

Chapter 7

"The caller didn't leave a message," Dakota said after checking. She couldn't help being disappointed, though not surprised.

"If Courtney left that phone under my bed on purpose—"

"Then that was probably her calling before to see if you'd found it," Dakota said.

"If she didn't, then someone else is looking for her. Might as well try the numbers she called and received calls from."

Dakota punched in the last number that had called.

The phone rang four times and went to voice mail. An electronic voice instructed her to leave a message.

She didn't.

She tried the only other different number. A male voice answered on the second ring.

"Where the hell are you?" the man demanded. "You leave in the middle of the night without a word? And what the hell am I supposed to do with your bar tab? If you think I'm picking it up, you're crazy."

Dakota looked over at Zane wide-eyed and mimed, "What do I do?"

"Talk?" he mouthed back.

She opened her mouth, but feared the man would hang up the moment she spoke. She let out a sigh, an impatient one like she'd heard Courtney do numerous times.

Silence.

"You're in trouble, aren't you?" he said, then swore angrily. "I told you not to get involved with these people." *These people?* Silence. "Courtney?"

"You were right," Dakota said, dropping her voice in the hopes she would sound enough like her sister.

Silence. Then he let out a curse. She heard the telltale sound of the phone disconnecting.

"Well," she said after repeating what the man had said, "Courtney's involved in something."

"Yeah, we kind of figured that. Bar tab, huh? Would you recognize the man's voice if you heard it again?"

"I think so."

"Sounds like she hooked up with a bartender at one of the local bars and ran up a tab," Zane said. "We might have to hit the bars."

Dakota nodded as she looked down at the list of phone numbers. "No other numbers we don't know."

The lime-green compact car was almost hidden in a stand of old junipers at the bottom of the ravine.

McCall found her deputy waiting for her beside a patrol car parked at the side of the road. As she walked over to the edge of the ravine, she noted the tire tracks where the car had gone off the road.

"No skid marks, no sign of the driver trying to brake," the deputy said as he joined her.

"Could have been going too fast and missed the curve, didn't have time to brake," McCall said.

"Yep, could have," he agreed.

That was, if Courtney Baxter had been driving the car.

"Got to wonder what she was doing way out here," the deputy said.

"No sign of the driver?" McCall asked.

The deputy shook his head. "I couldn't find any tracks, but then we had that big storm down this way the other night. Could have covered 'em."

"Let's go see," McCall said, and saw the deputy shoot her a look.

"It's pretty steep," he warned.

She ignored him and started down the slope. It *was* steep, the ground unstable. The dirt moved under her, an avalanche of soil. She began to slide and realized too late how she'd let her pride overrun her good sense.

Fortunately, the embankment ended at the edge of the junipers. She slid to a stop near the bottom of the ravine, grabbed a branch on one of the juniper trees and used it to keep from sliding any farther.

She felt the baby kick and smiled. That had actually been fun, she thought as she moved around the junipers to the side of the lime-green vehicle.

One glance told her what she already knew. The car was empty.

McCall glanced around, checking the ground for footprints. The only ones in the dirt were the deputy's. Either he was right about the storm erasing them, or no one had been in the car when it had gone off the road.

McCall pulled on the latex gloves from her pocket and opened the driver's side door. She caught the smell of something sour and felt her stomach roil. She'd been this way since the beginning of her pregnancy. No three months of morning sickness for her. Every smell affected her.

As she drew back from the odor, she noticed that the keys were in the ignition and the car was in Neutral. She checked the seat. It was pushed all the way back.

Whoever had last driven this car was long-legged, possibly longer-legged than Courtney Hughes aka Courtney Baxter.

McCall suspected that someone had pushed the car off the road into the deep ravine. Hoping it wouldn't be found?

Hard to hide a lime-green anything, though.

Holding her breath, she leaned into the car to check under the seats. She found the bloody rag stuffed under the passenger seat. It was wrapped around something heavy. Carefully, she turned back the dark-stained edges of the rag to reveal a gun.

The grip was stained with what appeared to be blood. The smell of the dried blood turned her stomach. She quickly wrapped the gun back up, leaving it on the floor of the passenger side, and stepped away from the car.

Taking large gulps of fresh air, McCall fought to

keep her breakfast down. The last thing she wanted to do was contaminate the scene. She took a few more deep breaths, steadied herself, then called to the deputy to contact the state crime lab.

After a few moments, she made the climb back up to her patrol SUV. The baby kicked again. She placed her hand on her stomach, felt the movement and made a promise to her infant and her husband that she would stop this—as soon as the undersheriff got back. Just a few more days.

"Everything is going to be fine," she whispered as much to herself as her baby.

But she feared that wasn't the case for Courtney Baxter.

Dakota drove part of the way back to the Lansing ranch while Zane slept.

She'd had a lot of time to think. Too much time apparently, since she'd found herself reliving Zane's kiss. A part of her wished she hadn't cut it off when she had. Another part of her, the logical, smart part, thought she should have stopped him sooner.

She was more than aware of Zane's reputation with women. She had no intention of becoming one of them. Last night, lying in her motel room bed, knowing he was only feet away in the next room, she'd had a terrible time getting to sleep.

Dakota hated that he still had that effect on her. She felt like that silly girl who'd trailed after him hoping for even just a smile from him.

As she turned down the road to the ranch, she knew she couldn't keep spending day after day with him.

Zane jerked awake as she pulled into the yard and cut the engine. Without a word, he was out of the pickup and striding toward the front door of the guesthouse.

She went after him. "Courtney's car isn't— Just a minute. I have the key...." Her words died off as she saw Zane try the knob. It turned in his hand and the door swung open.

He glanced back at her, all his fears culminating in his expression. He seemed to brace himself as he waited for her to join him before he stepped inside.

Dakota wasn't sure what she expected. She had a pretty good idea that Zane might have anticipated finding Courtney sprawled dead on one of the Navajo rugs gracing the hardwood floors.

The small living area was empty. So were the kitchen and bedroom and bath, as well as the closet.

"She's cleared out," Zane said, turning to look at her.

Dakota stared at the empty closet in surprise. When Courtney had shown up at their father's funeral with evidence that she was her half sister, Dakota had been afraid Courtney was after half the ranch.

After the shock of having a sister had worn off, Dakota had decided that Courtney deserved half interest in the ranch and their father's business. She was Clay Lansing's daughter, after all, and she'd missed out on a lot. Why shouldn't she have a chance to live on the ranch if she wanted to?

"I always wanted a sister," she said.

Zane gave her an odd look.

"I was just getting used to the idea." She sighed. "She would have noticed that her suitcase and money were missing, don't you think?"

"Unless she wasn't the one who cleaned everything out. Whoever gave her the money might not know what she did with it."

"Why would someone else remove all her things?"

"To make us think she is still alive."

Still alive. Dakota felt a chill at his words.

"If Courtney came back and realized her suitcase was missing, I'm sure she'll be in contact with you soon." He didn't sound as if he believed that was going to happen any more than she did.

She watched him search the small guesthouse. "What are you looking for?"

"Anything she might have left behind. You didn't happen to write down her license plate number, did you?"

"No, I had no reason to." But now that she thought of it, it would have been a good idea. She had just assumed that her biggest worry was that her sister would try to force her to sell the ranch so Courtney could get her share.

So what had changed?

Zane, she thought as she watched him move the bureau away from the wall. Zane and ten thousand dollars, is that what had changed? If they were right and her birth mother had contacted her, was it possible she'd put Courtney up to this? But why? It made no sense.

No, Dakota thought. This had to have something to do with her and Zane and Courtney being spiteful. But how far was her sister planning to take this? That's what scared her.

She stepped closer to see what Zane was reaching for. "You found something?"

"A credit card receipt. Looks like it was for food and drinks at the bar in Zortman." He held it up. "Is it yours?"

"I can't imagine how it could be. What is the date on it?"

"A week ago."

She shook her head. "I hardly ever get down to Zortman." It was a small old mining town an hour to the south.

"Has anyone else been in this room since then?"

"No. Just Courtney."

He met her gaze. "This could be the bartender who called. He apparently knows more than we do about what Courtney's been up to. How do you feel about hitting that bar down in Zortman? I need to check in at home first. I'm surprised that my brothers don't have the National Guard out looking for me."

"Give me a call when you're ready and I'll drive over to Whitehorse later," Dakota said. "I need to take care of a few things around here first." The lie seemed to hang between them.

"Sure. You know you don't have to go. I can go down and talk to the bartender on my own."

Dakota hesitated, caught between wanting to find Courtney and wanting to put distance between her and Zane and the old feelings he evoked in her.

"No," she said, finding Courtney and her diary winning out. "Just give me a call."

When Zane's cell phone rang, he thought it was Dakota calling to say she'd changed her mind. He'd seen that she hadn't wanted to go with him to Zortman. He didn't blame her. They'd been together now for almost forty-eight hours. Clearly, she'd had enough of him.

He mentally kicked himself for kissing her as he took the call. Had he thought she was still that starry-eyed girl who'd had a crush on him? What had he been thinking?

"Just received those DNA results from the cell phone," Doc said by way of introduction, then paused.

"Yes?"

"Whoever's blood is on the phone, I can tell you that the person is female and related to Dakota Lansing."

"Could it be a sister with the same father, different mothers?" Zane asked.

"Definitely could be from what I see in the DNA report," Doc said.

So Courtney really was her sister. He'd been so sure she wasn't and that she'd been pretending to be Clay Lansing's love child as part of some elaborate scam—a scam that somehow involved him.

And the blood *was* Courtney's. That thought was slow coming, but hit him like a brick. There hadn't been a lot of blood, but enough to scare him.

He had hoped it had been staged and would end up being animal blood.

"You still there?" Doc asked.

"Yeah, sorry, I'm just surprised. Thanks." As he hung up, he turned down his lane and saw the sheriff's SUV sitting in front of his house. He swore under his breath.

He glanced in the rearview mirror and saw his face. It wasn't that much better than it had been yesterday. The scratches were starting to heal, but still shocking.

Worse, he couldn't explain any of it, including the blood on Courtney's phone. Glancing over, he saw the bagged phone sitting on the seat where Dakota had left it. He pocketed the plastic bag with the phone inside and parked next to the SUV, hoping the sheriff wasn't here with bad news.

As he climbed out, he caught a glimpse of McCall's expression and knew whatever she was here for wasn't good.

"Zane," the sheriff said as she climbed awkwardly out of her rig.

He saw the exact moment she got a good look at his face and the scratches. Her expression darkened even more.

"Want to tell me how you got those scratches?" She sounded angry and disappointed.

He was pretty sure she now knew that he'd been hiding in the bathroom the other day so she wouldn't see his face. He swore silently. He looked even more guilty. Worse, the sheriff would know Dakota had been in on it.

"I don't know how I got the scratches," he said honestly. "But I'll tell you what I do know."

She nodded slowly. "Maybe we better step inside your house. You have a problem with that?"

He shook his head. He knew he should probably call the ranch lawyer. At the very least make her get a warrant. But he feared that would only make matters worse. He knew McCall, knew the kind of sheriff she was. All he could do was put his cards on the table.

Once inside the house, he offered the sheriff a seat as well as something to drink. Not surprisingly, she wasn't in the mood for either.

He told her everything, leaving out nothing but making sure he covered for Dakota.

When he finished, McCall said, "Where is this suitcase with the money in it?"

"It's in my truck behind the seat."

"Let's go get it," the sheriff said.

While he dug out the suitcase, she stood behind him.

"If you don't mind, you can put it in my car," she said, opening the passenger side door of the SUV for him to load the suitcase. "Then I'd like to have a look around your house. With your permission."

"Fine with me," he said as he led her back to the house. As they entered, he told her, "There's a broken lamp on the other side of the bed. I have no idea how it got broken."

"And the cell phone you found under the bed?" she asked.

Reluctantly, he produced it from his pocket.

She raised a brow when she saw that he'd placed it in a sandwich bag—and that it had what she must recognize as blood on it.

"The blood belongs to Courtney Baxter, although that's not her legal name, according to her mother. It's Courtney Hughes."

The sheriff didn't seem surprised at that news. "You should have come to me right away."

"I knew even less then than I do now. I wanted to find Courtney first."

McCall looked around the small house, going into the bedroom last. The covers on the bed were still rumpled; everything looked as it had when he'd awakened from what he now thought of as his mystery date from hell.

He watched McCall awkwardly bend down to look under the bed, saw her freeze and felt his heart drop. What of interest could possibly be under the bed? There'd been nothing under there when he'd found the phone.

She rose long enough to pull on latex gloves, then bent down again to pull out a red dress—the dress Courtney Baxter had been wearing when she'd appeared at his door two nights before.

Even from the bedroom doorway, he saw the dark stains on the silken fabric. More blood.

"That wasn't under the bed when I left here yesterday," he said, his denial sounding hollow, his voice tight with dread. "I'm being set up. I swear to you...."

McCall pushed herself to her feet and turned to face him. The rest of his words died off as he saw her expression.

"Zane Chisholm. You have the right to remain silent," she began as she bagged the dress, then reached for her handcuffs.

Chapter 8

Emma looked forward to trips into Whitehorse even though Mrs. Crowley was far from a fun companion. She spoke little and became irritated quickly if Emma tried to force conversation.

But being a recluse, Mrs. Crowley made it easy for Emma to have some free time away from everyone. It was their secret that Mrs. Crowley dropped her off to do her errands and picked her up hours later. For that Emma was eternally grateful.

Hoyt would have a fit if he knew. But Emma felt safe in Whitehorse. She still carried a pistol in her purse and kept on the lookout for anyone who didn't seem familiar.

It hadn't taken long to tell the locals from the occasional tourist passing through town. Whitehorse didn't get a lot of tourists. Most people came to Montana to see the mountains, towering pine trees and clear, fast streams. They had little interest in the rolling prairie, which was short on mountains, pines and streams.

Today though, Emma found herself wondering where Mrs. Crowley spent those free hours. The housekeeper never complained. In fact, she seemed to enjoy the time alone. Or maybe she just enjoyed being shed of Emma after the twenty-mile trip into town.

Emma knew she talked too much. But after being around so many men at the ranch, she was thankful to find herself in a woman's company—even Mrs. Crowley. She was excited at the idea of spending some hours on her own. The past year had been difficult. She had always been extremely independent. Being tied down and required to always have someone with her had been hell for her.

Not that she ever regretted marrying Hoyt. That was why she tried hard not to complain. This wasn't his fault, and she didn't want him blaming himself.

Today she had thoroughly enjoyed herself in town and was almost sorry when Mrs. Crowley pulled up in the truck for the ride home.

As she climbed into the passenger side, she noticed that Mrs. Crowley looked disheveled, which was completely out of character. Also the cab of the pickup smelled odd. She glanced more closely at the woman behind the wheel.

"Is something wrong?" she asked, taking in the death grip the housekeeper had on the steering wheel.

"I'm fine," Mrs. Crowley snapped.

Emma bit her tongue; however, she couldn't help

noticing that there was dirt under the woman's fingernails. How odd.

It wasn't until she got out of the truck at the ranch
that she saw the shovel in the pickup bed. It was covered with dark soil.

Zane thought about using his one phone call to contact the ranch lawyer. Instead, he called Dakota.

"I've been arrested," he said the moment she answered her cell. "When I got back to the house, the
sheriff was waiting for me. She found something under
the bed that wasn't there yesterday."

"What was it?" Dakota asked, sounding scared.

"It was the dress Courtney was wearing the night
she showed up at my door. Dakota, it looks like there
is blood on it."

"Oh, Zane. You're sure the dress wasn't under the
bed when you found the phone?"

"Positive." He never locked his house. Hardly anyone
around Whitehorse did. But he mentally kicked himself
for not thinking to do it yesterday when they'd left. He
had made it too easy for whoever was trying to frame
him. He'd thought the damage was already done. He'd
been wrong about that.

"Someone is definitely setting me up. I'm just scared
that something has happened to Courtney. Could you
call my dad? I used my one call to phone you."

"Of course. And I'll follow up on that receipt we
found behind the bureau."

"No, don't. Please. It's too dangerous. Whoever is
behind this… I'm afraid they're playing for keeps."

"You think Courtney is dead." Her voice broke and he could hear how scared she was that it was true.

"I hate to be the one to tell you this, but I heard as I was being led into the sheriff's department that Courtney's car was found in a ravine south of town. That was apparently why the sheriff was waiting at my house. I think McCall found more evidence against me in the car." He hesitated. "There's something else, Dakota. Doc called me. The DNA test results? Courtney *is* your sister."

Dakota hung up, shaken by the news. Zane in jail on possible murder charges. Courtney *was* her half sister— just as she'd claimed. And now she might be dead, her car in a ravine and more evidence against Zane in it?

She felt a sense of panic mixed with worry and heartfelt pain. She hadn't trusted Courtney. Still didn't. All she could hope was that her sister was alive and behind some scheme to make it appear Zane had done her harm.

It still made no sense. Courtney wouldn't take sibling rivalry this far. There had to be more to this.

Dakota reminded herself that her sister wasn't working alone. Who was this other person? Her birth mother?

She shuddered at the thought of Courtney's bloody dress being found under Zane's bed. Whoever was setting him up was building a strong case against him.

Dakota hurriedly called the Chisholm ranch, anxious to let Emma and Hoyt know what was going on so they could get Zane a good lawyer.

A woman answered the phone, her voice a little gravelly. "Chisholm Ranch, Mrs. Crowley speaking."

Mrs. Crowley? Zane hadn't mentioned anyone by that name. "I'm calling for Hoyt Chisholm."

"I'm sorry, he isn't in. May I take a message?"

Dakota heard someone ask, "Who is it?" then "I'll take it, Mrs. Crowley."

"Hello? This is Emma Chisholm, can I help you?"

Dakota introduced herself and quickly told her what had happened. "I'm sorry to have to tell you this over the phone."

"No, I appreciate you calling for Zane. It's just that... I'm shocked," Emma said.

"I'm sure Zane will fill you in on everything that's happened. You'll make sure his lawyer is called?"

"Of course. Thank you for letting me know."

Dakota hung up, unable to shake her fear for Zane—and Courtney. The way this was escalating, she couldn't believe Courtney had known what she was getting into.

As she glanced around the empty ranch house, she realized that she was spooked. She'd never been scared living out here so far from any other houses. The ranch had always been a safe place.

Until Courtney showed up, she thought with a shiver.

Zane had told her not to drive to Zortman and talk to the bartender, but when she considered all the evidence stacking up against him, she knew she couldn't just sit back and do nothing.

She didn't believe for an instant that Zane would hurt Courtney. It scared her though. If Courtney's car had been found and there was even more incriminating evidence in it... Was Courtney still alive? She shuddered at the thought that it might be too late for the sister she hadn't even gotten to know. Ultimately, blood was thicker than water. Whoever was behind this was going to pay.

Dakota reached for her purse. Maybe she couldn't save her sister; maybe no one could. But she would move heaven and hell to prove that Zane was innocent of this. She'd never been to the Miner's Bar in Zortman, but she'd heard stories about how rough it was when the gold mine had been up and running.

Still, she knew it would be at least a while before the ranch attorney could get Zane before a judge, and there was always the chance he wouldn't be able to make bail.

Dakota feared that whoever was behind this would be tying up any loose ends. If Courtney was still alive, then Dakota had to move quickly. She felt as if the clock was ticking, the noose around Zane's neck tightening as well.

As she headed for her pickup, Dakota tried to imagine why Courtney would agree to be part of this. Ten thousand dollars? There had to be more to it. Courtney had grown up in a nice house with two parents who loved her and provided well for her. Also, Courtney hadn't thought enough about the money to put it somewhere safer than under the bed—or take it with her.

It had to be something more alluring than cash.

Courtney's birth mother. With a start, Dakota realized what a pull that could have had on her sister. Courtney was an only child who had never known her father or mother.

Dakota knew what it was like not having a mother. What had it been like for Courtney not knowing either of her birth parents? Maybe she had yearned for that connection, someone who she resembled, more than her adopted mother had known.

Family. Was that the hook that had gotten Courtney involved in what she might have thought at first was innocent?

Clearly she hadn't realized how dangerous it was. Now, if Courtney was still alive, she would definitely be a loose end.

Dakota called Miner's Bar on her way to Zortman. She figured that even if the bartender wasn't working, he wouldn't be that hard to find.

Zortman was a small, old mining town, even smaller than Whitehorse. It squatted at the edge of the Little Rockies, surrounded by pine trees and rock cliffs.

"He ain't here," said a male voice as if this was his standard, humorous response when answering the phone. Dakota could hear chuckling in the background. It was an old bar joke, the typical line when a woman called.

She recognized the man's voice at once. It was the same man who'd answered the number on Courtney's cell phone earlier.

He laughed a little too long at his own joke. "Sorry, Miner's Bar. What can I do you for?" More chuckles.

Apparently the crowd was eating it up or was drunk enough to laugh at anything. Dakota figured it was probably the latter since it was late afternoon.

"Hello?" he said, his voice becoming muffled as if he'd turned away from the crowd at the bar. "Anyone there?" His tone changed. "Court?" he asked in a whisper.

Dakota snapped the cell phone shut and looked down the long straight road toward the Little Rockies. She didn't mind the drive south. This time of year the rolling prairie was lush and green, the sky a crystal clear, blinding blue. Only a few large white cumulus clouds hung on the horizon ahead.

A hawk called to her from a fence post as she passed. She'd just seen a bald eagle near a group of antelope. The antelope had spooked. She'd watched them race to the nearest barbed wire fence, scurry under it and take off again, disappearing over a rise. The eagle still hadn't moved, she saw in her rearview mirror.

As she drove through the ponderosas into Zortman, she spotted Miner's Bar among the other log buildings. It appeared old, the logs weathered. She parked, got out, breathed in the scent of pines and went over again how she was going to play this.

She was Courtney's sister. That much wasn't a lie. Dakota was betting that if the bartender knew about the people her sister had gotten involved with, then the sister wouldn't come as a surprise.

Pushing open the door, Dakota was hit with the smell of stale beer. The bar was like so many in this part of Montana. Small and dark, a bunch of regulars on stools along the bar, a sad Western song playing on the jukebox.

And like bars in out-of-the-way places in Montana, everyone turned as she came in. She felt their gazes as the door shut behind her. Only a few were still staring at her as she made her way to an empty stool at the far end of the bar.

Once people didn't recognize you, they usually went back to their drinking. Only a couple of the younger cowboys at the bar leered at her longer.

"Go get her, Wyatt," one of them said, loud enough for her to hear, as the bartender stopped what he was doing to head in her direction. The others at the bar laughed. Clearly they'd had a few drinks and were looking for some fun.

Dakota studied the bartender as he made his way down the bar. Wyatt was tall, broad-shouldered and not bad looking. There was stubble on his jaw. His blond hair was rumpled and he had a look in his blue eyes that she recognized. She would bet he was exactly Courtney's type.

"What'll you have?" he asked, giving her a grin. She'd also bet someone had told him his grin was irresistible to women. It wouldn't be the first time the man had been lied to, or the last.

She could feel the group down the bar watching now. They'd probably been watching him in action for as long as he'd worked here.

"Whatever you have on tap," she told him.

Wyatt raised a brow. "Gotta love a woman who drinks beer," he said, flirting with her as he poured her one from the tap nearby.

"Does my sister drink beer?" Dakota asked quietly as he set down a bar napkin and her glass of beer.

He leaned toward her as if he wasn't sure he'd heard her. "Your sister?"

"Courtney," she said, still keeping her voice down.

He froze, then picked up a rag and killed some time wiping down the scarred surface of the bar. She could tell he was sizing her up, figuring out what to say, afraid he'd mess up.

"I know she spent some time here. With you." She met his gaze. She figured those nights Courtney had come in late she'd been down here. From Wyatt's expression, she'd figured right.

Wyatt put down the rag, wiped a hand over his mouth and asked, "She told you about me?"

"I'm her sister."

He seemed to relax, even let out a small laugh. "The uptight daddy's cowgirl."

The uptight daddy's cowgirl? So that was how Courtney had described her. Maybe her theory about the sibling rivalry wasn't that far off. Courtney *had* resented the fact that Dakota had had their father all those years and she hadn't. She bristled at the "uptight" part, though.

"And you're her latest sucker," Dakota said to Wyatt, and took a long drink of her beer.

He frowned, angry now. "Hey, watch it. I'm no sucker," he said in a tight whisper.

Dakota lifted a brow as she put down her beer. It was cold and tasted good. She wiped the foam from her upper lip. "So you're saying she didn't stick you with her bar bill?"

He leaned against the bar. "Are you trying to tell me she won't be back? Is that what this is about? She sent you with a message for me? Or didn't she get the money?"

"She got the money, but she seems to have disappeared. Actually, I'm looking for her myself."

He laughed. "She owes you money, too, huh?"

"She's part con artist, no doubt about that. But I'm afraid we're both going to be out of luck if I don't find her. I don't like the people she's…involved with."

"Yeah, me either."

Dakota took another drink of her beer. She had to go slow. If she rushed this, he might spook. But if she gave him too much time to think…

"Of course, she could be lying to both of us."

Wyatt shook his head. "Not if she already got the money. It must just be taking her longer than she thought it would."

So Courtney *had* been paid to do something. Dakota was dying to ask him if he knew what she had to do for the ten thousand dollars. "You think the money is why she's doing this?" Dakota let out a disbelieving sound and took another drink.

"Why else?"

She shrugged. "I think her birth mother has her hooks in her." She took a chance, winging it.

He looked surprised. "She told you about her?"

Dakota didn't bother to answer. "Courtney was worried she couldn't trust the woman. What do you think?"

She could see that he liked being asked what he thought. He even gave it a few seconds of thought before he spoke.

"I think family's what it's all about. Court got choked up even talking about her. It's her *blood,* you know what I mean?"

"Yeah. I get that." She held his gaze.

"Sure, you're her sister. So you're going to do right by her." The last came out almost sounding like a question. Courtney must have told him about the ranch and the business. She'd been eyeing it along with whatever else she was up to, just as Dakota had suspected.

"Still, I'd like to meet her mother, make sure she's on the up-and-up."

"Yeah, me too, but Court wasn't havin' it. I said, 'bring her down to the bar,' but she said her mother doesn't get out much." He shrugged.

"But if the mother's staying in Whitehorse…"

"Up north near the border, I think. Court never really said. I just got the feeling she wasn't in town."

"She mention what her mother wanted her to do for this money?"

He looked wary. "Nope." He didn't ask if Courtney had told her. Clearly, he knew Courtney had no intention of telling *her*. Did that mean he knew her old connection to Zane Chisholm?

Dakota tried a different tactic, seeing that she was losing him. "I would have thought she'd have told you how she had to earn this money her mother was giving her."

He smiled, proving he wasn't as stupid as he appeared. "I should get back down the bar."

"I know Courtney was worried. She took one of our father's pistols."

Wyatt tried to hide his surprise but failed. He held up both hands. "I don't know anything about it." One of the regulars called to him for another drink. He took a step in that direction.

Dakota put a twenty on the bar along with one of

her father's business cards with the house's landline number on it. "My name's Dakota Lansing. If you hear from Courtney…" He started to argue. "She's already called me once saying she was in trouble and needed help. Unfortunately, the line went dead right after that."

He looked scared now. Another regular hollered at him, told him to quit flirting and bring them something to drink, but he didn't move. "I had a bad feeling about this. But I swear, she didn't tell me what she had to do for her mother. Just that she had to do it. She swore it was no big deal. Kind of a prank, really."

A prank? Dakota watched him hightail it down the bar. His hands were shaking as he reached for a couple of bottles of beer in the cooler. He'd suspected it was more than that. Who got paid ten thousand dollars by their mother to be part of a prank?

Wyatt had to know at least a little of what Courtney had been up to, Dakota thought as she left the twenty and her father's business card and walked out of the bar.

"Guess you didn't get far with that one," one of the regulars said, and they all laughed as the door closed behind her.

The state crime techs found the body buried under about six inches of dirt, fifty yards away from where Courtney Baxter's lime-green car was discovered.

McCall got the call late in the afternoon and drove south to the ravine. Coroner George Murphy was already on the scene.

"What have we got?" she asked after trudging through the cactus and sagebrush to the shallow grave. All the crime tech had told her on the phone was that they'd found a body in a shallow grave near where the car had gone off the road.

"The body was dumped here and hastily covered with dirt." George looked a little green around the gills. McCall knew the feeling. She never got used to violent death. It had gotten worse with pregnancy.

"Time of death?"

"I would estimate sometime in the past twenty-four hours. It appears the body was either thrown or rolled off that bluff," George said, pointing to a spot up by the road.

"It wasn't carried?"

He shook his head.

"So the killer might not have been very strong," McCall noted. "Could be why the body wasn't buried more deeply."

"Could be," he agreed. "I suppose you want to see the body." He didn't wait for an answer. He simply unzipped the black bag and stepped back.

McCall let out a surprised, "Who's that?" She'd expected to see Courtney Baxter.

"Your guess is as good as mine," George said. "He didn't have any identification on him. The crime techs took his fingerprints. He has what looks like prison tattoos, so they're pretty sure they'll get an ID on him as soon as they run his prints."

The man, short and slightly built, had been hit in the face with a flat, blunt object; his features were no longer recognizable. Blood was matted in his thinning, dark hair, his fingernails were dirty and broken, his clothing soiled from spending at least twenty-four hours under a pile of dirt.

McCall leaned away from the body, motioning for George to zip the bag up again. Her stomach lurched and she had to turn away from the smell not to be sick.

George handed her a mint. She mumbled her thanks and gazed up at the road, then over to the junipers where Courtney Baxter's car had been found.

"The crime team is broadening its search," George said. "They seem to think there might be another grave out here."

"Courtney Baxter's," McCall said, glad her stomach was finally settling down. "Unless Courtney's the killer."

"McCall, you are the most suspicious person I know," George said as he came over to stand by her. In the distance, crime scene techs were using cadaver dogs to search for more bodies. "I hope I never get like you."

"You will. If you stay at this long enough," she said.

Zane dialed Dakota's cell phone number the moment he made bail. One of the benefits of being a Chisholm was that his father was a powerful rancher and had pull when it came to the local judge. Thanks to his father, he wasn't going to have to spend even one night in jail. At least not yet.

Hoyt Chisholm and the ranch lawyer had convinced the judge that Zane wasn't a flight risk. So far, all the sheriff had was incriminating evidence, but no body.

Zane knew that if Courtney was found dead it could change everything. He didn't even want to think about that. Whoever was behind this was bound to hear he'd made bail. He didn't doubt they would step up their plan to frame him.

As he listened to Dakota's phone go to voice mail, he knew he was waiting for the other shoe to drop.

He had to find out who was behind this before any more "evidence" appeared. His brother Marshall had dropped off his pickup when he'd come in with their father for the bail hearing. He started the engine as he listened to Dakota's voice mail message. Where was she?

He left a message saying he was out on bail and had to see her. He couldn't help being worried about her and didn't like the idea of her staying at the Lansing ranch by herself.

After a moment, he tried the number again. This time when it went to voice mail, he left a message saying he was headed for her ranch and for her to sit tight. He had to see her.

He knew his father and brothers, along with Emma, were anxious to see him. They wanted an explanation. He wished he had one to give them.

But he was too worried about Dakota to do that right now. Worse, he feared she might have decided to do some investigating on her own. She'd mentioned going down to Zortman to talk to the bartender. He'd told her not to go. Unfortunately, he feared that might have been like waving a red flag in front of a bull.

He quickly placed a call home. "I have to make a stop before I come there," Zane told his father when he answered.

"Zane—"

"I'll be there as soon as I can. This is important. Would you ask Emma to make sure one of the guest rooms is ready? I'll be bringing a friend with me." He hung up before his father could question him further.

The hard part would be convincing Dakota to come back to the Chisholm ranch with him. The woman was independent, which he liked. But the more he'd thought about everything while in jail, the more he feared she was in danger.

Chapter 9

It was late by the time Dakota left Zortman. Clouds scudded across a black velvet sky, giving her only fleeting glimpses of a sliver of silver moon.

Exhausted after a long, emotionally draining day, she drove back to the ranch. She was anxious to talk to Zane so she could tell him what she'd found out. She hadn't been able to get any service while on her way to Miner's Bar or on the way back until she reached Chinook.

She checked her messages. Both from Zane. He was out on bail and was headed for her ranch? She half expected to see his pickup when she pulled into the yard. *He must be on his way,* she thought as she climbed out and went inside.

It had been a long day. She wondered if she had time for a hot bath before Zane arrived. She was anxious to talk to him, even more anxious to see him.

Dakota sensed something was wrong the moment she walked into her father's ranch house. She hit the light switch and nothing happened. For just an instant, she thought the bulb in the overhead light had simply burned out.

Then she smelled him.

The hair shot up on the back of her neck. Goose bumps skittered over her flesh as she started to turn, her mouth opening as she tried to find her voice.

Her throat contracted and before she could squeeze out a sound, he was on her. His large hand clamped over her mouth, his arm wrapping around her, snatching her back against him in a viselike grip.

She kicked, tried to free her arms to fight him, but he was so much larger, so much stronger, that she was pinned. He dragged her toward the back of the house, knocking over a chair, then a lamp. The lamp broke, sounding like a shot, as he carried her away in the darkness.

Dakota heard a vehicle coming up the road. She tried to scream, but he had his hand over her mouth and his arm around her, pinning her own arms at her sides.

He shoved her through the open side door of a dark-colored van. She tried to scramble away from him. He caught her leg, dragged her to him and then hit her with his fist.

Stars glittered before her eyes just before the darkness closed in.

"Dakota?" Zane knocked, then tried her door. It swung open. He glanced back at her pickup parked outside. After he'd parked, he'd walked by her truck, felt heat still coming off the engine. She couldn't have been home long.

His fear was that she'd gone down to Miner's Bar in Zortman and put herself in even more danger. "Dakota?"

It was pitch-black inside the house. He tried the light switch. Nothing. Only a faint sliver of moon lit the sky outside, but was quickly extinguished by the cover of clouds. It did little to illuminate the interior of the house even though the curtains were all open. Out here in the middle of nowhere, curtains were seldom closed. No point.

"Dakota?" he called louder as his pulse took off.

The modest ranch house was single-level, the layout allowing him to move swiftly through it. "Dakota?" He heard the growing fear in his voice. Then, in a sudden shaft of moonlight he saw the upended chair and shattered lamp scattered across the floor, and felt the cool breeze coming through the open back door.

He raced to the door, his heart in his throat. In the distance, he heard a vehicle engine turn over. Swearing, he rushed outside into the darkness. He cleared the edge of the yard in time to see a van roar down the road.

Zane tore around the side of the house to his truck, leaped behind the wheel and cranked the engine over. He hadn't gone far when he felt the pickup lean to the right and heard the *whap whap* of the back rear tire.

Even before he stopped and got out he knew what he was going to find. Someone had cut his tire.

He stared after the taillights of the van as they dimmed on the horizon, his heart pounding with fear.

Someone had Dakota. One sister was already missing. Now Dakota.

Call the sheriff.

As he reached for his phone, it rang.

"We have Dakota," a deep male voice said.

Zane had to tamp down his relief. He'd been expecting a call about Courtney and that one had never come. He'd feared the same might be true of Dakota.

"Who's *we?*" he asked, not expecting an answer but needing to fill the silence.

"If you ever want to see her again, you will do exactly as I say. Call the sheriff and I kill her."

"I won't. But don't you hurt her."

A hoarse chuckle. "Then you do what I say." He proceeded to give directions to an old mission cemetery outside of Whitehorse. "You know the place?"

"Yes." The mission building had been boarded up for years and the cemetery was surrounded by an iron fence. Both sat on a hill in the middle of nowhere. The perfect place for an ambush, especially on such a dark night.

"Twenty minutes? Bring the money."

"I'll be there."

"Come alone."

"Of course."

"And unarmed. You'd better get that tire fixed and get movin'. Time is running out for this cowgirl."

"I'm not movin' until I know that Dakota is all right."

The man started to argue, then swore. Zane could hear the scrape of his boot soles on the ground, then the groan of the rusty van door as he opened it.

A moment later, he heard what sounded like duct

tape being ripped from her mouth. Dakota gave out a small cry.

"Tell him you're fine," the man ordered.

"Zane, don't—"

Another cry from Dakota, what sounded like a struggle, then the man's deep voice again. "Happy? She's fine as long as you do what I say."

Zane's free hand balled up in a fist. He couldn't wait to get his hands on the bastard. He hung up and dug out the .38 pistol he kept under his pickup seat, making sure it was loaded.

Then he stuffed the weapon into the pocket of his jean jacket and slipped his hunting knife in its scabbard into the top of his boot.

Twelve minutes later, he'd changed his pickup tire and was headed in the direction of the old mission. He didn't have the money. The sheriff had confiscated it. Apparently whoever had taken Dakota didn't know that.

So that would change how things went down, he thought, as ahead he saw the old mission etched against the dark sky.

Mrs. Crowley heard the commotion shortly after the ranch phone rang. She glanced at her clock. Something was going on, since it was late in the evening. She'd been in bed, but not asleep, her drapes closed, making her room dark as the inside of a coffin.

Easing out of bed, she made her way to the door. Her room was in an empty wing away from the rest of the house. That was a blessing—and a disadvantage. She had to leave her room and sneak down the hallway to the stairs to hear anything that was going on.

Getting caught was not an option. But she was more than a little curious. She crept down the hallway to the top of the stairs, then settled herself into the deep shadows to listen.

"That's all he said?" Emma's insistent voice was followed by Hoyt's low rumble.

"I just know he was arrested because some woman he went out with is missing. He promised to come out here and tell me what's going on. But as you can see, he isn't here."

"Why would he want a guest room ready unless he was bringing someone with him?" Emma had dropped her voice. They were both on the lower wing where the guest rooms were located.

"I have no idea. Believe me, I'd like to know what the hell is going on as much as you do. I'm worried that something else has happened."

"Should we call the sheriff?" Emma asked.

"No. We'll wait and hope for the best."

Mrs. Crowley heard them go toward the kitchen. She knew Emma would make a pot of coffee, then probably bake something. The woman couldn't quit baking.

Sighing, she sneaked back to her room. Normally she never looked out her window, and kept the drapes shut tightly. But now she opened them a crack and peered out.

A breeze stirred the tall, old cottonwoods next to the house. Through the leafy limbs, she caught glimpses of moon and starlight. A dark night. Her favorite. She opened the window a crack and breathed in the air even though it tasted bitter to her, the scent too familiar, too painful.

She closed the window quietly and climbed back into bed. She knew she wasn't going to be able to sleep. As she lay staring up at the ceiling, she smiled to herself. Apparently there was trouble in Chisholm ranch paradise. There would be no lovemaking tonight in that king-size bed on the second floor of the other wing, or out in the barn.

Mrs. Crowley rubbed a hand over her smooth face. She would be glad when she no longer had to pretend to be someone she wasn't. And that time was coming. Soon.

Zane slowed at the turnoff into the old mission. His headlights caught on a dark-colored van parked in the shadow of the church. It sat at an odd angle, the side door open. As the headlights hit it, Zane saw that the van was empty.

As he drove in, his headlights slashed over the terracotta-colored stucco of the church structure, then picked up the bone-white of some of the gravestones higher up the hill.

He parked next to the van, killed his lights and engine and sat for a moment, listening with his side window down.

Clouds played peekaboo with the crescent moon and sky full of stars, keeping the night dark with floating shadows across the landscape. An owl hooted from its perch on the ridge of the church roof. Back on the highway, a semi roared past. Silence followed.

Zane eased his door open and, grabbing an old duffel bag from behind the seat of his pickup, stepped out. The bag had a couple pairs of his old leather branding gloves in it. Ten thousand dollars in hundred dollar bills didn't take up a lot of space. He figured it would be enough weight to fool the kidnapper since Zane had no intention of ever letting the man look inside the bag.

The kidnapper couldn't be inside the church, since it had been boarded up for years. That didn't leave many hiding places.

Moving slowly, Zane climbed the slope toward the graveyard. At the edge of the building he stopped to make sure the kidnapper wasn't hiding in the shadow of the church.

The moon came out from behind a cloud, painting the side of the church in silver. No sign of anyone next to the church, but they could have moved around to the highway side.

He had his doubts about that. A man holding a woman at gunpoint could be seen in the glare of lights from the highway. Zane doubted the man would take that chance.

Turning his gaze back to the graveyard, he continued up the hillside. There could be only one other place the kidnapper was hiding with Dakota.

Most of the gravestones were too small and narrow to hide behind. But as he climbed higher, he saw several larger tombstones, these closer together and deeper in shadow.

"I'm here," he called as he moved toward the larger moss-covered gravestones.

Something moved in the dark twenty yards in front of him. He could make out the man's huge shape against the black sky and see the man's arm locked around Dakota's neck. As he moved closer, he caught the faint glint of a gun; the barrel was next to her head.

"Keep your hands where I can see them," the man called out. "Did you bring the money?"

Zane held the bag out away from his body as he moved toward the man, keeping his gaze on Dakota. She had a strip of duct tape over her mouth and her hands were bound behind her.

As Zane approached slowly, the moon and a few stars broke free of the clouds, casting an eerie, ghostlike glow over the graveyard. He locked eyes on Dakota and saw the determined gleam burning there. The man hadn't hurt her, but he had made her furious.

He smiled to himself in relief. Even after the years apart, he knew this woman. From the look on her face, she was ready for whatever he had in mind. With the relief came a surge of love. Dakota had always been strong. He needed her to be strong now as he prayed that he didn't get her killed.

When he passed one of the taller headstones, he pretended to stumble on the uneven ground and surreptitiously dropped his gun behind the gravestone before taking a few more steps toward the kidnapper.

"That's close enough," the man said.

Stopping ten feet away from the man, Zane set down the duffel bag and took a step back from it. "Now let her go."

The man shook his head. "Not until you hand over the money. Throw it to me."

Zane took another step back, now within feet of the tombstone where he'd dropped his weapon. "We had a deal. I brought your money. Let her go."

He could see the man's indecision even in the dark. He wanted the money badly. He was nervous and afraid; clearly this wasn't something he did every day.

Zane watched as the man took a step toward the bag, dragging Dakota with him. She was making it as difficult as possible for him to keep the gun on her and move her forward.

The man swore and released her, giving her a push that sent her sprawling between two old, bleached-white gravestones.

The moment she hit the ground, she disappeared into the darkness. Zane heard her scramble away from the man.

The kidnapper swore and hurried to the bag as Zane backed up to the gravestone where he'd dropped his pistol.

As the man reached for the bag, Zane reached for his gun. Slipping behind the tombstone, he raised it to aim at the kidnapper's chest.

The man, intent on the money, didn't seem to notice at first that Zane had suddenly dropped down behind a gravestone ten feet away.

But when he did, he brought his gun up and got off a shot. The bullet ricocheted off the crumbling stone inches from Zane's head. The man started to dodge toward one of the headstones for cover. But even moving, he made a large target. The first bullet didn't seem to faze him.

Zane fired again, dropping the man to his knees. He'd dropped the bag a few feet from him. He made a move for it. Zane fired into the dirt next to the duffel bag and the man jerked his hand back.

"Where is Courtney Baxter?" he called to the kidnapper. "What have you done with her?"

The kidnapper looked up, surprised by the question. "You're asking the wrong person," he called back as he made another lunge for the bag.

Zane's next bullet caught the big man in the leg.

He let out a howl, stumbled awkwardly to his feet again and charged, getting off two shots that pelted the gravestone around Zane and sent rock chips into the air.

Zane fired once more, the man just feet from him. The final shot stopped the kidnapper cold. He stood like a lumbering pine swaying in the wind before toppling, coming down with a crash that stirred the dust around him.

Zane kicked the man's gun away from him and then knelt down to check for a pulse. He found none. The air smelled of gunpowder, the night suddenly deathly quiet again.

"Dakota," Zane called as he got to his feet.

She stumbled out of the deep shadows of the gravestones. She had managed to cut the tape around her wrists on something she'd found in the cemetery and was freeing her hands as she came out of the dark.

He took her in his arms. "Did he hurt you?"

She shook her head, removed the tape from her mouth and pressed her face into his chest.

"Did you recognize him?" he asked.

"I'd never seen him before."

With one arm holding Dakota, Zane pulled out his cell and was surprised to get service this far from a town. He punched in 911.

* * *

Emma talked Hoyt into going to bed after Zane called to say something had come up. "He said he would see us in the morning. Whatever is going on, apparently it is going to have to wait until morning."

Hoyt tried Zane's number. It went straight to voice mail. He finally went to bed and instantly fell to sleep.

Emma felt as if she'd just closed her eyes when she heard a vehicle. She checked the clock and was surprised to see that she'd slept for hours. It was almost three in the morning.

She went to the window, expecting to see Zane and whoever he'd wanted the guest room for.

"Mrs. Crowley?" What could the woman possibly be doing out this late on these nights?

Even as she told herself it was none of her business, she watched Mrs. Crowley slip into the house. For a long moment Emma eyed the pickup the woman used. Finally, knowing she wasn't going to get any sleep if she didn't, she pulled on Hoyt's dark robe and sneaked downstairs.

At the bottom, she stopped to listen. Not a sound came from Mrs. Crowley's wing of the house. Still, she waited. She would have a hard time pretending she'd merely come downstairs for a glass of water if Mrs. Crowley caught her.

Of course, there was always sleepwalking. Emma shoved that thought away with a snort. Mrs. Crowley would see right through that. The woman had an uncanny ability when it came to reading people.

Still not a sound.

In the kitchen, she slid open the utility drawer and

felt around until her fingers closed on the small flash-light Hoyt kept there.

She ran the beam over the extra keys on the peg by the door until she found the spare key for the pickup Mrs. Crowley had been given to use.

Then she quickly turned off the flashlight and stood, gripping the key and listening.

She hated sneaking around her own house. But she knew that thought had more to do with her own guilty conscience, given what she was planning to do.

Snugging Hoyt's robe around her small frame, she tiptoed through the living room to the front door. The house was never locked—until Aggie Wells had come into their lives with stories about Hoyt's first wife coming back from the dead.

Emma eased the door open slowly. It creaked and her heart stopped. She listened, then slipped out onto the porch. The night air felt good. She breathed it in, studying the horizon.

She never got tired of the view of rolling grasslands, the Little Rockies in the distance, a dark purple smudge in the starlight. Emma loved the smell of fresh earth and new, green grasses. She loved Montana and Hoyt, she thought as her heart gave a small kick.

What was she doing spying on their housekeeper?

She almost changed her mind and went back inside. But then she noticed the muddy tires of the pickup they'd given Mrs. Crowley to drive.

There hadn't been any rain this far north, but she'd heard a storm had blown through down in the Missouri Breaks.

Maybe Mrs. Crowley had gone sightseeing.

Until three in the morning?

The air suddenly felt cold. She pulled the robe tighter and made her way quietly to the pickup, keeping to the shadows of the house.

Mrs. Crowley's room was on the far side of the wing, but she had access to every room in the house.

Emma glanced up. All the curtains on this side were open, the glass dark behind them. Fortunately Mrs. Crowley always parked the truck at the end of the wing in the darkest part of the yard.

Emma quickly slipped around the side of the pickup farthest from the house and eased open the passenger side door.

The dome light came on. She quickly turned it off. Then, leaving the door open, she slid across the seat and behind the wheel.

She didn't want to turn on the flashlight, so she felt around until she found the ignition. She slipped the key in after a few awkward attempts and turned it.

When she heard it click, she pulled the tiny flashlight from the robe pocket and, shielding it with her hand, shone the light on the dashboard.

After quickly memorizing the mileage, she turned off the light, removed the key and slipped back out of the pickup.

As she started to ease the passenger side door shut, she caught a smell that made her stomach roil. It smelled like something had died in the cab of the truck. She thought about the shovel caked with fresh soil and the dirt under Mrs. Crowley's fingernails after the last trip to town and shuddered.

The pickup door clicked shut. She pushed to make

sure it had latched and then sneaked back along the house. When she reached the porch, she took one of the chairs and sat for a moment, her heart pounding.

I'm too old for this.

The thought made her chuckle to herself. She would never be too old for this. A sense of satisfaction filled her. She was going to find out what Mrs. Crowley was up to at night, if for no other reason than her own curiosity.

The woman had way too many secrets.

Chapter 10

"Oh dear, what happened to the two of you?" Emma cried as she ushered Zane and Dakota into the house.

Dakota knew they both looked a mess after what they'd been through last night. They were both dirty and exhausted, Zane's scratches still prominent.

They'd spent the rest of the night at the sheriff's department answering questions and being grilled about the dead man. Zane had been anxious to get to the ranch, so they hadn't even eaten since yesterday at noon.

Hoyt stepped up to his son, reached for his hand and then pulled him into a quick hug. Dakota saw the fear in the older man's face and knew how relieved he must be. Her own father would have felt the same way. She thought of him and felt her eyes blur with tears.

"What you must have been through," Emma said to

Dakota. Dakota shuddered as she remembered being taken captive last night. "Oh, sweetheart, it's all right."

Zane put an arm around her and pulled her close.

"The sheriff called and told us some of it," Hoyt said. "But I'd like to hear it from you."

Zane nodded. "This is Dakota Lansing."

Hoyt Chisholm's eyes widened in surprise. "Clay's girl. I was sorry to hear about your father."

She nodded numbly, and Emma ushered them into the kitchen where she served them hot coffee and cranberry coffee cake. Dakota ate two pieces; the cake was the best she'd ever eaten.

"Can I fix you breakfast?" Emma asked, no doubt seeing how Dakota had scarfed down the coffee cake.

"Not now," Hoyt said, and waved a hand at her. Then he quickly smiled over at her. "I'm sorry. This is all so upsetting. First Zane is arrested and now this?"

Dakota listened as Zane filled them in on everything, from the woman he'd never seen before showing up at his door for the bogus date, to the shooting last night at the old mission graveyard.

"This woman is your *sister?*" Hoyt asked, frowning. "I guess I never knew Clay had another daughter."

"Neither did I," Dakota said. She explained how she hadn't found out until her father's funeral.

"How old is this sister?" Emma asked, sounding as shocked as Dakota had felt.

"Not quite two years younger than me."

Hoyt got up and went to the cupboard over the sink. He pulled down a fresh bottle of bourbon and poured himself a drink, took a swig, then turned to ask if anyone else would like some.

"Hoyt, it's eight in the morning," Emma said, glad she'd dismissed Mrs. Crowley for the rest of the day. She'd hoped the housekeeper would go into town but as far as she knew, the woman had only gone as far as her room.

"How is it you never knew about this sister?" Hoyt asked. His voice sounded strained as he ignored his wife's scolding.

Dakota explained about her father's affair. "It had to be about the time my mother was dying or right after."

"Thirty years ago," Hoyt said more to himself than to anyone in the kitchen. He finished his drink and poured himself another.

Emma got up and went to him, touching his arm. Dakota heard her whisper, "Are you okay, honey?"

He nodded and turned back to Dakota. "Did your sister say anything about her mother?"

"No, and I didn't ask. Then when she disappeared…"

Zane took up the story, explaining about the trip to Great Falls, meeting Camilla Hughes and finding out about Courtney's trip north.

"We think her birth mother contacted her because she was going by the last name of Baxter," Dakota said. "The mother's name was Lorraine Baxter."

All the color drained from Hoyt Chisholm's face. The glass in his hands slipped from his fingers. It hit the tile floor and shattered, glass shards skittering across the floor.

Emma let out a small startled cry as the glass broke at her husband's feet.

"What's wrong?" Emma cried as she grabbed his

arm. He was visibly shaking, pale with beads of sweat breaking out on his forehead.

Dakota feared he was having a heart attack.

"Did you know her?" Zane asked as he stared at his father.

Hoyt swallowed. "I was married to her."

McCall had put off calling Courtney Hughes's parents until she got the DNA test results from the blood found on the red dress she'd discovered under Zane Chisholm's bed.

She was anxious after everything that had happened. Zane Chisholm was adamant that he was being framed and Courtney and her birth mother were in on it. McCall didn't know what to believe. But she had a missing woman, an apparently abandoned car, evidence of possible foul play and two dead men.

The men had both been identified as escapees from a California prison. She had put a call in to the warden to see what she could find out about the men. Hopefully he might have some idea how they'd ended up in Montana, involved with Courtney Hughes aka Courtney Baxter.

When her phone rang, she jumped. The baby kicked as she reached for it. Just a few more days. In the meantime, she hoped to get some answers. She hated to leave this case for her undersheriff, who would be coming in cold on it.

She was relieved when she saw the call was from the state crime lab.

"The DNA found in the blond hair from the car matches the DNA found in the blood of the dress," the tech told her. "Same woman."

Time to call the young woman's parents.

"What was unusual," the tech continued, "was that the DNA search brought up a flagged comparison test from about thirty years ago."

"Flagged comparison test?"

"Another missing woman. This one was believed to have been drowned, but her DNA was sent to us and flagged in case any DNA test should produce a match."

Drowned, missing victim? McCall swallowed, her heart pounding so hard she could barely hear herself think. "Are you telling me that a relative of Courtney Hughes is in the system?"

"Courtney Hughes's DNA results were a close enough match that the other one came up. Definitely related. I'd say mother and daughter. Interesting, huh?"

McCall thought about what Zane had told her. Courtney had been contacted by her birth mother. They suspected the Whitehorse Sewing Circle had been involved.

"You're saying that this other missing woman was Courtney's birth mother?"

"From the results, that is exactly what I'm saying. I pulled up the file. It's from a missing person's case from your area. A woman by the name of Laura Chisholm."

Emma stared at her husband. "There is another wife I don't know about?"

Hoyt shook his head and took her hands in his, his gaze filling with pain. "Lorraine Baxter was Laura Chisholm's maiden name. She thought 'Lorraine' sounded too old so she went by Laura. She had it changed legally, I think, at some point."

Everyone in the room fell silent as they let that sink in. Emma finally found her voice again.

"Courtney Hughes is Laura's daughter?" She looked over at Dakota. "You said she is about thirty-one or thirty-two? That means Courtney had to be born after Laura allegedly drowned," Emma said, even though she could see from everyone's faces that they'd all figured that out themselves.

Zane nodded. "So Laura Chisholm didn't drown, just as Aggie Wells said."

Emma felt sick to her stomach as she shooed her husband out of the way and cleaned up the broken glass. She needed the diversion. Her mind was spinning. Aggie had tried to warn her and now she was dead, all because no one had believed her. She reached behind her husband for the bourbon and poured herself a glass.

"I don't understand this," Hoyt said as he moved to the table and sat down heavily in one of the chairs. Some of his color had returned.

"It's pretty clear." Emma took a sip of the bourbon. It burned all the way down. "This is a message from Laura. All of this, setting up Zane, using Courtney—she wants you to know she's alive."

"Not just alive," Zane pointed out. "Capable of destroying our lives."

Hoyt rubbed a hand over his face. "Laura was so insecure, so needy. I was trying to build a ranch so I wasn't around enough. We were in the process of adopting the boys...."

"We have no proof that Laura is Courtney's mother," Emma said, knowing she was clutching at straws.

"I saw a birth certificate. It had both their names on it, but I suppose it could have been forged," Dakota said.

Hoyt shook his head. "Laura told me Clay was the father of her child."

Emma thought her husband couldn't surprise her further. She'd been wrong. She stared at him as if seeing a stranger. "When—"

"That day on the lake." He met her gaze. "I'm sorry I didn't tell you, but I couldn't bear to relive any more of the past than I've been forced to. Laura knew how badly I wanted a houseful of children. Her final blow was to tell me she was pregnant with Clay Lansing's baby."

"Did he know?" Dakota asked in a small voice.

"No. She told me she wasn't going to have it. I saw then that she had so little respect for human life and that was really the last straw. I told her I didn't love her and that I wanted a divorce. She went crazy."

"That's when she fell overboard," Emma said.

He nodded. "I wanted her out of my life but I didn't want her dead. I tried to save her...."

The room had fallen silent again.

Emma moved to her husband and wrapped her arms around him. "She's sick, obsessed and mentally unbalanced." None of those words came even close to describing Laura's kind of sickness.

"You realize we have no way of proving any of this," Zane said. "All we have is Camilla's word that the birth mother's name was Lorraine Baxter. Courtney has the birth certificate with both Lorraine's name and Clay Lansing's, and if Clay didn't know about the baby, then it is a forgery."

"She had the baby and gave it up for adoption?" Emma asked.

Dakota nodded. "We suspect through the Whitehorse Sewing Circle, so there will be no proof to find there."

"But surely one of the members…" Emma said. She'd heard about the group of women and what they'd done for years. It hadn't seemed like such a sinister thing to do, providing babies to good loving homes.

Now she feared that they might never know the truth. Unless Laura was found. She almost laughed at the thought. Laura would find them. She was probably close by, enjoying the pain she was causing them all.

"I'm worried about what she did to my sister," Dakota said.

"If we're right and Courtney is her daughter, then Laura wouldn't hurt her," Emma said with more conviction than she felt. Her words were met with silence.

Hoyt took her hand and squeezed it gently. "If Laura is alive, she's a murderer."

"How can you say *if?*" Emma demanded.

"Because I don't want to believe it," Hoyt said.

She softened her expression as she looked at him. Of course he didn't want to believe it. "Whatever she's done, it has nothing to do with you."

His laugh held no humor. "Emma, it has everything to do with me. I'm at fault. She didn't believe that I loved her enough. She turned to another man. Everything she's done is because I failed her."

"The woman is insane," Zane snapped. "You just happened to be the man she became obsessed with."

Dakota hadn't spoken for a while. When she did,

everyone turned to look at her because of the anguish they heard in her voice.

"I think Laura might be responsible for my father's death," Dakota said. "I was so hurt that Courtney was with him when he died and not me…." Her gaze came up. Her eyes welled with tears. "If Courtney was with our father when he died, then it was her mother's doing. I wouldn't be surprised if Laura was there when he had his heart attack. I can only imagine my father's reaction to finding out what Laura had done and meeting a daughter he hadn't known existed."

Zane put his arm around her as a vehicle pulled up outside.

Emma glanced out the window and felt her stomach roil with dread. "It's the sheriff."

Zane opened the door at the sheriff's knock, worried that she was here to take him back to jail.

"Sheriff Crawford," he said, hoping he was wrong because he couldn't leave Dakota, wouldn't leave her without a fight.

"Zane. I need to have a word with your father. Is he—" McCall looked past him.

"Please come in," Hoyt said. Zane moved aside to let her enter the house.

The sheriff glanced at Dakota, then Emma, and said, "I'm glad you're all here. I have some news on the DNA test the crime lab ran on Courtney Hughes's blood sample."

"Please sit down," Emma said. "Can I get you—"

"Nothing, thank you." She sat down and waited for everyone else to sit as well.

"Apparently when your first wife drowned, you gave the crime lab a sample of her DNA?" McCall asked Hoyt.

He nodded. Zane noticed how he stole a glance at Emma. They all seemed to know what was coming.

"The crime lab in Missoula ran Courtney's DNA. It brought up another close match. Laura Chisholm's," the sheriff said. "It appears that Courtney Hughes is Laura Chisholm's daughter."

She looked to Hoyt. He said nothing. They'd wanted confirmation. Now they had it.

"You already knew this?" the sheriff asked, looking around the room at them.

"We just learned that Laura Chisholm was Lorraine Baxter before she married my father," Zane said. "We hadn't known that she was definitely Courtney's birth mother."

"I don't think I have to tell you what this means," McCall said. "If Zane is right, then Laura Chisholm is behind her daughter's disappearance."

"She orchestrated all of this," Emma said.

The sheriff shook her head. "The only thing we're lacking is proof of that."

"She's not finished with this family," Hoyt said, his voice breaking with emotion.

"You have to find her," Emma said. "If she's using her own daughter to hurt my family…"

"I'm circulating copies of that age-progression photo Aggie Wells gave you not only locally, but also through-out the state," McCall said. "I'm doing everything possible to find her *and* Courtney." She didn't need to add,

"If she is still alive." Everyone in the room had to be thinking the same thing.

"I'll make sure Emma is never alone," Hoyt said. "I'll have one of the boys stay with her as well as Mrs. Crowley."

The sheriff's cell phone rang. She glanced at it. "I need to take this." She got to her feet and stepped out of the room.

A few moments later, she came back into the room. Zane saw the expression on her face and felt his heart drop.

"Is it Courtney?" Dakota asked before anyone else could speak.

McCall shook her head. "That was the warden at the prison in California where the two dead men did time. Both are escaped criminals." She seemed to hesitate. "Three prisoners walked away from a work area last week."

"Three?" Zane said.

"The warden said they'd all three had a visitor a few weeks before. He described her as a woman in her late fifties to early sixties, blonde, blue-eyed. She was going by the name of Sharon Jones and used a Billings, Montana, address."

"Sharon Jones? The woman Aggie found and swore was Laura Chisholm," Emma cried.

"What more proof do you want that this whole thing is some sort of vengeance against our family?" Zane demanded.

"Until she is caught, all of you need to be very careful," McCall said. "There's a third man out there, not to mention Laura herself. I think everything going on with Zane is merely a diversion to bring the focus off the real target, Emma."

The sheriff turned to look at Emma. "If we're right and Laura is responsible for Hoyt's other wives' deaths, then Laura will be coming after you."

Chapter 11

Dakota was still stunned by everything that had happened in the past forty-eight hours.

"I'm not letting you out of my sight until this is over," Zane said as they left the Chisholm ranch.

She smiled over at him. His words were music to her ears. He'd saved her at the cemetery, risked his life. She couldn't help but think about the kiss as they went back to her ranch where she packed up what she would need.

From there, they drove back toward Whitehorse. "We can stay out at the home ranch with my folks, but I need to go by my place first."

She didn't say anything as they pulled into the yard of his house. There were no other vehicles around—just like at her house. She reminded herself that Courtney's car had been found.

But the third escaped prisoner from California was

still at large. She wanted to believe that by now he had crossed the border into Canada and was long gone. Believing that Courtney and her mother had also skipped the country was a little harder to swallow.

"Doesn't look like anyone has been here," Zane said as he unlocked the door and stepped inside. "If you just give me a minute…"

"Zane." He stopped and turned to look at her, concern in his expression.

She stepped up to him and pushed a lock of his blond hair back from his handsome face. "Thank you."

He shook his head. "I got you into this."

"No, this started long before us. I just want to thank you. You saved my life last night."

His gaze locked with hers. "Dakota." The word came out like a prayer. She felt warmth rush through her. "Don't you know by now how I feel about you? I was half in love with that kid you used to be. Now…" He shook his head as if he couldn't put what he felt into words.

She leaned toward him and brushed her lips over his.

He drew back. "You sure about this?"

Had she ever been more sure of anything in her life? And yet, she knew that this would change everything between them—and possibly not for the better.

She'd taken chances in her life, plenty of them, but that was on the back of a horse in an arena or with the rough stock business. This was a whole different matter and she knew she was way out of her league.

He brushed her cheek with the rough pads of his fingertips, turning her face up to his so she couldn't avoid his blue gaze. She saw the cool blue and the heat behind it. With Zane Chisholm it would be all or nothing.

She nodded slowly and his hand slid behind her head, his fingers burying themselves in her long hair. He pulled her toward him until his mouth hovered over hers. Her breasts pressed against his hard chest, and his hold was strong and sure.

Her heart pounded like a war drum as he drew back to meet her gaze again, as if searching for something to stop this before it got out of hand.

She met that steely gaze with one of her own. The one thing she had never lacked was courage. Those long-ago embers now fanned to a flame so hot she felt her blood catch fire.

Funny how nothing had changed and yet everything had. She was no longer that girl. He'd said men were going to want to kiss her. And they had. Just none of them had been Zane Chisholm. Until now.

His mouth dropped to hers in a stunning kiss that left her breathless. "That has been a long time coming," Zane said, sounding just as breathless.

She realized why he hadn't kissed her all those years ago. Nothing about Zane Chisholm was safe. She was just smart enough to know it now.

Zane swung her up in his arms, kicked open his bedroom door and carried her inside. As he laid her on the covers, she wrapped her arms around his neck and pulled him down, unable to go another moment without kissing him.

When she touched his lower lip with the tip of her tongue, she felt a shudder rock through him. With a curse he let her pull him down to the bed.

For a moment he stared down at her as if seeing her for the woman she'd become instead of that cowgirl she'd been.

Then he dropped his mouth on hers, taking possession of it, stealing her senses and proving that his earlier kiss was only a prelude of what was to come.

He grabbed her Western shirt and pulled the two sides apart with a jerk that made the snaps sing. A moan escaped his lips as he gazed down at her breasts straining against the lace fabric.

He undid the front hook with two fingers and she felt her breasts freed. His gaze took them in, then those blue eyes shifted to her face.

"You are so beautiful," he said, his voice sounding hoarse. He lowered himself to the bed beside her, his fingers brushing one hard nipple and making her shiver with a desire she knew only he could quench.

His mouth dropped to the other breast and she arched against him, silently pleading with him not to stop.

He trailed kisses, damp and sweet, over her body, making her wriggle in pleasurable agony until at last he shed his jeans and she felt the heat of his body against hers.

He took her in his arms and slowly made love to her with ever-deepening kisses. The release came like a train gathering speed. She clung to him, crying out as she felt wave after wave of ecstasy.

Zane collapsed next to her, his hand spread on her damp stomach. They lay like that, breathing hard, both of them knowing they wouldn't be going to the Chisholm home ranch tonight.

* * *

Emma had a terrible time getting to sleep. Zane had called to say that he and Dakota were staying at his place. Emma hadn't argued. She'd smiled as she'd hung up the phone. It was clear Zane was crazy about the girl.

And to think that a year ago, Emma had thought she was going to have to help her stepsons find the perfect women for them. Somehow they'd all done it on their own. She guessed that was the way it was meant to be.

Of course, each of them had fallen in love with a woman in trouble. So typical of Chisholm men, she'd thought as she'd climbed into bed next to Hoyt.

It was a little after two when she woke. She slipped out of bed and went to the window. The pickup Mrs. Crowley used was gone. Earlier, the housekeeper had complained of a headache and gone to her room. Which had relieved both Emma and Hoyt. They didn't really want her to know what was going on.

But apparently Mrs. Crowley had felt well enough later to go out after Emma and Hoyt had gone to bed.

"What are you doing?" Hoyt asked from the bed, making Emma jump.

"I couldn't sleep," she said when she found her voice. She didn't want him to know she was spying on their housekeeper. He'd think she had enough problems without that.

He blinked. "So you are just sitting in the dark?"

"Go back to sleep. I like sitting here. If it bothers you, maybe I'll go downstairs and read for a while."

"You sure you're all right?" he asked, sounding worried.

"I'm fine." She got up and went to the bed, leaning

in to kiss him. "Go to sleep. I'll be back before you know it."

He smiled and closed his eyes. "You can read up here—I don't mind the light."

"I left my book downstairs." She waited for him to put up more of an argument but a moment later she heard him snoring softly.

As she crept downstairs, she admitted that spying on her housekeeper helped keep her mind off Laura Chisholm. But she knew that was only partly the truth. Mrs. Crowley was too smug in her secrets. Emma was determined to solve this one.

Moving to the living room window, she didn't dare turn on a light. Mrs. Crowley might see it. Instead, she sat patiently in the dark, hoping Hoyt didn't awaken again and come looking for her.

Twenty minutes later, she saw headlights in the distance.

Emma waited another five minutes after Mrs. Crowley had parked the pickup and gone inside her wing before tiptoeing into the kitchen for the flashlight and spare truck key.

She knew she wasn't being as careful, but she had to put an end to this nightly spying. With the key and flashlight, she padded out of the kitchen, across the living room and out the front door.

It was colder out tonight. The sky was dark and the wind smelled of rain. She hurried along the side of the house in the shadows, feeling the bite of the wind. Rain was imminent.

It would serve her right to get wet, she thought as she slipped around the back of the pickup and through the passenger side door. If Hoyt caught her drenched in rain, how was she going to explain that?

This time, she didn't take the time to wait and see if anyone might have seen her. She turned the key and snapped on the flashlight.

The beam shone on the odometer reading.

Emma blinked and did quick subtraction. Eleven miles? Eleven miles round-trip, she realized. That meant the woman hadn't even left the ranch.

It was more puzzling than when she hadn't known how far away the woman went in the middle of the night.

And more troubling somehow.

Rain pinged off the truck roof, making her jump. She hurriedly climbed out, slamming the door harder than she meant to.

Thunder rumbled in the distance. She hoped anyone who might have heard the slammed door would think that was what it had been.

As she started around the truck, a bolt of lightning splintered across the sky, lighting up the yard like daylight.

For a moment, Emma was blinded. She blinked and when her eyes focused again, she found herself face-to-face with Mrs. Crowley.

Dakota woke to thunder that was so close it seemed to reverberate inside her chest. In the darkness she shivered and rolled over to face Zane. His features were lit by the light of the storm. He couldn't have looked more handsome than he did right now, she thought with a growing ache inside her.

Earlier she'd gotten up to get a drink and had pulled on his T-shirt. It smelled of him, filling her senses. As she'd slipped it over her head, her skin had tingled. Now she remembered the way the T-shirt had fit him, accenting the hard muscles, the washboard stomach, the tanned skin. She couldn't help but remember the way his jeans had hung on his hips, the fine blond line of hair that ran from his chest to disappear at the large rodeo belt buckle.

She had looked away, but not before he'd seen her looking. A fire had burned in those blue eyes, hot as a welder's torch.

At just the thought of their lovemaking, she felt a fire burning in her. She'd never known this kind of passion, this kind of desire. Zane had been her childhood fantasy, the rodeo cowboy she'd planned to marry.

At the thought of her diary, she cringed inwardly. It embarrassed her that her sister, and who knew who else, had read about her longing. No doubt the reason it still embarrassed her was because that longing had never gone away.

Zane was the reason she hadn't gone through with her engagement. She'd felt as if there was something missing with her fiancé. Dakota had hated breaking it off, telling herself she was making a huge mistake still being in love with a fantasy cowboy.

But the truth was, Zane had corralled her heart and held it captive all these years.

In a flash of lightning that lit the bedroom, Zane opened his eyes. He smiled at her. "Nice shirt," he said.

Raindrops struck the partially open window next to them. Dakota felt the cool breeze rush over her bare skin as she brushed her lips over his, then pulled back a little to look at him. He seemed to be waiting to see how far she would go.

She shifted against Zane, feeling her aching nipples grow even harder beneath his T-shirt as she reached for the hem. Pulling his T-shirt up and over her head, she tossed it away.

He grinned. "You are insatiable."

She nodded as she wrapped her arms around his neck and pressed her naked breasts to his hard chest.

His hands came around her waist and drew her into him until not even the cool breeze of the rainstorm could come between them. As his mouth dropped to hers, thunder boomed again as loud as the pounding of their hearts in the old ranch house.

"Mrs. Crowley!" The words flew from Emma's mouth with obvious surprise.

"Whatever are you doing standing out in the rain?" the woman demanded from beneath the umbrella she held.

Emma had been so careful the other time. Now she'd been caught red-handed. "The thunder and lightning. It woke me up."

Mrs. Crowley was giving her a sideways look that said, "And that explains your behavior how?"

"I woke up, couldn't sleep and wandered out on the porch. I thought I saw the dome light on in the pickup," Emma said. It was the only thing she could think of since she was pretty sure Mrs. Crowley had seen her in the truck.

"Really? Do you have trouble sleeping often?"

"Must have been the thunder," Emma said.

Mrs. Crowley glanced toward the pickup. "The dome light must have a short in it. I noticed it wasn't working the other night."

So she *had* noticed. Of course she had, Emma thought. The woman never missed anything.

"I'll have Hoyt take a look at it," Emma said.

"Don't bother. It's off now. Let's just leave it that way." Mrs. Crowley gave her one of her twisted half smiles. "You really should get in out of the rain."

With that the woman turned and went back inside.

Emma stood for a moment, staring after her before she turned her face up to the rain. It felt good as she walked back to the front porch before entering the house.

Inside, she locked the door. Even as she did so she wondered what she was locking inside her house.

She shuddered at the memory of looking up to find Mrs. Crowley standing in front of her. Why did that poor woman scare her so?

Well, she'd never admit it. Especially to Hoyt.

Eleven miles, she thought as she went to the guest bathroom and dried herself off with a towel. Hoyt's robe was soaked. She hung it up.

Her nightgown was damp. She would change it upstairs.

As she headed upstairs, she mulled it over in her mind. Eleven miles round-trip. Where would that take you on the ranch?

Upset with herself, she knew she really *wouldn't* be able to sleep now. Retracing her steps, she went into the living room, turned on a lamp and picked up the murder mystery she'd been reading.

She was through spying on the poor woman, she told herself as she wrote down the mileage in the back of the book and wondered again where an eleven-mile round-trip would take a person on the Chisholm ranch.

The next morning the storm had passed. A brilliant glowing sun shone in the window from a sky of cloudless blue. Zane stirred to find the bed beside him empty. For one heart-stopping moment, he thought Dakota was gone.

Then he smelled bacon and heard the faint sound of music coming from his radio in the kitchen. He smiled and tried to still his pounding heart. Last night had been incredible. What surprised him was that it hadn't been like this with other women he'd known. He knew it sounded clichéd, but with Dakota it hadn't been just sex.

As he lay in the bed, it hit him like a boulder off a cliff. He loved her.

He'd never said the *L* word to any woman because he'd never loved any of them. For a few moments, he was shocked. But he realized this wasn't a spur-of-the-moment emotion. This had been coming for a long time.

Pulling on his jeans, he looked around for his T-shirt. Not seeing it, he grinned. He had a pretty good idea where he could find it.

Sure enough, as he stepped through the kitchen doorway, there was Dakota making breakfast in nothing but his T-shirt.

He moved behind her, put his arms around her, breathed in the scent of bacon and the woman he loved.

"I hope you're hungry," she said with a sexy chuckle.

"Hmm," he said into the side of her neck. She felt warm and soft, rounded in all the right places. He loved her strength as much as he loved her soft places.

Turning off the stove, he turned her in his arms. "What would it take to get you to come back to bed with me?"

Emma had slept. She woke sprawled on the couch with a crick in her neck and a page of her murder mystery pressed against her right cheek.

At first she didn't know what had roused her. Then she heard the phone and realized it wasn't the first time it had rung.

Still in her nightgown, she hurried to it, aware that it must be very early. Not even Mrs. Crowley was up yet.

"I just got a call from the Butte Police Department," Sheriff McCall Crawford said when Emma answered. "They've picked up a woman who matches Laura's description from the age-progression photo we sent around the region."

Emma couldn't help being afraid to get her hopes up. She'd prayed for this for so long. "But they aren't sure?"

"No, but they did find some evidence in her possession that makes them believe it's her," the sheriff said. "She had Courtney's number and Great Falls address on her and some gas receipts from a Westside convenience store in Whitehorse."

"Are they going to bring her to Whitehorse?"

"No," McCall said. "They need Hoyt to come to Butte to make a positive identification. They can only hold her for forty-eight hours so he needs to come as soon as possible."

Hoyt would have to face his first wife? Emma couldn't bear him having to do that. But if this was Laura and they couldn't hold her any longer because of lack of evidence...

"I'll tell Hoyt." She hung up and hurried upstairs only to find their bed empty. Hurrying back downstairs, she checked the kitchen and then headed for the barn.

She found him with his horses—the place he always headed when he was worried or upset. So he hadn't been able to sleep after all, she thought, wondering how long he'd been out there.

Emma watched him brushing one of his favorite horses. She could hear him talking softly to the mare and felt such a rush of love for him it almost floored her.

She took a step toward him, hating to interrupt. He looked so peaceful and she knew that this news would kill that instantly.

"Emma?" Hoyt seemed surprised to see her. "I thought you'd be asleep for hours." He smiled, making it clear he'd seen her sacked out on the couch. She probably still had the crease on her cheek where the page of her book had been pressed.

"I just got a call from the sheriff," she said. Hoyt put down the brush and stepped toward her. She quickly repeated what McCall had told her and watched an array of emotions cross his face.

"Then it's her," Hoyt said, sounding so relieved she stepped to him and put her arms around him. He pulled her close and she could hear the ragged emotion in his voice as he breathed words of love into her hair.

Wrangled

"I have been so worried about you, Emma," he said when she pulled back. "I have to go to Butte today? Why can't they just check her DNA since it is still on file?"

"I don't know. Apparently it would take too long. Or maybe she refused to take a DNA test. I hate for you to have to go, but if this woman is Laura…"

"Yes," he said. "It definitely sounds like she is. I'll do whatever I have to. I just want this to be over."

"Me, too," Emma said. She thought they would all be able to breathe again once Laura was locked up for good.

"I'll call one of the boys to stay with you until I get back," he said. Hoyt still referred to his sons as boys, even though they were all almost thirty or older.

She started to argue that it wasn't necessary. She had Mrs. Crowley. But her husband didn't give her a chance.

"I'd feel better if one of our sons is here with you until I'm positive they have Laura behind bars. Let's not forget that there is a third prison escapee still on the loose."

She hadn't forgotten. But with Laura locked up, she doubted they had to worry about the other escapee. By now he could already be across the border into Canada.

Chapter 12

Zane swore at the sound of the phone. He thought about not answering it. Right now the last thing he wanted was an intrusion from the outside world.

He glanced over at Dakota on the bed next to him. Her body felt so warm next to his, he never wanted to leave this bed.

The phone rang again. He reached for it and checked to see who was calling. When he saw that it was the ranch he quickly slipped out of bed.

He answered on the third ring. "Hello?"

"Zane, it's Dad." Zane listened as he filled him in about the trip to Butte and the woman the police there had behind bars. "Marshall is going to be staying with Emma, but I wanted the rest of you to know what's going on."

"They really think it's her?"

"Apparently she had Courtney's number and address on her and some gas receipts from the Westside here in Whitehorse."

"Then she'll be able to tell the police where Courtney is," Zane said, and heard Dakota come up beside him. She was wearing his shirt again and nothing else. At this rate, they were never going to eat the breakfast she'd cooked.

"Let me know what happens." He hung up to take Dakota in his arms and tell her the possible good news.

"Has this woman they arrested said anything about Courtney yet?"

"Apparently not. But she did have Courtney's address and phone number and some gas receipts from Whitehorse."

Dakota snuggled against him, wrapping her arms around his waist and burying her face into his bare chest.

"Dad promised to call when he knew something definite."

She pulled back to look up at him. "I'm just so afraid that the more time that goes by…"

"I know." He thought about Courtney's car being found in that ravine—and one of the escaped prisoners' bodies found nearby. He regretted that he'd had to kill the other escaped convict last night before finding out anything about Courtney.

Zane swung Dakota up into his arms and carried her back to the bedroom. Putting her down gently, he lay beside her on the bed.

She was so beautiful. He touched her face, running

his thumb pad over her smooth cheek. Her eyes widened and he saw desire stir in them.

"If we don't eat that wonderful breakfast you cooked pretty soon…"

Hoyt refused to leave until Marshall arrived. Emma was relieved when she saw Marshall drive up and Hoyt go out to talk to him. She and Hoyt had already said their goodbyes. She could tell Hoyt was just anxious to get to Butte.

A pilot friend had offered to fly him and was now waiting for him at the small airport outside of Whitehorse. It was no more than a wind sock, a strip of tarmac and an old metal hangar. But by flying, Hoyt could get there sooner—and get back just as quickly.

"Where's Mrs. Crowley?" Marshall whispered as he came through the back door and looked around the kitchen. Emma waved out the window to Hoyt as he climbed into his pickup. His gaze locked with hers for a moment before he started the motor and drove away.

"She wasn't feeling well and went to her room to rest," Emma said, turning from the window. "I'm worried about her. This isn't like her. But I don't dare go down to her room. She called me to say she had one of her headaches and asked if I would mind if she stayed in bed a little longer."

"She must have known I was coming over," he said. "She doesn't like me."

"That's not true," Emma said. He raised a brow and she laughed. "She doesn't like anyone," Emma whispered conspiratorially. "Sit down. I baked your second-most favorite cookies."

"I thought I smelled lemon." He smiled and slid into a chair at the table. "Dad eat all the gingersnaps?"

Emma closed the kitchen door so they would have privacy and turned on the radio to the country music station.

"Mrs. Crowley hates this kind of music," she said as she gave him a mug of hot coffee and a plate of lemon cookies and took a chair across from him.

He grinned at her. "How can you stand her?"

"Well…" She studied her stepson for a moment. "Can I tell you something? You just can't tell your father what I've been doing."

He made a cross with his finger over his heart and laughed. "If you've been slipping Mrs. Crowley happy pills, I've got some bad news for you. They aren't workin'."

Emma shook her head and leaned toward him. "I've been spying on her. And guess what? She sneaks off at night after we're asleep and she doesn't come back until the wee hours of the morning."

He frowned, clearly not expecting this. "Where does she go?"

"Well, that's what's so interesting. She only drives eleven miles, round-trip."

"That wouldn't even get her off the ranch."

"Exactly. But I think I've figured out where she goes. I just can't imagine why…unless she's meeting some man—" Emma realized "—at the old water mill house."

Emma realized Marshall wasn't listening to her anymore. He was looking past her out the kitchen window one moment, the next he was shooting to his feet, a curse escaping his lips.

She spun around to look out the window behind her, half expecting to see Mrs. Crowley's face pressed to the glass.

"Fire," Marshall said reaching for his cell phone. "Grass fire."

Emma saw it then. Smoke on the horizon. She'd learned about grass fires since moving to the ranch and knew how dangerous they could be, especially if pushed by wind. Outside the window she could see a brisk wind stirring the branches of the cottonwood trees.

She listened to Marshall barking information into the phone. He placed five more calls to his brothers.

"Go," she said when he snapped his phone shut. "I'm fine. Mrs. Crowley is here."

Marshall shook his head. "Zane is bringing Dakota to stay with you."

Emma liked Dakota and would be glad to spend some time with her. "Well, you don't have to wait for them to get here. Mrs. Crowley is in her room and I have your number if I have to reach you. You'll only be down the road."

The kitchen door suddenly opened. "What's going on?" Mrs. Crowley asked as she filled the doorway.

"Are you feeling better?" Emma asked.

"What's going on? I heard all the racket," the housekeeper said in answer.

"There's a grass fire. The boys have gone to fight it."

Mrs. Crowley went to the window and looked out as if she'd known where it was, had already seen it. "So what are you waiting for?" she demanded as she turned to face Marshall. "Shouldn't you be out there fighting it?"

He didn't get a chance to reply.

"I'm here with your stepmother now," Mrs. Crowley said in her no-nonsense tone. "Go."

"She's right," Emma said. "We'll be fine."

Marshall didn't have to be told twice. "Dakota is going to drop off Zane, then come here. She should be here soon," he said. "Call if you need me."

"I will," Emma said as she pushed him out the door. He took off running toward the ranch truck with the water tank on the back. A few minutes later, he was roaring down the road toward the dark smudge of smoke along the horizon.

"Marshall didn't even eat one of the cookies I made for him," Emma said. She turned to find Mrs. Crowley making tea.

"You must be feeling better," Emma said, looking out the window at the fire.

Mrs. Crowley could hear the woman's fear about the fire, but it was so like Emma to ask how *she* was feeling.

"I am better, thank you." Her employer turned in surprise at her words. "I appreciate how nice you've been to me. I know I haven't made it easy."

Emma's eyes widened a little as if she wasn't sure the words had really come out of her housekeeper's mouth.

Mrs. Crowley nodded, not having to pretend a look of chagrin. "You have been nothing but kind and I have rebuffed that kindness at every turn. I'm sorry."

Emma appeared not to know what to say for a moment. "I just wanted you to feel at home here. I have a tendency to come on too strong."

"I do feel at home here." Emma had no idea how

much. "Please, let me make us a cup of tea and visit until your friend gets here."

"Are you sure you feel up to making the tea?"

"Yes. I only had a headache earlier. I'm fine now." She turned her back on Emma and began to fill the teapot, hoping the woman would take a seat and not insist on helping.

To her relief, Emma was more interested in the grass fire.

Mrs. Crowley tried not to hurry with the tea but time was of the essence. Dakota Lansing would be arriving soon. She had to get at least one cup of tea into Emma before that. This opportunity might not present itself again.

"I suppose you won't be needing me soon," Mrs. Crowley said.

"Why would you say that?" Emma asked.

"Your husband's trip to Butte. I couldn't help overhearing. Is it really possible his first wife is alive?"

"I'm afraid so."

Mrs. Crowley shook her head as the teapot whistled. "I admit I did read a few things in the newspaper before I came here. I felt as if you and I had a lot in common actually. We are both haunted in a way by the past."

"That's true," Emma agreed as she poured a small pitcher of milk and prepared the cups.

"What I can't understand is why this woman would do what she's been accused of." She carefully filled Emma's cup and slipped in a fresh tea bag. "She must enjoy making other people miserable," she said as she watched the tea steep.

"I feel sorry for her," Emma said and Mrs. Crowley had to bite back a laugh. Of course Emma would.

"How can you possibly say that?" she demanded as she slipped a tea bag into her own cup, then took both cups over to the table, making sure she didn't accidentally mix them up as she saw the dust of a vehicle coming up the road in the distance.

"She must be a very unhappy person," Emma said.

"Maybe she just couldn't let go of her husband," Mrs. Crowley said as she pulled out a chair and sat down across from her. "Isn't it possible she loved him too much? That he was her life and she didn't need anything or anyone else?"

Emma took a sip of her tea and looked up in surprise. "You think she resented the children he adopted?"

Mrs. Crowley shrugged and sipped at her tea, watching Emma over the rim of her cup.

"I think she didn't want him but she doesn't want anyone else to have him," Emma said, then took one of the lemon cookies off the plate on the table and dipped it into the tea. She took a bite, then said, "That is the most selfish of all love."

Emma didn't like the taste of the tea and wondered how Mrs. Crowley could mess up even a simple cup of tea.

The woman was no cook. If Emma'd had her way, she wouldn't have let her in the kitchen. Every time Mrs. Crowley insisted on helping, nothing had turned out like it should have.

Emma prided herself on her cooking, especially her

baking. Fortunately, Mrs. Crowley hadn't insisted on helping with the baking.

She took another sip of the tea. It tasted bitter. She tried not to grimace with the woman watching her.

"I think I need a little of that sweetener my future daughters-in-law insist on," Emma said.

Mrs. Crowley was being so nice, she rose quickly to get it.

Emma used the diversion to dump some of the tea out in the plant on the windowsill. She would have poured out more but Mrs. Crowley was too quick for her.

"Thank you," she said as she took one of the packets, tore it open and poured it into her cup under Mrs. Crowley's watchful eye.

Emma hated sweetener, but she had no choice now but to drink the tea. Mrs. Crowley knew she didn't take her tea with milk, but she added a little anyway, hoping it would make the brew go down easier.

Mrs. Crowley was making an effort to be friends. Too late if the woman in Butte turned out to be Laura. Emma would feel badly about having to let Mrs. Crowley go. Well, not that badly. She would never know, though, where the housekeeper went in the middle of the night.

Emma promised herself that she would give Mrs. Crowley a decent recommendation for her next job and make Hoyt give her a large severance package.

Even as she thought it, Emma knew she probably wouldn't have done that if the woman wasn't disfigured. She wondered if Mrs. Crowley was often overly compensated by her employers not for her work but because of her injury. Emma supposed that, too, could have made the woman the way she was.

Or at least had been. She'd been so pleasant today it was almost…spooky. Emma could feel Mrs. Crowley studying her. Now that she thought about it, many times since the housekeeper had arrived here she'd felt her studying her like a bug under a magnifying glass.

Another benefit of her injury, Emma thought vaguely. No one dared stare at Mrs. Crowley, which made it easier for her to stare at everyone else.

Emma put down her cup. She'd been forced to drink all but a little of it. She suddenly felt light-headed. She could barely keep her eyes open.

Mrs. Crowley concentrated on her tea, letting Emma drink almost all of hers. A breeze stirred at the open kitchen window, bringing with it the smell of smoke. Hoyt was in Butte and by now all the Chisholm boys would be fighting the fire.

But the wind also carried the scent of dust. As she listened, Mrs. Crowley heard the vehicle she'd seen down the road approaching. It was only a matter of minutes before it reached the ranch house.

Mrs. Crowley glanced toward the window and the pickup that pulled into the yard. It was just a neighbor coming to refill the water tank in the back of his truck.

She looked over at Emma again. There was still time.

Emma was staring into her teacup as if reading her future in the small sprinkling of leaves at the bottom.

All things considered, not much of a future, Mrs. Crowley thought.

"I think Laura was scarred in ways none of us will

ever understand," she said. "Did you know that her father deserted her when she was six? He was her life.
Her mother remarried, of course, after transforming
herself into whatever that man wanted her to be. The
marriages never lasted so she kept having to become
someone new for someone else."

Emma looked up and blinked as if having a hard
time focusing.

"Laura's mother cared more about the men who
traipsed through the house in a steady flow than she
ever did about her daughter," Mrs. Crowley continued
as she rose to take Emma's cup.

"You wouldn't know what it's like growing up feeling that you're not enough, that your love isn't valuable enough, that you're not even enough for your own
mother. But I think you can imagine what something
like that can do to a person," Mrs. Crowley said.

Something was wrong. Emma had been trying to follow the conversation but Mrs. Crowley's words weren't
making any sense.

She stared across the table at the woman. Mrs. Crowley looked different this morning, but Emma couldn't
put her finger on what it was. She reached for a cookie,
but hit the small pitcher of milk. Milk splashed onto
the table.

"Here, let me help you with that," the housekeeper
said, moving the pitcher out of her reach.

"I'm not feeling well." Her head was spinning and
she could barely keep her eyes open.

"You must have what I did earlier. Headache? Light-
headedness? I was so tired I could barely stay awake."

Emma looked into the woman's face and had a moment of clarity. "Did you put something in my tea?"

Mrs. Crowley smiled. "It's all right. I only gave you a very strong sedative. It will knock you out, but it won't kill you. That comes later."

Emma tried to stand, but the housekeeper was on her before she could get out of the chair. She struggled to throw her off, but Mrs. Crowley was much stronger than she looked.

Nor was she limping, Emma thought as the housekeeper half dragged her toward the pantry. She gave up fighting to free herself from the woman's grip, realizing it was useless.

She was too weak. But she still fought to stay awake. Dakota was on her way. If she called out—

Emma opened her mouth, but only a low groan came out as the housekeeper dragged her into the pantry.

Emma's eyelids drooped and the last thing she heard as she lay on the floor was the hurried slamming of the pantry door. Then darkness.

Mrs. Crowley looked down the road. No Dakota yet. She sat down, poured a little milk into her tea and idly stirred it with her spoon. It was dangerous, this game she was playing. She had let it go on too long. She'd been in this house since March. It was now June and she hadn't accomplished what she'd come here to do.

With a curse, she knew why it had taken her so long. Emma. The woman had intrigued her. Each day she'd relished watching her employer. Emma had an insatiable curiosity and a need to comfort. Mrs. Crowley smiled at the woman's pitiful attempts to befriend her.

The curiosity could have turned out to be a problem, though. While she was watching Emma, Emma had been spying on her. She chuckled to herself at Emma's attempts to find out where she'd gone at night. Taking a sip of tea, she almost spilled it as she recalled Emma's face when she'd caught her coming out of the cab of the pickup last night.

Feeling good for the first time in a long time, Mrs. Crowley considered having one of Emma's cookies. Normally she didn't allow herself the pleasure of sweets. She had just taken a bite when she heard the sound of a vehicle. Looking out the kitchen window, she saw the driver of the pickup park in front of the house and climb from behind the wheel.

Dakota Lansing. Before the other night, she hadn't seen her since she was a cute little two-year-old, Clay Lansing's pride and joy.

She watched the now beautiful young woman head for the front door and felt a stab of remorse. Clay Lansing never knew it, but she could have fallen for him all those years ago. There was something so broken about him after his wife died. She'd been drawn to his pain and thrown caution to the wind.

She would have left Hoyt for Clay if it hadn't been for Dakota. It was ironic. She hadn't wanted a child, and in her reckless abandon had become pregnant with one.

She listened, but no sound came from inside the pantry. Smiling, she went to answer the knock at the door.

The fire had raced across the prairie, fueled by the wind and the tall grasses, and left charred, black ground.

Smoke still billowed up along the horizon and could be seen for miles, but the flames had been knocked down.

This was the wrong time of the year for grass fires. Unfortunately an early spring, hot temperatures and abundant grass had kept the blaze going.

When Zane arrived he found his brothers, along with neighbors who had seen the smoke and come to help. They'd managed to get the fire contained and were now busy dousing any grass and brush still smoking.

Another truck pulled in equipped with a water tank in the bed. Zane saw that his brothers had almost emptied their tanks and would need to make a run back to the ranch to refill soon unless they got the fire completely out with this last tank of water.

Zane backed up his pickup and jumped out to grab the hose from the back and turn on the faucet of the water tank. The spray felt cold and blew back in his face as he began to douse the grass along the edge of where the fire had burned. Down the way, more neighbors were working along with several small community volunteer fire department crews.

Zane was thankful that his brothers were already winning the battle against the blaze. What he wanted to know now was how it could have started out here in the middle of nowhere—especially after a rain last night. Unless it had been started by a lightning strike and taken this long to get going.

After emptying the tank in the back of the truck, Zane moved across the blackened ground to the spot where the blaze appeared to have started. He hadn't gone far when he saw the containers of accelerant and the boot prints in the soft earth.

Hunkering down, he studied the track and then, on an impulse, looked to the horizon where the foothills rose in small clusters of pines. Zane caught a flash of light in the pines along the foothills not a half mile away.

Binoculars, he thought. The arsonist is watching to see how much damage he's caused.

A moment later Zane realized the arsonist had seen him and knew he'd been spotted. A pickup roared out of the trees in the distance. The driver was making a run for it.

Swearing, Zane sprinted for one of the ranch trucks. The bastard wasn't getting away.

As he neared the truck, Zane called to his brothers. "The man who started the fire. I saw him watching us from the trees. He's taking off."

Zane jumped behind the wheel. His brother Marshall climbed into the passenger side as the truck engine roared to life, and Zane swung it around and headed for the county road to cut the man off.

Dust billowed up behind them as they raced across the pasture. Zane could see the blue pickup's driver careening down the road, hoping to escape before Zane could catch him.

"Can't this pickup go any faster?" Marshall joked, hanging on as the truck bounced over the ruts, fishtailing onto the road.

For a moment it looked as if the blue pickup would beat them to the spot where the two roads joined.

Zane feared that if the driver of the blue truck got there first, he might be able to outrun them. After all, his truck didn't have a water tank in the back.

He pushed the pickup harder, keeping his eye on the road as he and the other driver raced toward the point where the two roads intersected—and the trucks were about to meet, neither driver letting up off the gas.

Marshall was on the phone to the sheriff when he wasn't hanging on to keep from being bounced all over the cab.

"I suppose you have a plan," Marshall said, sounding a little anxious. "He doesn't look like he's going to give an inch."

Zane didn't answer. His mind was racing. Why start a grass fire? What had been the point?

Suddenly he knew. "Call our brothers," he cried. "Tell them to hightail it to the house. The fire was a diversion!"

The truck was almost to the intersection and so was Zane.

Marshall made the call and then braced himself for the collision. He must have seen that his brother wasn't slowing down—and neither was the driver of the other pickup.

Mrs. Crowley answered the front door on the second knock. She loved to see the expressions of people when they first saw her. Shock, then horror, then a nervous twitch of the eyes as their gazes slid away.

The young woman was even more striking close-up. She couldn't help but think of Clay's last words before his heart attack.

"Don't hurt my daughters." He'd grabbed her arm. "Laura, swear to me you won't hurt my daughters."

Fortunately he'd died before she had to answer.

"Is Emma here?" Dakota asked.

"She's lying down right now, but please come in. She told me to take care of you until she wakes up."

"I don't want to be a bother," Dakota said.

"Don't be silly," Mrs. Crowley said as she stepped aside to let Dakota into the house. "You're no bother. Come on back to the kitchen." She closed the door behind them, surreptitiously locking it. "Emma baked lemon cookies. She insisted you try one with a cup of my tea while you're waiting."

Chapter 13

Hoyt Chisholm stood in the Butte Police Department, shaking inside with both anger and fear. An officer had brought him into a small room and told him to wait, and that he would bring the prisoner in.

Glancing at the chair on the other side of the table, Hoyt was too anxious to sit. He kept reliving that day on Fort Peck Reservoir. Huge waves had rocked the boat as the wind gathered speed and churned up the water from miles down the lake. He'd never seen waves like that and wanted to turn back but Laura had insisted they keep going.

Nor would she wear a life jacket even though she'd told him she couldn't swim. He hadn't wanted the day to turn into one of their horrible fights, so he hadn't made her put the life jacket on. For all these years, he'd regretted that maybe the most.

If she'd been wearing a life jacket, she wouldn't have drowned. Or been able to escape and perpetrate the cruel and inhuman hoax she'd pulled on him.

If she was really alive.

He knew she had to be. Everyone else believed it now, even Sheriff McCall Crawford. Aggie Wells had believed it. Emma, too.

Was the reason he didn't want to believe it because it would mean he'd not only fallen in love with a monster, but he'd married her?

He thought of how he'd nearly drowned diving into the water looking for Laura. Shuddering, he remembered the cold darkness of the water and felt the horror that Laura was down there fighting for her life and he had let her die.

In a body of water as large as Fort Peck, no one had been surprised that her body was never found.

He closed his eyes, hating that he'd married so quickly after her death. By then the adoption had gone through and he had six sons to care for. Tasha had loved them all so and he'd wanted so badly for the boys not to have to grow up without a mother.

Tasha's horseback-riding accident had been ruled just that, an accident. But he knew that if Laura was alive, she'd killed her. Just as she'd killed the next woman who'd come into his life, Krystal.

Laura had tried to frame him for Krystal's murder—just as she was now trying to frame his son. That thought sent a tidal wave of rage roaring through him.

He opened his eyes, fury trumping his terror at coming face-to-face with his dead wife. Whatever Laura's problem, it was with him. She'd taken it out on his wives and now one of his sons. He would stop her. If he had to do it with his bare hands.

He heard footfalls outside the room. The echo grew louder and he braced himself. Was a man ever ready for something like this? The footfalls stopped outside the door. The knob turned, the door swung open and two police officers escorted a dark-haired woman into the room.

She had her head down, but he recognized something familiar in the way she moved. She was the right height, the right body type and even appeared to be close to the age Laura would be now.

One of the police officers motioned for Hoyt to move behind the table.

He stumbled into the chair, gripping the sides as the other officer brought the woman all the way into the room and instructed her to sit down.

She did as she was told.

He watched her slowly lift her head. Her gaze met his.

Hoyt flinched as he looked into the familiar bright blue of her eyes. A sound came out of him, half cry, half curse. *"Laura."*

"I'm sorry Emma wasn't feeling well," Dakota said as she took a seat at the kitchen table. She could see the smoke from the grass fire and silently prayed that Zane and the rest of the firefighters would be safe.

"You don't mind staying with my stepmother?" Zane had said on the way to the ranch.

"Of course not. Emma is delightful."

"She is, isn't she?" he'd said with a laugh. "I have to

warn you, though. She'll ply you with cookies or cakes and try to find out everything about the two of us. She'll have us married by the time we get the fire out."

Dakota laughed.

Zane had taken her hand. "Do I need to tell you how crazy I am about you?"

She'd met his gaze and shaken her head. Looking into those blues, she had seen how he felt about her. She was just as crazy about him.

"Well, just in case you don't know, I... I... I'm crazy about you."

She'd laughed, shaking her head. "I love you, too, Zane," she'd said as he pulled up to where the others were battling the fire.

Marshall had come up to Zane's side window then. The next thing she knew she was driving one of the ranch pickups with an empty water tank on the way back down to the house and leaving Zane without another word.

He hadn't said he loved her. She tried not to think about that as she watched the billowing smoke on the horizon, her heart in her throat.

"Do you take milk in your tea?" Mrs. Crowley asked, drawing her attention back to the kitchen.

"No, thank you." Actually, she didn't drink tea, but she wanted to be polite so she said nothing more. One cup of tea wouldn't kill her. She just hoped Zane and the rest of the men were able to get the fire out, and soon.

Something about Mrs. Crowley made her uncomfortable, she thought as she looked over at the housekeeper. The woman had come as a shock. When she'd opened the door, Dakota had been taken aback not so much by the disfigurement, though she hadn't been expecting it, than the look in her one dark eye.

The woman seemed to look through a person.

Dakota shivered at the thought.

"Would you like a sweater?" Mrs. Crowley asked. She had her back to Dakota but she'd seen her shiver?

Dakota realized she'd seen her in the reflection in the microwave door next to her. The woman had been watching her. If Dakota hadn't been creeped out enough by the housekeeper before, she was now.

Mrs. Crowley hurriedly made a cup of tea for Dakota Lansing. She could feel time running out and knew she was cutting this one way too close. Anything could go wrong. She was usually much more organized. Maybe she was losing her touch.

She had planned on ending this quickly—her first day on the Chisholm ranch. Being back in this house had been excruciating. At the time, she hadn't been able to stand even the thought of spending another day here with Emma and Hoyt.

She'd waited until she'd heard Emma coming downstairs that first day. She'd been ready, the coffee made, a cup prepared for Hoyt's fourth wife.

The moment Emma walked in, she'd turned and said, "I have your coffee ready." She'd turned, cup in hand, knowing that Emma took hers black and strong.

"I thought *I* was an early riser," Emma said, clearly unhappy that she didn't have the kitchen to herself.

"I like to get an early start." She was still holding the cup of coffee out, a small tasteless dose of poison carefully stirred into the black brew. Fast and simple sometimes was the best.

"I really don't want you waiting on me," Emma had said as she took the cup. "I appreciate your thoughtfulness, but coffee's been bothering my stomach."

Mrs. Crowley had watched in horror as Emma poured the contents of the cup into the sink. She proceeded to wash out the cup, then pulled down a mug to make herself a cup of tea.

"I can do that," Mrs. Crowley said, trying to keep the frustration from her voice.

"Like I said, I won't have you waiting on me or Hoyt. We like doing for ourselves. I'm sure we explained that you are merely here to help with the housework and some of the cooking, when I need help."

All Mrs. Crowley had been able to do was nod, but she'd been fuming inside.

"I don't want you working too hard," Emma had said.

"I'm capable—"

"I know," her boss said, cutting her off. "But I hope you will be more of a friend than a..."

"Servant?" She could have told the impossible woman that there was more of a chance of that than ever becoming Emma's friend.

"No, more like family," Emma had said, and gave her a smile. "We really want you to feel at home here, Cynthia."

That's when she'd corrected her. "I prefer you call me Mrs. Crowley."

Not that it had stopped Emma from trying to get close to her. Her plan a failure, Mrs. Crowley had become intrigued by the woman and found herself amused enough that she'd felt no need to rush this. She began studying Emma Chisholm, curious about Hoyt's fourth wife.

And all that time, Emma had been curious about her, studying her, spying on her. When she thought about it, the whole thing was actually funny.

But now as she fixed Dakota's tea, she reminded herself that she was finally taking actions that would culminate in the end she had needed for so long.

She would have to hurry, though, and that made her a little sad. But all good things had to come to an end, she told herself as she turned with two cups of tea in her hands. "Emma says I make the best tea she has ever tasted. I hope you like it."

Hoyt Chisholm was glad he was sitting down. He stared at Laura, unable to believe his eyes. She'd aged, of course, in the past thirty years. They both had.

But she still looked enough like the woman he'd fallen in love with and married that he would have known her anywhere.

"How did you survive that day in the lake?" he asked. "I dove and dove for you and…"

She stared back at him. "I don't know what you're talking about. My name is Sharon Jones. I've never seen you before in my life."

He looked into her blue eyes. He was still so shocked to see her again that he knew he wasn't thinking clearly. Everyone kept telling him she was alive, but he hadn't believed it until this moment.

"If you don't know who I am, then…" Then she couldn't have been the one who had terrorized him and his family. She couldn't have killed his other wives. She couldn't have framed Zane.

"You're…lying," he said, telling himself this woman was Laura. He felt the weight of what that meant. It brought with it all the ramifications of what this woman had done to him and his family.

What scared him was whether or not the police would be able to prove it. What if they couldn't lock this woman up and throw away the key? He and Emma and his sons would have to live the rest of their lives in fear of what Laura would do next.

"You're a liar and a murderer," he said.

She shook her head slowly and gave him a small half smile. "You're…mistaken."

She even *sounded* like Laura. No one could look this much like his first wife or sound so much like her, unless…

He'd been so shocked to see her that for a moment he'd forgotten what the woman was capable of doing to him. She'd always messed with his mind. Her faked death, her affair with Clay Lansing—she'd put him through hell and had no intentions of stopping.

"She's Laura," he told the cops as he got to his feet. "Get a DNA sample from her and you'll be able to prove this woman is lying. She's wanted for murder in White-horse. I'll testify that she is my first wife, Lorraine Baxter Chisholm."

The woman looked up at him as one of the cops helped her to her feet. "You're wrong. Dead wrong."

He shook his head. If she wasn't Laura, then she was her twin sister. "It's her."

As the officer started to take her out of the room,

she leaned toward Hoyt and whispered. "Are you really willing to stake your life on it? Or Emma's?"

Her words didn't surprise him. But when she gave him that half smile again, he realized where he'd seen it before—and where the real Laura Chisholm was right now.

Dakota took one of the lemon cookies as Mrs. Crowley placed a cup of tea in front of her.

"Emma tells me that you recently lost your father," Mrs. Crowley said.

"Yes."

"I'm sorry. I understand he raised stock for rodeos."

Dakota didn't really want to talk about her father. "Yes." She wished Emma would wake up from her nap soon. The housekeeper continued to stare at her with that one dark eye, making her nervous.

She looked toward the kitchen door, hoping to see Emma's friendly face. Instead, she saw something odd.

Part of an apron was sticking out from the under the door of the pantry.

Mrs. Crowley followed her gaze. Dakota couldn't miss the change in the woman's expression.

"Why don't you finish your tea and I'll check on Mrs. Chisholm," the housekeeper said.

Dakota nodded mutely. Emma kept her kitchen spotless. Dakota had noticed when she'd helped her with the desserts the other night. She'd commented then about what a wonderful kitchen it was.

"It's my domain. Everything I wanted in a kitchen. Everything in its place," Emma had said. "I have my sons and husband trained not to touch anything in here.

I try my best to keep Mrs. Crowley out as well." She'd made a face. "The woman never puts anything back where it goes. I swear, she'd rearrange everything if I let her."

Mrs. Crowley rose from her chair. Dakota picked up her teacup. She hadn't taken more than a sip. The tea tasted bitter and she didn't want any more of it. She pretended to drink, hoping she could get rid of it when Mrs. Crowley went to check on Emma.

Dakota waited until the woman left the room, then quickly got up and dumped the tea down the drain before hurrying back to the table.

She'd barely sat down again when Mrs. Crowley appeared in the kitchen doorway. Dakota jumped, even more nervous now. She'd come too close to being caught. Why hadn't she just told the woman she didn't like tea?

She hurriedly picked up one of the cookies and took a bite, hoping Mrs. Crowley didn't notice that her hand was shaking as she did.

Mrs. Crowley stood at the end of the kitchen table watching her. "You like her cookies?"

Dakota nodded. "They're delicious. She told me she loves to bake."

"Can't keep her out of the kitchen," Mrs. Crowley said.

Dakota noticed the housekeeper had her hand in the pocket of the apron she wore and she seemed to be standing more upright than she had before.

"You remind me of your father."

Dakota's gaze shot to the woman's face, settling on the one dark eye. "What?"

"Your father. I knew him."

Dakota stared at the woman. "You knew my father?"

"You didn't drink your tea," Mrs. Crowley said.

The swift change of topic threw her for a moment.

"I'm sorry, I thought you just said you knew my father."

"As a matter of fact, we had a very short, intense affair when you were two."

Dakota felt her eyes widen in alarm at the woman's words—and the gun she pulled from her apron pocket. It was a short, snub-nosed revolver and it was pointed right at Dakota's heart.

"You could have made it so much easier if you had only drank your tea like a good girl," Mrs. Crowley said. "I cared about your father. I could have been happy with him had it not been for you. I've never liked children."

"Courtney." The word had slipped out.

"Yes, your sister."

"She's your daughter?" Dakota was still trying to make sense of what she was hearing—and seeing.

"I gave birth to her, if that's what you mean."

"You're…"

Mrs. Crowley smiled. "I used to be Laura Chisholm. Get up. We're going for a ride."

"Where's Emma?"

"Don't worry, she's coming with us."

The gravity of the situation was just starting to sink in. Hoyt was in Butte, his sons were fighting a grass fire and Dakota was looking down the barrel of a gun held by a crazy woman and known killer. She hated to think what this woman had done to Emma, let alone Courtney.

"What are you going to do with us?"

"If it makes you feel any better, before your father died he pleaded with me to promise that I wouldn't hurt you," Laura Chisholm said, then laughed. "Unfortunately he died before I promised him anything."

"You were there when he died." Hadn't she known that was the case? "You and Courtney. You must have taken him to the hospital. Or Courtney—"

"Don't be naive. I gave him something that caused the heart attack, why would I try to save him? Courtney took him, but not until I was sure he wouldn't survive."

Dakota took a step toward the woman, her anger overpowering her common sense. She wanted to take the gun away from this woman and—

"I wouldn't do that," Laura said. "I don't care where you die but if you ever want to see your sister again, you will do what I tell you."

Dakota watched as Laura popped out the white contact from her eye without ever letting the gun trained on Dakota waver. She popped the other contact out and stared at Dakota with two familiar blue eyes. Courtney had inherited her mother's blue eyes.

Emma stirred, eyelids flickering. Her body felt like it was made of lead weights. She didn't think she could move and didn't try for a few moments.

As her eyes finally managed to stay open, she looked around and saw that she was lying on the floor of the pantry.

Had she fallen? Fainted? She tried to sit up and found her muscles so lethargic it took all of her effort.

She was partway up into a sitting position when memory flooded her and she froze, listening.

Voices. She listened, recognizing Mrs. Crowley's monotone. It took her a moment to place the other voice. Dakota Lansing.

Emma sat up the rest of the way, thinking only that she had to save Dakota. She felt her head spin from the sudden movement and thought she might pass out.

She took a moment, trying to clear her head, her thoughts. How did she think she was going to save Dakota when she wasn't even sure she could get to her feet?

As she listened, she felt her blood turn to ice. Mrs. Crowley was Laura Chisholm. The woman had been living in their house all this time? Her heart pounded at the thought of the murderer this close to them.

But hadn't she known something was wrong? Hadn't she been spying on the woman? She would never have guessed, though, that Mrs. Crowley was Laura Chisholm. Her disguise was too good. Now Emma understood why the woman had kept them all at arm's length. Finally, Emma knew the woman's biggest secret of all.

She heard Mrs. Crowley say, "I guess I don't need to check on Mrs. Chisholm. I hear her getting up now."

She'd heard her moving in the pantry.

From the conversation, Emma knew she didn't have much time. Mrs. Crowley had drugged her, and now the woman had Dakota and was planning on taking them to Courtney.

Emma, even through the haze of whatever she'd been drugged with, was betting the drive would be eleven miles round-trip.

She struggled to her feet. She knew she couldn't fight off the woman she'd known as Mrs. Crowley. All she could do was try to leave a message for Hoyt or the boys when they returned.

She looked around for something to write with and spotted her chalkboard on the back of the pantry door where she made her grocery lists.

Hurriedly, she grabbed a piece of chalk and as quietly as possible, began to write.

Chapter 14

Hoyt called the house immediately, his heart dropping when the phone rang and rang. He left a message for Emma to call him at once.

Then he started to call Sheriff McCall Crawford as he watched the police take the woman he'd thought was Laura back to her cell.

She turned once to look back at him and mouthed, "Too late."

And then she was gone through a door.

Hoyt thought if he had to look at her another minute, he would have gone for her throat.

He'd call the sheriff and his sons on the way to the plane. He needed to get home as quickly as possible. Fortunately, he'd be flying back, but still it would take him too long. That had been the plan, though, hadn't it?

Hoyt couldn't take that thought any further because

he knew the rest of her plan. Emma. The thought of losing her was almost his undoing. Ahead he saw the plane and pilot waiting for him.

As he hurried to the plane, he knew this was all his fault. He'd invited the woman into his house. Once as his wife. Now as his housekeeper.

Laura must be ecstatic that she'd fooled him so easily. She'd played him, getting him out of town, far from the ranch and Emma. He prayed he was wrong, but the more the thought about it, he knew Mrs. Crowley was Laura. He racked his brain. Had Laura ever mentioned a twin sister?

He couldn't remember, but the woman he'd just seen at the police station was a close relative, there was no doubt about that. And right now, the woman wasn't going anywhere. The police would be able to hold her until they could get to the bottom of this.

If Laura hurt Emma…

His heart ached from trying to hold in his terror. He had married a monster. Or had he made her that way?

Hoyt didn't know. He just hoped he'd get a chance to ask her—before he killed her.

McCall hadn't gotten much sleep last night. The baby had kicked the entire night, it seemed. She'd called in and told the dispatcher she'd be running a little late.

"Can you stay within cell phone range today?" she asked Luke.

"The baby?" His eyes lit when he asked. He smiled as he placed a large hand on her abdomen and felt the baby kick.

She smiled and covered his hand with hers. Her undersheriff Nick Giovanni would be back tomorrow to take over. She was more than ready.

She was hoping for a slow day at the office when her cell phone rang.

Luke shot her a look. "Whatever it is—"

"Sheriff Crawford," she said, taking the call. She listened, avoiding Luke's gaze and trying not to let her true feelings show in her expression. "Don't worry, Hoyt, I'm on my way."

"Hoyt Chisholm? I thought he'd gone to Butte to identify his first wife."

"She wasn't Laura. But he thinks he knows where Laura is." She reached for her shoulder holster.

"I'm going with you."

She started to argue but felt the baby kick. Her stomach cramped and for a moment she held her breath, knowing Luke was watching her intently.

"All right." Even though Luke was a game warden, he'd had the same law enforcement training and was often called in when there was a need.

"Where does he think Laura is?" Luke asked as they headed for her patrol SUV.

"Chisholm ranch. He thinks Laura has been masquerading as his housekeeper, Mrs. Crowley."

Luke let out a low curse. "And Emma?"

"Hoyt tried the house and couldn't raise anyone, but they could all be at that grass fire I heard called in earlier. It's under control, but apparently Emma is missing and so is Mrs. Crowley."

Zane could see the driver of the pickup and knew the man wasn't going to slow down. He was betting that the man driving the truck was the escaped prisoner from California and had nothing to lose and everything to gain if he got away.

"Zane." Marshall sounded worried. "Zane, I quit playing chicken when I was fourteen."

At the speed that they were traveling, the two pickups were going to meet at the same time where the two roads intersected.

"I'm not letting him get away," Zane said, and kept the pedal floored.

He watched the pickup out of the corner of his eye growing closer and closer. He saw Marshall reach for the dash to brace himself for the crash they both knew was coming.

At the last moment, the driver of the other truck veered to the left. Zane hit his brakes and cranked his wheel to the right, but he was still going too fast to keep from hitting the other truck.

The driver's side of Zane's pickup smashed into the passenger side of the other truck, driving it farther up the road and out into the open pasture. As Zane fought to keep control of his pickup, the other driver hit a dry irrigation ditch.

Zane swerved away, tires digging into the dirt, the truck rocking wildly.

"He's losing it," Marshall said as the other truck rolled. It churned up a cloud of dust as it rolled a second time and came to rest on its top out in the middle of the pasture.

When Zane got his pickup stopped at the edge of the road, he and Marshall jumped out and ran toward the truck. The driver had kicked out the windshield and was trying to climb out. The man matched the mug shot the sheriff had provided them of the third escaped prisoner so they could keep an eye out for him.

The escaped felon crawled out, bloody and bruised. He was hurt badly enough that he didn't put up a fight, just lay on his back in the grass.

"I need a doctor," the man cried. "You almost killed me."

"Where is Courtney Baxter?" Zane demanded.

"I'm not saying anything without a lawyer," the man said.

"I'll take care of him," Marshall said, no doubt seeing that his brother wanted to beat the truth out of the man. He grabbed some rope from the back of the pickup and began tying up the escaped prisoner for the ride to the sheriff's department.

Zane's cell rang. "Is everything all right at the house?" he asked when he saw that it was his brother Dawson calling.

"No one's here."

"What?" He looked at Marshall. "He says there's no one there."

"Wait a minute," Dawson said on the other end of the line. "I just found a note from Mrs. Crowley saying that they have gone into town."

Zane was shaking his head. "I'm going to the house," he called to Marshall, who signaled him to go.

Running to his pickup, he leaped in and tore down the road toward the ranch house. Emma wouldn't go into town, not with her stepsons fighting a grass fire burning down the road. She'd be baking something for when they finished with the fire.

He prayed he was wrong about the fire being a diversion. But the timing of the fire was too much of a coincidence. And now Emma, Dakota and Mrs. Crowley were gone?

He could see the house in the distance. Zane raced toward it, his heart in his throat. He kept seeing Dakota's face, remembering their lovemaking.

Why in the hell hadn't he told her that he loved her?

As the house loomed ahead, he prayed Dakota was all right.

"Did she hurt you?" Dakota asked Emma as they bounced along the road in the ranch pickup. Dakota was driving; Emma sat in the middle with Laura Chisholm holding a gun on her.

"No." Emma had been pretending to doze off and on from the time Dakota had helped Laura put her in the pickup.

"Just keep your eye on the road," Laura snapped. She'd peeled the scar off her face and no longer looked anything like Mrs. Crowley.

"Why are you doing this?" Dakota asked, trying to keep the fear out of her voice. She'd heard all about Laura Chisholm, knew at least some of the horrible things she'd done and suspected there was even worse they didn't know about. Dakota couldn't bear to think of this woman with her father.

"You wouldn't understand," Laura said, and leaned down a little to look into Emma's face. Emma had her eyes closed and her head on Dakota's shoulder.

As they'd been leaving the house, Emma had leaned heavily on her and seemed completely out of it. Until she'd whispered, "Be ready once we reach the well house." Then she had touched her fingers to her lips.

Dakota had nodded and squeezed her hand.

Now she wondered how Emma had known where they were going even before Laura had begun barking out orders.

"Can you drive any slower?" Laura snapped.

Dakota gave the pickup a little more speed. The road was narrow and bumpy as it cut through pasture. As they dropped over a hill, the house disappeared behind them.

"No one is coming to save you," Laura assured her as she caught Dakota looking in the rearview mirror. "That's a nasty fire that could destroy most of their pasture on that side of the ranch. They aren't going to stop fighting the fire to save you."

Clearly, this woman was behind the fire. She'd managed to get everyone away from the house. Dakota wondered how the housekeeper had started the fire and realized it must have been the third escaped prisoner from California.

"Emma, I'm surprised you don't want to ask about me and Hoyt," Laura taunted.

Emma seemed to stir. "Hoyt?"

Laura laughed. "You do realize that you're not even legally married, since I am alive and well?"

Alive, yes. Well? Dakota thought not. She was just grateful she hadn't drunk the tea the woman had made her. She feared neither she nor Emma would still be alive for this little trip.

As Dakota drove over another hill, she saw the creek through a stand of pines and beyond that, what appeared to be a small stone building with an old waterwheel on one side and a cistern on the other.

At the house, Zane threw the pickup into Park and jumped out. As he was running toward the door, he noticed that the truck Mrs. Crowley drove was gone. Someone had left, maybe all three of them, but they hadn't gone to town. Of that he was sure.

He hit the front door, burst through it and into the house, already calling Dakota's name as he ran.

"Dakota!" The house felt empty long before he reached the large kitchen.

He glanced upstairs. "Dakota?" Taking the stairs two at a time, he charged up to the next floor, all the time telling himself there was no one here. But he had to be sure.

He hadn't passed anyone on the main road but that didn't mean anything. There were numerous back roads on the ranch.

At the bottom of the stairs, he glanced toward the kitchen and noticed two teacups sitting on the table along with a plate of cookies.

Emma would never leave her kitchen without cleaning everything up.

He stepped in and noticed another teacup in the sink. The pantry door was ajar as well.

His phone rang, making him jump. For a moment he thought it was going to be Dakota. He imagined her telling him that she and Emma had gone for a drive with Mrs. Crowley to see the fire.

"Zane?"

It was his brother Marshall. "Is everything all right there?"

"No one's here, just like Dawson said. The pickup Mrs. Crowley has been using is gone."

"Zane, earlier Emma was telling me that she'd been spying on Mrs. Crowley. Apparently the old gal's been going out late at night and not coming back until the wee hours of the morning. She was telling me about it when I saw the fire. She thought Mrs. Crowley might have been meeting a man somewhere on the ranch."

Zane didn't even want to ask why Emma had been spying on the housekeeper. Racing to the far wing, Zane knocked at the housekeeper's door. No answer. He tried the knob. Locked. If he was wrong, his father would not be happy.

He stepped back, lifted his leg and kicked at the door. One more kick and the frame shattered, the lock broke and the door swung in.

The room was immaculate. In fact, it didn't even look as if anyone was staying here.

"Mrs. Crowley?" He stepped in. "Mrs. Crowley?" The bathroom door was ajar. He pushed it all the way open. Empty.

As he turned to leave, he spotted the framed photograph and froze in midstep.

It was a photograph of his father and a woman he'd never seen before. Why would Mrs. Crowley have a photograph of his father and some woman?

He stepped over to the picture and picked up the silver frame. His father looked incredibly young. Behind him was the original ranch house before the later additions, so that meant the woman in the photograph had to have been his father's first wife, Laura.

His gaze went to the woman in the photo. He felt his heart drop to his stomach. The frame slipped from his fingers and hit the floor, the glass shattering.

Laura Chisholm was Mrs. Crowley? She'd been living here all these months, right under their roof?

His cell phone rang. His father. He quickly answered it.

Emma continued to act as if she was still suffering from the drug Laura had given her. Through her half-closed eyes, she watched the landscape she had come to love blur past the window of the pickup.

Laura had a small, snub-nosed pistol pressed against her side. Emma felt the cold, hard metal with each bump that the pickup hit as Dakota drove them away from the prairie and up into the foothills.

Out of the corner of her eye, she saw the blackened, scorched earth from the grass fire off to the east. By now her sons would have the flames out and possibly be heading back to the house. She could only hope that they would find the note she'd left in the pantry.

"Don't you want to talk about it?" Laura asked.

Emma raised her head just a little to glance sideways at the woman. She looked so different now without the scarred face, the sightless eye. What gleamed in her two blue eyes was a brittle hatred that made her inwardly flinch.

"I would think you'd have questions for me. Don't you want to know how I survived, how I killed Tasha and Krystal, how I framed your stepson with the help of my daughter?"

Did any of that matter now? Emma didn't think so. "You're sick."

Laura laughed. "I'm no sicker than your friend Aggie."

That reminder stirred something in Emma. She had to tamp it down to keep from showing Laura that she wasn't as drugged as she was pretending.

"I know you killed her," Emma said, slurring her words.

"I hated doing it, though. I admired Aggie. We had a lot in common."

Aggie would have looked beyond Mrs. Crowley's disguise and not been fooled, Emma thought, then remembered that Aggie was dead because Laura had ultimately fooled her somehow as well.

"Why don't you just kill me?" Emma said. "Let Dakota go."

Laura smiled. "I'm afraid I've had to change my plans. You know, if you had drank that first cup of coffee I fixed you the morning after I started my job, it would have been all over right then. No one else would have gotten hurt."

Emma remembered the anger and frustration she'd seen in Mrs. Crowley's expression that morning. She'd misinterpreted it as the woman simply trying to establish herself in the house, the kitchen in particular.

"You could have poisoned me at any time after that," Emma said.

Laura chuckled. "You amused and intrigued me. I

liked watching you, knowing that I could kill you at any time—and you had no idea who I was."

"That must have made you very happy." They were close to the old well house now. Emma cut her gaze to Dakota. The young woman was strong and determined, her hands on the wheel sure. Emma knew she could trust Dakota to put up a fight when the time came. She just hoped that she didn't get her killed.

"Park here," Laura ordered. She couldn't help being disappointed. She'd expected more out of Emma. She regretted giving her a drug that, while it had allowed Emma to regain consciousness, made her pathetically docile. She'd hoped for more fight out of her.

"Give me the keys," she told Dakota, who turned off the ignition and handed over the keys.

Laura saw them both looking expectantly toward the old stone well house and stone water tank.

"Let's go see Courtney," Laura said. "I know how badly you want to see your sister. But remember. If you try anything, I will shoot Emma, then shoot you *and* Courtney."

"You would kill your own daughter?" Dakota demanded.

"I told you. I don't like children. Especially my own."

"What did my father ever see in you?"

Laura laughed. "I was beautiful and sexy and he was broken after your mother's death. I was touched by that kind of anguished love and wished Hoyt loved me half as much."

That got a small rise out of Emma. "Maybe he would have loved you more if you hadn't cheated on him."

Laura opened the pickup door and, keeping the barrel of the gun buried in Emma's side, pulled her out.

"You know nothing about it," she snapped, hating that she'd let Emma get to her. She couldn't have been more jealous of Emma than she was at that moment. Hoyt adored Emma. The two couldn't keep their hands off each other. He'd never been like that with her.

At the door to the well house, she tossed the key to the padlock to Dakota. The stone building had been perfect for her needs. It had no windows, only one door and was almost six miles from the ranch. Nor did anyone ever come up this way.

Laura remembered it because Hoyt had brought her out here the only time she'd ridden a horse with him.

"Open it."

Dakota caught the key. Laura still had the gun pressed into Emma's side, a hand gripping her arm. Emma gave a slight shake of her head. Apparently she didn't want to try to do anything until they got inside.

She inserted the key into the padlock, fearing what they would find inside this odd building. The door was made of metal and had rusted over the years. She had to push hard to get it to open.

As it swung in, Dakota blinked. The only light in the stone structure came from the now open doorway and from four small openings high above in the circular stone walls.

The walls were smooth and there were several old watermarks on them. Dakota realized that this was part of the cistern used for water storage.

She spotted her sister in the shadows and felt a surge

of relief. Courtney was alive. For a moment, that was all that mattered. Then she heard the rattle of chains and noticed the handcuff around Courtney's right wrist. The other end of the chain was attached to a pipe that ran along the wall.

Courtney began to cry at the sight of her. "Dakota, how did you—" The rest of her sister's words died on her lips as she saw Laura and Emma come into the room.

"A little family reunion," Laura said.

Courtney seemed to cower, a look of despair on her face. Dakota noticed that she was dressed in a pair of old jeans, a soiled T-shirt and sneakers. There were several containers that looked as if they had contained food stacked in the corner.

"You've kept my sister here chained to a pipe like an animal?" Dakota said, turning on Laura.

"Let's not forget that *your sister* was in on framing your boyfriend," the woman said.

"I haven't forgotten," Dakota said.

"I thought it was just a joke," Courtney cried. "I didn't know…." Her eyes filled with tears again as she bit off the rest of the lie. "Oh, Dakota, I'm so sorry."

As Laura started to shove Emma into the room, Dakota caught her signal. Emma whirled around, taking Laura by surprise, and knocked the gun from her hand. It skittered across the concrete floor. Dakota dove for it.

She heard Emma let out a cry and heard Courtney yell a warning. As her hand closed over the gun she was kicked hard in the side, knocking the air out of her.

Then Laura was on her, slamming her head against the concrete floor. Dakota felt blood run down into her left eye as she tried to fight the woman off. For her age, Laura was surprisingly strong and she fought dirty. She grabbed a handful of Dakota's hair, jerking her head back as she wrenched the gun from her hands.

In an instant, Laura was on her feet and holding the gun on them.

Dakota rolled over, wiping blood from her eye. Emma had gotten to her feet, but Laura had been too fast for her to intervene. She backed up as Laura swung the barrel of the gun toward her.

"Stupid. Stupid. Stupid," Laura said, sounding breathless and yet excited. "I should just shoot you right now. If Dakota moves a muscle, I will."

Dakota froze where she was on the floor as the woman backed her way to the open doorway.

"You aren't going to leave again," Courtney cried. "Please, Mother."

"Don't call me that. You were just a mistake of nature," Laura snapped. "My use for you is over. You wanted to get to know your sister? Well, now's your chance."

"Who is the woman the Butte police have in custody?" Emma asked.

"My cousin. People always thought we were sisters, we're so much alike. She owed me a favor," Laura said with a shrug.

Emma was just thankful that Hoyt was in Butte. By now he would realize he'd been sent on a wild goose chase, but he'd be safe from this woman.

"You know Hoyt will never remarry," Laura said.

"Yes, I know. Is that really all you want, for him

to never find happiness with another woman?" Emma asked.

"You make it sound so simple." Laura shook her head. "I *loved* him. I should have been enough, but then suddenly he tells me he's adopting three infant sons and talking about getting another three who needed homes."

"Hoyt loves children," Emma said.

"Yes, but I don't."

"Clearly," Dakota said. "Anyone who could chain up her own daughter and keep her prisoner out here…"

"Don't judge me," Laura snapped, and waved the gun at her.

"You have what you want," Emma said quickly. "Let Courtney and Dakota go. By the time they walk back to the house, I'll be dead and you will be long gone."

Laura smiled. "I thought killing you would be enough, but I was wrong. By the time Hoyt gets back to the ranch, you'll be gone and so will his sons. He will have nothing left. Only then will he finally know how he made me feel."

With that, Laura stepped out through the door, slamming and locking the airtight metal door behind her as she plunged them into semidarkness.

"She's leaving us to die here," Courtney cried.

"No," Emma said as she quickly moved to Dakota and helped her up. "She's not. Are you badly hurt?"

Dakota shook her head as she heard what sounded like the crank of an old metal wheel. "She's not through with us, is she?"

Emma shook her head.

"What?" Courtney cried. "What are you whispering about?"

Before either could answer they heard the water. It cranked and creaked through the ancient pipes for a few moments before it began to fill the chamber where the three of them were now trapped.

Chapter 15

Courtney let out a scream as water began rushing in around her feet. She tried to pull away but she was still hooked to the old pipe that ran along the wall.

"Stay calm," Emma ordered as she and Dakota hurried over to Courtney.

"I think if we both pull on this pipe we might be able to dislodge it," Dakota said. She met Emma's gaze as they both grabbed hold of the rusty pipe. They could feel the water surging through it. Once it broke, the chamber might fill even faster.

But the water was rising quickly and Courtney was manacled close to the floor. She would drown if they couldn't get her free.

"On the count of three," Emma said. "One, two, three!"

Dakota pulled as hard as she could. She heard Emma straining next to her. The pipe gave only a little.

Courtney began to scream. Water was lapping around their ankles now. A leak had sprung in the pipe. A spray of rust-red water showered over the three of them, drenching them to the skin.

"Courtney," Dakota snapped. "You can help. Grab hold of the chain and pull on the count of three. One, two, three!"

The pipe came lose and the three of them were sent sprawling in the rising water.

"Okay, we can't panic," Emma said as even more water began to flow into the tanklike room. "I left a message. Someone will find it."

But they both knew there was little chance of Hoyt making it back in time. The rest of the Chisholms were fighting the fire. She and Dakota shared a look.

"Zane will come for me," Dakota said, praying it was true. Courtney was crying, pushing at the water with her hands as it rose to their thighs.

"All we have to do is swim when it gets too deep to stand," Emma said. "Once we reach those small windows up there, the water will rush out. We'll be able to breathe."

Dakota looked up at the four slits in the rock, then at Emma. Neither said anything, but Dakota knew the water wouldn't be able to rush out fast enough to save them, because the slits were too close to the top of the tank.

Their only hope was being found before they drowned.

* * *

Luke had insisted on driving. "You'll be more comfortable in the passenger seat," he'd said, and McCall knew he'd been watching her. Nor was she feeling well enough to argue the point. She tried to get comfortable, but it was impossible with the baby being so active.

Time was of the essence if Hoyt was right and his housekeeper was Laura Chisholm. As far as Hoyt had known, the two were alone in the house, she told Luke.

"Hasn't this woman been working for them for several months?" Luke asked as he drove toward Whitehorse. She and Luke lived south of town on Luke's folks' old place. He'd built them a beautiful home, which he'd made her wedding present.

"So why would Emma have something to fear now, is that what you're asking?" McCall said. She'd been thinking the same thing. "I wonder if it doesn't have something to do with Zane." She had told him about Courtney Hughes aka Courtney Baxter. "Laura's her mother."

Luke shook his head. "If this Mrs. Crowley is Laura Chisholm, then where is Courtney?"

That was the question, and had been since she'd disappeared the night after her "date" with Zane. He was out on bail and if Courtney didn't turn up, or worse, turned up dead…

"Have you thought any more about what you want to do after the baby is born?" Luke asked.

McCall had her hand on her abdomen. She loved the feel of their child inside her. Safe. But once the baby was born… She flinched as she felt not a cramp, but what could only be a contraction.

"Honey?" Luke said, glancing over at her. "McCall?" He sounded alarmed.

"It's nothing. Just a twinge." That was all it had been, right? The baby moving so much must have caused it.

Suddenly she was scared. She would have gladly faced killers every day than to think about being the mother to this baby.

"Talk to me, McCall. I know something's going on with you."

"It was just a twinge," she said, hoping it was true. She needed to carry this baby to term. It was a month too early.

"I'm talking about right now. I'm talking about the last eight months," Luke said. "I know you're worried about the baby because we lost the first one, but—"

"I'm scared." The words were out before she could call them back. She hated to admit to Luke how she was feeling. "I'm not sure what kind of mother I'll be. Look at my mother. Ruby was…well, Ruby."

"That's ridiculous," Luke said. "Is that all that's been bothering you? You're nothing like Ruby, thank heaven." He looked over at her and said, "McCall?"

She had another contraction, this one much stronger than the first one. "I think I'm in labor. It just came on so suddenly." She remembered losing the other baby. It had started much like this.

"I'm taking you to the hospital."

She nodded as she heard Luke on the patrol SUV radio calling the sheriff's office. "Halley Robinson is the closest to the Chisholm place. Have them send her," McCall said.

Luke passed on the message as he raced toward the hospital.

McCall prayed her baby would be all right. She was almost to term. But what would she do once the baby was born? She was terrified she might become like her mother.

After the call from his father, Zane raced back downstairs to the kitchen. Hoyt had already figured out somehow that Mrs. Crowley was Laura.

"You have to stop her," his father had pleaded. "Whatever you have to do."

Zane knew what he was saying. But first he had to find them. If Emma was right and Mrs. Crowley had been going somewhere on the ranch at night…

In the kitchen he noticed the partially opened pantry door—and the hem of Emma's apron sticking out. He quickly moved to it, heart in his throat as he prayed he wouldn't find her—

The pantry was empty. He breathed a sigh of relief, then saw the note on the chalkboard.

Well house. Laura/Crowley. Hurry.

The well house was an old cistern system that hadn't been used in years. Water had been diverted from the creek for storage for low precipitation years back when the ranch was started.

Zane placed a call to his brothers as he ran to his pickup. He told them everything, including what his father had said as he drove toward the well house. "Marshall has taken the third prisoner escapee into jail."

"We have a section of fire we're fighting near the house," Dawson said.

"I can handle this. I just needed you to know. Dad is flying in. He's going to be heading straight for the ranch the minute his plane touches down."

"Find them," Dawson said.

"I will." Zane snapped the phone shut and drove as fast as he could up the road toward the foothills.

Laura could see dust in the distance. She'd told Rex to pick off one after another of the Chisholm brothers.

Now she had a bad feeling he hadn't done as he was told. She should have killed him instead of his mouthy cellmate Lloyd. Lloyd would have gotten the job done.

As she started to climb into the ranch pickup, she saw the flat tire. For a moment she just stood looking at it.

A flat? It seemed inconceivable that something so ordinary could foil her plans. For years she'd gotten away with murder, literally, because she'd planned every detail meticulously.

Laura glanced toward the road down in the valley again. Dust boiled up behind a rig headed this way fast.

She looked around for a place to hide, telling herself fate was playing right into her hand. She needed a vehicle and someone was bringing her one.

All she had to do was pull the trigger when the time came and then get out of here.

She could hear the water filling the tank and imagined the three women inside panicking. Especially Courtney.

For just an instant, Laura felt badly that Clay Lansing's daughters were part of the collateral damage.

But there was no way Laura could leave the girls

alive. Courtney especially was like a loose thread. One little tug and everything would come unraveled.

As the vehicle coming up the road grew near, Laura looked around for a good spot to hide in wait to ambush whoever it was. She needed their vehicle and, one way or another, she planned to get it.

They would have to swim soon. The water was rising faster now. Emma realized Laura must have closed off the main cistern tank. With the floodgates open, this tank was filling fast.

Creek water lapped at her waist. The three of them had moved to the edge of the tank closest to the door. They had tried to break down the door but to no avail. Now they were just saving their energy for when they would have to swim.

"I'm so sorry," Courtney said, not for the first time. "When she contacted me I was just so glad to finally meet my birth mother."

"It doesn't matter now," Dakota said.

"We're going to die, aren't we?"

"No, we're not," Emma snapped. She wished Dakota's sister had her strength and courage. The young woman seemed to have been pampered much of her life. A little hardship and struggle seemed to hone a person for times like this. Courtney hadn't been tested and now, facing the biggest test of her life, was ill prepared.

"Do you hear something?" Courtney asked suddenly.

Over the sound of the water filling the tank, Emma listened. A vehicle.

Courtney brightened. "Someone is coming to save us, just like you said." She was all smiles now.

Emma shared a look with Dakota, who seemed to share her own worry. She hadn't heard Laura leave and now feared that whoever was coming was about to walk right into a trap.

Zane slowed as he saw the ranch pickup parked next to the well house. He'd pulled his shotgun down from the rack behind the pickup seat and had it and his pistol within reach.

Slowly, he pulled up behind the pickup and saw the flat tire. He killed the engine, listening through his open side window.

Where were they? More to the point, where was Laura Chisholm?

That's when he heard the water sloshing around in the old cistern tank. What the hell?

And in that instant, he knew. Jumping out of the truck, he ran to the door.

"Dakota? Emma?" he yelled. He could hear water running in from the creek and the faint sound of voices on the other side.

He tried the door, but it opened inward so the water in the tank would make it impossible to open.

There was only one option. He had to close the headgates on the creek, divert the water back into the creek and drain the tank as quickly as possible.

He rushed around the side to the headgates. Someone had jammed a crowbar into them, locking the gates open. He was struggling to free the crowbar when he heard the first shot.

A bullet whizzed past his ear. The second shot splintered the wood next to him.

Diving for cover, he used the momentum and his weight to dislodge the crowbar. But the gate was still open, water still filling the tank, just not as quickly.

He peered out, trying to assess where the shots had come from. He didn't need to ask who had just tried to kill him.

Another bullet whizzed past. Laura had to be in the trees up on the side of the hill. He could still hear the water flowing into the tank. In order to drain the tank, he had to get from where he was across twenty yards without cover.

She'd fired three shots, but he didn't doubt she'd come with plenty of ammunition. Nor could he wait her out. The flow into the cistern had slowed almost to a trickle but he had to drain the tank. He didn't know how long Dakota and Emma could stay afloat in there. If they were even still alive.

The thought forced him to move. He pulled out his pistol and hoped he was right about Laura being in the trees on the hillside. It was a chance he had to take. Once he got the drain opened…

He got ready, then, firing as he ran, sprinted toward the cistern. If he could reach it and get on the far side…

Deputy Halley Robinson saw the smoke and the men putting out the last of the grass fire as she raced down the road toward the Chisholm house.

She recognized her fiancé, Colton Chisholm, on the fire line but she didn't stop. Her orders were to get to the house as quickly as possible and arrest the woman she knew only as Mrs. Crowley.

Halley had to ask the dispatcher to repeat what she'd said.

"The housekeeper is believed to be Laura Chisholm."

Halley still couldn't believe it. She'd seen the cantankerous Mrs. Crowley on numerous occasions when she'd been out to the ranch house. Everyone gave her a wide berth. Halley wasn't sure she'd ever looked the woman in the eye or really studied her face.

Now, as she neared the house, her only thought was of Emma. She'd fallen in love with Colton's stepmother, everyone had. If this report was right, then Laura Chisholm was a killer hell-bent on killing Hoyt's fourth wife—as she had his other two.

Halley parked in front of the house, noticing that the pickup Mrs. Crowley drove wasn't anywhere around. But there was a ranch pickup out front.

Climbing out, she unsnapped her holster, her hand on the butt of her weapon as she mounted the stairs, crossed the porch and knocked at the door. No answer.

She tried the knob. "Hello?" No answer again.

She made her way to the kitchen, Emma's domain. The house had an eerie feel to it that she didn't like. The moment she saw the cluttered kitchen she knew something was wrong.

Then she saw the note. Mrs. Crowley had written that they had gone into town. But that was marked out and below it was scrawled "Well house, Laura has Emma and Dakota." It was signed "Zane."

Fortunately Colton had taken Halley up to the old well house once on a horseback ride. She ran for her cruiser, called in her ETA and a request for backup she knew wouldn't be coming in time as she raced up the road toward the foothills.

* * *

McCall glanced at the clock on the wall and felt another hard contraction coming. "Check and see if there has been any word from Halley," she said, her voice strained.

She was worried. There'd been no word on what was going on out at the Chisholm ranch. More and more, she suspected that Hoyt had been right. The housekeeper *was* Laura Chisholm, and everyone knew what that woman was capable of.

"I checked a few minutes ago," Luke said. "Honey, there is nothing you can do but have this baby. Halley can handle herself. So can the Chisholm men."

McCall nodded and tried to breathe through the contraction. Luke was right. There was nothing she could do for Emma or anyone else. She was about to have their baby. She tried to concentrate on breathing.

Just think about your baby.

"Did you call my grandmother?" she asked as the contraction ended.

Luke laughed. "Of course. She'd made it clear she was to be notified the moment you went into labor, and I'm not about to cross Pepper Winchester. Or your mother. Ruby and Red are on their way. Hunt's driving your grandmother in from the ranch."

She smiled and looked into her husband's handsome face. She could feel their baby inside her, ready to come out into the world and make them a family. *This is your world, right here in this room,* she thought.

Another contraction hit. Dr. Carrey stuck his head in the door. He was wearing his Stetson but he'd changed into scrubs.

"Pepper called to tell me not to deliver the baby until

she got here, but I've got a rodeo tonight so let's get this baby born," Doc joked as he took off his hat.

McCall saw Luke step outside the room to take a call. She caught his expression before the door closed and realized he was as worried as she was about what was happening at the Chisholm ranch.

"What?" she asked when he came back in.

"Halley, she called in. She's all right."

"And Laura?" McCall asked, her voice breaking as another contraction gripped her.

He shook his head. "They'll get her."

Chapter 16

Zane sprinted toward the cistern, firing the pistol toward the trees as he ran. The air filled with the reports of shots, his and Laura's. He still couldn't tell where she was firing from and right now it didn't matter. As long as he reached the drain and could get it open…

He was ready to dive over the side of the hill to open the drain at the base of the cistern, when he felt the searing heat of a bullet. His left leg collapsed under him and he rolled, still firing. Fortunately, his momentum took him over the edge of the hill.

Rolling down the slope, he came to a stop at the bottom of the well house next to the drain. He knew he was hit; his leg felt on fire, but he was able to crawl over to the drain valve.

He didn't have much time. In order to open the drain he would have to use both hands. And even then he feared it wouldn't be enough. The valve wouldn't have been opened in years. His fear was that he wouldn't be strong enough without some sort of tool.

Blood soaked into the thigh of his jeans. He quickly laid down his pistol and grabbed the valve handle with both hands. It didn't budge. With a curse, he pulled himself up and put all his weight into it. The handle turned a few inches.

He heard the sound of footfalls on loose gravel. Laura was coming. Any moment, she would be down the hill and around the cistern.

Zane put everything he had into turning the handle.

Laura knew she'd hit him. She'd seen him go down. He'd been heading to the backside of the cistern where the drain was located. He'd managed to stop the flow of water into the tank. She couldn't hear the women. They would have to be swimming by now. The creek water was cold. They couldn't last long.

By now Courtney would have drowned. That thought gave her a moment's pause as she came off the hillside. Two to go—if she could stop Zane.

Laura smiled to herself. This would be over soon. She had just reached the road when she saw the dust and heard the roar of a vehicle engine. Company. Even from this distance she could make out a sheriff's department patrol SUV. McCall.

"Make my day," she said under her breath. This day was just getting better.

She could hear Zane trying to open the old drain. *Good luck with that,* she thought as the patrol car zoomed up the road. Laura crouched down in front of her pickup to wait. There was time. Even if Zane got the drain open, it would take a while for the water to drain enough to get the door open.

The handle turned. Zane heard a *clunk,* the sound of the lock released. He fell back, pulling the drain lid open. Water began to gush out. Inside the cistern, he heard the faint sound of women's voices. He couldn't make out the words but there were at least two women in there, still alive.

The water was rushing out quickly. If they could just stay afloat a little longer...

Picking up his gun, he knew he couldn't stay here. He would be a sitting duck. Actually, he was surprised Laura hadn't already found him. She would know where he'd been headed. So where was she?

He listened. That's when he heard the sound of a vehicle coming. But there was another noise as well. He looked up and saw a small plane headed in this direction.

Deputy Halley Robinson slowed as the well house came into view. Two pickups. The one Mrs. Crowley had been driving. The other must be Zane's.

She didn't see anyone as she pulled up behind Zane's truck. She cut her engine and opened the door, pulling her weapon as she did. Staying behind the driver's side door, she peered around the edge. She could hear water running.

"Zane!" she called. "Zane?"

He appeared at the lower edge of the cistern. She could see that his left leg was soaked with blood. He leaned against the stone structure, a gun in his hand, and motioned for her to stay back.

"Mrs. Crowley is Laura. She's got a gun!" he called.

Halley took in what she could see of the area. No sign of the housekeeper. Or anyone else.

She listened and heard running water. Closer, crickets chirped in the tall grass. The sun beat down. Nothing moved.

Halley never heard her. At the last minute, she sensed the woman behind her. She felt the hair rise on the back of her neck. As she started to swing around, she felt a viselike arm come around her neck. The barrel of a gun jabbed into her back. Her own weapon was wrenched out of her hand.

In the SUV's side mirror, Halley caught a glimpse of the woman she'd known as Mrs. Crowley. The scar was gone. So was the one white eye, the one dark eye. Two very blue eyes burned too brightly from a face that was surprisingly attractive.

She'd always wondered about the first Mrs. Chisholm and what it would be like coming face-to-face with a monster. Now she knew.

"Don't think for a moment that I won't kill you," Laura said.

Halley didn't. She'd almost been killed by someone much tamer than this woman when she worked on the West Coast.

"Zane!" Laura called. "I have Halley." She jabbed the deputy hard in the back.

Halley let out a cry.

Zane appeared at the bottom edge of the cistern again.

"I need you to throw down your gun," Laura said. "Then I need you to toss me your truck keys. If you don't, I will kill your future sister-in-law."

Zane hesitated only a moment. He tossed his gun away from him, then reached into his pocket and pulled out his keys. He threw them up on the road just a few yards from them.

Halley heard the airplane. It sounded as if it was going to land on them as it zoomed just over their heads.

"Today is your lucky day," Laura said, and gave Halley a shove that sent her over the edge of the road and rolling down the slope to the creek.

A moment later, Halley heard a pickup engine fire. Gravel pelted the patrol SUV as Laura spun the tires on the truck and took off down the road.

Dakota heard the sound of someone trying to open the door. The water had drained down until they could stand, but the cold creek water still pooled around their ankles. They were weak from the exertion of swimming. The cold water had zapped all their strength and all three of them were shivering convulsively. She worried that if they didn't get out soon, they would die of hypothermia.

When the door swung open, the first thing Dakota saw was Zane's face in the bright sunlight that poured in.

She stumbled to him, only then seeing the bandana tied around his thigh, the blood-soaked jeans and the lack of color in his handsome face. He grabbed her, holding her tightly against him as Halley wrapped a blanket around Emma and Courtney and helped them out into the sunshine.

Dakota began to cry as she pulled back to look into Zane's face. She'd feared that she would die in the cistern and never get to see him again. She'd known he'd come for her, prayed that he would be safe.

"We have to get Zane to the hospital," Halley was saying. "He's lost a lot of blood."

As Courtney and Emma climbed into the patrol SUV, Halley helped Dakota get Zane into the back. Halley gave her a blanket from the back and Zane held her. She couldn't stop shaking.

Halley slid in behind the wheel and took off toward Whitehorse.

"Laura?" Emma asked, her teeth chattering.

"She got away," Halley said.

"I don't think so," Zane said as he motioned out the side window. In the distance they could see the pickup barreling down the road, a cloud of dust boiling up as it went.

A small airplane was coming from the other direction. It was headed right for the pickup.

Laura saw the plane coming directly at her. Hoyt. So this was how it would end, she thought, and sped up. She just hoped she got a good look at his face before she died—and he got a good look at hers.

As the plane roared toward her, sun glinted off its windshield. She squinted, trying desperately to see the man behind the controls as she braced herself for impact.

She'd been so sure he would kill himself before he'd let her get away that she hadn't been paying attention to the road ahead.

At the last minute, the pilot pulled up. The plane's belly practically scraped the top of the pickup's cab—he'd called it that close. It happened so fast. All she could see was the plane out the pickup windshield, then it was gone and she was staring not at the road ahead but open, rugged country.

The road had turned and she hadn't even noticed. She hit the brakes but the pickup was going too fast. It began to skid and hit the edge of the road hard, slamming her against the door.

She fought to get control as the truck dropped down into the ditch. She could see the embankment coming up and braced herself as the pickup went airborne.

The truck plummeted over the embankment and nose-dived into the ground at the bottom. Her head snapped back hard. She saw stars, then darkness before the pickup came to a stop half-buried in dirt and sagebrush not two miles from the Chisholm ranch house she'd once called home.

When she opened her eyes, Hoyt was beside the pickup, staring at her through what was left of the shattered side window. He had a gun in his hand.

"You can't kill me," she said, sneering at him.

He raised the gun as she fumbled for her own weapon. Hadn't she always known this was the way it had to end?

She pulled out her gun, but never got to aim before he fired.

* * *

"Would you like to see your daughter?" The nurse brought the blanket-wrapped bundle over to her and put the infant into her arms.

McCall stared down at her daughter and felt tears rush to her eyes. "She's beautiful."

"Just like her mother," Luke said as he leaned over to look at his daughter.

All McCall could do was stare at the infant in awe. "We did this?"

Luke laughed. "Yes, honey, we did."

"I wondered how I would feel when I held my baby." She looked up at her husband. "There are no words."

"You're going to be a great mother. You know that now, don't you?"

McCall nodded, too choked up to speak. She didn't know if she would be great, but she did know she would give it everything she had. And, unlike her mother, she had Luke.

"They said I have a great-granddaughter," Pepper Winchester said as she stuck her head in the doorway.

McCall smiled at her grandmother and turned the bundle in her arms so Pepper could see her. Pepper's eyes filled at the sight of the infant. She reached for McCall's hand and squeezed it.

McCall fought her own tears at the sight of the grandmother she'd never known until recently crying over this new life. *Strange the twists and turns life takes,* she thought. Her daughter would know her great-grandmother. She would have more family than McCall would ever have been able to imagine. Dozens of cousins, loads of people who loved her.

As if on cue, her own mother came into the room. Ruby stopped a few feet away and seemed to be waiting for an invitation.

"Well, don't just stand there," Pepper snapped at the daughter-in-law she'd denied for twenty-seven years. "Come see your grandbaby."

Ruby smiled and came over to the bed. Her eyes widened. "It's a girl?"

McCall nodded.

"Have you chosen a name?" Pepper asked.

"Tracey, after my father," McCall said, and heard Pepper let out a sob. "Tracey Winchester Crawford." Pepper covered her mouth with her hand for a moment, tears spilling from her eyes, as if fighting to keep from bawling.

Her husband and the man Pepper had loved since she was sixteen came up behind her and put an arm around her. She turned to press her face into his broad chest. Hunt smiled at McCall over his wife's shoulder and mouthed, "Thank you."

"Is that all right with you?" McCall asked her mother.

Ruby nodded. "I know your father would have liked that."

Epilogue

Zane woke in the hospital room to find Dakota asleep in the chair next to his bed and Dr. Carrey standing nearby, writing something in his chart.

"She refused to leave here," Doc said of Dakota, keeping his voice down. "I got her into the only dry clothes we had."

Dakota was dressed in hospital scrubs. She couldn't have looked cuter.

"The bullet didn't hit any bone so I think it should heal nicely," Doc was saying. "You just won't be running any footraces for a while."

"Are Emma and Courtney all right?" he asked. He'd been surprised to see Courtney come out of the cistern, surprised and thankful. All charges against him would be dropped now.

"They're fine. Both were treated and released. You

do have another visitor, though. He's been waiting for you to wake up."

Doc left. A moment later, Hoyt came in. He glanced at the sleeping Dakota and smiled. "How are you, son?"

"Doc says I'm going to be fine. Emma and Courtney are all right, too, he said."

His father nodded.

"Did Laura…"

"She's dead."

Zane studied his father's face. "I'm sorry."

Hoyt let out a sound like a cross between a laugh and a sob. "I'm not. I'm just sorry she put my family through so much."

"We're Chisholms. We're pretty resilient."

His father smiled. "Yes," he said. "We are. Well, I best get home. Emma's got the rest of the family building on to the dining room. She says the current one isn't going to be able to hold all of us." He glanced toward Dakota, who was starting to stir. "I suppose she's right about that."

Dakota opened her eyes to see Zane grinning at her. She was reminded of the boy she'd known, that cocky rodeo cowboy who used to grin at her just like that.

"Hey, beautiful," he said as he reached for her hand.

She took it and let him pull her out of the chair and into his arms. "Easy, you're injured."

"Doc was just here. I'm fine and as soon as I get out of here…" His grin widened.

She shook her head, wanting to pinch herself. Hadn't this been her girlhood dream? She thought about the diary Courtney had taken, no longer caring if it came to light. She'd been afraid of her feelings for Zane, afraid that he could never feel the way she did for him.

Wasn't that what had made Laura so crazy? She'd believed that her love was greater than Hoyt's and it had driven her insane. If she wasn't half-crazy before that.

"There's something I need to ask you," Zane said, suddenly serious. "This isn't the way I planned it. All the way, racing up to the well house, I had this romantic plan how I was going to ask you to marry me." He shook his head. "But when I woke up to find you asleep in that chair next to my bed…"

"Your sanity came back?" she joked.

His gaze locked with hers. "I realized anywhere is the perfect place and I can't wait another moment. Dakota, marry me. I know this might feel sudden, but we've known each other since we were kids and—"

"Yes," she said, leaning down to kiss him.

He laughed and pulled her down for another kiss.

"Easy, cowboy."

"I love you, Dakota. I've always loved you from the first time I saw you try to ride a sheep. You must have been five at the time. I'd never seen a little girl with so much grit." He laughed. "I was so impressed when that sheep stopped and you did a face-plant in the dirt, and got up and didn't even cry as you dusted yourself off and walked away."

"I went behind the rodeo stands and cried. Mostly I was mad at myself for not staying on longer." She touched his cheek. "I've always loved you. As a matter of fact, I kept a diary and in it I said that someday I was going to marry you."

"And now you are," he said, and started to kiss her again but was interrupted by a sound at the door.

They both turned to find Courtney standing there.

"I'm sorry to interrupt, but I wanted to say good-bye and how sorry I am for everything," her sister said.

"Where are you going?" Dakota asked.

"Back to Great Falls. My mother…" Her voice broke. "My *real* mother, Camilla, wants me to come stay with her awhile until I figure out what I want to do with my life."

"I'm going to walk Courtney out," Dakota said. Zane squeezed her hand.

"Again, I'm sorry, Zane."

He nodded. "Put it behind you, Courtney. We have."

Dakota walked her out. "How are you getting home?"

"I'm taking the bus." Courtney looked away. "Do you think things like this happen for a reason? I mean, that they can completely change your life?"

"I do."

Her sister raised her gaze. "Sometime, I'd like to know more about my father."

Dakota nodded. "We're sisters, Courtney. The same blood runs through our veins. When you're ready, come back. I've always wanted a sister." She stepped up to Courtney and hugged her. Her sister hugged her tight. "Be happy."

"You, too," Courtney said. "You and Zane belong together. Send me a wedding invitation," she said with a grin.

"I won't need to. You're going to be standing right next to me as my maid of honor."

* * *

Emma looked around the large dining room table. *Glad I talked Hoyt into adding on,* she thought with a smile as she took in her family.

A little more than a year ago, she'd come here as a new bride to find she had six rambunctious and wild stepsons all in need of a woman to tame them. To think she'd thought she was the one to find them the perfect mates.

"What are you smiling about?" her father asked. Alonso had finally decided he'd better fly up from California and see how his daughter was doing.

"It's a long story," Emma said as she reached over and took his hand. "Isn't this all wonderful?"

He laughed softly. "God has blessed you."

"Yes." She couldn't have agreed more as she met her husband's gaze at the opposite end of the table. She took in Halley and Colton, Billie Rae and Tanner, Jinx and Dawson, Alexa and Marshall, Blythe and Logan, and finally Dakota and Zane.

In the past year she'd come close to losing all of them. But the Chisholms had prevailed. They were a strong, determined bunch, just like those who had settled this part of Montana before them. They'd weathered rough storms and yet here they all were, laughing and talking all at once around this table.

Once they got through all the upcoming weddings, there would be grandchildren before long. Hoyt was already talking about getting some small saddles and gentle horses for them. She'd never seen her husband more happy. He'd faced his worst fear, and now here he was among the people who loved him.

Her eyes filled with tears and she had to hastily wipe them as Hoyt rose, tapped his glass to get everyone's attention and said, "I'd like to make a toast."

The room fell silent, all eyes on her handsome, wonderful husband.

"To my family," he said, his voice breaking with emotion. "The Chisholms and the future Chisholms. Long may they live on this ranch and prosper."

"And multiply," Colton said with a grin as he looked over at his wife. Halley blushed.

"Hear, hear," Emma said, and felt tears rush into her eyes. She couldn't wait to be a grandmother, and apparently she didn't have long to wait.

*   *   *   *   *

USA TODAY bestselling author **Barb Han** lives in north Texas with her very own hero-worthy husband, three beautiful children, a spunky golden retriever/standard poodle mix and too many books in her to-read pile. In her downtime, she plays video games and spends much of her time on or around a basketball court. She loves interacting with readers and is grateful for their support. You can reach her at barbhan.com.

Books by Barb Han

Harlequin Intrigue

An O'Connor Family Mystery

Texas Kidnapping
Texas Target

Rushing Creek Crime Spree

What She Did
What She Knew
What She Saw

Crisis: Cattle Barge

Kidnapped at Christmas
Murder and Mistletoe
Bulletproof Christmas

Visit the Author Profile page at Harlequin.com for more titles.

DELIVERING JUSTICE

Barb Han

This book is dedicated to: Allison Lyons
for making every single book better. Jill Marsal
for always being there and ready to answer
every question.

The great loves of my life: Brandon,
Jacob and Tori, the best people I could ever
hope to have in my world (I feel crazy blessed!).

Patricia Allsbrook for the last-minute save
(thank you, thank you!) and always being such
a steady, calming force. And her daughter, Paulina,
for her quick wit (what are you, a twenty-year-old?)
and warm smile.

And Babe for *always* being the one
I can't wait to talk to every night.

Chapter 1

For a few seconds as Tyler O'Brien scaled Diablo's Rock and pushed up onto its crest, everything in the world was peaceful. Looking out onto the land that breathed life into his soul, he couldn't imagine a better place to be.

Tyler's gaze swept down and he muttered a curse as he stared at an overturned four-wheel ATV with an unmoving body splayed out underneath.

A dead body was not part of Tyler's lunch plans.

Tyler hated accidents. He and his five brothers had inherited the cattle ranch two months ago after his parents had died in an "accident." New evidence had the sheriff opening a homicide investigation before the will was out of probate.

"You okay?" he shouted, wishing for a response but not really expecting one. Not with the way the body was pinned under the ATV. It was too far away to get a good visual on the person. Yet Tyler had seen enough scenes like this one to get a good feel for how it would turn out.

Cell phone coverage was nonexistent on this part of the ranch so he couldn't call for an ambulance or the sheriff. He'd left his walkie-talkie with Digby, his gelding. Most ranchers used ATVs and pickup trucks for convenience when checking the vast amount of fencing on a ranch the size of The Cattlemen Crime Club. But Tyler figured his horse needed the exercise and it made him feel connected to the land to do things the way his father had. His ranch hands used ATVs, and for a split second he feared one of them might be below, but the area around Diablo's Rock was Tyler's to check.

Maybe someone had their wires crossed. Or a group of thrill seekers had wandered onto the land and one got separated.

His pulse kicked into high gear as he moved into action, digging the heels of his boots into the rocky forty-foot drop one careful step at a time. He scanned the horizon looking for the rest of the ATV party. There was no sign of anyone else as far as the naked eye could see.

Diablo's Rock wasn't a good area for people new to ATVs and only an idiot would come out here alone. There were black bears and copperhead snakes, badgers and all manner of wildlife running around this part of Texas. The land was beautiful and its danger only enhanced Tyler's respect for it. It was a reminder that people weren't always at the top of the food chain. An unprepared person could end up at the wrong end.

The closer Tyler descended toward the body, the more his pulse spiked. He could tell that the figure was smaller than a man, and that definitely ruled out one of his employees.

As he approached, he could clearly see the creamy skin of long legs, which meant the woman either had on shorts or a dress. He assumed shorts considering the fact that she wore running shoes. Neither outfit was appropriate this time of year, which struck Tyler as odd if she'd been planning on this excursion. Wouldn't she dress for the occasion? Thanksgiving was right around the corner. The average temperature in November was in the sixties in this part of Texas and this week had been colder than usual, barely breaking fifty with a blanket of cloud coverage most days.

A good part of the reason he'd intended to eat lunch on the rock was that the sun had finally broken through and its heat would reflect on the surface, offering a warm place to eat.

Then again, maybe the visitor hadn't planned on being out there at all. When Tyler got closer, maybe he'd recognize her face. The notion she could be someone he knew pricked his throat as if he'd swallowed a cactus.

People wandered off trails and did all kinds of random things while on scheduled hunting expeditions, but there was nothing on the calendar and the safety record on their land was unblemished. Right up until now, he thought.

The ATV had flipped over and was on top of her. At first blush, she looked trapped. He shoved thoughts that she could be a young runaway or in trouble to the back of his mind while he moved around the ATV, trying to get a better look at her positioning.

Her body was positioned awkwardly and close to

the handlebars, but she wasn't being pinned by them as he'd first suspected.

On closer appraisal, the ATV wasn't touching her at all. And that was the first positive sign he'd had so far. He couldn't tell how bad the damage was to her body from this angle and he didn't see any signs of her breathing.

As soon as he rounded the side of the vehicle, he noticed blood splattered on the rocks next to her head. He was no expert at analyzing an accident scene but he'd heard enough stories around the campfire from their family friend Sheriff Tommy Johnson to know the splatter most likely came from an injury to her head. An impact hard enough to create that amount of blood wasn't good.

She was facedown in the dirt with her head angled toward the side he was standing on. Not that he could see past that thick red mane of hers.

This didn't look good at all. He'd make the short hike back to Digby in order to use his walkie-talkie to call for someone to pick her up. And it was such a shame that a young woman's life had been cut short.

"We'll get you out of here soon," Tyler said softly, dropping to his knees to get a better look at her face. She wasn't wearing a backpack nor did she have a purse. A physical description might help the sheriff identify her.

Tyler brushed her hair away from her face, expecting to see her eyes fixed, and then checked her neck for a pulse. She blinked sea-green eyes instead and mouthed the words, *Help me.*

She was alive?

Shocked, Tyler nearly fell backward. His pulse

pounded even faster as he located hers on her wrist, which was strong.

"You're okay. I'm going to get you out of here." Tyler had enough training and experience to know better than to move her. He needed to reposition the ATV so he could better assess her injuries.

Just as he pushed up to his feet, her arm moved and then her leg. Was she trying to climb out from under the machine?

"Hold still, there," he said. "Let me get this out of the way."

Tyler dropped his backpack and hoisted the ATV upright and away from her body. It popped up onto all four wheels. His right shoulder pinched at the movement, the old injury liked to remind him of the reason he didn't have a pro baseball career anymore, and he rubbed the sore spot trying to increase blood flow.

The mystery woman had managed to roll onto her side and was trying to climb away.

"I'm not going to hurt you so you don't have to go anywhere," he said. "I have water. Are you thirsty?"

She nodded. Based on her pallor and the freshness of the blood on the rocks, she couldn't have been out there for long. That was the second good sign so far.

He had medical supplies in his saddlebag, enough to dress a field wound. He could tend to that gash and try to stem the bleeding while they waited for help to arrive. It wouldn't take long to scale Diablo's Rock, get to his horse and then return with provisions. But he didn't like the thought of leaving her alone.

"What's your name?" He went down on a knee next to his backpack, pulled a bottle of water out of the main compartment and unscrewed the cap before offering her the bottle. He shrugged out of his denim jacket, draping it over her.

She looked like she was drawing a blank in the name department as she took the water and poured the liquid over her lips. They were pink, which was a good sign. She couldn't have been out there for long.

It didn't surprise him that she'd temporarily forgotten her name and other details about her life, given the blow she'd taken to her head. Tyler had witnessed plenty of concussions out on the baseball field. The good news here was that she could recover, a huge relief considering he'd started the afternoon thinking he would be reporting a body.

"Do you have ID?" he asked.

She looked panicked and disoriented.

"Mind if I check in your pockets?"

She shook her head, angling the bottle to get more water into her mouth than her last attempt. Again she failed miserably.

He scooted closer to her.

At this distance, he could see the dirt on her clothes. The cotton long-sleeved shirt was a deep shade of green that highlighted her lighter-colored eyes.

"Let me help you." He cradled the base of her neck with his right hand, ignoring the spark of electricity shooting through him. He shouldn't be feeling attracted to her. A sexual current couldn't be more inappropriate under the circumstances. He didn't care how beautiful she was. And she was beautiful, with her sea-green eyes, creamy complexion and heart-shaped mouth. He'd force himself to look away from her lips if it didn't mean that he'd spill water all over her face.

But feeling a real attraction to a woman he'd found lying helpless on his land a few minutes ago?

Nice one, O'Brien.

When she signaled that she'd had enough to drink, he set the bottle within her reach and then pushed up to his feet. "Okay, I'll just check for that ID, okay?"

She nodded her agreement and winced with the movement.

"Did you come out here with anyone?" he asked, chalking his physical reaction up to his overreactive protective instincts.

Looking startled, she glanced around.

Then she shook her head. Another fact she might be fuzzy on, given that hit she'd taken to her forehead.

"A group?" he continued.

The only thing he knew for certain was that she wasn't from around Bluff. It was dangerous for tourists to get lost on a massive ranch like his. She was darn lucky he—and not a black bear or hungry coyote—had found her.

She squinted her eyes. A raging headache was one of the side effects of a concussion. Luckily, that could be dealt with by popping a few pain relievers. Tyler had those in his pack, too, but the doctor would want him to wait to give them to her.

Tyler didn't want to notice her full hips or sweet round bottom as he checked her back pockets.

If he could think of another way to search her front pockets, he'd be game. As it was, he had to slip his fingers into them and ignore the way her stomach quivered.

It was safe to say that she had no ID. For the moment, neither of them knew who she was. Maybe her handbag or backpack had gone flying when she'd crashed. He scanned the ground, taking a few steps in one direction and then another.

No cell phone or purse could be seen anywhere and that struck him as odd. Tyler couldn't think of one woman he knew who would go anywhere without her cell. And that fact put a few more questions in his mind that he didn't have answers to. Like, if she was alone why wouldn't she have supplies or ID?

The panic in her eyes didn't help matters, either. Of course, waking up to a stranger and not being able to remember who she was or where she'd been would cause a certain level of panic in any normal person. Hers bothered him and he wished there was more that he could do to put her at ease.

He pushed his feelings aside as just needing to offer comfort to a stranger. It couldn't be anything more than that. He'd only known her for ten minutes, and when it came right down to it, he still didn't know her. He didn't even know her name.

"I'm going to send for help," he said.

Her eyes pleaded, filled with more of that panic he didn't like seeing, but she didn't argue. Then again, she hadn't said anything except "help me" since he'd found her.

"It's okay. I'm coming right back. I promise," he added to ease her concern. He whistled, hoping the family's chocolate lab, Denali, was somewhere within earshot. He could keep her company. After a few seconds of quiet and no Denali, Tyler said, "My horse is tied up on the other side of that rock and I need to get there so I can contact my men and send for medical attention."

She didn't relax but she nodded, wincing again at the movement. That was going to be one helluva headache when the dust settled.

As Tyler got to his feet, he scanned the area for any signs of wildlife. In her weakened state, he doubted she could fight off a flea. He pulled out his pocket knife anyway and her hand met his faster than he'd thought possible for hers to move.

"It's okay, I'm here to help."

She nodded as she took the knife.

"I'll be back in a few minutes." He filed her reaction away as another interesting thought. If she'd come out alone, what was she really afraid of? Him? Animals? She'd come out by herself without identification or a way to defend herself. This patch of land wasn't anywhere near a road. Clearly, he'd never met the woman before but he didn't have to know her to realize that she didn't look the type to wander off on her own on a four-wheeler. Not that she looked weak or like she couldn't handle herself in most situations. But the type of clothes and shoes she wore didn't fit with the activity and those expensive running shoes belonged out here about as much as a woman wearing a light jacket in the cold.

She didn't give the impression that she was a bandana-wearing thrill seeker. Nor did she particularly strike him as a granola-eating nature girl. Especially since the latter wouldn't be in the driver's seat of a four-wheeler.

There was another thing that bugged him as he walked away from the accident. He'd noticed another set of tire tracks when he scanned the ground for her personal belongings, which meant there could have been another person involved.

If she and a friend had ventured onto his land by mistake, what kind of jerk would leave her alone in her condition?

Then again, with no cell service the other person might've been forced to go for help.

And it wasn't like Red was talking. All she'd said so far was, "Help me." Pretty much anyone in her situation would say the same thing.

Tyler quickened his pace. If there was someone on his land searching for reception, he needed to get a search team out while there was still plenty of daylight. The accident might've already been called in. If the person wasn't familiar with the area he or she might not be able to lead rescuers to Red.

Even so, a person would have to be new at this to panic and leave an injured person alone with all the dangerous wildlife here on the ranch. A darker side of him also noted that this would be the perfect way to cover up an attempted murder.

Tyler wrote the sentiment off as the result of learning that his parents had been murdered. He would like nothing more than to solve the case that had been made to look like an accident. Thinking about it made him angry. Who would want to hurt his family?

He shelved those thoughts for now.

Another one struck him about the mystery woman. If the scene back there had been an attempted murder, then the murderer could still be around. With her lying there vulnerable and alone, it wouldn't take much to finish the job.

Tyler crested Diablo's Rock and took the back side just as fast shivering in the cold breeze. He'd tied Digby to a tree in a spot where his horse could decide if he wanted to be in the shade or not.

The gelding was standing in the sun, right where Tyler had left him. He blew out a breath as he pulled his walkie-talkie out of his saddlebag and got hold of his foreman, Russ.

"What can I do for you, boss?" Russ asked.

"There's been a four-wheeler incident at the base of Diablo's Rock. A woman took a pretty bad hit to her head. She's not going anywhere without help."

"You don't know who she is?" Russ asked. It was more statement than question.

"Never seen her before. She doesn't have any ID on her and I'd put money on the fact she has a concussion."

"Sounds like a mess," Russ agreed. "Hold on for one second, boss."

Tyler would never get used to the title even though he owned just as much of the ranch as his brothers. Together, they had a ninety-five percent interest—or would as soon as the will was out of probate, which would take another ten months. The other five percent had been divided between Pop's only living brother and sister a few years ago. Uncle Ezra and Aunt Bea didn't agree on much of anything except being taken care of. The two of them were as alike as a water moccasin and a frog.

Pop had included them both in ownership of the ranch to help take care of them financially as they aged, since Bea's daughter had left for California and Ezra's only son had died before his tenth birthday. The family cattle ranch was the biggest in Texas, both in land and net profit. As if that wasn't enough, the hunting club brought in more money than they could spend, much to the benefit of the many charities their mother had loved—a tradition Tyler and his brothers had every intention of continuing in her honor.

Even though the family had money and the boys had grown up knowing that they stood to inherit the highly successful family business, none had relied on that inheritance. All six O'Brien brothers had a deep-seated need to make their own way and depend on themselves. None were like their aunt or uncle, who seemed content to ride their successful brother's coattails. Especially Uncle Ezra, who had been angling to sell his interest or be given more control over the hunting club in recent months. Tyler's older brother Dallas figured the man was getting bored in his old age and wanted more to keep him busy.

Tyler hoped that was all there was to it, especially since it was his job to keep the peace. Of all the sons, he was the best negotiator and he'd talked Ezra down for the time being. They'd already set aside one percent of theirs for Janis, their housekeeper, who would be wealthy enough not to work for the rest of her life. Although, she'd said she was way too young to retire.

"I have emergency personnel on their way to the Rock," Russ said, interrupting Tyler's heavy thoughts—thoughts he'd volunteered to ride fences to try to stem in the first place.

Ranch hands called Tyler a Renaissance man for

doing things the old-fashioned way, but the truth was that it was as good for Tyler's soul as it was for Digby's health. Being out on the land on his horse made him feel connected and whole in a way he couldn't easily explain, nor did he care to examine.

"Let Tommy know about this, will you? Someone might be sick with worry looking for her," he said. The sheriff had been Dallas O'Brien's best friend and like a brother to the rest of the O'Brien boys. He'd grown up on the land. His uncle, Chill Johnson, had worked for Pop as long as Tyler could remember. Tommy had come to live with his uncle after his parents died.

"Will do, boss. I'll see if the sheriff can meet you at the hospital to take statements. Maybe he can help figure out who she is." Russ knew Tyler well enough to realize that he wouldn't be able to walk away until he knew the mystery woman was all right.

Silence meant Russ was taking care of that phone call right now, which was good because if someone had already reported her missing, then Tyler might be able to bring back more than medical supplies. He might be able to give her an identity. And if that second set of tire tracks had someone frantically searching for help, Tyler could ease that burden, as well.

"Sheriff said no one called in an emergency or missing person's report," Russ said.

Tyler feared as much.

"Said he'll meet her at the hospital since he's tied up on another interview right now," Russ continued.

If no one was looking for her, then Tyler had to consider other possibilities for those tire tracks.

"Much appreciated," he said to Russ. "Have someone ready to take Digby from me so I can head to the hospital as soon as I get back to the barn. And send out a search team in the chopper to make sure there's no one out here lost."

Tyler thanked Russ before ending the transmission and starting the journey back toward the redheaded mystery. He couldn't completely ignore the fear that he'd return to a lifeless body. She'd been upright and responsive so he'd take those as positive signs. Being away from her while she was vulnerable had his blood pressure spiking faster than a pro volleyball player. He picked up his pace, needing to see for himself that she was still okay.

At the faster speed, he crested Diablo's Rock in half the time. Part of him wondered if she could have managed to crawl away. She'd seemed determined and half-scared out of her wits—a combination that could be dangerous—or deadly—and left him wondering what really had her so freaked out.

He found her right where he'd left her. His pulse had slowly wound back to a decent clip when he saw that she was still conscious. And yet something else he couldn't quite put his finger on was eating away at him. What was the creepy, fire-ants-crawling-on-his-spine feeling about anyway?

Danger, for one thing, in the form of poachers. Sure, there were poachers in South Central Texas. People looked for trophies and illegally hunted on the large ranches in the area, which created a dangerous situation for all involved.

The O'Briens worked diligently to keep the land free of people who trespassed to hunt or steal game, so that risk should be minimal. If it wasn't poachers, then what was it? The fact that so many things didn't add up?

A beautiful single woman alone on a four-wheeler in territory she didn't know and wasn't dressed for? Yep. That made about as much sense as a deer eating barbeque.

"Help is on the way," he said, trying to give her hope to hold on to, wishing he could do more. He knelt next to her and opened his medical supply kit.

"Thank you," she managed to get out.

"My apologies if this hurts." It was going to hurt. That gash on her forehead was deep and had him worried. He poured clean water over it and then dabbed antibiotic ointment onto an oversize gauze bandage, pressing it to her forehead to stem the bleeding. She seemed determined not to give in to the pain. Or maybe she was just too weak.

It didn't take long for the cavalry to arrive. Tyler heard the chopper moving toward them before he got a visual on it. A helicopter was the only logical choice for rescue workers to use in order to access this part of the land. Otherwise, they'd have to take her on one helluva bumpy ride to get her to a main road, and that could jeopardize her condition.

Tyler saw the chopper moments before the pilot landed.

From there, it was only twenty yards to reach him and Red. The land was flat enough to manage easily on foot.

As emergency personnel neared, the mystery woman squeezed Tyler's hand.

He glanced at her and saw that same look of fear in

her eyes. What was that all about? Didn't she realize this was the help she needed?

Depending on how bad that blow to the head was, she might not recognize them as the people who would help her. That had Tyler more worried than when he'd found her. Just how badly injured was she?

The blow she'd taken to the head looked bad. He'd give anyone that. But her panic looked like she was in one of those horror flicks being chased by an ax murderer.

"It's okay. I know these men. They'll take care of you," he tried to reassure her. Tyler had known the EMTs, Andy and Shanks, for years. They were good guys. Dougherty would be piloting the chopper. Tyler didn't need to see him to know that.

So what was up with the way she kept squeezing his hand, looking like she was trying to say something?

Chapter 2

The heel of Tyler's boots clicked against the white tile floor in the hospital hallway as he neared room 367 to check on Red.

He removed his gray Stetson before crossing the threshold, pausing long enough to finger comb his hair and chew on the facts. No one had reported the mystery redhead as missing or reported the accident. That had not been the news he was expecting and it made him worry that some other outsider was on his property, hurt, lost or just a damned fool who was hunting illegally and ditched the redhead when her ATV overturned. Something he couldn't quite put his finger on had his radar on full alert and it was more than just finding her in the condition he had.

Tyler pushed open the door at Bluff General and walked inside Red's room. Her eyes were closed. The bed had been raised so that she was halfway sitting and she had an IV attached to her left arm. He'd seen enough of the inside of hospital rooms to know the IV most likely contained fluids and possibly antibiotics to stem infection. All good things that her body needed to recover.

In fact, the fluids seemed to be working magic already because there was a rosy hue in the creamy complexion on her cheeks now. Her forehead had a proper bandage on it and his makeshift head wrap had been replaced with clean, white gauze.

Since she looked to be resting peacefully and he didn't want to disturb her, he figured this would be a good time to visit with her doctor and find Tommy to see if he'd managed to get a statement or put a name to Sleeping Beauty here.

Her eyes fluttered open and he felt like a fool for staring at her.

"How are you?" he asked, for lack of anything better to say. Even through the gauze and tape she was stunning.

"Better," she managed to squeak out. Her throat sounded scratchy. It was the dry air.

He set his cowboy hat down on the chair and moved next to her bed. Now that she seemed able to speak, maybe he could find out if there were others on his land or if he should call off the search.

"What's your name?" he asked.

She made a move to speak but coughed instead. Her gaze locked onto a large white mug situated on the wheeled table next to her bed just out of reach.

"You thirsty?" he asked as he moved to the mug.

"Yes, please" came out on a croak.

At least she was talking and making sense. Those were good signs.

"Were you alone earlier?" he asked as he held the oversize mug filled with ice water toward her. She eagerly accepted but didn't answer.

After a few small sips, she leaned her head against the pillow, but her eyes never left Tyler's face. Those sea-green eyes stayed fixed on him, panic and fear still there.

"Do you know who you are?" he asked, setting the mug down on the tray and then repositioning it so that she could reach water whenever she wanted.

"Jennifer," she said, throat still scratchy but sounding much better. Her voice had a nice pitch to it. "Who are you?"

"Tyler O'Brien. My brothers and I own the land you were on earlier."

Her gaze darted toward the door and then her eyes widened in fear, so Tyler turned to follow her line of sight.

A decent-looking man in his early thirties walked in. His gaze ricocheted between Jennifer and Tyler. He was several inches shorter, so Tyler guessed he was around five foot eleven. He was on the thin side, built like a runner, and had sandy-blond hair. A fresh-looking pink sunburn dotted his tanned nose and cheeks.

Tyler didn't recognize him.

"Honey," the man said with a sigh and he seemed to pour on the drama if anyone asked Tyler. "I've been so worried about you."

Tyler glanced at Jennifer in time to see a moment of

sheer panic, so he stepped in between them, blocking Tan Face's path.

"Name's Tyler." He stuck out his hand.

"What happened to you, honey? Are you all right?" Tan Face said, sidestepping Tyler and his hand.

"Hold on there, pal," Tyler said, placing his hand on Tan Face's shoulder, ensuring he couldn't get to Jennifer's bedside. "I didn't catch your name."

"James Milton," he said, puffing out his chest like a cobra, looking none too thrilled that Tyler had put a hand on him.

"Do you mind?" he asked. "My fiancée is lying in a hospital bed and she's none of your business."

Fiancée? Tyler didn't normally misjudge situations. His instincts were usually spot-on. Red seemed scared of the man. But if the two of them were engaged then he needed to take a step back. Some lines shouldn't be crossed no matter how irritated the man's presence made Tyler.

He let go of the man's shoulder. It might be better to take a wait-and-see approach to this one. Tyler told himself that he'd leave as soon as he knew she was going to be fine. Besides, he needed to make sure she had no intention of suing him for having an accident on his land. As crazy as that sounded, he'd heard of people doing that and more.

He ignored the little voice that said he was lying to himself about why he was sticking around and that it had to do with an attraction.

Milton made a dramatic scene of rushing to Red's side once he was free of Tyler's grasp. The man was fresh-from-a-shower clean and had on dress slacks and a button-down shirt. Not exactly the kind of clothes one would wear on an ATV adventure, so the logical question was why would he let Red go alone if he cared about her as much as he professed?

"I didn't know what to think when you disappeared," Milton said to her.

Tyler folded his arms and leaned against the wall. The panicked expression on Jennifer's face intensified. He'd probably regret this later, but he had to ask, "About that, James. What happened exactly?"

"I'm fine," Red interjected, her gaze darting from Tyler to Milton.

Tyler didn't have a strong reading on the guy other than general dislike and her reaction wasn't helping. Milton's concern came off as insincere. Tyler had learned long ago to trust his instincts. This guy looked like he was putting on a show.

The door opened and the sheriff walked in.

Milton turned and the look on his face when he caught sight of the sheriff was priceless. Also, it strengthened Tyler's intuition that this guy was up to no good. This was about to get interesting.

Tommy introduced himself to Jennifer and Milton, and then shook Tyler's outstretched hand.

"I've been worried sick about you, darling," Milton said, turning to Jennifer, and Tyler thought the man was overselling.

She managed a weak smile.

Tyler noticed that she stiffened when Milton took her by the hand. Not exactly a warm reception for her fiancé, and that got Tyler's mind spinning with scenarios, none he liked.

"Do you have ID?" Tommy asked.

"Did we do something wrong, sheriff?" Milton produced two Louisiana driver's licenses. His and Jennifer's.

"Just routine under the circumstances in which—" Tommy glanced at one of the plastic-covered cards "—Ms. Davidson was found."

When Tommy took down the information and then returned the cards, Milton refocused on Jennifer.

"I can't believe I almost lost you," he said, his voice had more syrup than Granny's pancakes when she'd started losing her sight but refused to wear glasses.

If anyone asked Tyler's opinion, and Tommy would as soon as they were alone, he'd say the guy was a fake. That didn't exactly make him a criminal.

"Mr. Milton, do you and Ms. Davidson mind answering a few questions?" Tommy asked.

"Don't take this the wrong way, Sheriff, but I'd like to spend some time alone with my fiancée," Milton said.

Tyler would bet his horse Milton would. He stifled a snicker.

"But I do understand that you're just doing your job," Milton added and Tyler was sure it was part of the concerned-fiancé act.

"Given that you seem to sympathize with my position, I hope you won't mind if I ask Ms. Davidson a question," Tommy said.

"Of course," Milton responded.

"Ma'am, would you be more comfortable giving me your statement alone?" Tommy asked. "I'd be happy to clear the room."

Milton balked at the request. Before he could puff up again, Tommy held out a warning hand.

"It's part of the job," he said to Milton. Then he turned his full attention to Jennifer. "Ma'am?"

She looked to be contemplating her answer.

"Why on earth would she want that?" Milton's cheeks turned a shade of red as he focused on Jennifer.

Her weak smile died on her lips as soon as he turned back to the sheriff and didn't that make the hair on Tyler's neck stand at attention. Was she being manipulated? Abused? Milton didn't seem to want her to speak up for herself.

Tyler ground his back teeth, thinking about a man being physical with the opposite sex.

"No, thanks," she said to Tommy.

"Were the two of you riding ATVs earlier today?" Tommy asked Milton.

"Yes, and I lost her on the trail so I left and went back to our motel to wait for her," Milton said.

Tyler's eyebrow shot up about the same time as Tommy's. Tyler also noted that she'd deliberately kept the truth from him earlier about being alone on the trail. He'd seen the tracks himself. What was she hiding?

The two of them might have gotten into a fight and it could have gotten physical. He could've taken off and then she could've chased after him before the crash.

"You decided to leave her unprotected in unfamiliar territory?" Tommy asked.

"We'd had a fight." James turned toward Jennifer with a stern look.

"I searched everywhere for her once I lost her on

the trail. I figured she was mad and needed to blow off steam."

"Do you realize there are black bears in these parts of Texas?" Tommy asked, incredulous.

"No. I didn't. I would never…" Milton let that sentence hang in the air. "I searched for her everywhere and couldn't find her so, like I said, I decided to give myself time to cool off, as well. I went back to my room, got worried, and when she didn't answer her cell I called around local hospitals."

"But not the police station?" Tommy asked.

Milton shook his head.

"Did you take off before or after she'd been in an accident?" Tyler asked, since he hadn't had a chance to brief Tommy on the situation yet.

Milton whirled on Tyler.

"What's that supposed to mean?" he asked.

"I was just wondering if you knew she'd been in an accident before you took off to 'cool down' as you said," Tyler elaborated.

"If I'd known anything had happened, I'd have stayed with her," Milton shot back, turning his attention to Jennifer with another overexaggerated look.

That rang more warning bells.

And there was another thing bugging Tyler. If these two were engaged, wouldn't she be wearing a ring?

"You said the two of you were getting married," Tyler began. "Set a date yet?"

"We're working on it," Milton said. "Why?"

"Just checking to see how far along your plans are," Tyler said coolly.

"And why would that be any of your business?" Milton asked, not bothering to hide his disdain. He'd been reasonably respectful to Tommy since he was the law, but the man must see Tyler as an inconvenience. A lot could be said about a man who treated people poorly if he saw them as beneath him.

Tyler shrugged, his casual demeanor was clearly getting to the guy. "Thought it was customary for the woman to wear a ring."

Milton's gaze shot to Jennifer. "We haven't made it that far. I just asked her."

Tyler studied Jennifer's reaction. Her expression was blank, her eyes dead as she forced a smile.

She was doing exactly what Milton said and yet she feared the man. Had Tyler read this situation wrong? Sure, none of it was adding up and she looked less than thrilled to be around Milton, but no one was forcing her to be with the guy.

Tyler couldn't figure why anyone would stay in a bad relationship. And yet it happened all the time.

"There are two sets of tracks leading up to the accident. And one left. How do you explain that, Mr. Milton?" Tyler asked.

"I can't because I wasn't there," Milton responded.

"Is that true?" Tommy asked Jennifer.

She glanced up at Milton first, and then nodded.

If she was going to corroborate Milton's story, then maybe Tyler needed to mind his own business. He'd tried to defend a few buddies who were in the middle of domestic fights and had learned just how quickly tempers could escalate. Tyler wasn't afraid of Milton; he could handle that jerk. But he couldn't make Red leave the guy.

If she wouldn't give him anything to work with, then he had to come at this from another angle.

"Have the two of you had any lifestyle changes lately?" Tommy asked Milton, picking up on Tyler's tension. "In preparation for the wedding?"

Milton's face scrunched up. "No."

"Haven't taken out any life insurance policies on each other? Named the other as the beneficiary?" Tommy pressed.

"No. Nothing like that." Milton's face looked ready to explode from anger. "Am I under arrest, Sheriff?"

Not yet, Tyler wanted to say.

"Can I see you in the hall for a minute?" Tyler asked Tommy.

"I was just about to suggest the same thing," Tommy said and then turned to Milton. "I'll be back as soon as I take a statement from the landowner."

The door had barely closed when Tyler turned around and asked, "How is it that a man could, first, leave his fiancée outside in a strange place alone and, second, not call the police when she's missing for hours?"

"Good questions," Tommy said. "He's a jerk. I just don't have anything that I can charge him with. I need something solid in order to take him in."

"Did you notice how scared she looks?" Tyler asked. "Or the fact that he was so concerned about her that he decided to take a shower before he bothered to figure out where she'd gone or what might've happened to her?"

Tommy frowned, nodded. "It's not illegal, though."

"His story doesn't add up and he'll most likely run

out of town the minute our backs are turned." Frustration ate at Tyler.

"You're right on both counts, but he has every right to go where he pleases for now. As far as I can tell no crime has been committed."

"He's hurting her." Tyler clenched his fists.

"Which is a shame, but not against the law unless someone witnesses it or she steps forward on her own to press charges."

"It should be." Tyler knew this guy was up to no good.

"I'll stay on him. If he so much as makes a wrong turn while he's in town I'll question him for it," Tommy said.

"There has to be more you can do than that," Tyler said.

"We can scare him," Tommy said after thinking about it for a minute. "We better get back inside. I don't want to leave him alone with her longer than we have to."

"I have a few more questions for him," Tyler said through clenched teeth.

Tommy paused before opening the door. "Go ahead and ask everything you want. See if you can get him to mess up and admit to something. Without her willing to go against him, we have nothing otherwise."

Milton stood, rising to his full height when they re-entered the room, which was still considerably less than both of the other men.

"Earlier, you said you lost your fiancée after a fight?" Tyler took up his position leaning against the wall near the doorjamb.

"She was tired and decided to turn back but I wasn't ready to go, so I told her how to find her way to our original meet-up point." Was Milton changing his story?

"I thought you said the two of you got into a fight," Tyler said.

Milton glanced down and to the right, a sure sign he was about to lie.

"That's what we fought about," he said, quickly recovering, as pleased with himself as if he'd just won the big stuffed animal at the state fair.

Clearly the man had just made another mistake. First he said he lost her, then he said that she turned back on purpose—which was it?

"You can't have it both ways, so pick one," Tyler said point-blank.

"Well, originally she said she was going to turn back, but then I got a bad feeling about her being out there alone in a place she didn't know and so I turned back to look for her, thus find her." Another satisfied smirk crossed Milton's features.

If that wasn't a sack of dung bigger than a bull, Tyler didn't know what was. Who did Milton think he was fooling?

Tyler's right hand fisted. He flexed and then forced it to relax.

"Good that you had time to clean yourself up, you know, while you were so busy being worried about your fiancée here," Tyler pressed.

Another frustrated pause.

"When I couldn't find Jennifer I figured she got angry at me for leaving her, so I decided to be ready to smooth things over when she came back to the motel," Milton said.

"Even though you couldn't find her when you went looking for her? You still assumed she'd be able to find her way back?" Tyler asked, not letting up. "And where was this meet-up point you mentioned?"

Milton didn't answer.

In all honesty, the man could walk out at any time. But then, that would leave Jennifer alone with Tyler and the sheriff. No way did James Milton want that.

"What are you doing in town, anyway?" Tyler continued.

"We came for the…nature. We wanted to get out of the city for a long weekend and decompress before kicking our wedding plans into high gear," Milton said. "Life from here on out is going to be crazy, isn't it, honey?" Milton shot another look at Red.

"What trail were you on? Do you remember anything about it that stuck out?" Tyler asked.

"Not really." Milton shrugged.

"Was it rocky or were there trees?"

"Trees," Milton said, trying a little too hard to sound convincing.

"Which direction did you come from?" Tyler asked.

"We came from the north," Milton supplied.

Tyler didn't immediately respond.

"You sure about that?" he finally asked.

"Yeah. North, right, honey?" Milton said, glancing down at Jennifer.

She managed a weak smile and a nod.

No one got to Diablo's Rock from the north on an

ATV. Tire tracks at the scene indicated the opposite. Tyler slanted a look at Tommy.

"That's impossible," Tyler said. "Tracks came from the south."

Anyone could get confused in an area they aren't familiar with, but this guy wouldn't be confused about direction because he was wearing one of those expensive compass watches.

"Guess I didn't notice." Milton shrugged. "If I'm not under arrest, then can we be finished with this conversation?" His lips flattened, indicating his patience had run out.

Well, guess what, buddy? So had Tyler's.

And they were far from done.

Chapter 3

"Where's the doctor?" Milton asked, rotating toward Jennifer and effectively turning his back on Tyler and Tommy. "How much longer do you have to stay in here?"

"In a hurry to go somewhere, Mr. Milton?" Sheriff Tommy asked, blond eyebrow arched.

"I'd like to get her home where I can take better care of her," Milton said. "It's impossible to get any rest in one of these places."

"And where is home?" Tommy asked.

"Louisiana, like on my license. You saw that earlier," Milton said. "You'd like to come home with me, wouldn't you, darling?"

There he went with that *darling* business again. Tyler wanted to vomit. Again, Milton was pouring it on a little thick.

While Tommy was finishing his interview, Tyler excused himself in order to talk to Jennifer's doctor, Dr. McConnell.

McConnell was a no-nonsense middle-aged woman who'd been working at the hospital since graduating medical school. A local, she wore jeans and boots under her white coat and she'd been a close family friend since longer than Tyler could remember.

"Is there any chance she's being abused?" he asked McConnell when he was sure they were out of earshot.

"I'm bound by oath not to respond to that question," Dr. McConnell said. "However, since you found her, I don't mind telling you that she has quite a few bruises on both of her arms."

"I'm guessing that's a yes," he said.

"She's been through a lot." McConnell frowned. "I'm not saying she's been abused, but even if she has there's no way to prove anything. And, of course, nothing can be done unless a victim is willing to talk about it or press charges."

"In theory, would you have offered that kind of help by now?" he asked.

"I would've. We're not talking about a child here, where I'd be forced to report suspected abuse and Tommy could step in," Dr. McConnell said. "I can only help patients who want it."

Tyler didn't like what he heard.

"When I see a patient with bruising like we've discussed, I'm always sure to have another conversation with her. I can promise that she'll know that there are folks who can help. I'll offer assistance, but it'll be up to her to accept," Dr. McConnell said, placing her hand on Tyler's shoulder. She had to reach up, considering she wasn't more than five foot three.

"Much obliged to you, doc," Tyler said.

"Before you go, any word on the investigation? It's been two weeks since I submitted the results from the third-party analysis of the toxicology report," she said, and he knew that she was talking about his parents. She'd been one of his mother's closest friends and he could see how much the doctor missed her in the dark circles under her eyes. The recent news that his parents had been murdered hit their friends hard, their children harder.

"Nothing so far, except that Tommy is reviewing the case file personally," he said. Tyler and his brothers benefitted the most from their parents' deaths so they'd be at the top of anyone's suspect list. There were no other leads at the time.

Dr. McConnell gave that a minute.

"Give your brothers a hug for me," she finally said.

"I will."

Walking toward Jennifer's room, Tyler's footsteps fell heavy. Even though he wanted to take James Milton out back and teach him a thing or two about why real men didn't hurt women, the reality was that there wasn't much else he could do at the hospital.

Tommy seemed to be wrapping things up by the time Tyler returned to the room. As much as it soured him to do so, Tyler shook James Milton's hand. Milton's wasn't moist or hot, indicating that he was fairly relaxed about the situation.

But should he be?

A man who hit a woman might be a practiced liar.

Tyler didn't care much for people who couldn't be bothered to tell the truth. And this jerk was poised to walk right out the door and go scot-free. He hadn't violated any laws that Tommy could arrest him for. Tyler could see Tommy's frustration written all over his face.

"One last thing," Tommy said to Milton. "Did you have permission to ride on the O'Brien ranch?"

"Permission?" Milton echoed. His eyes widened when he heard the name O'Brien. Most people knew it and had a similar reaction.

"The land that you and your fiancée were riding ATVs on is owned by the O'Brien family," Tommy continued. "It's protected by a fence and No Trespassing signs are posted everywhere. I've been out hunting on that property myself. So, my question to you is, were you aware that you were breaking the law when you took your recreational vehicles on the land?"

"Well, no, we hadn't planned on being on his property. We got lost. Is that a crime?" For the first time in the interview, Milton looked like he might break a sweat.

"Being lost? No. Trespassing on someone else's land and destroying their property? Yes." Tommy turned to Tyler. "Will you be pressing charges today, Mr. O'Brien?"

Tyler might not be able to stop Jennifer from walking out of the hospital with this jerk but he could slow them down.

"As a matter of fact, I will," Tyler said, shifting his gaze to Milton. "You say that you innocently got lost, but how do I know that you weren't out on my property, illegally hunting?"

"I don't own a gun, for one," Milton shot back.

Tyler figured that Tommy could check the gun registration database all day long and not find a gun registered to James Milton. That didn't mean he wasn't carrying one anyway. There was no shortage of illegal guns on the black market and in the hands of people who had no business with them.

"I can't know that for sure. Besides, you might've ditched it when you realized you were close to getting caught. In fact, I have another scenario worth the sheriff's consideration," Tyler said.

"Care to enlighten me?" But Milton's gaze said the opposite.

"How about this? You take your fiancée here on a hunting trip on my land. We offer excursions but you don't want to pay the price. You decide to do things on your own. But then you hear someone and you know you're about to get caught. Rather than risk it, you take off, leaving your fiancée to fend for herself. You go hide in your motel room waiting for her to come back. You clean up because you don't want to risk anyone realizing you might've been outside. But here comes the problem. Your fiancée gets herself in trouble and ends up in the hospital, so you make up this wild story about the two of you fighting to cover for the fact that you were illegally hunting on my property," Tyler said, his gaze zeroed in on Milton.

"You can't be serious." Milton's gaze darted from Tyler to Tommy as he took a step back. A few more and he'd be in the corner.

"Sure I can," Tyler shot back, watching Milton's reaction.

"Can I see your hunting license, Mr. Milton?" Tommy asked.

Milton balked. "I don't have one. I've already told you that I don't even own a gun."

"Did you realize that you'd need one?" Tommy continued.

"I didn't come here to hunt. I wasn't out looking for game on his land." Milton shot daggers toward Tyler before narrowing his gaze when he looked at Tommy again. "I'll ask again. Am I under arrest?"

"If you were, we'd be having a different conversation right now, Mr. Milton. One that would include reading your Miranda rights to you. Since I haven't done that yet, you're free to go." Tommy turned toward the door. "But I have every intention of investigating Mr. O'Brien's complaint. In which case, I'm advising you not to leave town until this dispute has been resolved."

It was weak. Tyler knew enough about the law to know that, but Tommy was betting that Milton didn't realize it.

"I have no plans to go anywhere until my Jennifer is better. And then I have every intention of driving out of this town and back to Louisiana," Milton said.

"Mind if I speak to you privately, Mr. Milton?" Tommy shot a wink toward Tyler so subtle he barely caught it.

Tyler immediately caught on. He grabbed the pen and paper off the wheeled tray table and jotted down his cell number. Then, he moved to the bed next to Jennifer.

"You sure you're okay?" he asked.

She nodded, looking resolved. If she was engaged to Milton, then wouldn't she seem more comforted by his presence? Tyler figured he could rack his brain trying to solve that and other mysteries for the rest of his life and still come up short. There wasn't much else he could do or say if he stuck around. Red... Jennifer, he corrected himself, seemed intent on staying with this jerk. Just in case she changed her mind and wanted a friend, he folded up the piece of paper into a tiny square.

"You change your mind or need anything, call me." He managed to slip it under her pillow before Milton returned.

Tyler figured it might help him sleep at night, knowing he'd done everything he could.

Heck, who was he kidding? Those sea-green eyes were going to haunt him.

Tyler's cell buzzed. He glanced at the clock on his nightstand. It was hours until the sun would rise. The noise should've jolted him awake but his eyes had barely closed all night thinking about Red.

He threw off the covers and walked over to the dresser where his phone sat on its charger, thinking what he really needed to clear his head was a night on the town and a stiff drink.

The number didn't look familiar but he answered anyway.

"I don't have anyone else to call. Please help me." The frail voice on the other end of the line belonged to Red.

Was she ready to talk? To get out of the relationship with Milton? To get help?

"Are you there?" she asked. Panic raised her voice a couple of octaves.

"Yes." he said. "As long as you're ready to tell me what's really going on."

"I'm sorry about before. It's just..." She paused, sounding almost too tired or scared to finish what she started to say. "If he finds out I'm talking to you, to anyone, then I'm dead."

"Seems to me that he's going to hurt you either way, Jennifer," Tyler said.

"My name isn't Jennifer. It's Jessica," she confided.

"I saw your driver's license," he said, chalking up the mistake to her head injury.

"Please, give me a chance to explain," she begged. "I'm not who I said I was. I know who I am and my name is Jessica."

Chapter 4

"Okay." The handsome cowboy paused as if he was seriously considering what Jessica had just said. "Is the license a fake?"

"No."

"Well then, I'm the one who's confused," he said, his voice gruff from sleep.

Jessica didn't know Tyler from Adam and yet his calming voice and masculine strength had her believing she could trust him. There was something about the tall cowboy that made her believe he would protect her.

Then again, it wasn't like she had a lot of options. The game had changed somewhere along the line and she hadn't expected Milton to try to kill her. He didn't even know that Jennifer had an identical twin, let alone that Jessica was posing as her sister.

"What's really going on?" Tyler asked.

How much should she tell him? *Could* she tell him? She needed to say enough to convince him that she wasn't crazy.

"I wish I knew," she said honestly. All Jessica thought she was supposed to be doing was subbing for her party-girl sister, Jennifer, in order to give her time to fix whatever needed fixing. Since no one in Jennifer's circle knew she had an identical twin, the two figured they could pull off a switch and no one would be the wiser. "I need to contact my twin sister and I can't do that while *he's* watching my every move."

"You're a twin?" Tyler sounded surprised but not shocked.

"Yes. Sorry for lying to you earlier," she said quietly into the phone, praying she wouldn't disturb Milton, who was sleeping ten feet away from her bed. Jessica despised lies. Anyone could ask her ex-boyfriend, Brent, about that. He seemed to be an expert at manipulating the truth when they'd been together.

Jessica refocused. She'd waited all night for Milton to doze off, and this might be her only chance to reach out for help. She'd be released sometime tomorrow afternoon and if she didn't get away from Milton it would be all over. Jessica's memory was still spotty but one thing was clear. She needed to get away from that man while she was still alive and connect with her sister before he figured her out. He kept asking her where she'd hid "it." Jessica had no idea what he'd been talking about. Her sister had warned her that Milton believed she had something valuable and had said to pick a place to take him. When she'd taken him to the O'Brien ranch and told him she'd buried it nearby, he'd slammed a rock against her head.

"What are you asking me to do?" he asked in that deep raspy voice.

"Get me out of here," she whispered. She was taking a huge risk in calling the cowboy. Milton could wake at any second. She had no idea what her sister had gotten herself involved in, but it must be pretty darn bad for that man to want her dead.

"Is he there right now?" the cowboy asked.

"Yes."

Milton stirred in his sleep and Jessica panicked. She hung up the phone before he could catch her. If hospital staff didn't show up every hour or so she figured Milton would've already found a way to finish the job. The fact that his earlier attempt to kill her had been staged to look like an accident made her believe that he didn't want to be associated with a murder investigation.

If Jessica didn't figure out what was going on and find her sister, they'd both be dead. Losing contact yesterday had settled an ominous feeling over Jessica. She wasn't sure who she could trust anymore, except the rich cowboy who seemed determined to help. He sent her pulse racing for a whole other set of reasons she didn't want to examine. But she'd called him as a last-ditch effort to try to help her escape and find her sister. Was that a mistake?

Milton rolled onto his other side in the chair next to her bed, causing her pulse to race.

Jessica had no idea how long she'd been lying there, staring at the white ceiling, when a pair of nurses walked in pushing a gurney.

Milton shot straight up and rubbed his puffy eyes. "What's going on?"

The nurse shot him a warning look before checking the chart affixed to the foot of Jessica's bed. "We're taking our patient for an X-ray."

Milton stood, blocking her path to Jessica.

"At this hour?" he asked, puffing out his chest, and Jessica noticed he'd done that earlier when he tried to intimidate Tyler. It hadn't worked with the rich cowboy.

"This is a hospital, sir. We run 24/7," the nurse shot back and she didn't appear affected, either. "Now, if you'll step out of the way on your own it'll save me the trouble of calling security and having you removed from the building. We can do this any way you want. It's your call."

Jessica grinned despite trying to hold it in. Luckily, Milton's back was to her so he couldn't see her face. The man frightened her.

The nurse could see her, though, and she winked at Jessica as she brushed past him.

Between the two nurses, they detached Jessica from the monitors and hoisted her up onto the gurney.

Milton made a move to follow them into the hall, but the lead nurse put up a hand to stop him. "I don't think so, sir. No one but the patient and X-ray tech are allowed where we're taking her."

His agitation was written in the severe lines of his forehead, and his eyebrows looked like angry slash marks. Jessica worried that wouldn't bode well for her later. Then again, he'd made his intentions pretty clear.

Milton stood in the doorway, watching, as Jessica was wheeled down the hallway. She could almost feel his eyes on her and she'd never be able to shake the horror of turning to find him standing there, rock raised in the air, and then a sharp pain before everything went dark.

With him in the room, she hadn't been able to sleep a wink for fear he'd make sure she never woke. But that didn't make sense, did it? Would he be so bold as to kill her in the hospital where he could be discovered? Especially now that their situation had drawn so much attention. He'd gone to great pains to make his first attempt look like an accident. Jessica had every intention of figuring out why he wanted to kill her sister and what she'd gotten herself into by agreeing to help.

The nurses made a right turn at the nurse's station and then broke into a run. Before Jessica could manage to get a word out, they stopped. A blanket was tossed over her head as she was ushered off the gurney. Her claustrophobia kicked into high gear but she resisted the urge to fight against it, taking a deep breath instead of giving in to panic. She could only pray that the nurses could be trusted.

"Don't say a word," Tyler said, turning the light on his phone toward Red as he took off the blanket.

"What are—"

"You asked me to help and that's what I'm doing," he said, hating how scared she sounded, looked. He expected her to argue or put up a fight. Instead, she wrapped her arms around him and buried her face in his neck.

"Thank you," she said, and he could feel her shaking. Tyler would do whatever it took to help Red. The mystery woman stirred up all kinds of unfamiliar feelings. And seeing her in an abusive relationship dredged up all kinds of bad emotions from the past…feelings he couldn't set aside as easily as he'd like. He'd told himself that he'd agreed to help her solely based on the fact that she was a woman in need, but there was more. The best Tyler could do was let Red explain herself. He intended to get to the bottom of what was really going on.

"Can I use that phone?" she asked.

"As soon as you tell me why you're with that jerk."

Shock widened her sea-green eyes. "I'm not. We're not. It's just that everything's so complicated right now. I'm not sure how to explain."

"Start at the beginning."

"I need to get ahold of my sister first, so I can sort this out. Please."

Tyler figured he needed to buy some goodwill so he handed over his cell.

Red made a phone call and it ran straight into voice mail.

"That's not good. She should be picking up." Exasperation ran deep in her voice. She called another number.

A sleepy-sounding woman answered.

"Where's Jennifer?" Red asked.

Tyler now knew that she'd been posing as her sister. It was a trick his twin younger brothers had played on the family more than once when they were growing up. It had all been good-natured fun. But Red's life was on the line.

And then a thought dawned on him. Red wasn't in a bad relationship with Milton, her sister was. Maybe she was giving her sister time to get her bearings enough to leave the jerk. She might've been the one to deliver the message. A guy like Milton wouldn't have taken news like that lying down. Had he gotten angry, found the nearest rock and bashed her in the head?

"What do you mean she just disappeared?" There was outright panic in Red's voice now as she spoke quietly into the phone. "No. Don't call anyone. Don't tell anyone. Promise me you won't look for her."

Red's shoulders slumped forward and tears rolled down her cheeks as she ended the call. She closed her eyes as if trying to shut out the world.

"Tell me what's going on and we'll figure something out." Tyler's fingers itched to hold her but making that move was a slippery slope. "Does he know who you really are?"

"No. And I have no idea what I've actually gotten myself into," she said, pinching the bridge of her nose. "My head hurts."

"You can start by telling me what your sister's relationship to James Milton is," Tyler said.

The mention of Milton's name got her eyes open in a hurry.

"We can't talk here." She glanced around. "Where are we anyway?"

Tyler didn't like the idea of taking her out of the hospital without knowing exactly what kind of danger she was in and from whom, but he had no choice under the circumstances. Milton would be asking questions soon and wouldn't be satisfied without an answer. Tyler needed to get her away from the building. He pulled out a bundle of clothing. "Here. Put these on."

"Scrubs?" she asked, and when he nodded she turned to face the other way.

He took the cue to untie the back of her gown and had to force his gaze away from the silky skin of her shoulder as she slipped out of the cotton material. In addition to the surgical scrubs, Dr. McConnell had provided a bra and panties and shoes. He needed to call her in the morning to thank her for arranging everything on such short notice.

Luckily she'd believed the story about Red wanting out of the relationship. Since she'd planned to release her the next day, McConnell didn't see the harm in giving Red an out tonight. She'd joked that it was already morning somewhere and made him promise to let her stop by his place after rounds to check on her patient. Lying to McConnell sat sourly in Tyler's gut. He'd explain the situation when he could. His first order of business was getting Red away from Milton and to safety. Then, the two of them would have a conversation about delivering justice to Milton.

"What now?" Red said, turning around to face him.

"Put these on." He handed her a surgical mask and hair covering. "And then meet me downstairs near the ER. If he sees me he'll think something's up. I want to give us as good of a head start as I can."

She took a deep breath and he assumed it was to steel her nerves.

"Okay. Let's do this," she said.

"You go first. That way, if he's wandering around and happens to see you, I won't be far behind," Tyler said. "Once you walk out the door, make a right toward the stairs. I don't want you waiting around for an elevator. The ER is on the first floor so you'll have to make it down eight flights of stairs on your own. Can you handle it?"

She nodded and all he could see were her eyes, the green stood out even more against the light-blue face mask.

"Okay, then. Once you're down, I'll meet you at the ER bay," he said. "Don't forget to take off the mask before you walk out of the stairwell."

Red stood at the door for a long moment. She pressed her flat palm against it but stopped short of opening it.

Then she stole a last look at him before walking out and to her right.

Tyler figured he needed to wait a bit before he followed. It would take all his self-control not to hightail it to Red's room and deliver his own brand of justice. Milton needed to see what it was like to fight with a man. But that would only alert the creep to the fact that Jessica was on the run. Since Tyler couldn't be in two places at once, he waited a few minutes, then pushed the door open. If Milton saw him at all, it could be game over.

Besides, there was a lot more to this situation than met the eye and Tyler needed to get to the bottom of what was going on before he let his fists fly. He'd take Jessica to the ranch for tonight. There wasn't a place around with better security than home.

Tyler made it down the hall and then to the elevator without incident. In the ER, Red was standing right where he'd told her to and a part of him sighed in relief. He couldn't be sure that she wouldn't bolt as soon as she had the chance and he had all kinds of questions that needed answers.

Then again, she was in a strange town. Running from the one person helping her didn't make a bit of sense.

So far, Red had told Tyler that she'd stepped in for a sister who was now missing. Twins. He shook his head as he walked toward her. Wouldn't his little brothers Joshua and Ryder have a field day with this? Red and her sister's trick would be right up their alley. Even though they weren't actually identical, his youngest brothers looked enough alike that they got away with a few too many pranks, switching places to confuse people.

Tyler took Red's arm and led her out to his waiting SUV.

"What has your sister gotten herself into?" he asked as soon as they were safe inside his vehicle. He turned the key in the ignition and backed out of the parking space.

As he meandered through the lot and onto the highway he expected her to speak. She didn't.

"We can turn back and I'll ask Milton, if that makes you feel better," he threatened. No way would he go through with it but she needed a little motivation to get her talking.

"I told you before, she's my twin sister. She's in trouble."

"What kind?"

"I don't know exactly what's going on," Jessica said, staring out the front window.

"Then start with what you *do* know," he said.

"I got a call from my sister three days ago asking

if I could take time off work to help her out," she said. "She needed me to step into her life and go on a trip with a friend of hers for a few days while she fixed a problem. She said go along with whatever he said, so I did. This isn't the first time I've had to bail her out of a bad situation, so I agreed."

"Is your sister involved in something illegal?"

"Before yesterday I would've been ready to fight if you asked that question about her. Now, I'm not sure what she's gotten herself into," Jessica said on a heavy sigh. "She's not a bad person. I normally get called in for a relationship that has gone south and she doesn't have the heart to break it off herself. I show up and help ease her out of it. At least that's how it started five years ago. It kind of grew from there."

"So you had no prior relationship with Milton?"

"We're not engaged, if that's what you're asking, and neither was Jenn," she said with an involuntary shiver. "I'd never seen the man before two days ago. My sister sent me with him. She said I could trust him and to go with him and pretend that I knew what he was talking about. We checked into the Bluff Motel and he started demanding that I tell him where something was. Some kind of box. I can't remember clearly." She touched the bandage on her forehead.

"Is that how you ended up on my property?"

"Yes. I picked a remote place thinking that he'd give up when we couldn't find the box right away. He got angry instead. Demanded that I tell him where it is, told me to stop playing games. I said that I'd tricked him and had no idea where the box was. The next thing I know I'm being hit in the head with a rock," she said, leaning back against the headrest. "Where are we going, by the way?"

"My ranch," he said.

"Maybe you should just take me to the airport and drop me. I can grab a flight or rent a car there and drive to Louisiana. I have to find my sister."

"In case you haven't noticed, you're in no condition to drive anywhere. Milton still has your ID so renting a car or getting on a flight is out of the question," Tyler countered. "And then there's the issue of him trying to kill you. We need to update the sheriff first thing in the morning."

"No. We can't."

Was she serious? She balked pretty darn fast when he mentioned Tommy.

"This is his town and he has a right to know the truth. You should be pressing charges against that jerk who tried to kill you," Tyler said. "In case you hadn't noticed, he seems intent on finishing the job."

"I have," she retorted, motioning toward her forehead. "But I have no idea what's really going on, I can't remember everything, and I've already put my sister in danger by leaving the hospital. All I know for sure is that Milton isn't the one in charge. Until I know who's trying to hurt her, I can't bring in the police. You can drop me off at a bus station."

She wouldn't last a day without money or transportation, and she seemed to realize it about the same time Tyler started to tell her.

"This must look bad to an outsider," she said. "But I have to ask you to keep everything I've told you between us. Give me a little time to figure out what happened to my sister and help her."

"She might be hiding."

"Or hurt," she said.

"In which case, doesn't it make more sense to bring in the law?" Tyler turned in to the ranch and security waved him ahead.

"This isn't a good idea. I shouldn't have called you and gotten you involved," she said, and he could hear the fear and panic in her voice. Not a good combination.

She looked exhausted, and his first priority was to get her inside where she could rest.

"Let's not make any decisions tonight," Tyler said, pulling up to his two-story log-cabin-style house. Their parents had built each of the brothers a home on the expansive ranch in hopes they would someday take their rightful places at the helm. Tyler's was on the south side to take advantage of the sun. Most people hated the heat in Texas but it couldn't get hot enough for Tyler. His mom used to joke that he had to be cold-blooded because of how much he loved summer.

He'd spent most of his childhood outdoors, throwing a baseball, football or whatever was around with one or more of his brothers. His childhood had been happy and filled with loving memories, and his blood boiled at the thought that someone had wanted his parents dead. They were kind, respected members of the community. His mother had one of those hearts that had no bounds. Pop was honest, albeit stern.

Tyler pulled into his attached garage and parked his SUV.

"Hold on," he said as he slid out of the driver's seat and then rounded the vehicle to open her door for her.

"Are you hungry?" he asked, offering a hand.

"I'm more thirsty than anything," she said, putting her fingers in his.

A frisson of heat fired through his fingertips and he noticed how small and delicate her hand was by comparison. He pushed those thoughts aside. His mind was still reeling over how much he'd misjudged his last girlfriend, Lyndsey. The last thing he needed was another complication in his life. "We can fix that."

There was a noise at the front door, a scratching sound.

Tyler opened the front door and let the family's chocolate lab inside. He patted his old friend on the head and scratched him behind the ears.

"This is Denali," he said to Red.

"Is he yours?"

"Denali?" Tyler glanced up. "Nah. He belongs to everyone. He drifts to each of our houses now that we're home, and he's been known to stay in the barn from time to time."

"He's beautiful." She hesitated. "And big."

"This old boy won't hurt you," Tyler said.

She moved a few steps closer and bent down. Denali jumped up at about the same time and her cheek met a wet nose. Jessica let out a yelp before reaching to scratch Denali behind the ears.

"You hit his favorite spot. Don't be surprised if he follows you around now," Tyler said.

She smiled as he helped her into the kitchen and for the first time could see just how weary she looked.

Even in an exhausted state, Red would be considered beautiful with those big eyes, thick lashes and creamy complexion.

"I have some homemade chicken soup in the fridge. How does that sound?"

"Impressive. You cook?" She eased onto a bar stool at the large granite island.

"Not me. I had some delivered from the main house."

"This ranch is amazing. Are you telling me there's even more to it?" she asked. She glanced around the room as he divvied up the soup into two bowls and heated them in the microwave.

Tyler couldn't help but laugh. "More" was an understatement. "Each of my brothers has a house on the ranch, and then there's the big house my parents lived in. They kept one wing open for guests of the hunting club we own."

"What kind of ranch is this?"

"We raise cattle and provide hunting expeditions."

"How many brothers did you say you had?" she asked as he set a steaming bowl in front of her.

"Five. Six if you count Tommy. He spent most of his childhood here. He and my older brother Dallas have been best friends since before I can remember." He took a seat at the island next to her. "Be careful. It's a little hot."

She blew on the spoon before taking a mouthful. "Either I'm *that* starved or this tastes even better than it smells."

Denali had gone to sleep at her feet.

"Probably a little of both but Janis Everly is an amazing cook. Her soups are a whole experience in and of themselves," he said with a smile. It was true. The woman could cook. "You should see the main house during the holidays. Everything's decorated to the nines and the whole place smells like cinnamon and nutmeg. Janis cooks every kind of cookie imaginable. She dresses up like Mrs. Claus and delivers them just about everywhere in town."

"She sounds like an amazing woman," Jessica said.

"She's a saint for putting up with us all these years," he said with a laugh, liking the smile his comment put on Jessica's face as she bit back a yawn.

He showed her to one of the guest rooms after she'd drained her bowl. A few hours of rest should clear her thoughts and let her come to her senses.

Then they could get to the bottom of whatever was going on. And even though she'd protested, he had every intention of bringing in the law.

Chapter 5

The *rap, rap, rap* against the front door shot Tyler straight up out of bed and to his jeans, which were laid out across a chair next to his bed. The machine-gun-like knocks fired again. Tyler hopped on one leg trying to get his second leg in his pants and stay upright.

He shook his head like a wet dog, trying to wake up, and glanced at the clock. Almost six thirty. What on earth?

He took the stairs several at a time and saw that Tommy was standing on the other side of the door.

"What's going on?" he asked as he opened the door and motioned for the sheriff to come in.

"I'm here on official business," Tommy said, and the tone of his voice didn't sound good.

For a split second Tyler thought his friend might be bringing news about his parents, except that he would've called all the O'Brien's together first. So this had to be about Red.

"You want a cup of coffee?" Tyler asked, moving toward the kitchen.

"No, thanks. I've already been on duty for an hour." Tommy followed. "I'm here to talk to you about a murder."

Tyler stopped in his tracks and spun around. Those words had the same effect as a good, strong cup of coffee. "Let me guess. Milton's dead?"

"No. He's missing. We haven't identified the victim yet," Tommy said.

"What does this have to do with me?"

"The body was discovered at the Bluff Motel," he said with an ominous sigh. "In Jennifer and Milton's room. I have to ask. Where were you an hour ago?"

"Here. Asleep," Tyler said, and he could see that his friend didn't like asking that question.

"Have you been here all night?" Tommy asked.

Tyler's phone records would tell the story so he decided to come clean. "No. I went to the hospital to check on Red after she called and said she was ready to leave the jerk. I brought her home with me."

Tommy's eyebrow arched severely.

"What else was I supposed to do?" Tyler asked, his shoulders and hands raised in surrender as he stood there in the kitchen in an athletic stance. "She reached out for help and I said I'd protect her. Dan Spencer was working the security gate when we came home and he can tell you that we arrived around three o'clock this morning. I fed her soup and put her up in the guest room, and that's all."

"She's here right now?"

Tyler nodded, motioning upstairs.

"Get your coffee. It's going to be a long day," Tommy said, taking a seat at the granite island.

A few minutes later Tyler joined him with a fresh mug filled with strong coffee. He took a sip. "You want me to wake her?"

"I'll need to talk to her," Tommy said.

"What happened to Milton?" Tyler asked. "He was at the hospital with her when she called asking for help."

"He must've left after you got her out of there," Tommy supplied.

Tyler took another sip, letting that information sink in. "He must've realized pretty quickly that something was up at the hospital."

"How'd you get her out of there without him knowing?" Tommy asked.

"Dr. McConnell arranged it on the condition she could check up on her at my house. She sent in a couple of nurses saying they were taking her for X-rays. I took over once they got her safely away from him." He paused long enough to take another sip. "I tried to convince Red to press assault charges a few hours ago."

"But she refused," Tommy finished. He knew the drill all too well. Except that this was no run-of-the-mill abuse case.

Tyler nodded. He'd let his friend make his own assumptions for now. But he had every intention of filling Tommy in as soon as he could.

"What happened at the motel?" Tyler asked.

"A couple in the room next door heard two men arguing, banging noises against the wall and then a few minutes later a car sped away. They didn't think much about it at the time, figured someone had too much to drink. The noise woke their baby and the husband got sent out to the car to get extra supplies from a diaper bag. When he returned he noticed the door next to his was still open. He thought it was strange and decided to check it out, make sure everyone was okay. That's when he saw a man splayed out on the floor, bleeding out. He tried to administer CPR and yelled for his wife to call 911," Tommy said.

"But it was too late," Tyler said.

Tommy nodded.

"Sounds personal," Tyler said.

"Very personal," Tommy echoed. "He stabbed him with a hotel pen, which means he grabbed anything he could find. Then he panicked and ran without thinking about closing the door behind him, which leads me to believe that he wasn't expecting the confrontation."

"Any chance this was a random mugging?" Tyler asked. Red was in more danger than she realized. If she truly was covering for her sister, and he believed her story, then Jennifer was into something very dark and dangerous. He also believed that Red had no idea what was going on and he found himself wanting to help her even more.

The truth lay somewhere between Texas and Louisiana, and Tyler had every intention of finding it.

"Nothing appears to be missing, although we won't know what happened for sure until we talk to James Milton." Tommy leaned against the counter. "If it had been a coincidence, though, he would've reported it."

"You're expecting to get the truth out of that man?" Tyler coughed.

"About as much as I'd expect a deer to drive a car. This whole scene looks like self-defense, but then Milton took off in a hurry, leaving behind his clothes, shaving cream, pretty much everything he brought with him as far as we can tell." Tommy dragged his boot across the tile floor. "And I'm left wondering why he would do that and not go straight to my office."

"Seems strange."

"Everything about Milton is off. From his fiancée ending up in the hospital and him expecting us to believe that lame story about losing her, to a man being stabbed to death in his motel room."

"What about the dead guy? Have you identified him yet?" Tyler asked, trying to absorb just how much danger Red was in. He also hated lying to Tommy, allowing him to believe that Jessica was her sister. He had every intention of clearing up the misunderstanding as soon as he spoke to Red. Tyler despised lies and they were racking up.

"No. He had ID on him but it was fake." Tommy's boot toe raked behind his other foot.

"What about transportation?"

"We're still working on the rest of the pieces." Tommy glanced up and tilted his head to the left. "We have no leads. Unless Jennifer knows what's going on."

"I can vouch for her whereabouts last night. She's been with me the whole time."

"The neighbor heard male voices. We aren't looking for a female." Tommy said. "And yet that doesn't rule out the possibility she might be able to fit the pieces together for me. Right now I have a dead stranger at the morgue with a fake ID, and a man on the run who could be anywhere or right under my nose looking for Jennifer. Based on his actions yesterday, I'd say the man doesn't want to leave town without her."

"I didn't trust or like that guy from the minute I laid eyes on him, but I'm just as confused as you are. She hasn't told me a thing since we got here." He glanced at the star-shaped metal clock in the kitchen. It was ten minutes until seven. "I'd hoped to give her a few hours of sleep before I talked some sense into her and brought her down to the station to press charges against Milton. At the time, I thought that SOB shouldn't get away with hitting women."

"That's not all he does," Tommy said on a heavy sigh. "The problem is figuring out what else he's into before I have another dead body in my town."

And if Tyler could save Red in the process that would be even better.

"It goes without saying that I'll need to speak to his fiancée to find out if he had enemies," Tommy added.

Why did the sound of the word *fiancée* string Tyler's neck muscles tight? He nodded, feeling the tendons cord and release.

"Did the witness hear what the two were arguing about?" Tyler asked.

"He said he was half-asleep but he thinks he remembers hearing him ask something about a necklace and where the girl was," Tommy said.

"They argued about Red?" Tyler did his best to act surprised. Damn, he hated withholding information from Tommy. But the surest way to lose Red's trust would be to go behind her back by telling his friend everything he knew. Tyler feared she'd strike out on her own and end up getting herself hurt again or worse... dead. She was in so far over her head she couldn't see right from wrong anymore, and Tyler was her best bet at finding the straight and narrow again. She seemed like a good person in a crazy situation, and Tyler of all people understood her need to protect her family.

"I believe I will take you up on that cup of coffee," Tommy said.

"Help yourself," Tyler said, draining his cup and pushing to his feet. "I'll go wake her so you can talk to her."

He could take a few minutes to prep her for what was to come, he thought as he knocked on the door of the guest room. He hated the idea of waking her before she'd had solid sleep. There was no movement on the other side so he cracked the door. "Jessica."

No answer. She must be out cold. His ringtone sounded from down the hall as he pushed open the door to her room. The bed was empty and there were no clothes to be seen. The door to the adjoining bathroom was wide open but he checked inside anyway.

Jessica was gone.

Tyler darted into his own room and answered his phone before it rolled into voice mail. The call was from Dan in security and Tyler knew right away that Jessica had hit his radar.

"What happened," Tyler asked.

"Sir, a white female is being detained in the guard shack. She was seen running across the south side of the land after exiting your house," Dan said.

Tyler needed to make a decision. Bring her in and let Tommy question her, or make an excuse and talk to her first? He opted for the second. "Take her to the main house for me and wait there with her."

"Yes, sir."

Tyler ended the call, threw on a shirt and made his way downstairs where Tommy waited in the kitchen.

"I'm afraid she's gone," he said, stuffing his cell in his pocket.

"What do you mean gone? Do I have anything to worry about with her?" Tommy asked, setting his cup of coffee on the counter.

"She's afraid and she's been traumatized. There's no way she could've been involved with the stabbing because she was with me. I know you have to handle this like every other case, so I already told you that Dan at the guard shack can corroborate our story. The only reason I didn't call you before is that she didn't want me to involve law enforcement even though I told her it was the right thing to do." Tyler hedged, hoping his excuse would hold water and Tommy would chalk her disappearance up to her being abused. "I'm sure one of the guards will see her. In the meantime, she's been through a lot and I'd like to get out and search for her myself. She doesn't exactly trust men right now."

"By all means," Tommy said. "Bring her by the station for a statement when you find her. Or give me a call and I'll come right over. Time is the enemy in a homicide investigation."

"I will," Tyler said, hoping he could convince her that Tommy was on her side. Having help from someone in law enforcement could prove beneficial.

"This mess could take a while to untangle. A man like Milton probably has a lot of enemies." Tyler grabbed his keys from the counter.

"I'd bet money on it." Tommy was already walking toward the door. "I'm heading over to the motel now. Maybe we'll know more once we process the scene."

"While I have you here, have you made any progress on your investigation into Mom and Pop?" He thought about Tommy's comment about time being the enemy of a murder investigation. Were all the leads cold on the O'Brien case?

"I'm sorry. I don't have anything new yet. You'll be the first to know when I do." Tommy excused himself and walked out the door.

Tyler grabbed a pair of socks from the downstairs laundry room and slipped into his boots. He was ready to head to the main house when someone knocked on the front door. He could see Red with Dan standing next to her.

"What happened?" he asked as soon as he opened the door.

"I'm not ready to talk to the sheriff. I decided to take a walk and this guy forced me to go with him," Jessica said, chin up in defiance. Determination filled those sea-green eyes.

"I'm sorry, sir. I tried to take her to the main house but she went ballistic," Dan said, looking exasperated. "Given her condition, I thought it was safer to bring her back to you."

"Thank you. I can take it from here," Tyler said to Dan.

"Yes, sir." Dan excused himself.

"Are you okay?" Tyler asked Jessica as soon as he closed the door behind her. He couldn't help but notice the red marks on her arms and wrists, still fresh from yesterday, as he ushered her into the kitchen. And she was shivering.

"Me, yes. At least for now. My sister is the one who is in trouble," she said, rubbing her arms to warm them.

"Pull another stunt like that and I might not be able to help you," Tyler warned, his anger raised from a place deep inside…a place that made him feel helpless and weak. He bit back a curse as he retrieved a blanket from the couch and handed it to her.

"I can't make any promises. I'll do whatever it takes to make sure my sister is safe." Jessica draped it around her shoulders before folding her arms across her chest in a defensive position.

"Come and sit down. I'll get you a cup of coffee." Tyler didn't wait for her to make a move toward the kitchen before he walked over to his counter. He poured two fresh mugs. He needed to tell her the news about what had happened back at the motel and he needed to find a way to do it without scaring the hell out of her. "You like sugar or cream?"

"Black is fine," she said, accepting the mug and taking a sip.

"You want to sit?" Tyler asked, motioning toward the bar stools at the granite island.

Red seemed to catch on to the fact that he had news. She set the cup on the counter and turned to face him, hands fisted on her hips. "What is it? What's happened?"

There was no good way to put this, so he decided to

come out with it straight. "A man was found dead in your motel room."

"Milton?" Red sank to her knees. Her skin paled. Tyler crossed the room and helped her onto the stool a few feet away from her.

"No. Not him." Anger tore through him again when he realized how badly she was shaking, this time from fear not cold.

"How?" she asked, looking utterly stunned. "Who?"

"Tommy doesn't know the answer. The guy had a fake ID so they'll start trying to identify him. As for how, he was stabbed to death after arguing with a man who we suspect was Milton," Tyler said. "A witness says the two were fighting about a woman and a necklace. I'm guessing the woman is your sister and you by proxy. Any idea what the necklace is about?"

"That's the first I've heard about it but maybe that's what is in the box," Jessica said. Hold on a second. Was it? A memory pricked, like a sudden burst, and then it dawned on her as she brought her hand up to the bandage on her forehead. The bump to her head must've confused her and made her forget. "My sister wanted him out of town. She needed to get him out of the way as she investigated something… I can't remember what. But she told me to go with him and agree to help him find the box. Once we got here, my sister told me she was getting close and to drag this out as long as I could."

"And that's exactly what you did," he said, and there was anger in his eyes.

"Right before I got my head smashed with a rock after telling him I'd tricked him and had no idea what he was talking about." She pulled the blanket from her shoulders and set it down.

"Feeling like he'd been duped must've made a man like Milton angry," Tyler said.

"He'd rented the ATVs and we were on your property by the time I fessed up. I remember that much. I'd stalled as long as I could. He got so frustrated his face turned red and he started demanding to know where the box was." She glanced at the bruises on her arms. "I expected him to be upset but I never thought he'd try to kill me."

Tyler's grip on the coffee mug intensified.

"He kept hinting at my neck when he talked about the box. I thought he was threatening me, you know, for show, because I never expected him to try to hurt my sister. Now I realize he must've been referring to a necklace."

Tyler's eyes widened. "I wonder…"

He retrieved his smartphone and pulled up a news story. She squinted at the screen to get a better look at the headline: Infinity Sapphire Stolen from Prominent Louisiana Family.

She quickly scanned the story. "This is the most famous necklace in America that isn't stored in a museum?"

"Seventy-seven-point-seven carats total weight," the handsome cowboy added. He stood so close that his scent filled her senses—a mix of woodsy aftershave and warmth, deep and musky—and it stirred up all kinds of inappropriate sensations.

"You know about this necklace?" She took a step

back, needing to put a little space between them, and tried not to memorize his unique aroma.

"The couple that owns the necklace attended an art auction hosted by my family recently. I didn't get a chance to talk to them. I prefer to be outside when all that's going on." He paused, turning the phone over and over in his hands. "Forgive the question, but I have to ask. Is there any chance your sister's a jewel thief?"

"None. Zero. I'd bet my life on it," she said, and she pretty much already had. "Whatever's going on can be cleared up as soon as I speak to her. She might not even know how much danger she's in. I have to find her before Milton or anyone else does."

Jessica was already up, pacing, when the cowboy touched her shoulder. It was all she could do to ignore the frissons of heat zinging through her.

"We will." His honest dark eyes seemed like they could see right through her. He was gracious to help her as much as he had already, but this situation had detoured to a very bad place and she didn't feel right putting anyone else at risk.

"It's too dangerous for you to be involved. Someone is dead because of this necklace. I can't ask for your help anymore."

"Let me be the judge of that," he said quickly. "Besides, I'm not going anywhere until I know you're safe."

Looking into his eyes, she could see he meant it and she figured it was most likely some kind of cowboy code. But she couldn't let anything happen to him, and especially not since he was being so generous helping her.

She started to protest but he stopped her with that same look.

"This is the situation as I see it. You have no transportation, no purse, and you have no idea who's after you. To make matters worse, you won't go to the law. So forgive me when I say that you don't have a lot of options right now. I'm willing to help and I'm your best bet to keep you alive and find your sister." He folded his arms and spread his feet in an athletic stance. "If those are your goals, and I believe I'm correct in saying they are, then I don't see how you're in a position to refuse my help."

He was right about all of it. There was no denying what he said was true. "I do want to live and you're absolutely correct about how desperate my situation is. But I still think it's a bad idea for you to get involved any further. Milton's out there, somewhere, probably looking for me. He must think that I know more than I'm saying or that I'm getting the necklace for myself."

The cowboy's slight nod said he agreed. He made a sound of disgust. "What exactly was his relationship to your sister?"

"All I know is that they dated a year or so ago. I thought he was out of the picture but I guess they stayed in touch. She dated society men and I'm sure it's a small circle."

"Did she mention anything specific about why she decided to leave him before?"

"There were a lot of things. Like, for instance, if a hostess said their table would be ready in twenty minutes and it wasn't, he would become and angry and didn't care who knew." She looked at Tyler whose dark eyes penetrated her poorly constructed armor. She wanted to lean on someone, on him, even temporarily. "I knew he was a creep, but Jenn didn't mention anything about him being physical with her."

"Violence can escalate." Tyler's boots scuffed across the floor as he paced. "I'm sure Tommy will run a background check on him as part of his investigation." Tyler stopped and held up his hand. "I know what you're going to say, so don't bother. But we will need to get Tommy more involved at some point."

She started to protest but he just shook his head. "I won't go behind your back, so don't worry. But we have to bring in the law. We'll talk more about that later. Right now, I want to hear more about Milton."

"Jenn said he was upstanding but she might not've known him as well as she thought she did. He is…let's see… I know she told me…oh, right. He's a lawyer."

"He didn't sound like one when Tommy interviewed him," Tyler said.

"Right. He's a corporate guy, mergers, I think."

"That explains the shiny shoes and his lack of knowledge about criminal law," Tyler quipped, walking past her and once again filling her senses with his scent.

"I don't know much else. I'm not even sure where he works but I'm guessing he's with a corporation in or near Baton Rouge where she lives." Jessica held up her coffee mug and breathed in the smell of dark-roasted beans.

"She said he was a jerk but she didn't give details?" He shot her a look of disbelief. "Sounds unusual for twins."

"I remember thinking she might've been too embarrassed to talk about him in detail, like he was seeing someone else while she thought they were exclusive or something along those lines." Jessica braided her fingers. "The relationship didn't last long. She didn't call me in to break up with him, so they might've remained friends or run in the same circles. That's about all I remember. I had no idea he was capable of actually hurting her. And now my memories are patchy about the past few days."

"Not surprising, after the hit you took to the head," he said.

"I think I'm awake enough for the day." She set down her empty mug. "Mind if I get cleaned up in the bathroom?"

He stopped pacing and stared at her for a minute. She knew exactly what he was thinking. "I'm not planning another escape, if that's what you're worried about."

His cheeks dimpled when he smiled. "There's a spare toothbrush in your bathroom. It's still in the wrapper. I'll have breakfast delivered."

She figured it would do no good arguing with a cowboy whose mind seemed made up, so she resigned herself to accepting his help.

"Tell me one thing, though," he said as she started to leave the room. "How'd you sneak out this morning? I mean, you were on the second floor and I didn't hear you leave."

"I couldn't sleep, so I heard the sheriff when he pulled in. The alarm code was easy because I watched you enter it last night. You seemed like a nice person but after being with Milton I had no plans to take that chance. I slipped out the side door."

She kept to herself how relieved she was that she hadn't gotten away for exactly the reasons he'd mentioned earlier. She was broke, alone, and had no means of communication. Not to mention the fact that she had no idea where she was and there would be all manner of wildlife outside that door. Plus, she was barefoot.

She was also desperate and she had a bad feeling about her sister's current situation. "Jenn might be trying to reach me on my cell. Can we go to the motel room and check if it's still there or is there no way now that it's a crime scene?"

"We can do whatever you want. But first, we're heading into the station so you can give a statement to one of the sheriff's deputies," he said matter-of-factly. "And if you want to stay above suspicion you'd better act like an unhappy fiancée."

Chapter 6

"Do you think he believed me?" Giving her statement to the deputy had taken Jessica all of fifteen minutes, mostly because she didn't know anything. She'd played the shocked fiancée as best she could, forcing tears that came only when she let herself think about her sister.

"You didn't give him a reason not to," Tyler said.

Jessica sank into the tan leather seat of the SUV as they drove to the motel room she'd shared with Milton. An involuntary shiver rocked her body at thinking about being in that place with him.

She should've been able to see right through that fake smile of his. Milton had charm in spades when he wanted to turn it on, and she could see why her twin would've been attracted to him. He was good-looking and had a professional job with what Jennifer would see as plenty of earning potential.

Jennifer had always wanted more out of life than the meager childhood they'd had in Shreveport. Both of their parents had worked low-wage jobs to support the family. Their mother had owned a cleaning service, her father had made a living doing seasonal yard work, and all three kids had had to pitch in to help summers. Jennifer had always imagined herself living in one of the grand Southern colonials they'd cleaned while Jessica had always been the more practical sister. She'd been able to see right through the men who dated Jennifer for superficial reasons and then dumped her when it was time to find a proper wife.

Tyler steered onto the highway. All makes and models of trucks blazed past them.

"I was remembering my last conversation with my sister. She said that she was involved in something and she needed to figure a way out, to clear things up. Or at least, I think that's what she said." Jessica gingerly fingered the wrap on her forehead.

"Which could mean that she is guilty of taking the necklace," Tyler said, and she couldn't argue with his reasoning. That's exactly what this would look like to an outsider. Except that she knew her sister better than that. Jennifer could be flighty and she definitely liked a good party and hanging out with the highbrow crowd, but she was honest.

Convincing the handsome cowboy of that was a whole different story. She couldn't prove that her sister wasn't involved. All she had to go on was how well she knew Jenn. *Twins for life!* had been their mantra since they were little girls and most of the time it felt like they could read each other's thoughts. Jessica had no such magic now and the silence was terrifying because she feared her sister was in grave danger.

"Jennifer might come off as insincere, and sometimes she is, but she's also good underneath all the layers. Freshman year she went to Houston for college. I helped her move into her dorm and we went shopping to pick up a few extra supplies. We get in the car and Jenn realizes that the clerk had forgotten to charge her for a twelve-dollar pillow. It was late August in one of the hottest summers on record in Texas. Jenn's car had no air-conditioning. But Jenn was worried that the clerk would get in trouble for the mistake. Drenched in sweat, she marched back inside to let him know."

She stared out the front window. "I consider myself an honest person, but I would've returned to pay for the pillow another day or waited until the sun went down. Not Jennifer. No amount of begging could change her mind. By the time she got back I was dripping so I made her stop off at the nearest gas station so I could buy a cup of ice to rub on my sizzling skin." And that was just one of many examples that came to mind.

Jessica could tell Tyler all day that her sister would never take something that didn't belong to her, but she had nothing concrete to prove it and he had no reason to believe her. "I can see how this looks and if I was you I'd probably assume the worst and that she was a bad person—"

"Hold on there. No one said anything about jumping to the worst-case scenario. We need to think through every possibility and I'm going to have to ask hard questions along the way. If you say your sister couldn't have stolen something then I believe you," he said. "Let's work with the assumption that she had no idea what was really going on but got herself tangled in this mess. That makes more sense anyway, because you two are close and based on my intimate knowledge of twins she wouldn't knowingly put you in danger. Someone could've used her. Even made it look like she was the one who took the necklace to cover for themselves."

"That necklace is worth a fortune. I'm betting Milton isn't the only one trying to find it, aside from my sister," she said. "With millions on the line, a lot of bad people would come out of the woodwork."

"Which could explain the man at the motel and if that's true, then I doubt Tommy will be able to identify him. He could be a treasure hunter or working for organized crime."

"One of how many?" She touched a sensitive spot on her head and winced.

"There will be a lot. Some of them will be official. Insurance companies hire interesting people to help investigate and recover merchandise like that, and a necklace worth millions would be insured to the nines," Tyler said. "And then there's the black market."

Just the thought made her head hurt even more. "And my sister is tied up right in the middle of this, of all these vultures."

"It would seem that way. Tommy is going to be following the same paths and I'm going to have to bring him in at some point," Tyler said, and she thought about it for a long moment.

"Okay. But not without discussing it with me first." She figured she could hold Tyler off long enough to get her bearings and for them to make enough progress for her to walk away and make sure he wasn't in danger. Eventually she'd have to break out on her own. "I need to speak to my sister. It's the only way to be certain of what we're dealing with. I talk to her and everything will be cleared up."

"You couldn't reach her earlier."

"True." She chewed on her bottom lip. "I need my cell. She may have left a message or a clue. I bet she's been trying to reach me and I haven't been able to answer. I hid my phone because Milton was creeping me out. That's why I didn't bring it with me when we went out on ATVs. I was afraid he'd take it and then he'd know." Jessica sat straight up in her chair, remembering a little more. "I find my cell and we get answers."

Three-inch-wide crime scene tape, Big Bird yellow with bold black lettering, stretched across the door of room 121 of the Bluff Motel. The sun was out and it was finally warming up a little.

A sickening feeling sank low in the pit of Jessica's stomach as she walked across the black asphalt toward the room she'd been forced to share with Milton. It was bad enough that a man had been killed only fifteen feet away, even a man who was after her sister or James Milton didn't deserve to be stabbed to death, but she could feel the sense of despair hanging in the air. Knowing what had happened and seeing the evidence right in front of her made everything that much more surreal. A man was dead. Her sister was missing.

Jessica's stomach clenched and she tried to stave off nausea. The sheriff ducked under the tape and moved toward them. He was holding a paper bag—evidence?—which he handed to a deputy.

"I couldn't be sorrier about what happened here," the sheriff said with a genuine look of compassion. "Has your fiancé been in touch with you?"

In the moment, she'd almost forgotten about keeping up that charade.

"No, he hasn't. But thank you very much, sheriff. This is all such a shock." That much was true. Everything about the past thirty-six hours had turned everything she knew upside down and twisted up her insides. "I'm afraid I lost my cell so I don't know if he's been trying to contact me."

Tommy nodded, which she took to mean neither he nor his deputy had found it.

"See anything in there that might help you figure out what happened?" Tyler asked, diverting the sheriff's attention, and she was grateful for that.

Jessica didn't have that same ability to fudge the truth with people that came so easily to her sister. In her heart, her sister was a good person incapable of hurting a soul. Of course, Jennifer never would have called it lying. She'd prefer to say something like *bending the truth*.

Tears leaked from Jessica's eyes. Her sister had to be all right. If she'd gotten herself involved with men worse than Milton, Jessica was even more worried.

"I ran James Milton through the system," Tommy said to her. "How well do you know your fiancé?"

"I learned a great deal more about him recently. Why?" Jessica wasn't sure where this was going and she didn't like lying to someone in law enforcement.

"What did you find?" Tyler asked, drawing the attention to him again.

Jessica shot him a grateful look.

"He has a record," Tommy said matter-of-factly.

"For what?" Tyler asked as Jessica gasped.

Tommy looked from Tyler to her. "I'm guessing by your reaction you had no idea."

"No. I would never have even guessed." Jessica didn't have to fake her reaction. She was genuinely shocked and even more worried for her sister. If the sheriff confused her reaction for feelings for Milton so be it. "You think you know someone."

"I made a call to Baton Rouge PD and he's pretty well known for having gambling issues."

"Meaning the issue is that he loses," Tyler added.

"They don't call it a problem when they're winning," the sheriff said wryly. "He's wanted for questioning in several cases the PD is trying to clear up, everything from small cons to extortion. They booked him on a small-time charge."

"I had no idea," Jessica said honestly as she tried to digest this news. She'd discovered that her so-called fiancé was a con man who'd set her up. More questions for Jenn were mounting. Jessica wondered if Milton had heard about the necklace and decided to steal it and cash in. Maybe he had debts to pay with the wrong people and one of those could've been the man that had been killed.

"Ever hear of Randall Beauchamp?" the sheriff asked.

"He's the head of one of Louisiana's wealthiest families," Jessica said. "And I've heard that he doesn't make all his money from legitimate sources."

Had Jennifer gotten herself mixed up with one of the biggest crime families in Louisiana?

"The Baton Rouge police chief seems to think that Randall Beauchamp is on the hunt for a stolen necklace worth millions of dollars on the black—"

Before Tommy could finish his sentence, Jessica sank to her knees. Nausea threatened to overwhelm her. Her world tilted on its axis as the reality of her sister's situation set in. Jennifer was as good as dead.

Was Milton working for the Beauchamps? Maybe he was greedy and wanted to sell the necklace in order to settle a gambling debt. Or maybe he needed the money to disappear.

Bile burned the back of Jessica's throat as she felt herself being lifted up by strong arms.

"You don't have to do this right now" came Tyler's masculine tone, and it sent a warm current running through her. "We can deal with all of this later."

"It's okay," she said as he led her to the passenger seat of the SUV. She turned to face him. "I need to do this."

The sheriff stayed put. A deputy had brought over something he must've wanted to show his boss and the two were engaged in conversation.

She and Tyler were just out of earshot. "I need to find my phone."

"Tommy or one of his deputy's might already have it."

Jessica shot him a look.

"No. There's no way Tommy will release evidence in a murder investigation. He can't."

Jessica looked him dead in the eyes. "I hid it in between the mattresses."

"Hold on" was all he said and then he walked away.

The deputy who had been talking to Tommy put an evidence bag in his cruiser as Tommy disappeared inside the cordoned-off room.

"Hey," Tyler said to Deputy Garcia. "Mind talking her off the ledge?"

Tyler motioned toward Jessica, hating that he was about to lie to his friends again. He'd known Garcia since middle school.

"What's going on?" Garcia asked.

"She's still in shock about all this. First, she decides to leave an abusive relationship and now a man turns up dead in her fiancé's motel room. I think she's blaming herself in some weird way, like if she'd stayed with him then everything would be okay," Tyler said, praying his friend bought into the lie. "And now finding out that not only was he abusive but he was a criminal seems to have put her over the edge."

"Not sure what I can say to help but I'll try." Garcia shook Tyler's outstretched hand before walking over to Jessica.

There were only two law enforcement officials on the scene that Tyler had noticed so far. Hopefully Jessica could keep Garcia occupied while Tyler worked on Tommy.

Tyler glanced at Garcia, who had his back turned to him, and then ducked under the crime scene tape.

The room had worn dark blue carpeting and two full-size beds with heavy bedspreads that looked exactly like the curtains in his Gran's old house. Beds, perfectly made, were to the right and there was a plywood desk and a dresser made of the same quality against the wall to the left. This was the sort of place that most likely bolted the furniture to the floor and nailed pictures to the walls.

Noise came from the bathroom beyond and Tyler figured Tommy was there collecting evidence and looking for clues.

He ran his hand along the box spring of the second bed, figuring that Milton wouldn't want Jessica sleeping closest to the door in case she decided to bolt.

Bingo.

He tucked the phone in his front pocket and then turned to sneak out.

"You shouldn't be in here," Tommy said, standing in front of the closet leading to the bathroom. His arms were folded and his feet braced.

"I was just looking for you." Damn. Tyler was a bad liar.

"I'll give you a hint. I'm not in one of the drawers of the nightstand." Tommy hadn't bought the line.

"This?" Tyler turned to the nightstand with the phone and alarm clock on it, stalling for a few seconds while he tried to think up an excuse. He saw a pen and notepad with the hotel logo on it. Snatching them up, he then turned toward Tommy. "I was looking for these."

Tommy's cocked eyebrow said it all. "Don't touch anything else. I don't need your fingerprints all over my crime scene."

At least he didn't seem to realize that Tyler had shoved something inside his pocket.

"What did you want with me?" Tommy asked.

"Glad you asked. I wanted to talk to you without Red in the room. Do you think there's any chance she knew what was going on?"

That seemed to ease Tommy's concerns. "Her reactions seem genuine to me. This is catching her off guard. Why? You think there's a chance she knew?"

"Not really. I just wanted to make sure I was on the same page as you after she reached out to me," he said.

"She thinking of leaving town anytime soon?" Tommy asked.

"Good question. She hasn't mentioned having family to take care of her. We already know she's from Baton Rouge. I don't think she's in a big hurry to go home, considering Milton could be there now."

"Men who abuse women like to cut them off from the rest of their family. So, even if there is someone she might not've spoken with them in months or years," Tommy said.

Tyler clenched his back teeth. "She may have had a dust-up with her family about him."

"She'll need counseling and a lot of support. Even though Milton can't hurt her anymore she needs help dealing with her emotions." Tommy's hands had relaxed and he'd slipped them inside his pockets.

"Milton's a first-class jerk."

"My guess is that the lawyer got himself in trouble with some gambling debt and that could be responsible for the timing of their trip. He might've hoped things would cool down back home," Tommy said.

"We didn't trust him from the beginning," Tyler added.

"Nope. He's a scumbag. I'm planning to dig deeper into whether or not he had a life insurance policy on Miss Davidson. She may not have known he'd taken one out and her *accident* seems even more suspect now. An insurance payoff could clear up any debt Milton had and set him up nicely."

"Good point. I didn't like him from the get-go and I like him even less now that I know about his background. She said he was an attorney and an upstanding citizen. Guess he put on a good act," Tyler said.

"Love is blind," Tommy quipped. "I see it all the time in my line of work." He paused. "She seems like a nice person."

Tyler nodded.

"I see that you're helping her out and she needs a friend. How far do you plan to go?" Tommy asked, accusation in his tone.

"Why wouldn't I lend a hand? She needs a place to catch her breath. It's been a crazy couple of days for her. I figure I'll help her get straight, maybe get Doc McConnell in to speak to her, and then send her back to Louisiana where she belongs."

"Be careful," Tommy warned.

"Of what? Her?" Tyler blew off the comments.

"Yes. I know you, Tyler O'Brien. You're not going to be able to turn your back on someone who needs a hand up. This woman's been through a lot and I'm warning you as your friend not to get too involved."

A throat-clearing noise came from the doorway. Jessica stood there. "Are you ready to go now?"

Tyler nodded and shot Tommy a warning look. Although he wasn't thrilled that Jessica overheard the conversation, he was relieved that she'd given him an out. He used it to walk out the door and past the tape.

Once they were safely inside the SUV and he was sure no one could hear, he said, "I found it."

"My phone?" There was a mix of apprehension and excitement in her tone. And fear.

He nodded. "We'll check it out as soon as the motel is safely in the rearview."

"Thank you," she said, adding, "and he's right, you know. A man is dead. This is dangerous—"

"That's not your fault," Tyler interjected.

"No, it's not. But I'm heading toward the people who killed him and that isn't safe for you." She didn't miss a beat.

"It's not for you, either. Will knowing that stop you?" he asked.

"No. My sister's in danger and I can't walk away. I have to find her. I don't have a choice," she said impatiently.

He took his right hand off the steering wheel once he got the SUV up to speed on the highway and squeezed her left. The contact sent a jolt of electricity up his arm. "Neither do I."

Tyler managed to dig into his front pocket while keeping the wheel steady. He produced a cell and placed it in Jessica's hand.

"Now, let's see what's on this phone."

Chapter 7

Tyler made sure no one was following them before exiting the highway. He located the closest parking lot, a Dairy Queen, pulled in and parked.

"There are three calls from my sister," Jessica said, and her face had gone bleached-sheet white.

"Put the phone on speaker," he said.

She did.

Sis, I'm so sorry that I got you involved in this mess. This is so much bigger than I imagined. I'm worried about you. Call me ASAP and get far away from James. He isn't who I thought he was. I gotta go. Call me.

Tyler shouldn't be surprised at the likeness of Jennifer's voice. After all, his twin brothers' voices were similar, too. And yet it still threw him off.

The message also confirmed what Tyler already knew, Jessica had no idea what was going on. He'd

trusted her and confirmation that he hadn't made a mistake in that trust eased a little bit of the tension cording
his shoulder muscles.

"She sounds good," Jessica said, wringing her hands
together. Fear, anxiety and apprehension were embed-
ded deep in her eyes.

*Are you okay, sis? You're not calling me back and
I'm starting to get worried about you. If James has hurt
you in any way... Click.*

"What's that noise in the background?" Tyler asked.
"Do you recognize any of the sounds?"

Jessica tilted her head to the left and leaned toward
the speaker. "I hear zydeco music and that must mean
she's with her friend. He lives in Spanish Town. That's
encouraging. She'd be safe with him."

"You said there are three messages," Tyler said, holding off his warm and fuzzy feelings for now. Jennifer
had already misjudged one so-called friendship but he
didn't want to burst Red's bubble of hope just yet. With
millions of dollars on the line, Jenn shouldn't trust anyone.

Sis, run. Jennifer sounded out of breath, like she was
running, and there was the sound of splashing water
in the background. There was a long pause. *Wherever
you are, run. Hide until I tell you it's safe to come out.
Oh, God, I hope you're okay. If James figured you out
don't believe anything he says. I had no idea what was
going on. Don't go to the police. Don't trust anyone and
especially not... NO!*

Jessica heard her sister scream.

*...I've gotta go. I'll figure a way out of this, I prom-
ise. And then I'll meet you on the bayou.*

Her words came out at a frantic pace now. Another scream came through the line and then there were sounds of a struggle. More screaming and a male voice telling her to stop kicking. He yelled a profanity and then came the sound of her phone being dropped in water.

A desperate Jessica held the phone so tightly her fingers lost color and now matched the pallor of her face. Anger quickly overrode all other emotions. She banged her fist on the dashboard. "They got her. It's the only logical reason the calls stopped."

"Do you recognize the man on the recording?" Tyler asked.

"No."

"What did she mean about the bayou?" he asked. Maybe he could nudge her out of an emotional state into logical thinking. Get her wheels turning.

"It's just a saying we have between us. Doesn't really mean anything." She turned to him, those sea-green eyes wide. "But they have her and now they'll kill her."

"Can I see that for a second?" Tyler peeled her fingers off the phone and scrolled through the call log. She was worth millions to them. They wouldn't kill her. He didn't see the need to bring up the fact that they would most likely torture her to get that information. "The last call came in while you were in the hospital."

"They got her so they no longer needed Milton," Jessica said. Good, she was using her anger to switch gears and think this through, and that was the best chance they'd have of finding Jennifer.

"That's one thought. Another is that someone else, a freelancer, has gotten in on the game. This necklace is famous and, like I said before, it's worth is going to bring people out of the woodwork to find it," he said, needing her to have a realistic picture of what they were facing and hoping he'd be able to convince her to bring Tommy up to speed. Tyler never went back on his word. He wouldn't go behind her back.

"She was at The Bluebonnet Swamp Nature Center during that last call," Jessica said.

"How do you know?"

"She's my sister and that's where she'd go if she was in trouble." Jessica's matter-of-fact tone had him convinced. "Plus, I heard her sloshing through water and there were sounds of nature all around her in the background. And I heard her slap her skin from mosquitoes a couple of times. This is the first place she'd go to hide because that's where I used to find her when she had a bad breakup with one of her boyfriends. She knows the area and probably figured it would be a good place to lay low, which also means she didn't want to involve her friends by staying with them."

"We'll start there." He handed her the phone and put the gearshift in Reverse.

"That's got to be a six-hour drive from here, at least," she said, sounding defeated. "Plus the call came in yesterday. She won't still be there, not if that jerk got to her, and I know he did. That's the only reason she wouldn't call again."

"Maybe she lost her phone. I heard the sound that it made hitting the water," he offered.

"She would've borrowed someone's to call and check in with me. We never go more than a day without talking and it's been at least twenty-four hours since her last attempt."

Tyler believed her, having witnessed the same phenomenon firsthand with Ryder and Joshua. Those two spoke daily.

"Baton Rouge is only an hour away from here by plane." He redirected the conversation. Last thing he needed was her dwelling on the negative.

Tyler made a few calls using the hands-free Bluetooth feature preloaded on his SUV and had set up their flight and itinerary by the time they reached the airstrip. He just hoped like hell they got to Jennifer first.

The flight went off without a hitch and a private car waited at the airport. Jessica's stomach had braided into an unbendable knot the second she'd heard her sister's voice on the third message and it hadn't let up.

"You said before that few of her friends know about you," Tyler said, ushering her into the backseat of a stretch limousine with blacked-out windows.

"That's right."

"I'd like to keep it that way," he said. "Especially since we believe she's been taken and others may not realize that."

"I wouldn't exactly call this incognito." She waved her arm in the air.

"Sometimes, the easiest way to hide is to be in plain sight."

The limo zigged in and out of traffic terrifyingly, but then southern Louisiana drivers were notorious for fast lane changes, tailgating and high speeds. Even being from Louisiana, Jessica had a difficult time navigating traffic in and around Baton Rouge. Don't even get her started on the bridges or thoughts of the alligators that lurked beneath them.

Rain threatened and a wall of humidity hit full force as they stepped out of the limo, stealing Jessica's breath. She'd get used to it in a minute, but those first few breaths after stepping out of an air-conditioned car were always staggering.

Tyler paid their entrance fee into The Bluebonnet Swamp Nature Center.

"I promise to pay you back as soon as the sheriff releases my personal belongings," she said earnestly, thinking about everything he was doing for her and hit hard by the realization that she'd never be able to equalize this debt.

He waved her off.

"No, seriously." It was important for Jessica to feel like she could cover her own bases. That was the only thing she didn't like about her sister. It was too easy for her to flash a smile and let someone else do the work for her. And even though Jessica had that same smile, she'd always known it would get her and her sister in trouble if used improperly.

Tyler mumbled something she didn't quite catch. She'd let it go, for now. A man as good-looking and wealthy as Tyler O'Brien was most likely used to getting his way. But he hadn't seen stubborn until Jessica put her mind to something. He'd learn just how persistent she could be when this was all over and she could put her affairs back in order. For the time being, though, she had to live off his generosity if she wanted to find her sister in time.

"There must be dozens of boardwalk trails here." He stood behind the Nature Center building looking at the maze of wooden paths.

"She likes a certain place. There's a bench close to an old cypress tree. The branch is huge. They built the walkway beneath it. Follow me," Jessica pushed past him, plucking at her shirt as beads of sweat rolled down her chest even though the temperature was barely seventy.

Jenn's favorite bench was a good ten minutes' hike from the Nature Center building. At their pace, they made it in seven. "There it is."

She ducked under the cypress branch, a good three feet wide, and dashed to the bench, wanting to soak in everything from the last place she knew her sister had been.

Tyler walked to the bench and dropped to his knees to get a better look at the water.

"I hope you're not planning on going in there," she warned.

"It's not like I want to," he said. "But we might be able to locate her phone."

"We?" No way was she getting in water with snakes and alligators. Jessica involuntarily shivered. "You know what's in there, right?"

"Sure do."

"I can't help my sister if I'm in the belly of an alligator chewed up into little pieces," she said, frustrated. Because she would do anything to save her sister, including jumping into that murky green water that scared her beyond belief.

Tyler's chuckle was a deep rumble in his throat and it

sent a sensual vibration skittering across her skin. She was about to be eaten by an alligator and the cowboy she'd brought with her was causing her to have inappropriate sexual thoughts.

"At least let me take my shoes off first."

"How deep do you think the water is here?" he asked.

"A few feet, four at the most."

"Look for bubbles before getting in." He was lying flat on his stomach on the boardwalk, watching the surface of the water. "I'd rather wait at least twenty minutes but we don't have that kind of time, so I want you to look hard."

Wasn't that reassuring? A serious case of the heebie-jeebies trickled down her spine as she moved to the other side of the boardwalk. Okay, she could do this. She needed to talk herself up for a minute to steel her nerves, but this was going to be no big deal. She scanned the water intently, watching for any signs of life.

"I think I should be good here," she finally said, stopping twenty feet from her original spot.

Tyler popped to his feet and moved a good ten feet from his first location. "All right, then. We're looking for her cell or anything that might indicate she was here."

He ducked through the slats in the wood and then she heard the splash that said he was in the water on the other side. Jessica took in a deep breath, held it, and then slid through the wooden slats on her side. The murky green water was cold against her stomach as she waded through waist-deep water. Moss gathered on her stomach and she nearly lost her cool. Every survival instinct inside her begged her to get out of there and run away.

Jenn needed her. The fear and desperation in her sister's voice would keep Jessica on the right path.

"Something just brushed past my leg," she said, letting out the breath she'd been holding.

"We better move quickly before someone sees us and kicks us out," Tyler said.

Jessica dropped down, trying to feel her way around in three-foot-high water. All she touched was slick rocks and she tried not to think about all the bacteria lurking around and what that would do to a cut in, say, her finger.

Every noise made her jump. Every animal sound made her heart race. Every scrape of her finger across a new surface made her pull her hand back.

After searching for what seemed like an eternity and coming up empty, she returned to the boardwalk and scrambled out of the water. She quickly checked her body for leeches or any other creepy-crawlies. "Did you find anything?"

"No." The water-sloshing sound came from the other side of the walkway.

"It's useless." And worse yet, felt hopeless. She should've known this would be a dead end.

The architecture of Spanish Town was mostly post–Civil War. Rows of early twentieth-century homes of wood construction lined the narrow streets. Houses were small but had large front porches and there was more pink in one place than Tyler had ever seen. "What's up with the flamingos on all the lawns?"

But "on the lawns" was an understatement. They hung in front windows and stood on porches. There was even one on a roof.

"People used to look down on this area as having questionable occupants, so everyone decided to give them something to stare at," Jessica said. "Mostly artists and musicians live here."

"And what do we think we'll find amongst all this plastic fowl?" he asked. Their shoes and clothes smelled like swamp. The limo driver hadn't wanted to let them back inside wet. Tyler had had to slip the guy extra money to convince him it would be a good idea. He'd also promised to pay for having the limo properly cleaned and aired out, which he figured he owed the guy.

"Jenn has a friend here. I might be able to trick him into thinking I'm her."

"The zydeco music playing in the background of the first message?" he asked.

"Yes. I'm hoping she confided in him, but she might have just wanted a place to lay low. His name is Elijah, by the way." She scanned the houses. "I'm just not sure where he lives, exactly."

"Do you think it's safe to go in like this?" he motioned toward their soaked clothing.

"Probably not, but what choice do we have?" she asked with a shrug.

"We need to play this smart. Not attract too much attention. Someone could be watching Elijah's place and we're soaked to the bone. Give me a few minutes." Tyler fished his cell from his front pocket and made a call. "Janis, can you book a room for me at the Hilton in Baton Rouge?"

"Fine but I'm putting you in the Presidential Suite," Janis said.

"Okay." Normally, he'd argue. There was no need to put him up in the best suite in any hotel. But this time, he had a lady with him and the two-bedroom suite would give her the privacy she needed. They were still practically strangers, even though it felt as if he'd known her for a lot longer than thirty-seven hours. Rather than try to get inside his head about what that meant, he requested fresh clothes in a woman's size five to six to be delivered to the hotel. And then he asked for men's. Janis already knew his sizes. "Casual stuff in a breathable fabric. Also, I'm going to need hats and maybe a few ladies' scarves. Think you can get all that to my room in the next hour?"

"Does a dog have fleas?" Janis quipped.

"Thank you, Janis. You already know I think you're the best." Tyler buzzed the driver who rolled down the partition between the cab and the backseat. "Can you take us to 201 Lafayette Street?"

"Yes, sir, Mr. O'Brien," the driver said.

"I'm going to need your services 24/7 while I'm in town," Tyler said. "Is that a problem?"

"No, sir." A smile lit the driver's face.

"Thank you. I'll double your current rate."

An even bigger smile curved the driver's lips. "You don't have to—"

Tyler put his hand up. "It would make me feel better for inconveniencing you on such short notice."

"I don't know what to say. Thank you."

"What's your name?" Tyler asked.

"Zander, sir."

"How about you call me Tyler? Every time I hear 'Mr. O'Brien' I look over my shoulder to see if my father's standing behind me."

Zander chuckled. "You're the boss, Mr.—" he glanced in the rearview with a sheepish look "—Tyler."

"Thank you, Zander." Tyler turned to Jessica. "You haven't eaten since breakfast. What sounds good?"

"Nothing, I'm okay."

"You need to keep up your strength." He placed a call to the hotel manager and arranged for soup, sandwiches and bottles of water to be waiting when they arrived. Tyler ended the call to Jessica's wide eyes.

"Can I ask a question?"

He nodded.

"I've seen your place and where you live is beautiful. There's more security than a…a…maximum security prison. So, I hope I'm not being rude, but just how rich are you?"

Tyler couldn't help but laugh. He never really thought of himself as wealthy. Rich in land and family, maybe, but not rich in the loads-of-money-in-the-bank rich. Maybe it was the way he'd been brought up. Pop had had his feet firmly planted in the soil and all the boys had followed suit. They cared more about running their horses—speaking of which, Digby needed exercising— than running up credit cards. But by all measures, they were loaded. "Guess I never think about it."

"How can you not?" she asked, eyes wide. "When I first met you I thought you were some kind of ranch hand, which was fine by me. You seem so…normal.

But now I see that you own your own plane and can fly it rather nicely, by the way. You can snap your fingers and have almost anything you want delivered or arranged…am I on the right path here?"

"Not everything," he said. "And nothing that really matters."

"Tell me one thing you can't make appear?"

"My parents." He didn't miss a beat. "No amount of money can bring them back. We're about to have the first Thanksgiving without them, without Mom's cooked goose and all the trimmings, and it feels odd. She was all the warmth in the holidays. Her meals. Her traditions that me and my brothers used to think were corny as kids. That's the stuff you miss, the little things. The way she used to make these maple cookies in the shape of leaves and the whole house smelled like pancakes and cinnamon. Now all I can think is how my own kids won't ever bake pies or cut out paper snowflakes with her."

"I'm so sorry." Jessica touched his arm, and it was as though her words reached into his chest and filled some of the emptiness in his heart. He'd heard those three words more times than he could count in recent months and yet this was the first time they'd had healing power.

"Your mother sounds like an amazing woman," she said.

Tyler nodded, fearing that if he said any more he'd get choked up. Next thing he knew, Jessica had braided their fingers together.

"There's no way to replace the people we love and no amount of money can fill that void. My sister has essentially turned her back on us trying to do just that—make a bank account somehow fulfill her life. I never understood that about her. I love her with all my heart, don't get me wrong, and money's nice. Living without it stinks. But just like that old saying goes, it can't buy love. It's refreshing to hear that your family has it right."

Tyler agreed. "Being close with my brothers helps, having their support makes losing our parents easier to get through. This first holiday will be hell for all of us, but we have each other and that makes a huge difference."

"I can imagine," she said. The empathy in her voice made it seem like things would be even better in the future. He wondered if she'd lost someone important to her.

Zander stopped in front of the Hilton and opened the door to the backseat. Tyler exited first and held out a hand to Jessica. "My lady."

She took the offering with a smile, glancing down at their swamp-filled clothes.

The hotel's manager greeted them at the door. "Mr. O'Brien, what a pleasure to have you back."

It must've taken great effort for her not to wrinkle her nose at the smell of the two of them, Tyler thought. He had to give her credit, she held strong. The manager was tall and brunette, curvy, in her late thirties. Her name tag read Annabeth Malloy.

"Thank you for having us, Miss Malloy," he said, shaking her outstretched hand. "This is my guest Miss Archer."

A bellhop arrived as Annabeth acknowledged Jessica. He'd given a fake name to make Jessica feel more comfortable. She seemed ready to climb out of her skin from the attention they were receiving.

"Devin will help you with your bags," Annabeth said.

"I'm having a few items delivered," Tyler said with a nod toward Devin.

"Of course. Devin will take you to your suite. Please let me know personally if there's anything I can do for you or Miss Archer."

Tyler thanked Annabeth and followed Devin to the elevator, taking Jessica's hand and pulling her close. It was the best way to shield her from any watchful eyes in the hotel lobby. The way she fit with his arm around her felt a little too right. And that was something else Tyler didn't want to think about too much. He had enough going on without further complicating his life. And keeping her alive long enough to find the truth was at the top of his agenda.

"You've been quiet since the car ride," Tyler said, handing Jessica a bag filled with clothes and undergarments, which she eagerly took.

"I feel bad about what I said earlier about your money." She hadn't meant to be a jerk, but she had been. She'd judged him solely based on his money and that made her exactly like the people she despised, the kind of people who only cared about superficial things. The cowboy was nothing like that. He hadn't even hinted at the kind of money he and his brothers had, and she figured he wouldn't have, either. He'd been kind to her and had done nothing but offer help. So what if his presence put her on edge.

"I don't think you're showing it off in any way. In fact, I was a little surprised you had any. No offense."

That deep rumble of a laugh broke free from his chest again and it sent sensual little tingles up and down her body. "I don't know what to say."

She'd showered and was covered head to toe in a thick cotton bathrobe provided by the hotel and yet she was keenly aware of being completely naked underneath.

"It's just that you look so…normal." His skin was olive colored and tan, and his hands were rough, as if he worked outside.

"What did you expect me to look like?" Thankfully, he seemed amused as he sat down at the expansive oak table in front of a wall of windows that she was sure would frame the best views of the city if the curtains hadn't been pulled shut.

She'd smelled the food the second she'd stepped out of the shower, and despite thinking there was no way she could eat under the circumstances her stomach growled. And he was right, earlier; she did need to keep up her strength.

"Fancy, maybe? Like J.R. Ewing or something," she said, and that solicited a full belly laugh from Tyler.

"Sorry to disappoint you," he said.

"You didn't," she said a little too quickly, and it caused her cheeks to burn. "What I mean to say is that I like that you're normal."

"I could always break out my bolo tie and Western shirts if you'd be more comfortable," he quipped.

"Great. Now you're making fun of me." She reached

across the table to slap his arm but he caught her wrist and held it. She didn't immediately move to take it back.

Suddenly the air in the room was charged, and her breath caught in her throat as he drew sexy little circles with his thumb.

Chapter 8

A tense expression crossed Tyler's features, like he was trying to figure out his next move. He let go of Jessica's wrist and picked up his sandwich instead. "I hope you like BLTs and soup. This won't be as good as Janis's but it'll keep us from starving."

"I'm just happy not to smell like swamp water anymore," she said awkwardly.

"I know you were hoping to find something there and I'm sorry we didn't," he offered.

"Anything would've been nice, some kind of direction." There was so much heat and intensity crackling between them it seemed odd to talk around it.

"Sometimes it's good to be able to rule a place out. My friend Tommy has the motto No Stone Left Unturned during an investigation. It's surprising how a small detail often means the difference between a trail going cold and cracking a case wide-open," he said.

"So, we go back and try to find Elijah's place in Spanish Town," she said.

"Does he know about you?"

"She kept me separate from the rest of her life, even her friends. I doubt she told anyone about me, so he should be quite surprised when her sister shows up on his doorstep."

"Or not."

She cocked her head sideways. "What do you mean?"

"Earlier you suggested trying to fool him into thinking you're Jenn." He paused long enough for her to nod. "She said not to trust anyone. I think we should take her advice to heart. We'll know if he's involved based on his initial reaction to you."

"I hadn't even considered the possibility that one of her friends could've gotten her into this mess, but you're right."

"Let's hope they didn't. But if she's innocent, and I believe you when you say she wouldn't steal, then she either tripped into this or someone set her up," he said. "There aren't a lot of people who would have access to the Infinity Sapphire. We'll track who might've come into contact with the owner over the past few weeks. I'd like to trace your sister's movements as well, but that is a little bit trickier since we don't want to bring you out in the open."

"Speaking of which, I need to do something different with my hair." She rolled a strand around her index finger.

"Supplies were delivered while you were in the

shower," he said. "There are hats to choose from. Scarves. We should probably dye your hair and have it cut but your natural color is beautiful."

Butterflies flitted through her stomach at the compliment and she was pretty sure her cheeks flamed. But Jessica wondered if there was anything he couldn't get at the snap of a finger. This was definitely a different lifestyle than the one she knew and it made her more than a little uncomfortable. A man with this kind of money was more Jenn's type. "Thank you."

She finished her sandwich and soup, surprised she was able to clear her plate and bowl. Her body was hungrier than she realized. After changing into linen shorts and a button-down silk blouse, she tried on a couple of hats before settling for one in taupe with a wide brim and a silk scarf wrapped around it. There were tan strappy sandals with just enough of a heel to give her a little more height. She looked in the mirror and hardly recognized herself. That was most likely a good thing, because even though all of what she wore was out of character for her, she didn't want to look like herself right now.

Jessica applied light makeup, more gifts from the generous millionaire, before walking into the living room where he sat at the desk on his cell phone. Tyler was so down-to-earth that she hadn't thought of him as being wealthy—at least, not until he started flying planes, ordering limousines and generally snapping his fingers to make pretty much anything show up.

None of that should have shocked her, except that he didn't fit the *millionaire* stereotype. Based on her sister's dating stories, rich men sounded like playboys or self-obsessed jerks.

She never could understand what Jenn saw in them. Jenn was beautiful and she could easily turn heads. Even though she and Jessica were identical, Jessica normally looked quite different from her sister. Jessica's hair was pulled up in a ponytail most of the time. She wore very little makeup. And her favorite outfit was a tank top and jeans.

Tyler was different from Jenn's usual men. He was almost staggeringly handsome and definitely good-looking enough to be a playboy, but she was pretty sure he'd laugh if someone said that out loud.

He finished his call and set his cell on the desk in front of him. "The owner of the Infinity Sapphire, Emma-Kate Brasseux, will be home this afternoon."

The idea that Tyler could be walking Jessica into the belly of the beast sat in his gut like shards of broken glass. On the other hand, he was darn certain there was no way she was going to let him talk to the owners of the necklace without her. There was far too much at stake. He'd have to be careful not to cross any boundaries with Tommy's investigation and local law enforcement would also be involved. Now that the stolen necklace was common knowledge and the motive in a murder investigation, Tommy would send someone to speak to the Brasseuxs, which was why Tyler wouldn't call ahead and make an appointment to speak with them. He wanted to check things out first.

On the ride over, Tyler wanted to know more about Jessica. "Where's your family, other than your sister?"

"Shreveport, where we grew up. It's just my parents. We had an older brother who died when we were in high school. It affected us both but Jenn hasn't been the same since."

"I'm sorry for your loss." Tyler couldn't imagine losing a sibling so young.

"My brother, Jeffrey, had just turned eighteen and graduated high school when he signed on to work the pipelines in Alaska. Dad had been out of work for a while and my parents were having a hard time keeping food on the table. Sending one of us to college was out of the question.

"Jeffrey noticed an ad in the paper and saw it as his ticket to help the family while getting out on his own. Times were tough and he couldn't find a local job. He hadn't been gone for three months when we heard the news there'd been an accident." Her voice broke, and he could tell that even now it was difficult for her to talk about it.

"Sounds like he was an honorable and brave young man, trying to do the right thing by his family," Tyler said.

Jessica nodded as a tear spilled down her cheek. Tyler thumbed it away. Contact while she was so vulnerable wasn't a good idea. And neither was taking her in his arms, but he did it anyway. He lied and told himself that his actions were purely meant to comfort her. There was so much more to it than that, though…bringing her into his arms calmed his own torn-up heart.

"We were all devastated but Jenn took the news hardest. Something inside her just broke after that. She stopped hanging out with our friends and slept all day for a solid month. When we finally convinced her to get out of bed she was different. She started wearing makeup and spending more time alone. Then she found babysitting jobs and used all the money to buy nicer clothes. In school the next year she started hanging around with rich boys. I think she associated our financial situation with losing Jeffrey. She couldn't get off to college fast enough, relying on school loans to make it happen. It lasted a year before she quit school and moved to Baton Rouge. Said she needed a fresh start. There, she kept her family, including me, under wraps and didn't want us to meet her new friends. I think she was ashamed of us."

Tyler could feel her shaking in his arms, so he hauled her tighter to his chest. The limo had stopped but he didn't care. The only thing that mattered right then was the shaking woman in his arms, the feel of her skin underneath his weathered hands and the way she looked up at him with those big eyes.

So he dipped his head and kissed her. Her body stiffened and then relaxed against him. The shaking stopped as she parted her lips for him and her breath quickened. She brought her hands up around his neck and tunneled her fingers into his hair.

Tyler knew this was charting a dangerous course. He'd cut out casual flings after his first year of college and this woman had already broken through barriers that normally took other women months to breach. He should back off, let go.

He couldn't.

So he deepened the kiss, ignoring all the warning bells trying to sound off inside his head. Jessica dropped her hands, clutching his shirt, and that quieted his internal protest.

Her hand wandered across his chest and he pulled her onto his lap.

The air inside the limo crackled with desperate need. *Desperate.*

Tyler didn't like the sound of that word when it came to him and Jessica.

He pulled back and looked into her eyes, a mix of desire and desperation staring back at him.

And that last part was a mood killer.

When they made love—correction, *if* they made love—there'd be nothing desperate about it.

"The car stopped," he said, unable to move...wishing he'd seen something else in her eyes—or just good old-fashioned lust.

"I know." She brought the back of her hand up to her lips and eased off his lap.

Tyler needed a distraction, so he signaled Zander to lower the partition.

"Where would you go to find someone if you didn't know their last name or address?" he asked, focusing on why they were there. The trip to Spanish Town hadn't taken long. Other than Elijah's name, they didn't have much to go on.

"And they live here?" Zander asked.

"Yes."

"Then I'd go to the market. It's a place up ahead where all the locals gather to eat," Zander said. "I can point you in the direction but you're not going to find out where someone lives if you pull up in one of these. It's a tightknit community."

"With lots of artists who have an affinity for pink flamingos, or so I've noticed," Tyler joked, trying to ease the tension.

Jessica smiled and that helped. He wasn't sure how he'd allowed things to get so out of hand in such a short time, but he vowed not to let it happen again.

"Here's what you want to do." Zander pointed to the street in front of them. "Go down here about two blocks. Make a right and walk halfway down the street. The market is dead center of Spanish Town. You can't miss it. If the person you're looking for lives around here, someone will know him or her."

Tyler thanked Zander and asked him to wait right there on the corner. The short walk in the thick humidity, even with cooler overall temperatures, had Tyler plucking at his shirt. Texas was dry in comparison even though his state had seen more rain last year than in any he could remember. He took Jessica's hand in his and she smiled up at him. With that second smile something happened in his chest and he chalked it up to residual feelings from what had happened in the limo. "I think we can get further if people believe we're a couple."

Damned if a hurt look didn't settle in her eyes that knocked the wind out of Tyler. He didn't want to care about Jessica beyond helping to save her and her sister. So what the hell was happening to him? He didn't do mushy feelings but he couldn't ignore the warmth in his chest every time he was near Red. He told himself that it was her situation tugging at his heart. Her brother was gone and her sister's moving away must've hurt like hell. He could never imagine Joshua and Ryder in that situation. But, hey, life was crazy sometimes. And, sometimes, strange things happened.

The market was a grocery-store-turned-eatery where locals gathered for breakfast and lunch. The building was painted fire-engine red and a retractable hunter-green awning covered the sidewalk dining space. The lunch crowd was running thin but Tyler asked for a table for two outside so he could chat up the waitress.

He ordered a shrimp po'boy and two cups of coffee, even though they'd just eaten.

"Will that be all?" the waitress asked. "Dorinda" was stamped on her gold-colored name tag in white letters.

"Yeah, I guess it will. Although, I wonder if you could help me out." Tyler hesitated and she leaned forward. "Our friend Elijah used to play around here. I got a new cell and lost all my contacts." He made an annoyed face that seemed to resonate with Dorinda. "I thought we'd reconnect while we were in town. You know where we can catch him?"

"You just missed him. He was in here a few minutes ago," she said with a small shake of her head.

"Think I can still catch him?" Tyler made a move to get up.

"Stick around long enough and he'll be back." She motioned toward a waitress inside. "He picks her up as soon as her shift's over."

That was even better news because they didn't know what he looked like. "Do you have any idea what time that will be?"

Dorinda glanced at the white plastic watch on her wrist. "I'd say another hour to an hour and a half."

"Thank you. I can't wait to see that old son of a gun," he said, a little worried he might be overacting.

"Can I get anything else for you, hon?" the waitress asked.

Jessica bent her head forward, face in her hands, as if she had the worst headache of her life. Wearing sunglasses and a wide-brimmed hat, she wouldn't be easily recognized. "Aspirin."

She lifted her head up and laughed. So did Dorinda.

"I told him to stop me after the third Ruby Slipper, but do you think he did?" Jessica said, feigning frustration. She coughed and shook her head.

"I hear you. I'll be right back with those coffees." Dorinda winked before she turned and walked away.

"I hope Elijah comes back soon," Jessica said, scanning the streets. She had to be uncomfortable out in the open like this.

"I have no intention of allowing anything to happen to you."

Chapter 9

"We should wait on the corner for Elijah," Tyler said. "We don't know what he looks like but we know who he's coming to pick up. This way no one will get suspicious if he walks right past us."

Jessica agreed as she followed him. He stopped and turned toward her, shielding her from the street.

"Are you doing okay?" he asked, and then brushed the tips of his fingers against her cheek in a move that sent sensual shivers skittering across her skin.

Her back was against the telephone pole at N. Seventh Street and Spanish Town Road, directly across the street from where they'd eaten. Cars twined down the skinny road.

Jessica nodded as she studied the activity. "This guy walked by a few minutes ago."

"Which one?" Tyler's gaze swept the sidewalk casually.

"This guy in the white pants, white hat." She intentionally looked in the opposite direction.

"He seems to be interested in us," he said, and he couldn't ignore the possibility that the police or others—men with guns—wanted to find the same person they were looking for.

The next thing Jessica knew, Tyler's hand had cupped her neck. He mouthed the words, *Trust me.* And then he dipped his head, hesitated, slicked his tongue across his lips and kissed her.

Her body instantly reacted. She reached for him, wrapping her arms around his neck and parting her mouth enough for his tongue to slide inside.

She thought she heard a groan from deep in his throat as his arm came around her waist and his free hand splayed against her back.

Deepening the kiss, he hugged her—her body immediately molding to his. Her breasts swelled and ached for his touch. Her body reminded her just how long it had been since she'd had good sex…and it had been far too long. She instinctively sensed that sex with Tyler would shatter her in the best possible way.

His body pressed hers against the telephone pole and she imagined how he would feel on top of her, pressing her into a mattress. She could feel his rapid heartbeat through their clothes.

He pulled back first and rested his forehead on hers. From across the street someone shouted, "Get a room!"

The comment made both of them laugh, his was that low rumble from deep in his throat and it was so darn sexy. He started to say something, then stopped, and she half feared that he was about to offer an apology. That was the best kiss she'd had in…in her whole life, and a part of her wanted to celebrate it, not feel awkward that it had happened.

"Damn," he said and his voice was low.

"I was just thinking the same thing," she said with a slow smile. His hand stayed steady against her back and she was grateful because he was the only thing holding her upright at this point. Her bones felt like Jell-O. She'd heard that a kiss could make a person go weak at the knees but this was the first time she'd experienced anything close.

"I've been wanting to do that again since we stepped out of the limo," he whispered.

"Maybe you should try it one more time." She tunneled her fingers into his dark curly hair.

He didn't seem to need much encouragement because he delved his tongue inside her mouth with bruising need. His body pressed against hers, sandwiching her, and desire sprang from deep within. In that moment, she got lost.

Tyler seemed to regain his senses first, pulling back. All the warmth in the cowboy's eyes turned to something else…something that looked a lot like confusion, and it caused her heart to squeeze.

"We should be watching out for Elijah. He could be here by now."

"Did I do something wrong?" she asked.

"You? Hell, no. But I just crossed a line that I shouldn't have, and I apologize," he said.

Where had that come from? And to make matters worse, he just apologized for kissing her.

Embarrassed, she sidestepped him. "Don't be sorry. I participated just as much as you did."

"Come over here. I'll kiss you, honey" came from a few steps away with inappropriate smooching noises.

If that didn't set her cheeks on fire, then waiting wordlessly with the cowboy standing next to her did. Sure he regretted their actions after having a chance to think about it. Jessica didn't doubt she was attractive, especially when she put on nice clothes and some makeup, but this wealthy cowboy was out of her league and he had to know as much as she did that it would never work between them. It would be smart to keep her guard up with him. As soon as she found her sister and settled this mess, she'd go back to her life in Shreveport, a life that made total sense.

The waitress, Elijah's presumed girlfriend, came out the front door, lit a smoke and leaned against the front glass of the restaurant. Someone knocked on the window from inside. She made a face and moved over to the newspaper boxes at the side of the red building.

A full twenty minutes later a vintage El Camino pulled up. It had been partially restored, looked like a work in progress and had the beginnings of a mural painted down the right hand side.

The waitress pushed off the wall of the market. Now on her second smoke, she looked at the driver of the El Camino. She hesitated, made another face and then started walking toward the curb.

Jessica pulled off her hat and glasses and rushed toward the El Camino. "Elijah."

The man driving was in his early thirties and fit the description of a Louisiana musician to a T. He wore a chestnut fedora with a white hatband and red feather. Both arms were covered in tattoos and he wore a dark tank underneath a denim shirt with rolled-up sleeves. He had a silver thumb ring on his left hand, dark hair and eyes, and a mustache and goatee.

"Jenn, where the hell have you been?" he asked, eyes bright.

A moment of panic engulfed Jessica. Could she pull off being her sister when so much was on the line? Sure, it had been easy enough when she was stepping in to ease Jenn out of a relationship. But this? This was so much more nerve racking.

Jessica smiled as she pulled Tyler over to the El Camino's passenger side so Elijah could get a good look. She came up with the best lie she could. "I met someone and we ended up at his place in New Orleans."

Elijah shook his head and smirked. "I should've known. You could at least answer my texts."

"Lost my charger." She shrugged, figuring that was exactly something that would've happened to her less responsible sister.

"Actually, she lost her phone altogether," Tyler said, sticking his hand out. "I'm George For... Ford."

Jessica, arm around his waist, pinched him. Seriously? That slip might've just cost them. It would be a miracle if Elijah bought that...

"Good to meet you," Elijah said, no hint of distrust at Tyler's hesitation.

Even so, Tyler didn't seem to be good at this under-cover thing. Or maybe lying didn't come naturally to him. That was a good thing considering her ex, Brent, had seemed to wake up with lies coming out of his mouth. Lies like *you're the one I love* and *what we have is real* were right up there with *she didn't mean anything to me.* Her name had been Katherine. And Jessica had believed him the first time. Then she'd stumbled across his secret email account and had been forced to ask him if Katherine had been the one he was talking about, or was it Naomi, Judy or Blanche?

Thankfully, Elijah didn't seem to notice Tyler's mistake.

"I see you've moved on from one millionaire to another," Elijah said with a wink.

Was she supposed to know what that meant?

The waitress pushed past them and plopped into the passenger seat, looking annoyed that she hadn't been acknowledged yet.

"My friend, Susannah." He looked from the waitress to Jessica.

"Girlfriend," Susannah interjected with an annoyed slap to his right forearm.

"Nice to meet you," Jessica said, appreciating the distraction. If Elijah didn't look too closely or ask too many questions then she could keep up the charade.

"Well, George, the next time you whisk my girl out of town without telling anyone make sure she checks in with me, okay? Big Beau's been looking for you, by the way." He made a face at Jessica.

The reference drew another blank.

Then again, Jenn had been secretive lately. She'd said she was dating someone important but didn't say who.

Tyler glanced from Elijah to her. He slid his arm

around her waist—she ignored the quiver that rippled through her stomach—and squeezed her so her side was flush with his. He repositioned her in front of him and wrapped his arms around her.

"Do I need to be worried about Big Beau?" he asked against her neck loud enough for Elijah to hear, his breath heating her skin.

She shook her head and her cheeks heated. Thankfully, her blush was authentic. Her body was a pinball machine of electrical impulses with Tyler this close. At least she didn't have to fake an attraction. Jessica might have the ability to sell a lie, she'd done it for her sister, but that didn't mean she enjoyed doing it.

Elijah looked at her and it seemed like he was really examining her. That wasn't good. "Are we good for Thanksgiving, then? My place?"

"Of course," she said raising her voice a few octaves like Jenn did when she was flirting. She twined a strand of hair around her finger and smiled, using all her sister's charms against him.

"You're not going to ditch me for him, right?" he asked, pain from the past still present in his eyes. She felt bad for him because she knew exactly what it was like when Jenn decided to make other plans. It was warm in the sunlight and cold in the shadows.

"Why would I do that?" she frowned. Exaggerating the expression was exactly Jenn's style and made Jessica want to throw up in her mouth a little bit. Her sister had a flare for drama.

Elijah shot her a glare. "Now, that's a good question. Why would you stand me up when we have plans?"

Jessica loved her sister and she'd never want her hurt,

but she could get easily frustrated with Jenn's personality and the way she treated people at times. Elijah stared at Jessica and she realized that she'd missed an inside reference between Elijah and Jenn. She'd missed a cue and now Elijah was suspicious. Frustration nipped at her. It was difficult to think straight with her back pressed against Tyler's pure muscle-over-steel chest.

This situation was getting sticky.

"I hate to take her away from you, but we have reservations," Tyler said, catching on.

Elijah had already looked her up and down as though suddenly realizing this was not an outfit Jenn would ever have on her body. Panic was beginning to set in. The exchange wasn't a total loss. They'd gotten the name Big Beau from him but who the heck was that?

The waitress in the passenger seat was looking a little annoyed. "Good. Maybe we can go now?"

There was a hint of jealousy in her tone. Did Elijah have real feelings for Jenn? Maybe that was the weird vibe she was picking up on from him.

"Stop by later," he said, ignoring Susannah, who looked even less thrilled now.

Tyler tugged at Jessica's hip. She almost forgot to blow a kiss to Elijah and that was something her sister always did before she walked away. Jessica turned and thanked heaven she had, because Elijah was staring expectantly. She blew the kiss and he smiled widely before pulling away.

"He almost caught me," she said to Tyler as they doubled back to walk to where the limo had parked. "My sister always blows a kiss. It's the silliest thing and I nearly forgot to do it."

Tyler squeezed her, keeping his arm around her as they walked. "You did good. He seemed suspicious at first when you missed that personal reference, but then he relaxed."

"I really thought I blew it," she said honestly. "Thank you for saving me."

"No problem. And now we have a name," he said with more than a hint of pride in his tone.

"Think we can go back to the market and ask around?" she asked.

"It's not safe for us here," he said. The weight of those words was heavy on her limbs. He was right. They'd dodged one bullet with Elijah and they needed to get out of Spanish Town.

"Big Beau. That could be anybody," she said under her breath.

"We'll have to ask around, but my guess is that someone will know who he is."

The limo was parked exactly where they'd left it. Zander stepped out as soon as he saw them and then opened the back door.

"Where to, Mister Tyler?" Zander asked.

"18008 North Mission Hills Avenue," Tyler said, conceding the *mister*.

"I'm probably just being paranoid, but do you get the feeling that someone's been following us?" Jessica asked.

"Yes, and I haven't decided if that's a good or bad thing yet."

18008 North Mission Hills Avenue was one of those luxurious, one-of-a-kind New Orleans–style estates.

Tyler had said the Brasseuxs lived there. The grounds looked like a park and it reminded Jessica of the grand homes of the old South. The place had been meticulously constructed with old brick, a slate roof and patios, and an oversize front porch with columns and one of those Southern-style front entrances. It was exactly the image that came to mind when Jessica thought of old Baton Rouge money. A golf course wound through the neighborhood and she guessed there had to be at least four or five acres of lush, flawlessly groomed grounds around this house alone.

Zander pulled up to the front gate and idled the engine. The partition slid down. "This the place where you're headed, Mister Tyler?"

"Doesn't look like we'll get past the gate without an appointment," Tyler said.

"No, it doesn't. What would you like to do?"

Tyler's hand was already on the door release. "I believe we'll get out here. Why don't you circle around the neighborhood? I'll call you as soon as we're ready to be picked up."

"Yes, sir," Zander said.

Jessica followed Tyler into the unseasonably sticky air, missing the air-conditioning as soon as she stepped out of the limo.

"I hope we make it to the main house. Security could be all over us long before we make it halfway across the yard," he said.

Surprisingly, they did make it. Majestic live oaks surrounded the house. As they neared, she saw something that made her heart jump in her chest—the partially painted El Camino parked at the side.

Jessica froze. "Elijah's here?"

Tyler shot her a look that warned her to be on guard. "We have no idea if we're here because we outsmarted security or if we're right where they want us. Either way, I'd like to get a closer look."

"He must be involved," she said quietly and mostly to herself. There must've been something she'd missed in their conversation. He hadn't missed a beat when he saw her. But then, she wasn't the best judge when it came to liars. Jessica had the sometimes unfortunate tendency to take people at face value. "Do you think this means my sister is somewhere safe?"

"It very well might." There was a note of sympathy in his voice. He was trying to give her hope and she appreciated it. She would hold on to it and not give in to the despair nipping at her heels.

The veranda stretched on for what felt like days, wrapping the entire front and left side of the mansion. There were half a dozen white rockers positioned to take advantage of the view of the front gardens. She followed Tyler to a window and peeked inside. She'd already seen the hand-painted stained-glass windows from the front yard. But what they could see through the window was the picture of opulence.

The crystal chandelier hanging over the foyer was fit for a king. Jessica moved to the next set of windows to the left and saw a receiving room that looked like something out of a Southern plantation magazine. A marble fireplace mantel was the focal point of the room. There were perfectly preserved vintage gold-leafed French furnishings. This place was the very epitome of grandeur—a world that was very foreign to Jessica. Even though it was beautiful, it was also intimidating and felt like something out of another time and place, albeit perfectly preserved.

"Whoever decorated this place must've died in the Civil War," Tyler joked, and she was once again reminded of how different he was from the picture of wealthy people that Jenn had painted.

She couldn't help but laugh and it felt good to break the tension. "I can't see Elijah anywhere."

"I don't like that one bit," Tyler admitted.

Jessica's stomach dropped when she heard the sound of a boot stepping onto the wooden porch. She whirled and there he was, fifteen feet away, the barrel of a gun pointed at her.

"Don't even think about doing anything stupid, cowboy," Elijah said as Tyler spun around.

"Funny seeing you here," Tyler quipped, holding his hands up in surrender. "I'm here to see the Brasseuxs. Emma-Kate's expecting us."

"She and Ashton aren't here right now," Elijah said with an ominous smirk.

Jessica thought when she'd first seen Elijah's El Camino that he was somehow in league with the Brasseuxs. Now she wondered if that had been a mistake. Maybe he was just a common criminal and they were innocent victims. "Where is she?"

"Who?"

"Don't play dumb. You know exactly who I'm talking about," Jessica said.

"Jenn? Let's just say she won't be in the way anymore." His voice held no emotion.

Jessica cursed and made a move toward Elijah, blinded by anger.

Tyler stopped her by grabbing her arm. "Don't. That's exactly what he wants. Don't give him any reason to shoot you."

She conceded but took another step forward, hoping she could get Tyler close enough to make a move. Elijah couldn't shoot both of them and she might be able to create a diversion long enough to give Tyler an advantage. She knew nothing about guns, though, so she had no idea if Elijah could fire multiple rounds in a few seconds or if he'd need to cock the hammer every time. Tyler squeezed her elbow and she took that as a warning.

"What do you want with me?" she asked, still trying to stall so Tyler could think of a plan. She knew he wouldn't make a move as long as that barrel was pointed at her chest. She didn't need to be an expert to know that a shot this close would do serious damage.

"Who the hell are you? Jenn never said anything about having a sister," Elijah said and his voice was a study in calm. His disposition, relaxed shoulders and steady hand said that he felt in control, and he was for the moment.

"It's none of your business who I am," she shot back, anger getting the best of her again. The gentle, reassuring squeeze to her arm came a second later. "Where is my sister?"

Elijah sighed. "That, I don't know."

"You're lying." Jessica ground her back teeth to keep from saying anything else that might provoke him. She saw a figure moving toward them using the live oaks as cover out of her peripheral vision. Zander?

"Now that you're here, I have to figure out what to do with you both," Elijah said.

She needed to distract him so Zander could get closer. "My sister trusted you. She thought you were a friend. Why would you do this to her?"

His laugh was almost a cackle. "Your sister looks out for number one. Just like I do. She, of all people, would understand me putting myself first."

"She wouldn't hurt a flea and you know it."

"Tell that to Mrs. Brasseux," he quipped. "After all, Jenn was sleeping with her husband."

Was her sister having an affair with a married man? Was that the reason she'd kept her new man's identity a secret?

"Take me to her. Please," Jessica begged, trying to process that last bit of information.

"He can't," Tyler finally spoke up. "He isn't the one calling the shots."

"That's not your concern. And that goes for both of you," Elijah shot back defensively. His lips thinned. His gaze narrowed. Tyler clearly had struck a nerve.

"Then tell me who is," Jessica said. Her sister had always spoken highly of Elijah. "If you cared about my sister at all you wouldn't do this."

"Move." Elijah motioned toward the porch steps.

Tyler urged her forward, moving his hand low on her back.

"Hands up where I can see them," Elijah said.

"Where are the Brasseuxs?" Tyler asked.

"Let's just say they're preoccupied at the moment.

Now move." Elijah gestured with the barrel of his gun. He was taking them to his El Camino. There was no trunk, thankfully, because Jessica was claustrophobic and she feared she'd have a panic attack.

As they rounded the corner of the big house, she noticed there was another car parked in front of the El Camino, a white sedan. The El Camino had been blocking the second car from view. Jessica heard a click and the trunk automatically opened.

Jessica's chest squeezed and the heavy air thinned as she thought about climbing into that trunk. No way would her claustrophobia allow her to go inside there willingly. Her body began to shake. If she could keep her cool, Elijah might take her right to Jenn. Then again, he could just take them into the bayou, shoot them and dump their bodies into the swamp for the alligators to pick apart.

More than anything she wanted to glance backward to see if Zander was making progress toward them but she couldn't risk giving him away.

Elijah made Jessica and Tyler walk in front of him, and he was giving them a wide enough berth to make it impossible for Tyler to disarm him. He sure thought like a criminal for someone who'd been parading around as a musician. If what Elijah had said was true and he had no idea where Jenn was, then Jessica and Tyler were in big trouble.

A struggle sounded behind them and a bullet split the air. Jessica instinctively ducked, but before she could get her bearings someone was on top of her and she was facedown on the concrete parking pad with a masculine body shielding her. Tyler's body. And he had a calming presence.

"Stay low," was all she heard him say before another shot fired. "Get behind the house as fast as you can. Don't look back."

Panic nearly closed her throat as the pressure of his body eased and she scrambled for cover. She couldn't help but look back to see if Tyler or Zander had been shot. All she could see clearly was Tyler diving into the fray. There was blood on the concrete and her heart stuttered as she rounded the corner, looking for something she could use to help the guys. No way would she leave them alone to deal with Elijah if there was something she could do to help.

There was nothing around so she ran to the back porch and tried the door. Locked. Dammit.

Another shot was fired and she ran to the corner of the building to see what had happened. Before she could get a good visual, Tyler was helping Zander toward her as the El Camino sped off. Blood dripped from the arm dangling at Zander's side and she rushed to help him. "What happened?"

Zander winced as he moved. "Bullet grazed my shoulder. I'll be fine. I saw you two in trouble and had to help—the police wouldn't have come in time."

"We appreciate it." Tyler helped Zander to the rear porch. "Where's your cell?"

"Back pocket." Zander eased to one side as Tyler fished out the phone.

"I'm calling for an ambulance. We'll stick around until they get close and then we have to go. Her sister's in danger and we can't afford to lose any more time," Tyler said as he pulled off his undershirt and tied it around Zander's shoulder just above the wound while checking to make sure Elijah wasn't circling back. "You're going to be fine. Have the police check on the family inside the house, if anyone's there."

Zander nodded. "Don't worry about me. Nothing but a scratch."

Wasn't that pretty much the same line all men gave? If the situation weren't so dire, Jessica would laugh.

"Keys fell out of my pocket. Heard them drop over there somewhere." Zander motioned toward a pool of blood. "Take the limo and get out of here."

Tyler handed the cell to Zander, who explained that he'd had an altercation and needed help.

Jessica located the fanned-out keys. "Got 'em."

"Then go," Zander pressed after ending the call.

"Not until help arrives," Tyler said.

"I'll tell the cops that I ran into someone in town who asked me to drop him off here. I'll give them the description of the man who drew a gun on you and Jessica. That way the police will be looking for him and not either of you." Zander took his cell phone and wiped it down. "Can't have your prints on here."

"What will you tell them about your limo disappearing?" Tyler asked, thanking Zander.

"I'll figure something out. Don't worry." Zander shooed them away as sirens sounded far in the distance. "I'm fine. Now go."

"We'll check on you later," Tyler said, embracing

Zander in a man-hug. "Thank you for everything you've done. We wouldn't be alive without you."

Jessica's sister, on the other hand, might not have been so lucky.

Chapter 10

"Do you think it's possible what Elijah said is true?" Jessica asked. The Louisiana humidity made it difficult to breathe.

"That your sister was having an affair with Ashton?" Tyler navigated the limo onto the highway.

"She had a new man in her life and she refused to tell me who he was," she said, tapping on the dashboard.

"Makes for a good story. Your sister is having an affair with a wealthy man. Tries to get him to leave his wife but he won't. She steals his wife's family heirloom for revenge," he said.

"When you put it like that, it sounds like something on a TV crime show."

"Exactly. And it sums everything up nicely except the part where your sister's not a thief," he said, and then glanced over at her. "You haven't changed your mind, have you?"

She hesitated. "Not really. I know my sister. But then I wouldn't have believed that she was involved with a married man, and yet she is."

"True." There was no conviction in his voice. "She may not have known he was married when she met him."

Good point. For all her social climbing, she was still a small-town girl at heart. A sophisticated liar could pull the wool over Jenn's eyes.

"Also, in the last message she said not to believe what Milton would say about her. Maybe the same holds true for Elijah. I think we need to talk to your sister before we jump to any conclusions," he said.

"What do you think the name Big Beau really means?" Jessica asked.

"He could've been throwing the name out to get a reaction from you," Tyler said.

"A reaction from my sister," she clarified. "Or so he thought at the time."

"My bet is that Big Beau is an actual person," Tyler said. "We'll start there. The only other clue we have is the bayou."

"I still don't know if that's significant." She couldn't help the desperation in her voice.

"Milton's still out there somewhere, most likely looking for you," he said. "It would help if we knew what your sister had been doing and where she'd been leading up to this. Does Jenn keep a diary or journal?"

"No. She's not really the type to actually write anything down. Her cell phone is a different story. If we could find that then we'd get more of the picture of what's going on. She and her cell are inseparable." Jessica pinched the bridge of her nose to stave off a headache. "Where to next?"

"We need to find a good place to hide this limo and get back to our hotel to clean up and figure out our next move." Tyler pulled a business card out of his pocket. He handed the card and his cell to Jessica, temporarily steering with his left hand.

Annabeth Malloy, the hotel manager?

"Call her number and put the phone on speaker," he instructed.

A few seconds later the familiar voice was on the line.

"This is Tyler O'Brien—"

"Of course, Mr. O'Brien, how can I help you?"

"I'd like to enter through the service door. A society reporter's been bothering my friend and I and we'd like to shake him."

"No problem at all, sir," she said. "I'll make the arrangements and have someone waiting for you."

"Excellent. Much appreciated," he said. "There's one more thing, I'd like my limo safely stored until I need it again."

"Absolutely," she said confidently.

"Much obliged, ma'am."

Jessica got lost in her thoughts for the rest of the drive, rolling over the new information about her sister.

The service entrance was dead quiet and empty, not a soul in sight. The sticky humidity made Jessica want to shower all over again. Adrenaline had faded. She was tired and hungry. At least the air-conditioning in their suite evened out her temperature.

"I need to clean up." She disappeared into the bathroom, not wanting the cowboy to see the tears brimming in her eyes. The past day and a half had been surreal and a very real fear engulfed her every time she thought about her sister. Some people believed in twin telepathy and there were moments when Jessica did, too. Instances like this one, when she was overwhelmed with fear for her sister and she was sure something bad was happening.

"If we put our heads together, we'll figure out where your sister is," Tyler reassured her as she stepped out of the bathroom in fresh clothes. This time, she'd opted for a simple T-shirt and cotton shorts with running shoes. Her hair was thrown up in a ponytail; it kept her neck cooler that way.

She nodded but didn't say anything. What could she say? Her sister had never felt farther away.

"You could get away with calling yourself a college student dressed like that," Tyler said in an obvious attempt to change the subject. He seemed to pick up on her mood. "LSU isn't far and that look should help you blend in."

"Thank you. I think."

"It was meant as a compliment. Order whatever you want from room service. Would you mind asking them to send up a burger and a beer for me?"

"Not at all." In fact, both sounded really good right now.

"Thanks. I'll just be in there taking a cold shower." He seemed to realize the implication in that last part and he cracked a dry smile. "For that reason, too, but I need to wash the blood off me."

Jessica couldn't help but smile. For a wealthy guy, he was the most down-to-earth man she'd met. The images of the type of men her sister had dated paraded around in her head. She imagined flashy suits and designer casual wear. This cowboy was pretty much the polar opposite. And he looked damn good in his jeans and boots, so much better than those superficial types.

Normally, she'd notice more about the handsome cowboy, but all she could really focus on right now was Jenn. Besides, her thoughts were only more confused about Tyler after the couple of kisses they'd shared.

Jessica absently dialed room service and ordered dinner. The sun was going down and they still had no answers. Questions swirled. All they knew for sure was that her sister was in trouble, so nothing new there.

Tyler joined her fifteen minutes later, wearing only a pair of jeans that sat low on his hips. His rippled chest was tanned and muscled. Working on a ranch sure as heck did a body good because he had a six pack below solid steel pecs.

"Food should be here soon," she said, trying to force her eyes away from his chest. "And I'm not any closer to figuring out where my sister could be than I was this morning."

The couch dipped under Tyler's weight as he sat down next to her. She'd pulled a notepad and pen from on top of the nightstand and made a few scribbles on it. Mostly, the word *bayou* sat in the middle of the page and she'd circled it over and over again until it looked like one thick mass of wires.

"We just need one break. That's all. And we'll figure this whole thing out. What else do you remember about coming here with her?" the handsome cowboy asked, and no matter how many hours she spent with him she'd never get used to the sound of his voice. Its deep timbre stirred her somewhere low in her belly, and the flutter of a thousand butterflies rippled through her every time he spoke.

"She used to order in a lot when I visited. I didn't really think about it much before but I guess she didn't want to be seen with me." She wrote down the words *Big Beau*. "Do you think Elijah was just trying to throw us off?"

Tyler shrugged as the phone rang. They both looked at the land line.

"Could be the front desk," Jessica offered.

Tyler answered. "It's Zander. He's calling from a phone at the ER."

She heard very little from Tyler's end, which meant that Zander was doing all the talking. The instant Tyler hung up, she asked, "Is he okay?"

"He's doing fine. Said one of the bullets tapped his shoulder and the other grazed the inside of his arm and his ribs, missing anything that could cause serious damage. The doctor said he's very lucky." Tyler walked over to the couch and she couldn't help but admire his athletic grace. Basic biology had her evaluating whether or not he could protect her, given that they were in such dangerous circumstances. "They're treating and releasing him."

"That's the best news I've heard all day." She sighed with relief.

A knock sounded at the door. Tyler shot her a warning look. "Get out of sight until I give you a green light."

She moved into the bedroom and stood behind the door where she could see through the crack.

Tyler pulled a handgun, she wasn't sure what kind, and held it behind his leg as he opened the door with his left hand.

"Come on in," he said to the room service attendant.

The attendant wore a white sous chef shirt and black pants. He looked legit as he wheeled in the tray. "Would you like me to set up at the table, Mr. O'Brien?"

"No, thanks. Just leave it there." Tyler pointed next to the table. "I can take it from here."

He pulled a few bills from his pocket and tipped the attendant without revealing what was in his other hand. "Smells fantastic."

"Enjoy, sir," the waiter said with a smile.

Tyler closed the door behind him. "It's safe."

Even though the waiter was gone and the coast was clear, the tension stayed in the room. Jessica hated living like this, afraid of her own shadow. But her identity had been revealed and soon everyone would know that Jenn had a twin sister.

"What are you thinking about?" Tyler placed the gun securely in the side table.

"How they're not going to stop until they find me. They know about me now. Our advantage is gone."

He motioned for her to sit at the table, so she did. He put a plate in front of her and pulled off the metal cover to reveal the best-looking hamburger she'd ever seen. Or maybe she was just that hungry.

"I also ordered a fresh pot of coffee," she said. After

that adrenaline rush, the beer didn't sound as good as coffee. She didn't want anything to dull her senses and she was a lightweight when it came to alcohol.

He must've been thinking the same thing because he set the beers aside in an ice bucket. "I'll keep these cold for later."

By the time she took the last bite of her burger, Jessica had downed a bottled water. She poured a cup of coffee afterward. "Want one?"

"I can get it."

"I'm right here." She cocked her eyebrow. She hadn't noticed it with all the drama going on around them, but this cowboy seemed to prefer to do everything for himself. "I don't mind. Really."

"Don't go to any trouble."

"It's none at all." She poured a cup and handed it to him. "See how easy that was?"

He chuckled. "My parents taught us to be independent. We grew up working the ranch right alongside Pop. Mom spoiled us but pretended not to. She always said we were blessed and not spoiled. Either way she managed to bring up six independent boys. Although," he smiled, "some might call us stubborn."

"Sounds like you grew up in an ideal family."

"We did. And it ruined us. We all have a difficult time letting others in," he admitted and there was something dark in his eyes now. Regret?

"Doesn't sound like such a bad thing. The situation I'm in now reminds me to be even more careful who I trust," she said. "Even someone with the best of intentions can hurt you."

* * *

"Trust can be a good thing. When it's earned." Had he trusted Lyndsey too soon? He'd believed that she knew him and understood his priorities. And then she'd demanded that he walk away from the ranch forever if he wanted a future with her. She'd said their life was in Denver, where her family lived. Needless to say, being given an ultimatum had gone over about as well as filthy ranch clothes in church and begged the question, why would she demand something like that if she really knew him?

She'd walked out and the nagging question remained: How could he have loved someone he knew so little? Even so, when Lyndsey had left he didn't think he'd ever breathe again. Surprisingly, his body functioned even when he wasn't sure he wanted it to. Losing his parents at the same time had been a double blow.

Speaking of family, when this ordeal was over and Jessica was safe, he needed to touch base with his brothers and Tommy about the investigation back home. It was easy to set aside his pain and focus on someone else's problem for a change. Tyler had focused on his own until he'd gone numb. All he could think about was the note Lyndsey had left behind. *Enjoy your life and try to put someone else first for a change.*

For the past few weeks he'd tried to figure out if there was any truth to what she'd said. He'd dated around since Lyndsey, but it had felt like he was ticking a box, making sure he was playing the field.

Tyler could be honest enough with himself to admit that Lyndsey hadn't been completely first in his life. He chalked it up to their differences. She was outgoing and liked to hang out with friends at the bar after a long day. She was flirtatious and he'd almost convinced himself that he didn't mind. He was the complete opposite. Tyler kept more to himself, preferring to trust only those who shared the O'Brien last name.

And after a long day, he wanted a good meal and a cold beer under the stars. If there was a woman involved, then he could think of other things he wanted to do, as well…things that involved both of them naked.

There was something special about looking up at the night sky in Texas, the wide expanse of midnight blue with bright specks.

Lyndsey was most likely right. He probably needed to make more of an effort with people. He was good at negotiating and analyzing all sides of a business deal to come up with a fair solution and that's why he was in charge of handling contracts and disputes. He had managed a temporary truce between Aunt Bea and Uncle Ezra recently and that had taken some serious skills. But dealing with emotions, especially his own, wasn't his strong suit.

Enough focus on the things he didn't have the first idea how to fix.

Tyler needed to straighten out his thoughts about the current situation. "Let's go back to the beginning and think this through. Milton was one of your sister's exes, right?"

"Yes. She dated him for a short while last year but they stayed friends after, or so she thought." Jessica sat on the couch and folded her right leg underneath her bottom. She sipped her coffee and set the mug on the table.

"Is that the reason she figured he wouldn't catch on that you were subbing for her? He must not've known her very well," Tyler said.

"He didn't. Not really. But then my sister's personality has many layers. I'm not sure I know all of her. I never imagined she'd be in any kind of trouble like this and yet here we are. And then there's the affair."

"We now know that Elijah is involved," he said.

"Up to his eye teeth," she added.

"How close were the two of them?"

"I'm guessing he reminded her of home, barely scraping by," she said. "He must've felt familiar to her and helped her miss us less."

"I can't help but wonder how a musician and a corporate lawyer would know each other. It doesn't seem that they would travel in the same circles," he said. "Not to mention the fact that Milton couldn't possibly be currently practicing law with his criminal record."

"That's a good question. My sister is the only connection I can find. She never dated Elijah to my knowledge." Jessica sipped her coffee.

"But that doesn't mean he didn't have feelings for her."

"No. You're right. In fact, I'm pretty sure he did based on the way he looked at me before. There was no way she'd go out with him, though," Jessica's eyes lit up just then. Her eyes weren't the only thing he noticed. There were other things, endearing quirks about her that he liked. For example, the corner of her mouth twitched when she was nervous. The movement was so slight he almost missed it the first time. He'd also noticed that her tongue slicked across her bottom lip when she was about to lie. He'd seen that a few times when she spoke to Elijah and was grateful that she hadn't done it while talking to him.

Her laugh was almost like music and made him want to hear it more often. He vowed to himself to take her out to dinner when this was all behind them and make her laugh until her stomach hurt. Also, she blinked when she wasn't sure what to say next.

But the main thing he noticed was how sweet she tasted when he kissed her. And just how right she fit when he'd held her in his arms.

"I'm worried about the Brasseuxs." She sighed sharply. "And I feel like a hamster on a wheel. Every time I ask questions I go round again."

"I keep wondering what they and Elijah have in common. Or Milton, for that matter." Tyler stabbed his fingers through his thick hair. "I mean, the Brasseuxs could've had some interaction with Milton socially. But Elijah? I can't find a connection there."

"I know one," Jessica said.

Tyler arched a brow.

"My sister," Jessica said quietly. "What if she's not as innocent as I want to believe? What if she stole the necklace to get back at Ashton and then her so-called friend Elijah sees an opportunity to make some money off of her? Everything could've gone sour and she got herself in more trouble than she could handle."

"You don't really believe that, do you?" he asked.

"I don't want to, but that's where the evidence points," she said. "You know what? I'm tired. I need to get some rest."

Chapter 11

Jessica tossed and turned in her bed, unable to sleep for the nagging feeling that she was missing something important. She drifted in and out, straining to think. At three o'clock in the morning it finally dawned on her. She bolted upright and must've screamed because Tyler burst into the room a few seconds later.

"What happened?" he said, his low, sexy voice still gravelly from sleep. He rubbed his eyes and moved to the bed.

"I didn't mean to wake you," she said, forcing her eyes away from his muscled chest. This wasn't the time to think about those ripples of pure steel and how soft his skin felt to her touch. Or the warmth his body possessed.

"I'm a light sleeper." The mattress dipped under his weight. He had on boxers and nothing else.

"It came to me in a flash and I realized what I'd been missing. Do you have your smartphone?" she asked.

He jogged into the next room, returned a moment later and offered his cell to her.

She pulled up the internet and entered *The Bayou* into the search engine. Hope filled her chest for the first time. "It's an actual place. The Bayou. She said that she'd see me in the bayou, which I assumed was a general reference, except that there really is a place. She took me there the very first time I visited and never again. It was one of the only public places we went. It's really far on the outskirts of town. Actually, saying it's near any kind of civilization is being generous."

"What kind of place is it?" he asked.

"A hole-in-the-wall that only locals know about. See?" She shoved the phone toward him with an address highlighted on Google Maps. "It doesn't have a website, per se, but it's listed as a business. This is the address."

He took the phone and examined the web page. "This is a good place to start."

In her excitement at this first real lead, she launched herself toward Tyler and threw her arms around his neck. The covers pooled around her knees.

"This place looks…interesting to say the least. It's literally surrounded by a swamp." His free arm circled her waist.

Jessica realized all too quickly that her thin cotton tank top was the only thing standing between them. She started to pull back.

He dropped the phone on the bed next to her knees.

"Oh, no you don't," he said, hauling her against his chest. His other arm wrapped around her bottom.

Before she could talk herself out of it, she kissed him. With a quick maneuver, he had her on his lap, straddling him, and she could feel the warmth of his erection pulsing against the inside of her thigh. Jessica deepened the kiss. Tyler was all hotness and fire and manliness. His hands palmed her bottom. She liked the feel of him…real…and rough…and still so surprisingly gentle. She scooted closer until her heat was positioned against his straining rod. The thought of sex with Tyler sent a thunderclap of need pounding through her, making her stomach quiver.

His hands roamed her bottom as she pressed her almost-naked breasts flush against his chest.

A throaty, sexy growl tore from his throat and she could feel his muscles as they flexed. Their breath quickened as her hands searched down his back, lingering on each ripple, memorizing his strong lines.

And then five words she didn't want to acknowledge wound through her thoughts. *Is this a good idea?*

She barely knew the guy and yet she'd already trusted him with her life. And a certain intimacy had come out of that, which couldn't be denied. But did she really know him? Sure, the sexual tension between them was thicker than the Louisiana humidity. She had no doubt sex with Tyler would be amazing. And then what?

They were from two different worlds. He'd go back to his life on the ranch. She'd go back to hers in Shreveport, helping her parents and running the family business, which wasn't much but enough to keep them going financially. She couldn't imagine leaving them to fend for themselves.

Her brain cautioned her not to get ahead of herself. The future was a long way away. She had tonight. She was feeling the effects of an exciting breakthrough. And there was nothing wrong with mindless sex.

The idea of taking a breather when Jessica's skin flamed against his touch was almost unthinkable.

Except that he cared about her and they were stuck in a weird space between needing to blow off steam and needing to be with each other. The former was a no-brainer. That's where Tyler existed most of the time. The latter scared the hell out of him.

Calling on every ounce of strength he had, he forced himself to slow it down a few notches.

The other side of the coin was that he realized she'd been through a lot and most likely needed an outlet for her stress. While that would normally be right up Tyler's alley, for reasons he couldn't explain it bothered him with Jessica.

"This is not a good idea right now." He lifted her up and set her on the bed next to him, doing his level best to squash the disappointment roaring through his chest and the little voice in the back of his mind cursing him out. That was the same piece of brain that controlled everything south and he'd learned as a teenager not to listen if he wanted to stay out of trouble.

"Oh" was all she said, and he could hear the surprise and disappointment clearly in her tone.

"You're beautiful, don't get me wrong. But anything

happening between us is not going to work," he managed to say.

"It's okay. You don't have to spare my feelings." Her cheeks blushed and that ripped right through him.

Did she think he didn't want to have sex with her? How could he not? She had all the attributes he admired in a real woman. She was smart, had sexy curves and was damned near irresistible. In fact, if he didn't do something to cool his jets in the next minute or two he couldn't trust himself not to haul her into his arms again and take her right then and there on her bed. Before he went all caveman on her, he needed a cold shower. He'd explain later…when he figured it out for himself.

"We're going to talk about this, but not right now." He pointed at the phone. "First, we find your sister."

Before she could protest, he walked out of the room and straight into a cold shower.

If that didn't rank right up there as one of Jessica's most embarrassing moments in life, she didn't know what did. Clearly Tyler wanted her. There was no denying the erection she'd felt against the inside of her thigh. Was there something horribly wrong with her that he couldn't follow through on that desire? Maybe he'd finally realized what he was doing and decided to put a stop to it. Everything had happened so fast that Jessica got swept up in the moment. The attraction between them was real, but there was more to a relationship than physical pull. And he was right. They needed to focus on finding her sister.

Guilt washed over Jessica for losing focus. Jenn

needed her and she'd gotten momentarily wrapped up with the handsome cowboy.

Shaking it off, she dressed in jeans and a cotton shirt. Throwing her hair in a ponytail she tried not to focus too much on where they were going. There'd be mosquitoes in the swamp. Alligators. Bacteria. And all sorts of creatures eager to feed off human flesh and blood.

And if thinking about that didn't give her pause, nothing would.

Then there were the people themselves to contend with…people who preferred life off the grid with no cell service or contact with the outside world.

She took a fortifying breath and turned toward the living room. Tyler stood there, dressed and fresh from a shower, staring.

"Ready?"

"As much as I'll ever be," she said, thoroughly confused by the mixed signal.

He picked his phone up from the bed and made a call.

"Who are you calling in the middle of the night?" she asked, slipping on her running shoes. If she was going to hike through the swamps in the middle of the night, then she figured that she'd need to be comfortable.

"It's not safe to drive around in Zander's limo anymore. I'm arranging transportation," he said.

"Let's give our eyes a few minutes to acclimate to the darkness before we head out." Tyler adjusted the seat of the SUV that had been organized for him by the hotel manager. He didn't normally play that card, the one that had him waking up a hotel manager in the middle of the night, but this felt like a real lead and waiting until morning could be the difference between life and death for Jessica's sister.

He'd also arranged for a flashlight but he wanted some peripheral vision as they made their way through dense woods to The Bayou.

"How far is it from here?" she asked.

"About twenty minutes on foot." He'd parked off the highway near the gravel road leading to the place. Any lights on that road would give them away and he didn't want anyone to know they were coming. He had no idea if The Bayou was a safe place or not. Given its coordinates, he couldn't imagine that it was…this was a place people went to fly off the radar. He grabbed a package of bug repellent wipes out of the bag he'd arranged to have in the vehicle, opened one and held it out. "Rub this on any exposed skin, neck, arms."

She took the wipe and her fingers grazed his palm. Again he regretted not following through with sex earlier. He still couldn't figure out what was wrong with him. The tension between them was a distraction they couldn't afford and he half figured a rousing round in the sack would help with that problem. Maybe then he could fully concentrate on finding Jenn instead of thinking about the curve of Jessica's sweet bottom in his hands.

Tyler tore open a packet of bug repellant and wiped his arms and neck. The last thing he needed was a case of West Nile to take home, and he sure as hell could use a distraction from thinking about Jessica's backside.

"We'll go in dark, meaning I'll cut off the flashlight when we get near the clearing to the building. If we're lucky, everyone on the premises will be asleep. If we're not, there'll be dogs and people with guns who will wake up when they bark. Based on the Google Earth picture, it looks like the kind of place there'd be Dobermans or pit bulls. So, not only will we go in dark but we'll go in quiet."

His eyes were adjusting to the darkness and hers were huge with fear.

"You want to wait it out here?" he asked, his voice more curt than he'd intended.

Her reaction was immediate. "No. I'd do more good with you and I'm not sitting out here alone."

He silently cursed at himself for not being able to stop thinking about their encounter in the hotel room. "You know how to handle a gun?"

"They scare me to death."

"Well," he conceded, "then we'll find something else for you to—"

"But that doesn't mean I can't get over it," she interrupted. "I'm not *that* afraid and especially if it means getting my sister to safety or keeping one of us from getting shot."

She held out her flat palm and he could see her hand tremble in the light of the full moon. He had to hand it to her. She got extra points for bravery.

"The safety is on." He molded her fingers around the SIG Sauer. "It's important to get a good feel for how it fits."

She brought her other hand up and cupped the butt. "I got this."

"You gave me the impression this was the first time you'd touched a gun."

"I said that I was scared to death of them, and that

part's true, but my dad taught me how to shoot when I was twelve because he kept guns in the house."

"Was he a hunter?"

"No. We lived in a bad part of town and he wanted me to be ready in case he couldn't be around." She opened the magazine and checked the clip. "This should do but I'm hoping that I won't need to use it."

"Make sure it's aimed at someone besides me if you decide to shoot," he said, only half teasing. After his stunt back at the room she had to be angry with him. Heck, he was angry at himself. He still didn't know why a bout of conscience had come over him.

Taking a beautiful woman to bed didn't normally have him getting inside his head about not being in a relationship with her. *Damn, O'Brien.* He'd really loused that one up. If he got another chance with Jessica, and he was pretty sure that wasn't going to happen based on the wall she'd erected between them, he wouldn't waste it like he had the first time. But then second chances rarely happened in the real world. Tyler muttered a curse.

"What did you say?" she asked, looking at him oddly.

"Nothing." He hesitated. "Are you ready?"

"As much as I can be," she said softly, and her blatant honesty pierced his heart.

Yeah, he was going to live to regret his actions in the hotel. Because walking away from a woman with that much strength and beauty was going to be the end of him. But, hey, just like his short-lived baseball career and his last relationship had proved, everything had an expiration date.

Tyler tried to let this thing with Jessica roll off

his back, ignoring the fact that it had more staying power than a determined bull on rodeo day.

The sounds of a swamp in Louisiana at night were not something Jessica would ever get used to. There was a clicking sound to her right as she navigated the dense forest of live oak. Everything sounded alive, even the trees, and more awake than in daylight. Something rustled in the undergrowth a little too close for comfort and her heart skittered as she stepped over gnarled roots.

Crickets chirped, her skin crawled and the sound of footsteps slogging through muddy water sent her pulse racing. This was home of the alligator.

Owls hooted in surround sound and she could tell they were literally all around her as she stepped in the marsh. Something moved underneath her shoe. She bit back a scream and reached for Tyler.

He positioned her beside him and she kept her gaze focused on the light beam that hit a tree and then bounced to the ground and back. Step by step she held her breath, trying not to focus on the chorus of insects. Heaven only knew what other creatures were lurking in the dark. She couldn't help but check for a set of eyes as the light skimmed the deeper water right next to them and she prayed they wouldn't end up waist deep as they trudged along.

Who in their right mind would come out this far from the city and into this unknown? If her sister had been taken, and Jessica was fairly certain that was the case, then this would be the perfect place to dispose of a body.

Focusing on the worst-case scenario wouldn't help their investigation or her mood, so she did her best to shove those thoughts aside as she plucked her heel from the slick soil. It was impossible to move through the vegetation without making a sound. Every time she stepped, it was as if the ground refused to let go.

Tyler squeezed her hand and stopped. The light from the flashlight disappeared, plunging them into utter darkness.

Jessica's heart beat in her throat as she took a tentative step forward. Trust wasn't her strong suit but desperation had her willing to do pretty much anything to find her sister. The total blackness ignited her claustrophobia and if it wasn't for Tyler she would've had to stop right there and turn around.

If Jenn had been on her own she'd have called. There was no doubt about that in Jessica's mind. It had been two days since her sister had gone silent. A lot could happen in forty-eight hours.

Her eyes adjusted to the darkness enough to see outlines by the time the trees thinned. She counted three sheds and her sister could be in any one of them. Then there was the main building, a relatively small two-story structure with a handmade sign on the porch that read The Bayou in big white letters on what appeared to be a large piece of driftwood. That was about the only thing she could see clearly because the trees around the house formed a canopy in the swamp making it impossible for light from the moon to shine through.

Two vehicles were parked in back, an old Toyota pickup truck and a Volkswagen van that looked like a relic from the sixties. Thankfully, there were no dogs on the premises or Jessica and Tyler's presence would already be known.

Tyler squatted down behind the Volkswagen and motioned for Jessica to come over. He flashed the light. The license plate on the VW read, Big Beau.

Jessica tried to wrap her mind around what this could mean. Her sister had mentioned The Bayou and then Elijah had referred to Big Beau. This had to be the place.

This could be a trap, a little voice said. Maybe she was right where Elijah wanted her.

Did that mean that Jenn was here somewhere?

Was this some kind of headquarters or meeting place for the group who was after the Infinity Sapphire?

A hand covered Jessica's mouth. Before she could scream she was dragged backward. She spun around out of her assailant's grasp, landed facedown and fumbled for the SIG Sauer she'd dropped in the struggle.

"Shhh. Don't scream. I'm here to help you and your sister. Don't say a word," the unfamiliar deep male voice said.

Tyler was there in the next beat, his gun at the man's temple. "Where do you think you're going with her?"

"Stay calm and we'll all get out of here alive," the man said.

From her vantage point, Tyler seemed the one in charge so it was bold of this guy to give orders. Her hand skimmed the surface of the ground until landing on her gun. She picked it up, sat up and pointed it directly at the male figure.

"I'm Big Beau. And if you want to know where your sister is, you'll keep quiet. We need to get out of here right now. If they know I'm talking to you I'll end up floating in that swamp. If the gators don't haul me off, the mosquitoes will."

"I have a car nearby," Tyler whispered.

She wasn't sure how Tyler knew to trust the guy. She had her own doubts, but desperation had her ready to do almost anything to find Jenn.

"Let's go before somebody wakes," Big Beau said. The guy was huge. Tyler was somewhere around six foot four so he was significantly taller, but Big Beau had the belly of a grizzly bear.

"Not so fast." Tyler patted the guy down to check for a weapon as Jessica scrambled to her feet.

"You won't find anything on me. I left my AR15 inside and there's more where that came from. But if you're smart, you'll move it along. If we wake anyone up or they know I'm helping you, I'm dead. And so is Jenn."

Chapter 12

At the SUV, Tyler kept his gun leveled at Big Beau. Getting a closer look at him Jessica saw what a big, burly man he was. A patchwork of scruff covered parts of his jaw and neck. He wore a flannel shirt with the sleeves cut off. His eyes were pale blue, his hair dirty blond. Jeans rode low on his hips, tucked underneath a pot belly.

"I know what you're thinking and I ain't like them others," he said, holding his right hand toward Tyler as if it could stop a bullet.

"Prove it," Tyler shot back, keeping his gun aimed at the big guy. "Tell us where she is."

"She ain't far. Unless they've moved her."

"Who has her?" Jessica asked defensively.

"It's complicated but I remember you from the first time your sister brought you here," he said.

"How? That was so long ago. I don't remember you at all," she said honestly.

Big Beau held back a laugh. "Your sister came out here and talked about you all the time since then. I hoped you'd figure out she was in trouble and come see me."

"If that's true, then why doesn't anyone else know me?" She seriously doubted Jenn spoke about her to anyone.

He rolled his big shoulders in a shrug. "Reckon she had her reasons. She never talked about you where anyone else could hear and always asked me to keep it a secret."

"Because she was ashamed of me," Jessica said quietly. Then she glanced up apologetically. She hadn't intended to say that out loud.

"Ashamed?" He shook his head. "Proud's more like it. She went on and on about how smart you are and what a success you've made out of your family's business to help your parents."

"I had no idea she felt that way." True, she had expanded the cleaning business from houses to office buildings so her mother wouldn't have to do the heavy lifting anymore. And she'd hired two dozen workers, jobs she was happy to provide to people in order to boost the local economy.

Big Beau looked like he was examining Jessica and it made her uncomfortable. "I'm sorry for staring, but you two look so much alike. I'm surprised at how different you think or that you don't know how proud she is of you. She talks about you like you walk on water."

"Me and my sister have always been close but I didn't

know." Jessica wiped an errant tear as it rolled down her cheek. She'd always loved her sister and had known on some level that Jenn loved her as much, but hearing that her sister was proud of her overwhelmed her with emotion.

"Jenn used to say all she had to work with was her looks," Big Beau continued. "And that she had to play her cards right or she'd end up with nothing. But you... she thought you hung the moon."

Jessica couldn't stop the sob that tore from her throat. Tyler moved to her side and put his arm around her protectively.

"I'm fine." She ignored the confused look on Tyler's face as she sidestepped out of reach. "Really. It's just very sweet to hear and my sister's in trouble. I let my emotions get the best of me but I'm good now."

Tyler eyed her up and down, clearly not convinced, but not ready to push the envelope either.

"Why didn't you do anything to help her?" she asked Big Beau, needing to redirect the conversation to something more productive.

"It ain't right how they're setting her up to look like she stole that necklace. They plan to kill her as soon as they get hold of it and make it look like suicide. As far as helping her, that's what I'm trying to do right now."

"She's innocent?" Jessica knew she shouldn't sound so surprised. She wanted to believe in her sister, but after learning about the affair, it was hard. "Who's behind this?"

She was so close that he could reach out and grab her if he wanted, but she didn't care.

"Ashton Brasseux. But now that Randall Beauchamp's involved it's a mess," Beau said, and turned toward Tyler. "She's my friend and I wouldn't do anything to hurt her. My family don't feel the same way. Everyone's afraid of Mr. Beauchamp so they do whatever he asks. They don't have no trouble with her personally but he said to find her, so they did."

"What's Beauchamp's involvement in this?" Tyler asked.

Big Beau shrugged. "All I know is he has a buyer for that stolen necklace and now that it's gone missing he'll do anything to get it back."

"Is she hurt?" Jessica asked Big Beau. "Did he do anything to her?"

"I can tell you where I believe he's keeping her, but that's as far as I can go. I have no idea what shape she's in. My guess is not good. If he knows anyone from my family helped you out he'll have us all fed to the gators." Big Beau shivered.

"But she's alive?" Jessica could barely ask the question.

"She was last I heard," he said honestly. "No way was she involved in this. Ashton used her."

That made a lot of sense.

"You can trust us. No one will know the information came from you," Tyler promised.

Big Beau half smiled and nodded. "My life depends on it."

"Why are you helping us?" Jessica asked.

"Your sister's a good kid." Big Beau's face broke into a smile talking about Jenn. She had that effect on people, and especially men. She was charming and beautiful, but there was something else about her that drew people to her. "She don't mean nobody harm. It's a shame what's happened to her and it's even worse that my family's to blame. I'll give you the address where we took her."

Big Beau relayed the coordinates of a place he said was in town.

"Elijah told us about you. He was trying to set a trap for us, wasn't he?" Jessica asked.

"He doesn't know Jenn and I are close, so I figure he thought he was sending you to your demise. Nobody's going to find out you were here from me," Big Beau said. "Unless the gators start talking, I reckon no one will ever know."

He winked.

"Thank you." Jessica hugged Big Beau. Not because he would cover their tracks but because he cared about Jenn and had opened Jessica's eyes to a whole new side to her sister. Jenn had always come across as so confident, letting everything roll off her. Inside, she was far more fragile than Jessica realized and she wanted to protect her sister.

He seemed taken back by the gesture and stiffened. "Go on, now. Find Jenn and get her out of the state until this whole mess settles down."

"Do you know James Milton?" she asked.

"He that no-good lawyer she messed with last year?" Big Beau asked.

"He tried to kill me when he thought I was Jenn," she supplied.

"I reckon lots of folks want to get their hands on that missing necklace," Big Beau said, his anger evident on his face. "That's a stupid move, though. Everyone knows Beauchamp wants it."

"I thought he might be working for him."

"Doubt it. He could be trying to get in his good graces, though," Big Beau said. "Or pay off a debt."

"He's a gambler," she said, remembering the news they'd received from the sheriff.

"Well then, he might be trying to get himself out of trouble," Big Beau said.

"My sister sent me with him as a distraction. She wanted him out of town. You know anything about that?" she asked.

"Sure don't."

"What else do you know about my sister?"

"Not much. She liked to mix with men who wore shiny shoes and fine suits. Most of them hang in the same crowd and do a little too much sharing. She didn't like to be reminded that she was really just one of us," Big Beau said. "A man with shiny shoes usually has a slick tongue in my experience."

Jenn must've liked having some reminders of her past because she'd made friends with Big Beau. Jessica was less trustful of men in general and rich men in particular. She'd seen the way prominent men manipulated others. That was half the reason she stuck around to run the business she'd grown with her mother. Greed was powerful and she'd seen the damage firsthand.

"I best get back," Big Beau said. "Be careful who you trust. Folks around here have a way of knowing each other. Families, connections, they sometimes make no sense but go way back."

"We will," Jessica reassured him, as if she needed

to be reminded there was no one she trusted besides Tyler and Big Beau.

Tyler set the coordinates in his phone as Jessica started toward the side of the SUV. She turned around to thank Big Beau once again but he wasn't there. He'd already disappeared into the bush. The thought of making that journey again sent a shiver down Jessica's spine.

Tyler had been expecting another place near the swamps and was shocked when he pulled into an upscale family suburb with rows of white colonials. If Jenn was here, she was being held in plain sight.

"You sure this is the right area?" Red asked, echoing his sentiments.

"These are the coordinates." Tyler motioned to his phone, which had been giving the directions aloud.

Tyler's ringtone sounded. He pulled to the side of the road, turned off his lights and kept the engine idling. He glanced at the screen. "It's my brother, Austin." He answered the call. "Yo, what's up, Ivy League?" His second oldest brother had gone to college in the northeast, earning the nickname.

"Russ called me because you didn't show up this morning," Austin said. His voice sounded as though he'd only been awake a few minutes. "Everything okay?"

Damn. Tyler had meant to touch base at the ranch and ask someone to cover his area for the next few days. "Yeah, fine. Had a last-minute trip. Personal business."

"Lyndsey?"

An awkward tension filled the cab of the SUV. "No. That's long finished."

"You sure about that?" Austin pressed.

Now was not the time to discuss her.

"Positive. That the only reason you called?" Tyler didn't mean to sound defensive.

"Can a man check on his favorite brother?" Austin scoffed, his sense of humor intact. "This is what happens when people wake me up before the sun comes out, by the way."

Tyler chuckled. Austin was no early riser. "Yeah. I'm good, though. No need to worry about me."

"Then I won't stress about the stranger who's been asking around in town for Tyler O'Brien," Austin said.

"You catch a name?" Tyler asked as Jessica shot him a concerned look.

"All I know is Tommy called and said you were helping out a woman who was in trouble. Next thing I know a stranger is looking for you and you're not showing up to work, which I don't have to say is unlike you," Austin said, more than a hint of curiosity in his tone.

"Janis didn't tell you that I'm out of town?" Tyler asked, thankful he'd remembered to talk to her. He wanted to tell his brother what was going on but needed to speak to Jessica about it first.

"It must've slipped her mind," Austin said.

"In her defense, I called after I left and never said I'd be gone long."

"Give Tommy a call when you can. He didn't sound himself," Austin said.

"I plan to touch base with him after breakfast." It wasn't a lie, even though Jessica shot him a cross look. She couldn't object to him bringing in Tommy after they found Jenn. Jessica's concern so far had been that whoever had her sister would kill her if the cops were chasing them. No one would get rid of her until they had that jewel.

"You hear about the Infinity Sapphire going missing?" Austin asked.

A pleading look came from the passenger seat. Jessica's hands folded into prayer position.

"I read something about it the other day." Playing dumb would only make Austin suspicious. He knew that Tyler read the newspaper every day, just as he did. They'd also had the Brasseuxs at the ranch, so Tyler would notice a story about the prominent family.

"I wondered about the Brasseuxs after the gala," Austin said.

"You did?" Tyler was shocked. He hadn't heard anything and his brother had been quiet up until now.

"I overheard him telling his wife that her spending was out of control," Austin said. "And then her necklace worth millions goes missing a couple months later."

"You think he was involved in an insurance scam?" Tyler wasn't sure if he should tell his brother that the Brasseuxs might be in trouble, but he was certain about that call to Tommy later. Maybe his friend had dug up more information.

"Who knows? The only thing I'm sure of is crossing them off the list for next year's gala." Austin chuckled and then paused when he didn't hear Tyler do the same.

Right. His comment was meant to be funny.

"You sure everything's okay?" Austin asked.

"Yeah. Why wouldn't it be?" Tyler tried to laugh it off. It was too much, too late but Austin didn't press.

"Get in touch with Tommy later. You have any idea when you'll be back at the ranch?" Austin asked.

"Couple of days should be enough to tie up a few loose ends here," Tyler said.

"I'll let everyone know." Austin paused. "Take care of yourself, brother. And call when you're ready to talk about it."

"I will." Tyler didn't like holding back from his family and the secrets were racking up. He ended the call and looked to Jessica. "Might be better to park here and walk to the end of the block."

The neighborhood had decent-sized yards and plenty of trees.

"Okay," Jessica said. She made a move for the door handle but stopped. "I'm sorry that you're lying to your family for me. I can tell how much it bothers you."

"It's—"

"Don't say that it's okay." Her hand came up in protest. "Because it's not fine for you to be dishonest with the people you love."

"I'd argue, but you're right. Austin understands and I didn't fool him for a second." He looked her in the eye. "And I need to make that call to Tommy later this morning. Right after we find your sister. I've thought this through and there's no reason not to tell him what's going on."

He really looked at her, expecting an argument.

"You're right. I want you to contact him as soon as we get my sister to safety," she said.

"He has no jurisdiction here, so whatever we're about to get ourselves into we're on our own anyway."

She nodded and brushed her hand against his arm.

"Thank you for taking this risk for my family. If you want out, though, I'd totally understand."

"We've come too far for me to walk away now." He was rewarded with a small smile—it was sweet and sexy at the same time.

There was very little security at the house. Tyler didn't want to tell Jessica his real fear, that none was necessary because Jenn wasn't perceived as a threat. She would be immobilized and he had no idea what physical condition she'd be in when they found her. He was prepared to carry her over his shoulder for the mile and a half walk to his SUV if that's what it took.

The sun would be up soon, so they had to move fast.

Tyler wished there was a way to prepare Jessica, to soften the blow of seeing her sister in such a vulnerable state as they closed the distance between the tree line and the house.

They could go in through the raised basement. Tyler pulled his gun and motioned for Jessica to do the same. He walked policeman-style, gun and flashlight drawn, down a half dozen stairs.

The door was locked but he'd had enough experience with barn doors to figure out how to pick it.

Inside, the place was dark and dingy, and the floor slanted downward, resulting in water pooling in one corner of the space. Tyler immediately looked for alternate exits in case the cellar door was no longer an option. An old wall that divided the space was half-torn down. The stairs leading to the main floor were old and wooden. There would be people up there. They couldn't go out that way.

Tyler scanned the room for any signs of life. A

woman sat crumpled over in a corner of the room. Her head was slumped to one side, her neck at an odd angle and for a split second Tyler feared the worst.

Jessica let out a little gasp before seeming to catch herself and going silent as she hurried over. She dropped down next to the woman and cradled her face. "Jenn."

Chapter 13

Tyler took a knee on the other side of Jenn and checked for a pulse. Relief washed over him when he got one. "She's alive."

Jenn's eyes fluttered open and she immediately drew back. A cut ran down the side of her left cheek and her right eye was swollen and bruised.

"Don't be scared. It's me. I'm taking you home," Jessica said soothingly.

It took a minute for Jenn's eyes to focus, but when they did she scrambled toward Jessica, hugging her sister around the neck. She was aware and that was a good thing.

Tyler glanced around the room. He was a little surprised they'd left her alone in the basement. The lock on the cellar door had been easy enough to pick. This was an upper class suburban neighborhood and they must not figure that anyone would tie this place to criminal activity. It was the kind of place where he half expected to find a grandma upstairs, having risen early and gathered vegetables to begin preparing the roux that would cook all day until used in a dish such as crawfish étouffée for supper.

"I'm going to pick you up and take you out of here," Tyler said.

Jenn pulled back, fearful, and shook her head. Her lips were dry, cracked and he wondered how long it had been since she'd had water. Getting her hydrated would be his first priority as soon as he got her out of there.

"It's okay, sweetie. This is my friend and he's here to help," Jessica said, her voice rising in panic. "What's wrong?"

Jenn shifted her position to reveal her ankles. Her feet had been tucked underneath her bottom so they'd missed the thick ropes around her ankles. Tyler followed the bindings to a three-inch PVC pipe climbing up the wall that disappeared into a hole in the ceiling. He pulled out his cell.

"What are you doing?" Jessica asked, placing her hand on his arm.

"Calling the police."

Jenn shook her head again and Tyler stopped, his finger hovering over the nine.

"I have no choice. I can't take a chance and I sure as hell can't leave you like this. We make any noise down here and I guarantee the room will fill with more men with guns than you can shake a stick at. What else do you think we should do?" he asked.

"I loved him," Jenn managed to say, her voice raspy

and she sounded so tired. "Get the necklace. Keep it safe."

"Or we get you out of here, find the necklace together, and then go to police," Tyler said, using a tone that said he was done talking.

"No police. Not yet," Jenn insisted. "Not while it looks like I did this. Who would believe that I'm innocent?"

She had a good point. Currently, evidence pointed directly at her involvement.

"The truth will come out," Jessica soothed her sister. She was putting up a brave front but it was clear to Tyler that she was fighting to keep her emotions in check. "All anyone would have to do is look at you to know you're innocent."

"I go to the police and I'm dead," Jenn said, and it looked like it took an incredible amount of effort to speak.

Her statement was true and he couldn't deny it. She was afraid for good reason. Tyler tucked his phone into his pocket.

"Then we find a way to get you out of here and figure this out," Jessica said emphatically, obviously not wanting to upset her sister with the information about Elijah and Milton. "But I am not leaving you here. Do you understand me? I won't do it."

Tyler slid his arm around Jessica's waist, trying to soothe her.

She smiled up at him and then scooted closer to her sister and out of his reach.

"Where's Ashton?" Jenn whispered. It was barely loud enough for Tyler to hear.

"I don't know," Jessica said.

Tyler searched the space for something he could use to cut the rope. Seeing Jenn like this, defenseless and in a basement, he understood why they didn't think they'd need security and this was just what he'd feared. They were hiding her in plain sight and were confident… too confident?

Even so, the move was pretty brilliant if anyone asked Tyler, and he'd have to keep that in mind moving forward. These guys were clever career criminals and neither Jenn nor Jessica would be safe until those men were locked behind bars.

There was nothing around to use to free Jenn. The sun would be up soon. That meant someone would most likely be down to check on her.

Old houses were notorious for having pipes that ran nowhere. Was it possible that the PVC pipe she was attached to would be the same? He stood and ran his fingers as high as he could reach on the PVC pipe. The ceiling wasn't more than seven feet high so he could reach fairly far into the ceiling. He curled his index finger around the end of the pipe. Jackpot.

Tyler twisted the pipe but it wouldn't budge. There was probably twenty years of grime holding it together. He clamped his back teeth together and gave another twist, netting a little movement this time. Digging deep, he squeezed the pipe and turned. This time, it gave. He pulled apart the pipes by threading one through the ceiling. They could worry about the ropes later. His first priority was getting her out of there. He scooped her off the floor and raced toward the cellar door.

Jessica went first, pushing through the door and into the beginnings of sunlight.

Two men in an SUV with dark windows burst from the vehicle. Tyler cursed and he heard Jessica do the same. They must've been reporting to work because they hadn't been there fifteen minutes ago.

"Run and keep running. No matter what happens," he said, figuring they still had a chance if Jessica could get away. She would have to call the police then. Of course, with criminals this smart, he and Jenn would be hidden in a new location.

Tyler had no intention of going down without a fight.

"Stop," one of the men shouted.

Tyler didn't look back. He ran on burning legs. At this distance, the men would have to be spot-on shots to hit him, although he liked his odds less since he was a good-sized target. Once he got to the trees, *if* he got to the trees, it would be even more difficult for them to get off an accurate shot. They could circle back to their SUV once they got away from the men. Try running there now and the men would catch them before they could get Jenn inside.

He could get to the trees, but then what? If he could set Jenn down, turn around and pull out his gun in time then maybe he could hold them off.

Carrying roughly a hundred and twenty pounds of woman put him at a distinct disadvantage. He chanced a glance behind. The men were closing in fast.

The trees were too far and he realized that there was no way he was going to make it in time. Either of the men could stop and fire at this point and have a good chance at hitting him. His best guess as to why they hadn't fired already was that they wanted Jenn alive because they assumed she knew where the necklace was hidden.

All his and Jessica's efforts to save Jenn wouldn't matter the second these guys caught up with them. He couldn't outrun them and he could hear their footsteps closing in.

The next second, Jessica spun around with her gun leveled. "Duck."

Tyler dropped to the ground, holding on to Jenn, whose arms were wrapped so tightly around his neck she was almost cutting off his ability to breathe.

A bullet split the air, Jenn screamed and Tyler half feared she'd been shot by mistake. He looked behind him to see the men had scattered in the opposite direction, running for cover. His chest shouldn't fill with pride for Jessica's quick thinking but it did. And he was darn grateful she wasn't a lousy shot or he might've ended up with a bullet in his skull.

He popped to his feet and blazed past her. "Let's go."

Only when they were deep in the woods and there was no sign of pursuit did he feel it was safe to stop and catch his breath. "Way to think on your feet back there."

Jessica smiled and it quickly faded as she put her arm around her sister. "I can't take her home. That's the first place they'll look. I have to figure out a way to warn our parents without telling them what's going on. And we need to stay out of sight until we sort this out."

Tyler waited for his breathing to slow before talking. "I can make sure your family is safe. I'll send someone to pick them up and take them away for an extended vacation. And I have the perfect place to hide while we figure this out. There are blind spots on my ranch and I know just where they are. We can pitch a tent on my land and stay under the radar."

"She's too weak and she needs medical care," Jessica said. "And these guys won't let up."

"I have other plans for her and those men with guns are exactly the reason we need to find a place to hunker down for a few days and give her time to recoup. She needs medical care and I know where she can get it and still be safe." He examined the cut on Jenn's face. "All the wounds are superficial so they'll heal quickly as long as there's no infection. In the meantime, I'd put money on the fact that necklace has to be somewhere in Texas and I'm betting it's near Bluff."

"Of course, that's why Milton believed me and took me there," Jessica said. "I guess he figured he'd get me to tell him where it was and then he'd take it back himself. And then he could collect a reward from Mr. Beauchamp or use it to get in his good graces."

"Gambling" was all Jenn managed to say. She needed water, food and a day's worth of rest before she could say much more. Nearly three days of who knew what conditions she'd been in other than the basement. The only good news was that she seemed otherwise healthy and should bounce back given a little time to recoup.

"What did you say?" Jessica asked, leaning closer.

"She said gambling. I'm guessing Milton's trouble had to do with a betting addiction," Tyler said.

Jenn nodded.

"But you didn't think he'd turn on you," Tyler clarified.

"No." A look of horror crossed Jenn's weary features as she looked at her sister. "I would never have—"

"I know. Don't try to talk right now. It's okay," Jessica soothed. "I know you would never put me in danger on purpose."

"We need to stay on the move," Tyler said as he moved toward Jenn. "And get her into the SUV."

He scooped her up and she wrapped her arms around his neck again. He'd rather go straight to Tommy than to the ranch. There was no doubt that Tyler could trust his longtime family friend. Jessica and Jenn seemed to have other ideas. He needed to help them see the light.

So far the only thing the three of them agreed on was getting Jenn out of the state and keeping her off the radar while she gained her strength. But Tyler had every intention of calling his friend. Jessica had greenlighted the connection before and nothing in their present circumstance changed his mind.

The flight home was smooth as the morning sun settled in the sky. Jessica was grateful to have her sister back. During the flight she'd racked her brain to put the pieces together. Milton had obviously been in some kind of gambling trouble and when Jessica couldn't deliver the necklace, he'd tried to kill her, believing her to be Jenn.

Jessica had an endless list of questions…would Elijah realize Big Beau had allegiance to Jenn now that she'd escaped? Elijah had figured Jessica out. But who stole the necklace in the first place?

Everyone seemed to believe that Jenn knew where this multi-million-dollar necklace was, but she was too weak to talk. Answers would have to wait until she was hydrated and feeling better.

"Checked the weather in Bluff before we took off," Tyler said, interrupting her hamster-wheel of questions. "It should be in the low sixties for the next few days. Perfect camping weather."

Images of the last time she was on his land flashed through her thoughts. Of turning to find Milton standing there, rock in hand, ready to bash her head in. That image was burned into her brain.

After settling the airplane in the hanger, Tyler helped Jenn into the backseat of his SUV. She was moving a little better now that he'd removed the ropes from her ankles. He'd given her ibuprofen and water from his emergency kit and Jenn had slept during the flight home.

Jessica was grateful for Tyler. She couldn't imagine doing any of this alone—and yet hadn't she been alone her entire life? Sure, she'd had her sister and her parents, all people who leaned on her, but who did she have to depend on?

Without the Texas cowboy she had no idea where she would've ended up. Dead, she thought. She would've died if she'd been left underneath that ATV. A wild animal would've gotten to her or she would've wandered around on the property, lost, until she succumbed to dehydration or, if she'd survived long enough, starvation. The important thing was that she and Jenn were together and her sister would be okay.

Tyler took a call, walking around to the back of his SUV out of earshot. A pang of jealousy tore through her, which was silly. She had no designs on the cowboy, even though the few kisses they'd shared in the past twenty-four hours had left a piece of her thinking otherwise.

Dating hadn't been a priority of late and especially since Brent. It was more than his infidelity that pierced her chest. It was the fact that she'd so easily given her trust to him, and how willingly he'd stomped all over it. Was she that bad a judge of character?

It would seem so, because she'd misjudged her sister, as well. It had taken a stranger, Big Beau, to tell Jessica what she really meant to Jenn.

How strange was that?

"That was my brother Dallas. Someone in a suit is still asking around for me in town," Tyler said, rounding the SUV to where she was sitting in the passenger seat with the door open.

"Why would they want you?" Then it must've dawned on her. "They must've figured out that you were helping me."

"When your sister wakes up, we need to talk to her."

"Do you think she'll be safe with us?" she asked. "I'm worried about her. She's been mumbling something and I think she's out of it."

"I was planning to call Dr. McConnell to have Jenn examined. We could check her into the hospital under a fake name. I can send security to keep an eye on her 24/7 while we continue to investigate. I'm certain the doc will accommodate us without asking a lot of questions."

Jessica chewed on that thought for a minute. She liked the idea of having her sister in a facility where she could be properly cared for. Looking at her in this condition was a cause for serious stress. Would Jenn fight them on it? Could she? As it was, she could barely lift her head and her ramblings were becoming more frequent and less distinguishable.

"She'll get well faster in a place she can be looked after properly," he said with a convincing look.

"Okay. Let's do that. If we can get her to agree," she said.

"Her eyes have barely opened since Baton Rouge. I doubt she has any fight left inside her." Tyler had a point. He walked away, presumably to give her time to think about it.

Jessica looked in the backseat. Her sister was resting comfortably but she needed medical care in order to get better. What if infection set in or she was bleeding internally? She already favored her right side, moving carefully as if one of her ribs was broken. She needed X-rays and an IV.

But that would mean leaving her in the hospital.

The thought of not staying with Jenn hit Jessica like a two-by-four to the chest. But what choice did she have? It wasn't like Jenn was waking up. She could have a concussion or worse. Even though Jessica couldn't imagine walking away from her sister, she wouldn't deny her medical service or put her in danger because of her selfishness.

Fighting tears, she walked over to where Tyler stood forty feet away. No way was she going to let the handsome cowboy see her cry again. This was the right thing to do for her sister. "Signing my sister into the hospital under an assumed name is the best way to go. Can you arrange it?"

Tyler took her hand in his and tugged her toward him. She leaned into his strong chest and he wrapped his arms around her. And in that moment, crazy as it might sound, she felt safe.

"You're making the right call. She'll be well cared for in the hospital and it's the last place Milton or anyone else will look since you've already been there."

She nodded. "Plain sight."

"That's right," Tyler said. "I'll call Dr. McConnell and set everything up."

Jessica wiped a rogue tear. "It's hard to see her like this. She's normally so strong and willful."

"We'll get her the care she needs and you'll be back to your twin antics in a few days," he said, an obvious attempt to make her smile.

It worked.

Chapter 14

Tyler pulled off the highway and then around the back of the Quick Gas Auto Mart on the outskirts of town where an ambulance waited. Dr. McConnell had insisted this would be the best and safest way to transport Jenn to the hospital, and he figured she was right on both counts.

Jenn could begin receiving fluids immediately and, given that she was severely dehydrated, that should make a big difference in her general health. Glancing at Jessica as he parked had him wondering if she would be able to walk away from her sister. Agony darkened her features and she was chewing on her thumbnail.

"They're going to take good care of Jenn and the doc said she'd call the minute your sister wakes up and is ready to talk," he said to reassure her, hoping she wouldn't change her mind at the last minute.

"You're right," she conceded. "It's just hard to leave her again."

Tyler waved the EMTs over. Andy and Shanks greeted Tyler as they went right to work helping Jenn out of the SUV and positioning her on the gurney.

Jessica was at her sister's side as Jenn's eyes fluttered open again.

"You're going to the hospital," Jessica said.

Jenn barely nodded.

"Everything's going to be okay and I'll see you very soon," Jessica reassured, rubbing her sister's arm.

Jenn opened her mouth to speak but looked as though she lost the energy. She took in a ragged breath and mouthed, *Love you*.

"Love you," Jessica parroted.

"We'll take good care of her, man, I promise," Shanks said to Tyler, looking from Jessica to Jenn. Tyler could almost see the question mark in his mind at the resemblance between the two.

Tyler patted Shanks on the back. "I know you will. And we'd appreciate it if you kept my involvement between us for now. In fact, if you could keep quiet about this whole thing."

"Doc mentioned something about this being tied to a criminal case and her being a witness, but that's all she could say." Andy's eyes got wide and sparkly with excitement. He lowered his tone when he said, "Is she going into the witness protection program or something?"

"I'd like to tell you more but I'm sworn to silence," Tyler said, trying to sound disappointed. He didn't want to quell Andy's excitement, and figured his response would serve as a good reminder of how top secret this had to be.

"Right-o." Andy nodded and wheeled the gurney to the back of the ambulance with a satisfied smile.

As soon as Jenn was out of sight, tears started rolling down Jessica's face. Tyler glanced around, feeling exposed in their current location. He hugged her before ushering her into the SUV.

"Why do I feel like I'm never going to see her again?" Jessica said, wiping the tears from her face as she apologized. "I'm sorry. I'm not usually a crier."

"Never say you're sorry for showing your emotions," he said. Tyler had been an expert at stuffing his below the surface for too many years.

"I've always been the strong one, you know. It's why my sister always comes to me and this makes me feel weak." She motioned toward a rogue tear sliding down her cheek.

"Crying doesn't make you any less strong. Tears are just saltwater. The ocean is filled with it and that doesn't take away from its magnitude. Real strength means pushing through your boundaries when you're afraid and never giving up. Trust me when I say you have that in spades."

She smiled through red-rimmed eyes. "Thank you."

Tyler started the engine and navigated onto the highway, heading home. His heart fisted in his chest. He was in trouble. And this time, going home had a new meaning. Rather than rack his brain trying to crack that nut, he fisted the steering wheel and focused on something that made sense...the road in front of him.

"You're quiet all of a sudden," Jessica said.

"I just have a lot on my mind." It was partially true. Tyler couldn't stop thinking about Jessica and wasn't it his trick to shut down emotionally when he got close to someone or something he wanted? But then he hadn't wanted anything like he wanted her in his life and it confused the hell out of him.

Another thing he didn't want to think about right then.

Tyler decided to take her to the easternmost tip of the property, furthest from his house, where people would least expect him to be. His SUV was made for off-roading and he'd need it to reach the location. The drive took another two hours. Jessica leaned her seat back and rested for the ride. He almost woke her half a dozen times to tell her that he was confused and wanted to sort out what was going on in his mind, but he stopped himself. She needed the rest and he liked having her there.

"This location will be out of the way for most of the ranch business and should keep us flying under the radar," he said when she finally sat up.

Pitching a tent didn't take long. He'd decided on camping next to Hollow's Lake, figuring they'd need a water source if they were going to be out there for a few days. This land wasn't near where they kept the cattle and therefore no one would be riding fences. There were no hunts scheduled on this side of the property in the month of November, so unless something had changed they'd be good. He had cursory supplies, including toiletries, in his SUV at all times in case he wanted to spend the night out on the range and sleep under the stars, which had happened often since hearing the news about his parents.

He built a campfire and offered Jessica a protein bar before making coffee.

"I'm impressed," she said, taking a sip.

"What you're tasting is the result of years of trial and error." He laughed.

"It's even more than that," she said, and he knew exactly what she was talking about. "What is it about a beautiful landscape that makes everything taste so much better?"

"Fresh air does something to food and drink."

She nodded. "Thank you for taking care of my sister."

"No problem," he said, but he could see that it was a huge deal to her.

Jessica didn't want to like the handsome cowboy any more than she already did. As soon as they figured out who was behind this crime and could prove it to the law she'd go back to Shreveport and running the family business so she could resume taking care of her parents. The thought made her sad. Not the part about taking care of her parents, but returning to Shreveport. The place no longer felt like home and the job had never before felt so lonely.

Could she convince Jenn to come home?

Jenn? Come home?

Jessica almost laughed out loud. Her sister hadn't been able to wait to get out of Shreveport. If Baton Rouge was no longer an option, and Jessica was pretty sure it wasn't, then maybe Jenn could get a fresh start in Houston or San Antonio.

Thinking about her sister brought on too much sadness, so she pushed those unproductive thoughts aside for now and tried to clear her head with another sip of coffee. They needed to figure out why Jenn was being set up.

"Have you heard from Zander?" she asked.

"He was released from the hospital last night and is doing fine." He sat staring with his back to the sun.

Had a wall come up between them? When Jessica really thought about it, Tyler clammed up every time they got close. What was that all about? He had feelings for her, or at the very least an attraction, and yet he shut down every time they tried to act on it. She made a mental note to ask him about it. Maybe it had something to do with his past.

"Did you really play pro baseball?" she asked, remembering a conversation with Zander.

"Yep."

"And what happened?"

"Nothing." He rubbed his right shoulder, a move she'd seen him make several times when they'd done something physical.

"Everything okay?" She motioned toward the spot where his hand was rubbing.

He stopped midrub. "Peachy."

She pushed to her feet, unsure what she'd done to make him stop talking to her. All of a sudden they were at one-word answers and he looked uncomfortable. "I'm going for a walk."

"You want company?"

"No." What had happened? One minute he was comforting her and now they were barely speaking. What was up with that?

Jessica pushed those thoughts aside as she walked toward the lake. Every step away from Tyler was a giant leap toward being completely stressed. How had she become so dependent on a stranger in just a few short days?

Anger and frustration formed a tight ball in her chest, making breathing hurt. She had no right to feel this way about him and she needed to walk it off. Heck, she didn't want to feel this way about any man. And yet she couldn't deny that was exactly what was happening.

So the handsome cowboy had done a few nice things for her. Let's face it, his actions were nothing short of heroic. But that didn't mean she had to put up with his roller-coaster emotions—one minute on and the next keeping her at a safe distance.

At least this was better than her relationship with Brent. He'd been practiced and cool the whole time. He knew exactly the right words to say to throw her off the trail if she was suspicious…and it had all been one big act so she wouldn't catch him cheating.

Jessica paced from a mesquite tree to the lake's edge a few times before she looked up and realized that Tyler was standing right there watching her. She let out a little yelp before she could quash it. "What are you doing sneaking up on me like that?"

"I'm sorry." His wry grin belied the sincerity in those words.

"Great. The man *can* put two words together," she quipped and then regretted saying what she was thinking. She should probably bow at the man's feet for how much he was helping her family, so why did she want to claw his eyes out right now instead?

There he stood, silent, for a long moment with his arms crossed as he leaned against a tree.

Jessica would be damned if she spoke first. Two could play at that game, so she planted her fisted hands on her hips and stared right back.

"You want to scream or something? Go ahead. No one will hear you out here," he said, as if he dared her to.

His stance was casual. Hers was aggressive. *Well, get used to it, buddy.* She had no plans to back down from a challenge.

"I would if it would help," she shot back. "Can't see how that'll make it easier to be around you, though."

"*I'm* the problem?" He almost sounded sincere but damned if that grin wasn't plastered into place on his face. It was sexy, she had to give him that, but a little sexy—okay a lot sexy!—wasn't about to make her cave. Besides, she was getting whiplash from his mood swings. One minute his hands were all over her, making her want things she hadn't felt before. And then the next he couldn't put enough distance or a bigger wall between them.

"Glad you see this from my point of view," she said, knowing full well his was a question not a statement. Well, he'd put it out there.

The smile faded from his lips and his hand flew behind his back at a sound behind her. "Get down."

She dropped to all fours at the exact time his gun came around and leveled at a spot where her head had been seconds before. A bullet cracked the air as fire flared from the tip of his barrel.

"Stay down," Tyler said, already on the move.

Jessica pulled her gun and crouched behind the tree where Tyler had been a few moments before, hoping to get a look at what he'd seen. She scanned the area next to the lake, the direction he'd fired, and couldn't see anyone. And now that it was getting dark, she'd lost sight of Tyler in the trees.

If anyone came near her, she'd have no qualms about shooting.

A few shots were fired at least forty feet away. She whirled toward the sound, trying to keep her hands from shaking as she gripped the gun and kept alert.

Rustling noises came from the same direction. Rather than move into the dangerous area, she maintained position. She wanted to call out to Tyler but did not want to compromise his position or hers. A thought crossed her mind. She was crouched in the spot from which he'd fired a few minutes ago. Her position was already compromised. She needed to move.

Staying low, she crawled toward the water.

It was eerie how everything had gone quiet.

Jessica sat near the water's edge, looking at her reflection in the moonlight. Still no sign of movement around her.

She completely stilled, quiet, for several minutes that dripped by like hours.

A hand touched her shoulder at the same time as he spoke. "It's okay."

She nearly jumped out of her skin. Using the momentum, she spun around on him. "It most certainly is not. I could've shot you."

That wry grin parted his lips. "You're not fast enough."

She let that slide, ignoring the sour taste in her mouth that came with knowing he was right.

Chapter 15

"What happened? Who were you shooting at?" Jessica asked, trying to calm her fried nerves.

"I saw movement in the bush and something charged toward me. Turned out to be a wild hog," he said.

Tyler O'Brien was no doubt capable of handling any situation he came across, but Jessica couldn't ignore the fact that the cowboy lit up more of her senses than was good for either one of them.

Another noise sounded behind her. Jessica jumped and scrambled into his arms.

"Don't tell me you're afraid of a hog?" he asked, leaning back to get a better look at her.

"You're not?" she asked.

"They're mean but, trust me, I can be worse. I'm not going to let anything happen to you," he said and his voice was gravelly. "But *this* isn't a good idea."

"What?" she asked, but she was being coy. "Is *this*?" She reached up on her tiptoes and pressed a light kiss to his lips. Sure, she was frustrated with him and she figured half the reason their frustrations had built to this degree was all the sexual tension crackling around them every time he got near her. It was crazy and impulsive but all she could think about was the feel of his arms around her and how right everything felt when she was this close to him.

His heart thundered against her chest, its rhythm matching hers.

He closed his eyes and took a deep breath. "I can't stop whatever's going on between us and it scares the hell out of me."

"You don't have to be in control all of the time," she countered. "Maybe it's time we both let go."

With that, he closed his arms around her and pressed her body flush with his.

"I'm glad you feel that way, because this thing between us seems to have a mind of its own," he said. "I'm tired of fighting it."

A trill of need blasted through Jessica. "Those are the best words I've heard all day."

He dipped his head and claimed her mouth. She parted her lips and his tongue slid inside, tasting her, needing her.

Tyler picked her up and carried her to the tent. He set her down long enough to pull the sleeping bag outside, under the stars.

She shrugged out of her shirt, dropping it onto the ground, and he groaned when he saw her blue lace bra.

All it took was one step for him to be there, his hands

on her breasts as her nipples beaded beneath the silk undergarment. He paused long enough to look into her eyes and she was certain he was searching for reassurance.

No words were needed as she tugged at the hem of his shirt. His joined hers on the ground a moment later and then his lips were on her neck, slowly moving down. He stopped at the heartbeat at the base of her neck, feathering little kisses there, and then slicked his tongue down the line between her breasts.

Her breath came out in little gasps as he explored her sensitized skin. She planted her hands firmly on either side of his shoulders to stop him.

"What? What's wrong?" he asked, and his voice was low.

"We're wearing too many clothes," she said, already grabbing for his zipper.

He shimmied out of his jeans and she did the same. Her bra came off a few seconds later and joined the other clothes on the ground.

Tyler stopped, his eyes dark and hungry, and looked at her. "You're beautiful."

"So are you," she said, tracing a line down the muscles in his chest. He was like touching silk over steel, raw power in physical form.

His hands roamed her breasts and she liked the rough feel of his fingers on her skin.

Her breath caught as he slipped her matching blue silk-and-lace panties down the sides of her hips with achingly slow movements.

She tugged his boxers off next and took a second to admire his glorious body in the moonlight. He was

muscle and hotness with just the right amount of gruff-
ness to be irresistibly sexy…damn. There was so much
more to Tyler O'Brien than a hot body, although he had
that in spades. He was warm, intelligent and caring…a
potent combination. And she was hooked.

When this was all over and he walked away, the pain
was going to be beyond anything she'd ever known…but
she had tonight. And a little part of her mind told her
she'd held back too long. She needed to take what she
wanted…and she wanted the hot cowboy. Hurt would
eventually heal and she would have this memory for
the rest of her life.

Jessica made a move toward Tyler but he stopped her.

"I'm not done looking at you," he warned, naked
and glorious.

She should be embarrassed but there was something
about his presence that made her feel completely at ease.
She glanced down at the makeshift bed on the ground,
smiled, and then took off running in the other direction, straight to the water.

The cool lake practically sizzled against her burning skin.

Tyler was behind her in the next moment, spinning
her to face him. She wrapped her legs around his waist
and eased him inside her.

"You're going to destroy me," he said, his muscles
taut as he thrust deeper inside her.

"In the best possible way," she said. "Now shut up
and kiss me."

He did kiss her, his tongue thrusting inside her mouth
as he filled her with his erection. One hand splayed
against her bottom, the other pressed and tugged at one

nipple then the other until she shattered into a thousand tiny pieces around him.

And then he detonated inside her as they, bare-naked skin to bare-naked skin, held each other in the moonlight.

Tyler woke before light peeked over the horizon, feeling a little too refreshed. There was a chill in the air that didn't penetrate his warm body—warm because of the woman in his arms. And a big part of him wanted to stay right there and hold her for as long as he could.

Good news about Jenn's condition would be a welcome relief for Jessica and he wanted to deliver it first thing. He needed to move to a spot on the north corner of the lake where he could check his cell phone.

Slowly, so he wouldn't wake her, he untangled their arms and legs with a satisfied smile. Last night had been right up there with…no, had been *the* best sex of his life.

When they sorted out Red's situation they needed to have a conversation about seeing each other on a regular basis, explore where this could go. He picked a few supplies out of his pack and moved to the water. After brushing his teeth, he replaced the supplies and hiked to the other side of the lake.

His first phone call would be to Dr. McConnell. It was early but she'd be up making rounds. He walked along the lake, checking various spots for bars until he got at least three. Immediately his cell phone started buzzing and dinging. Fifteen missed calls and a half dozen text messages. Not good.

The first was from the doc. She was direct, as usual,

saying that hospital security had been breached and her patient had gone missing.

Tyler immediately phoned.

"It happened an hour ago," she said, not bothering wasting time on perfunctory greetings. "I had to call the sheriff."

That second statement was a given. Jessica might be upset at first but she'd see that the doc had no choice.

"What did Tommy say?" he asked.

"He figured it was connected to the murder at the motel. I didn't link you to my patient. That's between you and Tommy," she said.

"What was her condition?" Jessica needed to know what they were dealing with. "Tell me in layman's terms."

"She'd had two bags of saline, so she was rehydrating. Overall, I've seen worse but I don't like her being gone before I had a chance to evaluate all her injuries." The doctor hesitated for a second. "How's her sister?"

"What gave her away?" Tyler asked.

"She doesn't have the same bruising on her arms, for one," Dr. McConnell said. "That was the first tell."

He should've known. "I apologize for not being up front. This situation is sticky and some information wasn't mine to share."

"You have your reasons," she said quickly. "I've known you a long time and I trust they're good ones."

He thanked her and asked if he could see the security footage.

"I'll have someone drop a copy of the feed off at the ranch," she said. "It would be best if you stayed away from here for now."

"Understood."

"On that note, the images are grainy. We don't have a need for high-tech security here so the equipment's old," she said.

"How many people are we talking here?" he asked, hoping to get a better frame around who they might be dealing with.

"Just one," she said, and there was an ominous quality to her tone.

"Did you recognize him, by chance?" he asked.

"I'd swear it was the man visiting her sister the other day."

James Milton.

"I better get ahold of Tommy and see what he's found so far." And he needed to come clean to his close friend. The best way to help Red and her sister was to lay all the cards on the table. On second thought, he'd shoot a text asking Tommy to meet at the cabin. It would be easier to explain everything with Red there.

"I'm here if you need anything," Dr. McConnell said.

"We'll be out of cell range for a bit this morning. You hear anything or if anyone connected to this shows up at the hospital, I'd appreciate a heads-up."

"Already have you on speed dial." She paused. "At the risk of sounding motherly, be careful."

"You know I will," he said before ending the call.

Tyler made a beeline toward the tent. Jenn had gone missing and Milton had her. Tyler had miscalculated the man and her disappearance was on his head.

Jessica needed to know.

Chapter 16

Tyler didn't like the idea of waking Red before she'd had a chance to get a proper night's rest, but this news couldn't wait. They needed to regroup and come up with a plan to find her sister, now. "I have news."

She blinked her eyes open.

"We need to talk," he said, kissing her on the forehead.

Red sat up, yawned and rubbed her eyes. "What's up?"

Bad news got worse with age so he didn't wait for the right words to come. "A man breached hospital security an hour ago and managed to get away with your sister."

The look of shock and horror playing out on her face fisted his chest. He'd let her down in the worst possible way.

"Who? How?" she asked, wide-eyed.

"I can't say for certain. Dr. McConnell is sending security films to the house. If we pack up now we should be there around the same time." Tyler was already gathering supplies. "She was doing better because she was getting hydrated, but doc said she didn't get a chance to get a full workup yet."

"And, let me guess, they have no idea who took her?" she asked again.

He looked her directly in the eyes. "Doc's pretty certain it was James Milton."

Panic crossed her features as she scrambled to her feet. "What do we need to do?"

"Pack up and go home."

Within ten minutes, the campfire had been tamped, the SUV packed and they were on the road. Tyler drove across the property, calling ahead to security to alert them he was coming. His next call was to his brother Austin.

"We have a situation and need to send out an alert to security," Tyler said as soon as his brother answered. "The woman I've been helping, Jessica, her sister is missing and they're both in danger. Everyone should stay vigilant and be on the lookout for Jessica's twin sister and a white male. If people want a visual, I'll be at my place in the next twenty minutes. I'm coming up from Hollow's Lake."

"I'll let everyone know. Dallas is in town this morning so I'll text him the situation. He'll want to meet up with us. The twins are in the barn so they'll be easy to round up. I'm not sure where Colin is, but he'll want to know what's going on and pitch in to help," Austin said.

Joshua, the youngest twin, had been traveling back

and forth to his job in Colorado. He'd been having the most difficult time with the transition to rancher, given that he loved his job in law enforcement. Tyler was glad to have the extra help. He thanked his brother even though he knew Austin wouldn't see it as necessary. "I'll see you in a few."

"We're all here for you. Just let us know what you need and we'll make it happen," Austin said. "In the meantime, I'll watch your back as you enter from the south end of the property."

Tyler ended the call with the push of a button on his steering wheel. Red didn't immediately speak.

She finally leaned forward and said, "I didn't know there were twins in your family."

It was a distraction from the helplessness they both felt being in the SUV driving home rather than being there to save her sister.

"The youngest boys, Ryder and Joshua," he said.

"Now I get why you seem to understand twins so well," she said with a hollow quality in her voice. She was talking, going through the motions, but her heart wasn't in the conversation.

He understood. Sometimes people needed to do something to keep busy or they'd go crazy. Given the current situation, Red had every right to be distant. And he had another bomb to drop on her. "Tommy's going to be at the cabin when we arrive."

Red shot a look at him.

"I didn't tell him anything. I said that I wouldn't go behind your back and I didn't. But he has to be involved now. He has resources that can help find your sister."

She started to put up more of a fight but seemed to lose steam as she blew out a defeated-sounding sigh.

"Whatever it takes to get my sister back alive," she said quietly. "I'll do anything to make sure she's safe."

Jessica could barely breathe. Ever since she'd heard the news about her sister it felt as if the air had thinned and the walls were closing in on her. If Milton had gotten to her, and it had to be him, then Jenn was as good as dead. The man had a violent background and nothing to lose. There would be no incentive to keep Jenn alive if she didn't cooperate.

Based on her sister's condition, Jessica wasn't sure if her sister would be coherent enough to say where the necklace was even if she did know.

And what if she knew exactly where the necklace was? What if she'd figured it out? If she told Milton, he'd kill her and dump the body just as ruthlessly as he'd tried before.

"You said you were going to take care of my parents."

"They're on a ranch in Montana," Tyler said.

"My dad's always wanted to go fly-fishing," she said wistfully, trying to absorb all the information coming at her.

"That's how we convinced him to leave. Also, he thinks his daughters are joining him there for Thanksgiving."

"Does he know about all this? He and mother will be so worried," she said.

"Thinks you two arranged the trip with the caveat they had to leave immediately," Tyler said, and there was a sad quality to his tone.

"I'm more than happy to reimburse you for the expenses," she offered.

"It's not that. He sounds like a decent man and I hated lying to him," he said.

Their worlds had never felt so different. She and her sister were running from the law while Tyler's best friend was the sheriff. He was a good person who stepped in to help when most would run the other way. Would she do the same for a stranger? She liked to think she would, but then she'd never been asked to dodge bullets for anyone before.

But that was for her blood, her sister. No matter how crazy things got, Tyler stayed the course and offered his life to help. She thought about how much she'd been asking of him, forcing an honest man to lie to the people he loved, and a hard knot formed in her stomach.

"You can take me to the sheriff's office to file a report and leave me there. You've done enough for my family," she started, but his hand came off the steering wheel long enough to stop her.

"Don't push me away." His fingers closed around hers as he temporarily steered with one hand.

Was she?

"Every time we get close, you tell me to leave," he continued. "There's only one thing you need to know about a Texan—we don't quit when life gets tough."

Those words, his support, wrapped around her, bathing her in warmth. She couldn't deny his point. Every time they got close and she started opening up, she found a reason to shut down. He'd never left her side. "I don't know how to let go of the feeling that you're going to walk away at some point."

"I can't promise forever, but I do know that I've never felt like this about anyone before," he said.

"Me, too. That's exactly what I'm afraid of."

"Can you take a step back once we get Jenn back and life returns to normal and see where this leads?" he asked as he pulled into an area that finally looked familiar.

"I don't know," was all she could say. He deserved the truth.

"Do me a favor," he said.

"If I can."

"Don't make any decisions right now." He pulled into the garage, turned off the engine and held on to the key. He didn't make a move to get out of the SUV. "Not while everything's turned upside down."

For her own protection, she needed to tell him that was impossible. That she'd already made her choice... to go home and try to forget everything that had happened these past few days. And yet it would be impossible not to remember last night.

Before he could say anything to change her mind, Jessica opened the door and stepped out of the SUV.

They came from two different worlds, knew very little about each other, and trying to convince herself they could somehow magically make it all work would be foolish.

"The door's unlocked," he said, moving from the driver's side.

She walked in and forced her thoughts away from the feeling that this was home. It wasn't home. Home was with her parents in Shreveport.

He grabbed her elbow as she crossed into the kitchen, spun her around and pinned her against the wall.

"I get that you've lost a lot and that you're scared. But give us a chance." His steady gaze, those dark eyes— she could lose all sense of time. Even forget how messed up her life was right then.

The doorbell rang.

He didn't move and she didn't speak.

"I'll take that to mean you're at least thinking about what I said."

She looked away. No way could she look into those eyes any longer with what she was prepared to do.

An urgent knock sounded at the front door. No doubt it was the sheriff. She'd most likely be arrested for lying to an officer of the law. Would Tyler still want to have anything to do with her then? He wasn't thinking clearly.

He kissed her anyway, slow and sweet. She molded against him.

"Tyler, I saw you drive in," the sheriff said through the door.

Tyler pressed his forehead to hers and closed his eyes.

The next thing she knew, he'd gone into the other room and opened the door. The sheriff walked in first, followed by three men who looked related to Tyler, and a woman.

"I'm Stacy," she said, offering a hand.

Jessica took it and then the tears came.

Stacy pulled her into a hug. "It's going to be okay, you hear me? These men will find your sister and bring her back safe and sound. They're good men and they'll look out for you."

Those words were soothing, and a sense of calm radiated from Stacy.

"Thank you," Jessica said softly. She took a fortifying breath and straightened her shoulders.

Thankfully, the men had moved into the kitchen, gathering around the granite island and passing out mugs of coffee.

"These are my brothers, Austin, Ryder and Joshua," Tyler said.

"Dallas is on his way and Colin must be out of cell range," one of the men said. She recognized the voice as the one on the phone, so he had to be Austin.

"Nice to meet everyone." Each shook her hand and it was easy to guess who the twins were based on the fact that they looked so much alike.

They huddled around the coffeepot as Tyler moved to her side and took her hand.

No one made her feel the way Tyler did. And a big part of her didn't feel worthy of that kind of love. Wow. Was that why she took care of everyone around her? She didn't feel like she deserved real love?

Before she could talk herself out of holding Tyler's hand, he put his arm around her and she leaned into his strength. It was time to bite the bullet and own up to her fraudulence. "I haven't been completely honest with you, sheriff. My name is Jessica and I've been covering for my twin sister, Jennifer."

"I know," Tommy said, and she almost thought she didn't hear him correctly. She must've shot him one wild look because he put his hand up. "I didn't at first, but I started piecing things together and when I dug into your sister's background and found you everything snapped into place."

"I understand if you need to arrest me or something," she said. "But I'd appreciate it if you let me help find my sister first."

The sheriff made a face. "Arrest you? For what? Being a witness to a crime?"

Tyler squeezed her and she'd never felt more safe in someone's arms. But her sister was out there with a crazed man who had nothing to lose.

"Tell us what you know," Tyler said to the sheriff.

"We've been able to ascertain that James Milton owes Randall Beauchamp a large sum of money. His interest in the Infinity Sapphire is twofold—clear his debt and get enough money to start fresh somewhere else. He's been studying for a real estate license in Nevada, so my guess is that he's been planning his exit from Baton Rouge for a while."

"So, we know that he's involved and that Jenn was set up. Why does everyone think she knows where the necklace is?" Tyler asked.

"Because she does," Jessica said. "She might not even know it, but she does. It's the only thing that makes sense."

"What do you mean?" Tyler asked, clearly confused.

A picture was finally emerging. "Jenn said that Milton kept asking about the box. Maybe Ashton asked her hide something for him but she may not have known what it was."

"It would also mean that she trusted the person who

gave it to her," Tyler said. "And we already know she was having an affair with Ashton."

One of the brothers set up a laptop on one side of the island and plugged in a thumb drive. "This is the footage from the hospital."

It was grainy, just as they'd been told, but it was so obvious that the person walking out was not James Milton. "That's Ashton Brasseux."

"How can it be? He and his wife, Emma-Kate were kidnapped," Tyler said, and then it dawned on him. "Or so he wanted everyone to think."

Jessica sipped from the mug she'd been handed earlier.

"Local police did some digging and found out that the Brasseuxs were having a little money trouble. Ashton and Emma-Kate were separating and she believed that he was seeing someone else," the sheriff said.

"My sister," Jessica said quietly. Jessica turned her full attention to the sheriff. "I know how this looks. All evidence points to Jenn taking the sapphire or at the very least being involved in stealing and hiding it. Other people seem to believe the same thing, bad people, but I know in my heart that my sister would never do that. She was in love with Ashton Brasseux and he set her up."

"I have to follow the evidence," the sheriff said. "But I promise to look at all the facts and keep an open mind."

She smiled, nodded. Under the circumstances, he was being generous. "Thank you."

"What's our next step?" Tyler asked. "We know that Jenn is in danger and we need to find her."

Tommy nodded.

"Do you know anything about the person who has been asking around for me?" Tyler asked.

"I tracked him down and he was an investigator for the Brasseux's insurance company," the sheriff said. "We just need to make sure he stays out of the way."

"Any chance that necklace is here on the property?" Tyler asked.

The doorbell rang.

Tyler excused himself and answered the door. "Janis, come in."

"I brought food," she said, carrying a full basket of muffins and pastries.

"Let me take that," he said, and she seemed to know better than to argue.

Janis followed Tyler into the kitchen. Her gaze moved around the island, stopping on Jessica.

"Good morning, Mrs. Templeton," Janis said. "I didn't know you were here."

Jessica shot Tyler a look. "I'm sorry, have we met?"

Janis stared, openmouthed. "You were here a couple of weeks ago with your husband."

"I'm afraid that I have no idea what you're talking about," Jessica said, but the light went on at the same time Austin turned the laptop around.

"Who'd she come with?" Austin asked.

"Her husband," Janis said, confusion knitting her eyebrows. "But I must be mistaken."

"Does Mr. Templeton look like this?" Austin asked, angling the screen toward Janis.

"Why, yes. It's a little blurry but that's him," she said emphatically.

"Which means that Jenn and Ashton came here, and Milton must've known she would come back to a place where they'd already been," Tyler said, and the sheriff nodded.

Tyler poured another cup of coffee. "Do you remember any details about their booking?"

"It's been a couple of weeks. Let me think," Janis said as he handed her a mug.

Hope blossomed for the first time since this whole ordeal started. If Jenn had been taken by Ashton, surely she'd be safe. If he loved her, he wouldn't do anything bad to her. Would he?

The man stole a family heirloom from his wife and gave it to his mistress to hide, promising her they'd be together forever. The short-lived burst of hope immediately died.

"If he gets the necklace, he'll hurt her," Jessica said. "We have to find them first."

"Is there anything specific you remember about the couple?" Tyler asked Janis.

"They stayed in their room most of the time. Didn't book a hunting trip, I remember that for sure because I thought it was odd this time of year," Janis said. "I remembered thinking that they must be honeymooners."

Reality hit Tyler harder than a ton of bricks. "She hid the necklace in the main house."

The sound of bar stools scraping across tile echoed as everyone stood at the same time.

"I can check the registry and tell you which room

they stayed in," Janis offered, and they were already making a move toward the door.

"We'll tear the place apart if we have to," Austin said.

As soon as the group left, Jessica said, "They won't be on the property. We might find the necklace, but with security here he's not stupid enough to risk coming straight at us. He'll take her somewhere else until he comes up with a plan."

"First, let's get the necklace. That's the best thing we can do to ensure your sister's safety. He won't do anything to her if he thinks she's useful."

She followed Tyler to the garage where he fired up the SUV and backed out.

The drive to the main house took ten minutes. Denali was on the front porch waiting.

"Hey, buddy," Tyler said as the chocolate lab trotted over to greet him.

"I'll just check the registry," Janis said.

The main house was set back, but they could see the road from the porch. An older model, white four-door Mazda pulled up in front of the gate, someone was pushed out and the car sped off.

"It's her," Jessica shouted. "It's Jenn."

Chapter 17

Tyler darted toward Jenn as the guards in the shack bolted outside. "She's clear. She's with us."

Most of the house emptied, with all the boys running close behind Jessica, and she had never felt so protected and secure in her life.

"Jenn," she said as she dropped down beside her sister, who was folded onto her side. She wore a jacket over her shirt, which was odd considering the weather had warmed up.

"Go," Jenn whispered, looking too weak to move. She made a grunting noise before repeating the word.

Sheriff Tommy knelt next to Jenn, his gaze sweeping over her. "Everyone back away."

"I'm not going anywhere," Jessica said, just as she noticed sweat beads on Jenn's forehead. She wiped them away. "It's okay. I'm here now and I won't let those men hurt you."

Jenn winced as she shook her head. "Go."

Her sister was weak and clearly not thinking straight. Jessica had no idea what those jerks had done to her sister but she hoped they rotted in jail for their crimes. She vaguely heard the sheriff in the background giving a description of the vehicle that had sped away.

"Everyone needs to step away," he said, unzipping Jenn's jacket to reveal a bomb strapped to her body.

Tears fell freely as Jessica held on to her sister's hand. "I'm not leaving you."

There was a piece of white paper sticking out of her jacket pocket. Jenn angled her head toward it.

"Sheriff—" Jessica started but was cut off.

"I see it. Everyone needs to get back," the sheriff demanded, leaving no room for doubt that he was serious.

The brothers did as instructed, except for Tyler. He didn't budge.

"I have protocol to follow, Tyler," the sheriff said.

"And I have my loyalties," Tyler retorted.

"If you're not going to make this easy, then scoot over so I can take a closer look," the sheriff said. He took out a pair of something that looked like tweezers and put on rubber gloves. He removed the folded piece of paper and peeled it open.

"It's easy. We get the necklace or she goes boom. You have one hour to leave it where you found her sister. No cops."

"He used the term *we*," the sheriff said. "We're dealing with a network."

"Which one of these guys has experience with explosives?" Tyler said.

"Chemical engineer," Jenn managed to say. "Ashton."

Everyone reacted to the news.

"She needs medical help." Jessica fought back tears as she whispered reassurances to Jenn.

The sheriff leaned back on his heels and evaluated the situation. "Ashton must be our guy. He's in charge."

Heads bobbed in agreement.

Tyler glanced up at his brothers and shooed them back into the house to search for the piece of jewelry.

"They must think we already have the necklace," Tyler said. "We'd have to hightail it to drive to Diablo's Rock in an hour. I can get there on Digby in forty-five minutes."

"Someone needs to show up whether we have the necklace or not," the sheriff said. "It'll be our best chance to nab them."

"They'll be watching for police," Jessica said. "We mess this up and they'll push the button."

"They can do that anyway once they get the necklace," Tyler warned, and he was right.

"This looks like pretty standard material." The sheriff rattled off names that didn't mean much to Jessica, then said, "They'd have to be using a wireless trigger mechanism."

"Cell phone," Jenn said through a coughing fit.

Both the sheriff and Tyler stiffened until she calmed again.

"So, if they need a wireless connection to detonate the bomb, then what happens if I take her out of cell range?" Tyler asked. "There are so many dead spots on the property, it would be easy to take her somewhere there's no signal. In fact, Diablo's Rock is a dead zone."

"We need to be careful moving her," the sheriff said.

"I'll get the SUV," Tyler said as Austin burst out the front door.

"Found it stuffed between the mattresses," he said, holding out the Infinity Sapphire. The brilliant stones caught the light just right, leaving sparkly streaks in the air.

"You're going to be okay," Jessica soothed, brushing Jenn's hair from her face. "You're here and we're not going to let anything happen to you."

"So stupid," Jenn managed to say. "Thought he loved me."

"I know, sweetie," Jessica said. "But he's not good enough for you. And we're going to make sure he spends the rest of his life in jail."

Jenn nodded and a tear streaked her cheek.

"Move her carefully," the sheriff said as Tyler moved to the other side of Jenn.

"You might want to step behind the SUV," Tyler said to Jessica, but she was already shaking her head.

"I'm staying right here by my sister," Jessica said. She expected Tyler to put up an argument but he nodded and kept going, gently moving Jenn into the back of the SUV on top of layers of sleeping bags.

"I'll need you with me," Tyler said.

She moved to the passenger side as soon as Jenn was secure. "I have no plans to leave her."

"I was afraid you'd say that."

* * *

"We have to approach the same way you did with the ATVs," Tyler said to Jessica as he parked the SUV a few yards from the rock. Her body language screamed fear. No doubt she remembered the last time she'd been there a few days ago.

His brothers were near, they'd fanned out around the area, but there was no cell coverage out there. Good for Jenn but bad for overall communication.

"Stay here," he said, handing her the Sig Sauer she'd used before. "Don't let on that anyone's in the back of the SUV. Don't even glance back there, okay?"

"I'm good." She palmed the weapon and then double-checked the chamber.

"Remind me not to get on your bad side later." He kissed her. "I need to check the area. The boys aren't far and they know how to hide. The tricky part will be communicating with them if we get in trouble."

"We're going to be fine. We have to be."

She didn't say that their lives depended on it but they did.

Tyler moved to the rock and dug his boots in, moving to high ground to get a better look at the area. As he crested the rock he thought about how much his life had changed since the last time he was there. Everything had been turned upside down, he'd never been in more danger and never been more in love. The danger part he could handle.

He saw the glint of metal coming behind a bush on the east side just as the telltale flash of fire followed. The bullet pierced him. Shock registered as he missed his footing and tumbled the forty-foot drop from Diablo's peak.

* * *

Jessica heard a gun fire. She bolted from the SUV in time to see Tyler tumbling down the face of the rock. Panic engulfed her and her pulse skyrocketed. Before she had a chance to rationalize her actions she was running toward him.

Please let him be okay.

Her stomach twisted as she got close enough to see him lying there, facedown, unmoving. All she could think about was getting to him and then she saw the blood through his plaid shirt.

There was no way to contact his brothers. Her own sister lay in the SUV, unconscious. All Jessica's hopes had been riding on the cowboy and now he was dying, leaving her, too. It was a selfish thought and she knew it. She tamped it down and spun around to the sound of footsteps running up behind her. There were three men, all with weapons pointed directly at her chest. She pointed her own gun at the ringleader, Ashton. "Stop or I'll shoot."

"Whoa," he said to the others, holding his hands out for them to stay behind.

They were out of cell phone range. Tyler's brothers had to have heard the shot, hadn't they? And all of them were about to die.

Well, she planned on taking a couple of these jerks with her.

"Back off if you want the necklace," she said, taking a step away as the men slowed their approach.

"You don't have a play here, honey," Milton said, and her skin crawled at the sound of his voice.

She retreated a few more steps until her back hit a

solid wall of rock. "Don't come any closer or I'll start shooting."

All three men stopped. The third fit the description of the man in the suit who'd been asking around for Tyler. It dawned on Jessica. The insurance adjuster must be in on it. Milton wasn't working for Beauchamp, he was in league with Ashton.

"How did they talk you into joining them?" she asked the third man.

"This guy?" A wide smile broke on Ashton's face. "Fraternity brothers forever."

He and Ashton were friends? He must've been offered a cut.

"My sister thought you loved her," she said as Ashton took another menacing step toward her. Anger burned through her chest. She hated the guy, but could she kill someone?

It was either kill or be killed.

Ashton ignored her comment and made a move to kick Tyler. "How'd this jerk get involved?"

Jessica closed her eyes and pulled the trigger. By the time she opened them a second later, chaos had broken out.

Ashton was on the ground, wrestling with Tyler, who had already shot Milton. She'd nicked the insurance guy who was diving on top of Tyler and Ashton.

Milton didn't seem to realize he'd been shot because he lunged toward her.

"Bitch," he said as he dived.

She whirled to the right and he smacked into the rock, shoulder first, but managed to knock the gun out of her hand. His thick hand clutched at her until he gained purchase on her shirt. He shoved her to the ground and she desperately felt around for the Sig.

Milton twisted until he was straddled over her. She glanced to the side in time to see that Tyler and Ashton were wrestling for a gun. Ashton's friend was rearing back to deck Tyler.

In a burst, the gun went off and Tyler managed to roll on top of Ashton.

There was so much blood.

Milton raised his hand high and she could see a rock in his palm.

And then she heard the footsteps.

"Put your weapons down," Sheriff Tommy's familiar voice said.

Milton ignored the request. She wiggled but he was too heavy to buck him off. And then another gunshot roared. Milton's eyes bulged after taking the second hit. He slumped to the side allowing Jessica to slide out from underneath him.

Austin wrangled Ashton's friend away, pulling him by the foot. But Tyler and Ashton were too tangled up. A shot was as likely to hit Tyler.

Jessica scooted away from Milton and gentle arms pulled her to her feet. She wasn't sure which one of the twins helped her, but she was grateful.

Tyler pushed Ashton off him and got in a solid punch.

Ashton's head bobbled and then he fell forward, unconscious.

The sheriff was by Tyler's side before she could open her mouth to speak. He zip-cuffed Ashton's hands behind his back.

Jessica ran to Tyler to see just how much blood he'd lost. His brothers were by his side as his eyes closed.

"He's going to be all right, isn't he?" Jessica asked, tears streaking from her eyes. She must've looked as torn on the outside as she was on the inside. Tyler was bleeding, unconscious. Jenn was alone in that SUV where anyone or anything could get to her.

"Austin is with your sister," the sheriff said, easing one of her fears as she heard the *whop, whop, whop* of the helicopter.

Chapter 18

Tyler blinked his eyes open, quickly closing them again. His arm came up to shield them from the bright light shooting daggers through his retinas. His eyes burned as if they'd been branded.

"Hold on there, buddy," Austin said, and the sound of his voice moved toward Tyler until he felt his brother's presence at his side. "Let me get the nurse."

"I'm fine," Tyler blew him off, knowing full well it wasn't the nurse he needed. "Where is she?"

"About that," Austin started.

Tyler's hand came up to stop his brother from delivering bad news. Thinking about losing the woman he'd fallen for hit him like a physical punch. "Never mind. How long have I been out?"

"Just two days," Austin supplied. "And you've been in and out."

"Really?" Tyler needed to get well so he could find Red. There was so much he wanted to say to her. He squinted and a figure in the corner caught his eye.

"Hi, there," Jessica said, moving to his side. She was wringing her hands and that wasn't a good sign.

Austin winked. "I'll leave you two alone to talk."

All the words he'd intended to say died on Tyler's lips when he made eye contact. "How's your sister?"

"Dr. McConnell says Jenn will be fine," Red said, stopping just out of arm's reach. "She's down the hall, already sitting up and chatting. She confirmed that she'd been dating Ashton and he told her that she needed to take care of something to secure their future. He'd said he and his wife were in a loveless marriage and that he'd been planning to leave her for months. He gave her the box and Jenn naively didn't open it. He'd already arranged for Milton to steal it so there'd be a double payoff. His fraternity brother had planned to help him scam the insurance company and was going to get a cut for selling the Infinity Sapphire to Beauchamp's people."

"But Ashton was only using your sister. Setting her up to do the time for the theft," Tyler said, his hands aching to reach out to her, hold her.

"He planned to let her do the time or be killed by Beauchamp. Milton had secretly set up another buyer, and that's who showed at the motel room in Bluff," she said, shifting her weight from her left to right foot. "When Milton didn't produce the necklace, the guy figured he'd been duped. Their whole plan fell apart. Jenn was the only one who knew where the necklace was this whole time. And it turns out we were right that Elijah wanted the necklace to make money off his own sale."

"It can't be easy for Jenn knowing the person she fell in love with was using her," Tyler said.

"Those wounds will be harder to heal," Red admitted. "But just as fast as Jenn falls in love, she can fall out of it."

"And how about you?" he asked. "Do you fall in and out of love quickly?"

She stared at the floor instead of answering.

It was now or never, he thought. "It's finally over. But what happens next? You go back to your life and I do the same? I've never felt this way about anyone before, Jessica. I'm in love with you and I don't want this to be the end."

A little gasp escaped before she suppressed it. "I feel the same way. I've fallen hard for you, Tyler. But it would be crazy to throw away my life and you certainly can't throw away yours. Especially not when neither of us can be certain this isn't a circumstantial romance."

"Do you really believe that's true?" He did his best to mask the hurt in his voice.

"No, of course not. I want to believe this is real, but I need more than a few days to process what's going on between us and make sure it can become something permanent," she said, and there was no covering the confusion in hers.

"Come here," he said and she did.

She eased onto the side of the bed and he put his arms around her. "Let's just agree to keep seeing each other as much as we can until we figure it all out. I don't want to spend another day without you in my life but I'll wait for you."

He brushed a tear off her cheek. "No more crying. This is a good thing. *We're* a good thing."

She leaned into him gently. "Yes, we are. I was so scared when you were shot. I was so afraid of losing you."

"You don't have to," he whispered into her ear and then kissed her neck. "I'm right here."

Jessica had waited six agonizing months for this day to come. She finished her breakfast and grabbed her car keys off the counter with giddy anticipation. Now that Jenn had returned to Shreveport and learned to run the family business, Jessica felt comfortable enough to let the employees know there'd be a change in the guard at Davidson Cleaning Services and Jenn would be taking over.

As she walked out the front door, she froze. "Tyler? What are you doing here? We aren't supposed to see each other until this weekend." And she'd been planning to drop the same bomb on him for weeks. She was ready. She knew that their love was real and could last.

"I couldn't wait to see you," he said with a smile.

She took the couple of steps from the porch quickly, ready to share her good news. Before she could reach him, he dropped down on one knee and produced a small velvet box.

"You are the love of my life. When you're not with me I'm empty in a way I've never known before. I want you to spend the rest of your life with me and our children," he said.

Tears were already flowing down Jessica's cheeks, tears of pure joy.

"You want children?" she asked.

"At least four, but I figured I needed to talk to you about the number before I started making plans," he said. "Jessica, will you marry me?"

She nodded as she wrapped her arms around him. "I love you, Tyler O'Brien, and I can't wait to start our life together."

He kissed her, tenderly at first, but need built quickly.

"Will you come home with me and stay this time?" he asked. "The past six months have been killing me and I don't want to spend another day apart."

"Yes, I'll marry you. And, yes, I'll come home with you. I can't imagine a better place to bring up our kids," she said. "And you know what? I was just on my way to let the employees know that my sister is taking over."

"Good. Because when you come home with me this time, I'm not letting you go."

"You can hold on to me forever," she said. And she couldn't wait to spend the rest of her life with her Texas cowboy.

* * * * *

"CHELSEA, WHAT'S GOING ON?" Johnny clutched his cell
phone to his ear and at the same time he sat up and turned
on the lamp on his nightstand.

"That man…that man is here. He tried to b-break in."
The words came amid sobs. "He…he was at my back
d-door and breaking the gl-glass to get in."

"Hang up and call Lane," he instructed as he got out
of bed.

"I…already called, but n-nobody is here yet."

Johnny could hear the abject terror in her voice, and an
icy fear shot through him. "Where are you now?"

"I'm in the kitchen."

"Get to the bathroom and lock yourself in. Do you hear me? Lock yourself in the bathroom, and I'll be there as quickly as I can," he instructed.

"Please hurry. I don't know where he is now, and I'm so scared."

"Just get to the bathroom. Lock the door and don't open it for anyone but me or the police." He hung up and quickly dressed. He then strapped on his gun and left his cabin. Any residual sleepiness he might have felt was instantly gone, replaced by a sharp edge of tension that tightened his chest.

Don't miss
Closing in on the Cowboy *by Carla Cassidy,*
available July 2022 wherever
Harlequin Intrigue books and ebooks are sold.

Harlequin.com

SPECIAL EXCERPT FROM

ⒽHARLEQUIN
ROMANTIC SUSPENSE

*One night of passion with Marcus Jones led to a
pregnancy Chloe Ryder didn't expect. And when a
serial killer they captured launches a plan for revenge,
Chloe wonders if she'll survive long enough to tell
Marcus about their child...*

Read on for a sneak preview of
The Agent's Deadly Liaison,
*the latest book in Jennifer D. Bokal's
sweeping* Wyoming Nights *miniseries!*

"You think this is a joke? I wonder how many pieces of
you I can cut away before you stop laughing."

On the counter lay a scalpel. Darcy picked it up. The
handle was still stained with Gretchen's lifeblood. Chloe
went cold as she realized that she'd pushed too hard for
information.

Knife in hand, Darcy slowly, slowly approached the
bed. Chloe pressed her back into the pillow, trying in
vain to get distance from the killer and the knife. It did
no good. Darcy pressed Chloe's shackled hand onto the
railing and drew the blade across her palm. The metal
was cold against her skin. She tried to jerk her hand away,
but it was no use.

Darcy drove the blade into Chloe's flesh.

The cut burned, and for a moment, her vision filled with red. Then a seam opened in her hand. Blood began to weep from the wound. She balled her hand into a fist as her palm throbbed, and anger flooded her veins.

Chloe might've been handcuffed to a bed, but that didn't mean that she couldn't fight back.

"Damn you straight to hell," she growled.

With her free hand, Chloe pushed Darcy's chin back. At the same moment, she lifted her feet, kicking the killer in the chest. Darcy stumbled back before tumbling to the ground. Had Chloe been free, she would have had the advantage.

But shackled to the bed? Chloe had done nothing more than enrage a dangerous person.

Standing, Darcy brushed a loose strand of hair from her face. She smiled, then scoffed before echoing Chloe's words. "Damn me to hell? Hell doesn't frighten me, Chloe. Nothing does—especially not you."

Don't miss
The Agent's Deadly Liaison *by Jennifer D. Bokal,*
available July 2022 wherever
Harlequin Romantic Suspense books and
ebooks are sold.

Harlequin.com

Love Harlequin romance?

DISCOVER.

Be the first to find out about promotions, news and exclusive content!

f Facebook.com/HarlequinBooks

𝕏 Twitter.com/HarlequinBooks

◉ Instagram.com/HarlequinBooks

𝕻 Pinterest.com/HarlequinBooks

You Tube YouTube.com/HarlequinBooks

ReaderService.com

EXPLORE.

Sign up for the Harlequin e-newsletter and download a free book from any series at **TryHarlequin.com**

CONNECT.

Join our Harlequin community to share your thoughts and connect with other romance readers!
acebook.com/groups/HarlequinConnection

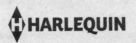

HARLEQUIN

Heartfelt or thrilling, passionate or uplifting—Harlequin is more than just happily-ever-after.

With twelve different series to choose from and new books available every month, you are sure to find stories that will move you, uplift you, inspire and delight you.

HNEWS20